C000075537

The Dreams that Make Us

andrew argyle

Published by andrew argyle publishing

Published by: andrew argyle publishing

ISDN: 978-0-9954665-0-0

First edition edited by: Amy Butcher Content. Montreal, Canada (www.amybcontent.com)

Cover design by: 'Rob Whitney Design', Lincoln, UK

Cover photography adapted from 'Cliffs Clovelly Coast West' by M Henbert CC BY-SA 3.0 (Creative Commons).

Author's website: **www.andrewargyle.com**

For Kim, the perfect wife.

The Dreams that Make Us

Even the person you trust the most isn't always who they seem to be

PREFACE

It was almost dusk, the time for lovers to stroll in bonded romance. I was sixteen, heading for a worrying seventeen, the day I sat in the long shadow of a sycamore tree near to the South West Coast Path. The way here was high above Sidmouth on the Devon coast and gave those determined enough outstanding views of both the Victorian seaside town and the English Channel as it lazed and shimmered in the dying summer sun below the towering red cliffs.

I glanced yet again at my watch. Would she honour her word and meet with me? It was well over twenty minutes since the last people I'd seen had drifted along the path some fifty metres from where I sat. A couple in their mid twenties. They hadn't seen me. At least I presumed they hadn't by the way they paused at the stile, kissed and giggled and how she allowed his hand to slip down inside her loosely buttoned shirt. My teenage eyes watched intently. And then they were gone, hand in hand, taking the steep path down to my peaceful hometown.

My exploratory hands hadn't got that far with my first girlfriend, but otherwise I was blessed to be dating her: my beautiful, stunning Juliet. A slim balcony figure to my ardent Romeo, and the first girl I had kissed, you know, tongues and all that. I did once, at a disco, actually touch one of her soft, exciting breasts, but only from the outside of her thin white blouse. As a teenage lad, I naturally wanted to do more and see those breasts naked, but she wouldn't let me. I ultimately respected her decision.

A sudden movement caught my eye. My angel appeared

by the stile with her long, brown hair flowing freely onto her dark blue cotton dress and matching summer cardigan. I rose from the dry ground, waved self-consciously, and hurried over to her. I remember thinking that my new Levi jeans and dark-blue shirt neatly complemented her own feminine clothing. We were truly meant to be a couple.

To my frustration she declined my kiss, turned and started up the path once more. 'Come on' was all she said.

I dutifully followed, but she was hockey-field fit and remained slightly ahead of me.

'We need to talk, Juliet,' I said with unfounded optimism, adrift in her wake.

'There's really no more to say,' she said, not even turning her head.

The dusk was deepening, and for the first time I noticed a slight chill in the air. Some two hundred metres on, Juliet suddenly came to a rest on the path and stood with her arms folded, gazing out at the intoxicating sea. I moved alongside her and wrapped my left arm around her shoulders.

'Come on, Jules.'

'*Don't* call me that,' she said, shaking off my arm. 'You know I hate it. I told you this morning it's over, Michael. Finished. How many times do you want me to keep saying it?' There was a harshness, a finality in her tone that seared into my heart. Burnt deep.

We'd been going out for four months and thirteen days by then, and now she wanted to end it. I guess in truth we'd never really started. All she'd done over that brief period of time was to light the blue touch paper of my male hormones, causing them to burst into a frustrating blaze of burning emotion. And now she wanted to walk away.

I moved behind her and tried to wrap my arms around

that narrow waist. I just wanted to hold her. She twisted round and faced me, shaking me off again in the process, swatting at my hands as if they were flies.

'Stop it, Michael. Let's go back. I shouldn't have come, shouldn't have agreed.'

'Give me a chance, Juliet.' I said, pleading with my watery eyes. 'Let's give it one more go. I really like you.'

She paused a beat and her voice softened, but the message remained firm, uncompromising. 'We've said it all, Michael. Everything. Now it's time to move on, huh?'

I inhaled a deep, silent breath and took her in, resisting with incredible difficulty the intense physical magnetism of her body. 'Okay, okay, it's over,' I said with a heavy sigh, my arms hanging loosely by my side as my shoulders sunk. 'But can we just have one final hug? Please? Just one?'

Her hesitation confirmed everything.

'Well, alright then. I suppose so. But that's it, okay? Then back down before I'm missed—right?'

I nodded, stepped forward, and wrapped her in my arms, but felt the stubborn, wooden resistance. No warmth, no affection. As the sun also gave its final bow, I pulled my head back, smiled at her, looked deep into her chocolate eyes, and thrust her backwards. Strong and sudden. She had no chance, because I'd given her that chance and she'd dismissed it, hurting me in the process. I stepped forward to watch her as she toppled backwards, arms flailing, over the cliff's edge. Shock silenced her. No noise. No sound at all. She disappeared from view below me and I was too wary to go closer to that short, dry grassy edge to peer over after her.

I glanced about again quickly. Still no one in sight. I scampered along the path until I could look back down, despite the gathering gloom, to the shoreline below. And there she lay. Still. No twitches. No one would have survived that fall. And Juliet was no exception. The evening walk had been clandestine. She'd not told her parents we were meeting. She'd slipped out. My parents had gone to some black-tie dinner, so it was easy for me to leave my home, Cliff House, and not undertake the exam revision that I said I'd be doing. I tracked back home, unseen.

And then I would wake up. Sometimes sweating.

I had this dream for several months after Juliet and I stopped going out. Although it had common elements, the dream would vary in detail. Sometimes Juliet fell from a Shakespearean balcony, sometimes from a high bridge, but from wherever she fell, she usually died. Sometimes however she did survive, but broke her back, condemned to spend the rest of her imaginary life in a wheelchair.

In reality I knuckled down to my exams and later went to university. Save for one occasion when I stood quite close to her, I didn't see Juliet again. I never even wrote to her. Her parents moved away, Cornwall direction as I recall it.

Some say dreams are arbitrary recollections of random experiences morphed into a night-time fantasy. Others say dreams are subtle premonitions or unexplained insights into the future to tantalise, to guide, to *warn*. I didn't understand that at the time. I'm not Freud. I'm just a regular guy negotiating the best path through life, tackling frequent obstacles and staying ever watchful for rare opportunities on the horizon.

The irony was that I was the one to find myself in a wheelchair, not Juliet. However, that necessity came when I was older, in my very early thirties. And I turned thirty-four recently. Maybe dreams really are premonitions. Who knows?

Life can throw tough stuff at you and present you with challenging times. I've heard it said that with murder, the victim isn't always the person who suffers the most. That may well be right. My friends of old might have wondered how someone like me could wax so lyrical on such a topic. Obviously Death has visited my family as he does every other, sometimes expectedly, like with my old grandma, sometimes suddenly, like with my parents. But a privileged only child getting involved in a murder investigation is by no means ordinary, which gives me an edge on the subject, I guess. Would you investigate a murder with a killer at large? But then, when did murder last touch your life? And if being involved in one murder is extraordinary, then being involved in more than one must be truly exceptional.

My name's Mike Miller, and now it's time to record something truly exceptional.

I've been asked what I found the most difficult: the loss of my parents in such a dreadful way when I was young; the brutal murder of my beautiful wife, Lindsey; or receiving from some madman a mortal threat to my own life whilst in a wheelchair as I defied the police and asked questions about Lindsey's death. Not easy to answer. Form your own view as I tell you about it.

There is an obvious point when telling you about these dramatic events. You know I survive. I could hardly write about them if I didn't. What you don't know, of course, is how I did survive—or whether it was a damn close thing that I'm even able to tell you the story at all.

I do, however, have an advantage. Fortunately not everyone takes my view about recording life's adventures. My close friend, Grace, recorded many of these events in some detail, but then ironically it was she who set us on this life-changing course. I've seen what was written. I've had to dramatise her own recollections a bit because they needed even more detail for these purposes, but I lived many of these days with her as she led, in her inimitable way, the unofficial investigation into Lindsey's death. She told me much more than she recorded, of course, so I've added bits in. I know the characters concerned and we talked a lot. I'm sure she wouldn't mind my using what she wrote.

You see, I'm not able to ask her.

But now I'm jumping ahead.

ONE

On a Sunday morning in early September, the visitors called round to tell me my darling wife would never be coming home again.

It was about nine thirty when they rang the doorbell of our marital home, an elegant, substantial bungalow on the edge of Westland. This chocolate-box village was some four miles from Tiverton—a popular tourist stop in England's beautiful West Country. The house itself was modern and expensive and constructed with some centuries-old material that gives rural Devon an indisputable English character— red roses round the door and all that.

Two casually dressed people stood on the bungalow's doorstep. Nearest to me was a tall, slim man with a summer-tanned face and neatly cut, dark brown hair. Slightly behind him, to my right, was a shorter woman with mousy hair, collected and pinned at the back of her head. Both young. Even though I was thirty-two, almost thirty-three, I thought they were young. Mid to late twenties maybe. The only giveaways as to their official status were the office-style identity cards slung on long lanyards round their respective necks. From a quick glance, I recognised the insignia of the Devon & Cornwall Police. These were detectives, not uniformed officers, on a serious, not a community, visit.

Their anxious expressions, body language and alert eyes told me they were bringing bad news. Somehow I knew it was about Lindsey.

'Michael Miller?' the male officer asked in a gentle

manner. He looked down at me where I sat, my left hand on the edge of the open door and my right hovering over the wheelchair's hand rim.

'Yes, that's me,' I said, looking up at his face for more clues. I saw friendly brown eyes and a firm well-shaven jaw, all set around a serious expression. 'How can I help?'

'I'm Detective Sergeant Johnson. And this is Detective Constable Williams,' he added, gesturing towards his colleague. 'Could we come in for a few minutes?' He looked at me expectantly.

To his left, Williams fidgeted slightly, rocking gently on her feet, her hands clasped together in front of her.

'Yes, yes of course,' I said, manoeuvring backwards. I'd always been told you should ask to see identification from anyone purporting to be an official who wants to enter your home, but I'd no idea what a genuine police officer's formal identification looked like, and the simple things hanging round their necks might have been the totality of it.

They both stepped with a respectful air into the spacious polished-wood hallway. DC Williams closed the front door with excessive care and they both looked at me for direction.

'Through here,' I said and wheeled my way down the hallway and turned right into the large farmhouse kitchen with its central breakfast bar island and quarry tile floor. It was all chrome and marble, expensively kitted out with spotlights in the ceiling and discreet lighting, both practical and aesthetic, in every conceivable nook and cranny. On the far side was a wide dining area with closed patio doors looking out over the developing garden. I trundled over to my chair-free space by the light wood table and motioned for them to sit on a couple of the wooden carvers opposite me. DS Johnson sat down and placed his arms on the surface in front of him. He was in Lindsey's chair.

'Mr Miller,' he said as he started to fiddle absentmindedly with his fingers. 'I understand you're married to... er... Lindsey Jane Miller. Is that right?'

I nodded. 'Yes, yes I am. What's going on?'

'Is Mrs Miller here?' Johnson continued.

'No, she's staying the weekend with a friend. Is everything alright? What's this all about?'

Johnson glanced round at Williams who took a black notebook out of her pocket but looked back at him in silent communication. Johnson looked me straight in the eyes. 'I'm sorry, Mr Miller, we have some distressing news for you.' He paused, as if summoning some mental courage. 'A body has been found and we think it's your wife, Lindsey. We're both very sorry.'

I must have looked shell-shocked because Williams leant forward and said in a soft voice with a hint of a Welsh accent, 'Mr Miller, are you okay? Can I get you something? Some water, or a cup of tea perhaps?' I just stared at the table. Forgive me, but I have to admit that my first thought was how her death would affect me, what with the wheelchair and everything. I know that sounds a bit selfish, but the thought flashed and was gone before I resurfaced to the true reality of the situation.

'Dead?' I said slowly, shaking my head ever so slightly and staring at Johnson with a look of incredulity. 'What do you mean dead? Has there been an accident or something?'

Johnson swallowed. I had the impression this whole notification thing was relatively new to him, and he wasn't enjoying it. Who would? Hardly reporting a lottery win, was it? He said in a matter-of-fact tone, 'It doesn't appear to have been an accident—'

'Oh, *not* an accident? What's happened then?'

Johnson lifted his right hand gently in a half-hearted stop gesture. 'If I may, Mr Miller, I'll come on to that in a minute.' He paused and scratched his chin. 'When did you last see your wife?'

DC Williams shifted uncomfortably on her seat.

'Last see her? Well, yesterday, early afternoon. About two fifteen, maybe a little later—yes, nearer two twenty. I don't exactly recall. This is all really... She left in her car to meet up with an old school friend for an evening out. She was to stay over in a hotel and was due back this afternoon, but no time was arranged—we were both happy with a degree of flexibility.' I paused. 'So what's happened?'

Williams wrote some notes in her pocket book.

'Did you speak to her?' Johnson said

'After she left?'

He nodded.

I recalled that we'd spoken later in the evening. Had said quite a lot in a relatively short time—personal stuff. Was it really necessary to ask all this now? I felt I had to keep going.

'Yes,' I said in a quiet tone. I paused and took a deep breath. Williams looked at me anxiously. 'She called me just to say that she was okay, that they'd been to some Italian restaurant, and she was back at the hotel.' I paused again, rubbed my hand once over my eyes in a rolling motion. 'I wanted to have what you might describe as quite an intimate conversation, but she said she was tired.' I felt my face reddening.

Johnson tactfully pressed on. 'I understand, sir. So she was visiting a friend. Who was that?'

'Julie Wycliffe. They met at school and kept in touch—

not just Christmas cards, but they'd meet up two or three times a year. Lindsey says… said… it kept her young having regular periods of reminiscing.' I paused, leant back in my wheelchair and stared at my hands as I rubbed my fingers gently together. Everything felt a bit unreal, kind of fuzzy.

The room was silent for a moment. Maybe they'd wordlessly agreed to give me a hint of respectful space. Maybe they just didn't know what to say next. I was grateful for the quiet to gather my thoughts.

I slowly looked up at Johnson. He was about to speak again, but I stopped him by asking quietly, 'So, if it wasn't an accident, what on earth's happened?' I felt a couple of tears welling in my eyes as the reality hit home further.

Johnson said nothing as if he, too, were gathering his thoughts. I noticed Williams shoot him a glance as if willing him to speak.

'We believe,' Johnson said eventually as he leaned forward across the table, 'that your wife has been murdered.'

I felt as if someone had landed a heavy blow in my midriff. My body went limp and I took a series of slow, deep breaths. Eyes cast down, hands clasped together. The detectives sat patiently waiting for me to respond. I sensed for a moment that Williams was going to stand up and come round the table to my side, but she stayed seated.

'You're not serious?' I knew it was a stupid comment as soon as I'd said it. I guess you don't get two solemn detectives calling round to your house on a Sunday morning to tell you your wife has been murdered when they're not serious.

'I regret we are being serious, sir,' Johnson said as if I'd asked a sensible question. He leant back in his chair while still fiddling with his fingers. 'Is there anyone who can be with you? A family member, or a friend?'

'Um, I don't know,' I answered. 'Maybe. Maybe I'll get in touch with someone soon, there's so much to take in just now. Please don't worry about me, I'm sure you have a lot of other people to look after, other things to do besides being with me.'

Johnson nodded gently. 'We'll ask a couple of family liaison officers to call, if you like. They're trained for this kind of situation...'

I said nothing, or maybe nodded slightly in grateful acknowledgement. Everything felt like a dream.

'We have to ask you to formally identify her body, I'm afraid,' Johnson continued methodically. 'Maybe in a day or two. I know this isn't easy, but it's a legal requirement. Can you do that, Mr Miller? We can assist of course with the... er... wheelchair and everything. An officer will need to be present in any event.'

'Thank you,' I said with a weak smile. 'I suppose I'll book a train to London, so if you can tell me where I have to go, I'll see what I can do. I have a friend there who can help me.'

Johnson looked surprised. 'London?'

'Well, yes,' I said, giving him a slightly puzzled look. 'London. Lindsey caught the train there yesterday. She was staying at a Premier Inn near Putney Bridge, as Julie only has a small one-bedroomed flat—you know what it's like living in the capital. They went to some local Italian, all according to plan, and she rang me on her mobile from her hotel room at about ten thirty. I presume the Met asked you to call on me as my local CID. So, where do I need to go...?' I shrugged gently with confusion.

Johnson and Williams both looked puzzled.

'I'm sorry, Mr Miller,' Johnson said. 'But we believe your wife died at about eleven o'clock last night. And she wasn't in London. She was murdered in Littleworth Wood, towards Tiverton, about three miles from here.'

TWO

Have you ever woken up to a normal day suddenly to have life's security blanket taken from you, leaving your world a scary place? The day a close relative is hurt in a car accident; the day you discover your spouse's affair; the day your teenage daughter announces she's pregnant without a boyfriend in sight; the day you're diagnosed with cancer… Life can never remain 'normal', I guess. Something lurks around the corner, drawing nearer as each day passes, and your life changes.

The two officers offered to take me to the Exeter Hospital mortuary when all was ready for me, but I thanked them and said I'd sort it out myself. Johnson gave me the usual spiel about having to notify me of the news. He added that a Detective Chief Inspector Goddard was handling the case and was already at the scene in Littleworth Wood awaiting the Home Office pathologist and investigating the area during these initial 'golden hours'.

'He's likely to visit you soon, as he'll want a more detailed statement,' he continued as we made our way back into the hallway. I thanked them for their condolences and kindness and watched them walk self-consciously to their car.

I was about to close the door but became abruptly mindful of the neighbouring village. The nearest property was another bungalow, now owned by a middle-aged guy— Craig someone or other as I then recalled it—who moved in after us and had little to do with anyone. The four new houses, all sold to professionals with young families, were round the slight bend in the close. Despite being at the end of the cul-de-sac, I was particularly grateful that I'd insisted on net curtains to give us both some privacy from prying eyes.

As the door closed, I had an intense feeling that Lindsey was standing behind me. I twisted my head, but the hallway was empty, of course. *Do* the dead watch you? I looked at the hallway as if seeing it for the first time and pictured that actual occasion when we had viewed it together. It was very late autumn, almost winter, the previous year that I'd found this particular bungalow. I showed Lindsey the property on a website, but she wasn't so sure, which was curious as we usually saw things the same way.

'It's a touch isolated, isn't it?' she'd said while squinting over my shoulder at the location plan.

'The four houses have gone, but the two bungalows are left—I like this one right at the end by the fields,' I said, pointing at the screen. 'It's part of an exclusive estate according to the agents and close to the village amenities. Look, it says the photos don't do it justice and it should be viewed.'

'There's a surprise.'

'Come on, Lindsey. If people rent isolated rural cottages for their precious fortnight's holiday, why not live in one all year round?' I said.

'For a fortnight, sure, but I like people around me the rest of the time.'

'That's why it's in a village…'

'*Edge* of a village.'

We talked it through, she apologised for being mardy and we had a hug. In the end she said my argument had some merit, and she agreed to at least view it. She was usually keen to please me—she was wired like that. She later admitted the agents had been right. As we looked out at the spectacular countryside beyond the fledgling garden hedge, I said with a smile, 'I love it,' and had reached round to her. She took my hand and gently stroked my dark brown hair with the other. 'Me, too.'

With one final look at the hallway, I headed for the office. What do you do when you're told that your wife has been murdered? If she'd died after a long illness, I'm sure I'd have felt different. We all think differently and handle stress and emotions in our own way. I felt a strong sense of being orphaned. Dying at just forty-three, Lindsey hadn't even reached half a century. An only child with no children. Her parents were both dead. She had a couple of cousins whom I'd never met who lived somewhere in Canada, but no other relatives. She had many friends, but perhaps her best friend was Grace Atkins who lived in Tiverton. I thought I should at least tell her. It crossed my mind to drive over there, but I remembered that my adapted car was in Tiverton being serviced and I didn't feel like venturing out anyway.

And so I decided to ring her. After all, it was only, as I saw it then, a telephone call.

THREE

I went into the office, flicked open the address book and dialled Grace's number. She answered promptly.

'Grace,' I said, leaning back in my chair with some relief that she'd answered, 'it's Mike. I have some dreadful news.'

I just came out with it until she told me to stop crying and said she would drop everything and come straight over. I wasn't in the mood to argue, and besides, I rather wanted her with me. Grace was the kindest, most thoughtful woman I'd ever met—after Lindsey, of course—but I'd also witnessed her inner core of steel that drew friends to her in times of crisis.

'That would be great, if you're sure it's no bother.' I gave a huge sniff.

As I waited for her to make it over from Tiverton, I busied myself in the kitchen and brewed up some coffee. Strong, with cream. My head filled with voices.

'You should have skimmed milk and watch your weight, Mike,' Lindsey had said once. 'You're hardly out jogging anymore.'

'I'm as fit as can be expected. I have my exercises and rehabilitation routine, don't I? My weight's under control so let me handle it, huh?'

'Of course it is, darling; I just want you to keep it that way. I love you just the way you are. It's so easy to put the kilos on, but incredibly difficult to lose them, isn't it?'

'My arms are certainly stronger than ever, aren't they?'

'That's for sure,' she replied, and pulled a mischievous face with animated eyebrows.

I smiled at her. 'Sorry, feeling ratty. Come here, you.'

As I stirred my coffee, I smiled again and felt that Lindsey would have allowed me the cream indulgence on an occasion like this, so cream it was.

I was in the sitting room when I heard Grace's silver Mercedes SLK pull up on the drive, its powerful 3.5-litre engine hardly designed for a subtle arrival. I was able to reach the door and open it just before she pushed the bell. She stepped into the house and bent down, and we had a slightly awkward hug. Somehow her sunglasses remained fixed to the top of her head. She remained stoical, but my own tears returned.

Eventually she pulled away. 'I'm so, so sorry, Mike. This is truly, truly awful. Awful. I really don't know what to say. I was trying to get my head round it as I drove over here, but I just don't get it—well, not yet anyway.' She took my hand briefly. 'Who on earth would do such a dreadful thing to poor Lindsey?'

I pulled a damp handkerchief out of my pocket, wiped my eyes and blew my nose. I gave a self-conscious hint of a shrug, 'Let's go to the kitchen. I've made some coffee.'

I turned the wheelchair round and was conscious that Grace was about to help me. I glanced up at her, and she would have seen my reddened eyes. A grateful 'Thanks' was all I could say.

She pushed me to the kitchen and left me at my spot by the kitchen table. While I stared out through the patio doors reflecting on what was happening, she busied herself around the kitchen and reheated the coffee in the microwave. She added skimmed milk—the indulgence was over.

'We'll sit out on the patio, Mike. It's such a warm day and it might give you some comfort, rather than being stuck in here.'

She carried the two coffee mugs outside and returned to the kitchen.

'My turn to push,' she said and took me into the fresh air. The chequered stone patio, level and abutting the house's floor for my sake, had been Lindsey's design. It was wide with plenty of room for the wooden table and six chairs, although I tended to keep two of those tidily to one side to allow space for my wheelchair. Lindsey used to refer to it as my 'landing strip'. The patio was edged with low stone walls that ran out from the back of the bungalow and were in-filled with a twenty-centimetre soil border containing a variety of tall, leafy flowering plants. They separated the patio from the lawn, and when the walls reached their respective corners, they each took a right-angled turn towards each other. They didn't meet, but left a two-metre gap to allow a level access onto the lawn. The position allowed us to enjoy the ancient sheep pasture that stretched some two hundred metres down to a leafy oak wood.

Releasing the handles of my wheelchair, Grace stretched and looked around.

'The garden's really coming on, Mike. These patio tubs have taken on a life of their own.' With a practised movement, she transferred her sunglasses from her head to her nose, and stepped onto the lawn through the break in the low wall. The September garden composed a symphony of scents bathed in warm sunlight and cool shadows. I watched her meander round slowly to the sound of a lazy woodpigeon, the tops of her fingers poking casually into the pockets of her tight denim jeans. She was a couple of inches taller than Lindsey, say about five feet seven or eight, and pretty slender. A passion for tennis kept her sportily fit. Her patterned red shirt matched the scrunchie around the stumpy ponytail roughly crafted from her dyed-blond hair.

We said nothing else until two or three minutes later, when she returned and took Lindsey's place at the head of the table to my left. Reversing her sunglasses back on to her head, she picked up her coffee and took a deep mouthful. If I hadn't known she was thirty-eight, I'd have put good money on her being no more than thirty, such were the absence of lines from her face.

She gave a determined smile and said gently, 'What's happening to us, Mike?'

I guessed the rhetorical question just summarised her typically logical thoughts. She'd lost her husband at the start of the year, and now her close friend. When I say 'lost' I don't mean he'd died or anything euphemistic like that. She'd lost him to some flirtatious, leggy bimbo of a secretary at work. She came home early from a Springsteen concert and found them in the spare room of their house. Broke her heart. An expensive mistake for Martin who, as a successful financial advisor, was worth a few quid.

She took a further swig of coffee and started again. 'You said on the phone that Lindsey was in London, so how come she was still in the area? What was she doing in Littleworth Wood anyway, particularly at that time of night?'

I shrugged.

'But you must have some idea, Mike. They're a geographical world apart after all. Are there really no clues at all?'

'You're sounding like those detectives, Grace,' I said

with a disapproving air. But she didn't seem to hear me.

'Was she seeing someone, Mike?' Her eyes didn't leave my face.

I was firmly of the view that Lindsey had been faithful to me. Okay, I wasn't the lover to her that I'd been to others, but, as I'd explained it in the early days to Lindsey, my incomplete lower-level spinal injury had fortunately not affected me adversely in that department. We'd last made love on Friday night and I certainly didn't notice any negative vibes or unwillingness then. Indeed, as I recalled it, she'd come on to me and had started the whole thing off when I was just contemplating sleep.

'No, of course not,' I said firmly. But it was a damn good question. Lindsey had an independent spirit, independent means, and, looking back, every opportunity to conduct an illicit affair. I took a final swig of coffee and held the empty mug in my hand.

'Penny for your thoughts?' Grace said with an empathetic expression.

'Look, Lindsey spent a long time trying to sort you and Martin out before it was clear he wasn't coming back, didn't she? You remember that, yes? She saw first-hand what damage an affair can do and was always passionately against such behaviour. Sure, we can all be hypocritical, but somehow I feel she was honest on this one. But even if she was having an affair, why on earth was she in Littleworth Wood when she had every opportunity for a romantic weekend in London? Doesn't add up, doesn't add up at all, does it?'

Grace nodded, 'Yeah, I guess not. Still…'

I tried to soften the tone. 'You're going to miss her, aren't you? She was your rock in the divorce.'

She smiled. 'Well, to the extent that she certainly encouraged me to fight rather than just let the bastard go, sure. I can't believe how stupid I was. I don't like to admit it, Mike, but that son-of-a-bitch is the only person to get inside my underbelly, and I've been trying to shake him out ever since. Never thought I had an Achilles heel until he crashed into my life. So, yes, I'll always be grateful to Lindsey for making me see sense on this one, else I'd have nothing today. It was evidently meant to be, since I'm now in a position to pop round to be with you at a time like this, which seems like an ironic payback, doesn't it?'

We fell silent. A single sparrow landed on the patio wall close by, suddenly saw us, and took rapid flight.

She looked over at me, as if she'd made some sort of decision. 'We're mates, aren't we?' she said.

The question threw me. 'Of course we are,' I said with a quizzical smile. Where was this going? I stared back down at the angled mug and started to rotate it, watching the final drop of coffee trickling round and round to pursue the elusive bottom.

'Lindsey was my best friend, the best friend I ever had,' she continued. 'We've been friends for over fifteen years. I knew her Dad when he was alive—and her Mum of course. You never met her Dad, did you?'

I shook my head and said nothing, focussed on the mug.

'We told each other a lot,' she continued. 'I always thought we could speak about anything…'

I looked up. 'Thought?'

'Yeah, thought. But you know what, Mike? I think that changed. Over the last few months, certainly since you two got yourselves hitched, something, or someone, was troubling her. She was less forthcoming, that was for sure.'

I sat forward on my wheelchair, put my mug down and leant my arms on the table. This was new, intriguing. 'Really? Have you any idea what it was?'

She shook her head slowly. 'No, no I haven't. I've no idea at all, which frustrates me. I've thought about it a lot—you know, tried to work out what the heck was going on with her, as I'm certain I wasn't imagining it. I even confronted her once and she was pretty evasive, even when I gave her the third degree.'

I looked out over the field as a lone rook laboured across the sky towards the wood. Maybe I could think what it might have been.

'And, if we are mates,' she continued, 'then I should tell you something else.'

'Go on.'

'When I last saw her—must have been Thursday just gone when she popped round to mine—I caught her on her mobile. She wrapped up the call pretty quickly when I came into the room with the tea as if she didn't want me to hear—or even know—she'd been on the call. I challenged her, of course.'

'And?'

'She made some mealy excuse. I made it clear to her that I didn't believe her.'

I shook my head dismissively. 'Might have been anything. She was as straight and honest as they come, Grace. Think of an angel—and then the angel's mentor. That was Lindsey. You must have it wrong.'

'I know what I heard, Mike,' she said, giving me a determined stare. 'Something about it registered with me, okay? She was being very friendly, almost whispering.'

'So? Doesn't mean anything, does it? She was popular

that's all. She was always using her mobile—you know, calls, texts and that tweeting thing.'

'I know that, Mike. Aren't we all glued to our phones nowadays? I only mention it now because of what's happened—might be relevant as I see it.'

I said nothing for a moment. 'So who *was* she talking to then? Did you hear anything?'

She paused and then said, 'Do you know a *Karl*, Mike? I heard her use the name Karl.'

I racked my brain but couldn't think of any Karl we knew, and certainly no Karl with whom she could have a flirtatious, secretive conversation.

'No,' I said, gently shaking my head. 'I can't think of anyone called Karl.'

She shrugged. 'Well, that just adds to it all then, doesn't it? It's got me thinking, Mike, and that's not going to stop until all this is sorted.'

I have to admit that it had got me thinking, too.

FOUR

So who on earth was Karl?

Grace stood up from the patio table. 'No more coffee for me, thanks, best get going and let Barney out. He's pretty good, but even Labradors have an endurance limit.'

'Martin will have you back in court for custody again if he hears you've been so cruel to that mutt.'

'Over my dead body,' she said, picking up the empty coffee cups. 'It's been good to talk things through Mike, even if we haven't yet come up with much as a team.'

Team. I liked that word. 'You've stopped me from being the lonesome widower and going through it all on my own.' I knew that I sounded nonchalant, but I just had to be strong—the alternative was not an option.

She gave me a kiss on the cheek. 'I'll ring you this evening to check you're okay, but call me anytime, won't you? Keep strong. I'll see myself out.'

'Remember the house phone has no answer phone—voicemail or whatever—but I'm marooned here anyway so I'll be in. Use the side gate, I think it's unlocked.'

'You *know* it's unlocked, Mike. Lindsey said you always leave it open. Check your insurance policy if I were you, else the insurers will wriggle out of any claim. Certainly would have done in my day. Not good for security, is it?'

'Well, I've hardly got much of that with bugger-all of a fence and hedge, have I?' I waved my arm towards the near open field. 'Besides, gives me a sense of freedom, doesn't it—you know, not being locked up in here.'

'Whatever,' she said. 'But a bit of a gambit in my view. Still, your call.'

After she left, I went inside and made myself another coffee. I looked at the biscuit barrel, but just didn't feel hungry—I wondered if I'd ever get my appetite back. I settled down on the sofa in the sitting room. It just seemed so odd, to be in the house, surrounded by all our things yet knowing I'd never hear Lindsey's key in the front door. That she would never enter the echoing hallway with a cheerful greeting. That we'd never even have another hug, another kiss—never make love again.

With a sigh, I picked up a framed wedding picture from an occasional table. We were married on a sunny day in March with the temperature slightly above seasonal, as I recalled it. That was almost six months ago.

'So, no photographer at all then?' Grace had asked as the four of us left the sour-faced registrar and paused on the steps outside the Registry Office.

'Didn't bother, did we?' Lindsey said with a smile as she stood behind me with both hands on my shoulders.

'You cheapskate,' Grace laughed. 'And with all that money in the bank. I always thought you'd have a mega fairy-tale wedding, Lindsey. Caribbean beach or Austrian castle.'

'Our original plan, but then Mike wanted to just get on with it. He's so sweet.'

'Hello,' I laughed, 'I might be in a wheelchair, but I can still hear you.'

Lindsey kissed the top of my head. 'Course you can, darling.'

As some guy wandered past, I held out my small

camera and called, 'Excuse me, could you do us a favour?'

I was positioned at the end of a low wall on which Lindsey seated herself with a spectacular smile as she held my hand. Instead of a traditional bride's dress, she wore a white satin suit and a feathery white fascinator. She never needed to pay much attention to her short brunette hair with its pixie cut, except to keep the creeping grey at bay.

I studied the photo. She looked wonderful, radiant as the cliché goes. I stroked her face through the glass, but she didn't react.

The fourth person at our wedding was Bronia Field, an old school friend of Lindsey's. After a gap of some twenty-six years, they'd met again by chance at the start of the year when Bronia had been appointed manager of the Tiverton hospice, where Lindsey volunteered. According to Lindsey, they hadn't got on well at school, opposing sort of gangs, but the connection and the exaggerated memories had seemed to create a growing bond. In the photo, Bronia was standing behind the bride.

As for Grace, she was standing behind my wheelchair on Bronia's right. I peered closer as if seeing her for the first time. Knowing what she'd just told me about her Achilles heel, it was hard to believe from her smile that just a few weeks before that day she'd caught Martin naked, taking treacherous advantage of both her absence and his office floozy.

I put the photograph carefully back on its table and stretched out on the sofa with my head resting on a soft cushion. The large room was quite ornately decorated with heavy fabrics, deep furniture and some paintings, principally oils, from a notable collection Lindsey's parents had accumulated after a lifetime of interest.

But who on earth was Karl?

The telephone rang.

Noting my watch said twelve fifteen, I stretched out a lazy left arm and plucked the cordless receiver out of its cradle to a number I didn't recognise.

'Mike Miller,' I said in a fairly subdued voice.

'Mr Miller, my name's Detective Chief Inspector Goddard. Is it convenient to talk?' The voice was deep and assured and clearly belonged to a man in control. I had the impression we were going to talk whether it was convenient for me or not.

'Yes, of course,' I said, with a hint of a pointless but instinctive nod.

'I'm sorry about your wife, Mr Miller. My deepest condolences. I've had some feedback from my two officers, Johnson and Williams. I need to come over, take some initial details as I'm not far away.'

I was dealing with a man on a mission, but then most people would want a man of action on the case, not a wimp.

'Of course. When?'

'I've got a couple more things to do here first. Let's say one o'clock?'

I thought for a few moments. I knew the Chief Inspector would want to see me, and I understood why the police had to get on with their enquiries as soon as reasonably possible. I knew I needed to cooperate, but I also needed some time. We were talking about my wife after all.

'Well,' I said, 'if talking to me would help you move the enquiry on, then that's fine by me, but could we say nearer two?'

That was agreed, so we said our formalities and rang off.

Yes, I knew an inspector would eventually visit, but there were some tasks I had to do before he arrived. I hadn't forgotten my conversation with Grace and the concerns she'd raised. A picture had started to form in my head, and the first thing I needed to do was to find where Lindsey had kept her most personal of things.

FIVE

'I understand you last saw Mrs Miller yesterday afternoon?' Goddard asked, tilting back slightly in his chair with his arms crossed.

The police arrived for their second visit of the day at spot on two o'clock. They sat at the kitchen table and declined even tea. My preference was for something a touch stronger, a beer perhaps, but that would have to wait. DCI Goddard had brought a skinny, pallid young detective sergeant named Ward who had outrageously thick red hair and appeared a little in awe, if not wary, of the senior man.

Goddard himself was a hint over six feet and was thick set, but fit. He had dark brown eyes behind silver-framed glasses. I guessed he was about forty-five or so, judging by his receding dark, greying hair and the experience and confidence of his angular face.

Goddard repeated his condolences and gave a perfunctory explanation for their early visit. I had every impression that he was going through the motions of ticking a box on a virtual procedural form he no doubt objected to with a passion.

I looked him in the eye. 'That's right, Chief Inspector, yesterday afternoon. And please call her Lindsey as everyone did. She loved marriage, but hated the "Mrs" bit. She couldn't get used to it having been a "Miss" all her life.'

I noticed DS Ward scribbling in a small black notebook. He wrote fast, his tongue protruding in a classic symbol of concentration. Never got that myself.

'I see,' Goddard said. 'Mrs... Lindsey hadn't been married before then?'

'No. She'd lived with a long-term partner, Peter, a few years back, but they never married. She had admirers of course, quite a few as I understand it, but she was always—how shall I put it?—fussy and wanted to wait for Mr Right.'

Dipping his head forward he said, 'And that was you?' No smile and posed like a serious question.

'I guess so, if you put it like that.'

'Well, it's how you put it,' Goddard said. He took his glasses off and let them swing lightly in his hand. 'So, yesterday afternoon?'

'Sorry?'

'You told us you last saw Lindsey yesterday afternoon and that she went to London for the weekend to see a friend.' His eyes didn't move from my face.

'Yes, that's right,' I said, feeling slightly uncomfortable for some reason.

'She often do that?'

'What, go see Julie?'

Goddard nodded.

'Occasionally, I suppose. She went two or three times a year and spent most of a weekend. Last went in June, I think, and before that late December—between Christmas and New Year anyway.'

'When did you last speak to her?'

I ran through what I'd told the detectives about the telephone conversation.

'Ten thirty's quite early, isn't it?' Goddard said.

I smiled. 'She joked that at her age she was losing her stamina and that even at their June weekend they'd made it to eleven thirty. But I knew she was tired as she's been doing long hours at the hospice.'

'The hospice?' Goddard asked, replacing his glasses on his face. He had a way of taking them off and putting them on without moving his eyes off me. It crossed my mind that I wouldn't want to be interrogated as a suspect by him. Was I a suspect? Did he think I'd done in my own beautiful wife? It was hard to see what he was thinking, but I dismissed the idea as rather silly.

'Lindsey volunteered quite often at St Chad's Hospice in Tiverton. Random hours—sometimes days and, on odd occasions, night shifts, getting back early hours of the morning. She loved it and found it very rewarding. Not my scene, mind you, as I've never been one for such places—it must be tough emotionally.'

I couldn't help but get the feeling Goddard wasn't too impressed by me. Evidently I wasn't manly enough in his book, but then we're all wired differently. He in turn might have had a phobia about finger-nailed black boards, or heights, or even frogs or spiders.

'You're aware that Lindsey died at about eleven o'clock last night in Littleworth Wood, not London, aren't you?' He said this in a matter-of-fact voice that I could just about handle, but which wasn't, in my view, textbook bedside manner for these circumstances. 'So how do you account for the fact that she managed to get from London to Devon in under thirty minutes? Physically impossible, isn't it?'

'I don't understand it,' I said. I glanced down and removed my handkerchief from my pocket. I took a deep breath and blew my nose. I wondered whether Goddard would see me as upset. Maybe he'd ease up, show some empathy. If he did notice, he showed no sign of adjusting his bedside manner, and he certainly didn't slow down.

'Forgive me, Mr Miller, but I need to ask you this. Where were you yesterday evening?'

'*Me*? Where was *I*? For heaven's sake I was here, what do you think?' I stared at him as I put away my handkerchief.

'I don't know what to think, that's why I'm asking. So you didn't leave the house?' A picture flashed through my mind.

'I've just said I was here, didn't I? I went out into the garden a couple of times, I suppose, if you want me to be precise. Had a beer on the patio and watched the sun go down, but that was the extent of it.'

Goddard said nothing, but stood up and walked over to the patio door as Ward continued to scribble in his book. He stood looking out at the garden and without turning said, 'Have you got a car?'

'Yes, an adapted one. A Ford Focus.'

He turned round. 'You didn't use it then?'

'Would have been tricky as it's in for a service. It went in yesterday morning and should be back tomorrow morning some time. Not exactly easy for me to go far without it.' I patted my wheelchair with both hands to emphasise the point—I often did that. 'The only other car in the family is Lindsey's and I obviously can't drive that. By the way, where is her car?'

'It's been recovered from the wood,' Goddard said, returning to his seat. 'Forensics are examining it.' He paused, looked somewhat uncomfortable, and then started to ask a question. I knew it would come up at some point and I wondered how he'd put it. Ever since I'd started using the wheelchair, I'd noticed how socially awkward most people became in dealing with a physical handicap. 'May I ask why you're in a wheelchair? Have you been using it for long?'

Even Goddard looked uncomfortable at his own question. Ward's tongue protruded even more as he concentrated on the note taking and he certainly didn't look up, as though saying, 'Don't look at me, I didn't ask that question.'

'Horse-riding accident,' I said. 'I borrowed a friend's horse and took it round a cross-country course. Worst twenty-five pounds I've ever spent.' I gave a watery smile at my go-to line. 'We approached a jump, and the horse decided at the last moment to go round it and didn't share his decision with me. I carried on, fell on the jump and landed awkwardly, you might say. I spent several weeks in hospital, underwent some rehabilitation, and now this.' I patted the arms of the wheelchair again. 'I'm paralysed in both my legs. Luckily, so to speak, type L1, so it could have been far worse. As you can see, I have full head and neck movement and I can use my arms, wrists and fingers. I'm independent for the basics, fortunately, but heavy household cleaning and maintenance tasks are beyond me. Many men would welcome that, I guess.' I smiled weakly. Goddard didn't react at all. 'Other paraplegics are much worse off, of course. I've been very lucky in the circumstances.' I paused. 'Unless there's a major medical advance, I'm told I won't walk again. Not easy being told that.'

Ward kept on writing. Goddard ran his hand through his hair and said, 'I'm sorry to hear that. When was this?'

'Two years, one month and five days ago,' I spelled out in a deliberate tone. 'I was living in Edinburgh at the time, then moved to Taunton.'

No one said anything for a few moments and the only sounds in the room were the gentle hum of the fridge and the ponderous clicking of the kitchen clock doing its rounds.

Eventually Goddard said, 'Have you any idea who would want to murder your wife, Mr Miller?'

If he'd asked me that question before my earlier conversation with Grace, I would have given a different answer, of that I was sure. Grace's comments had, however, changed things as they'd given me something to think about, something to do. I eased back in my chair and pulled a piece of paper out of my pocket. It was plain A4 with typed writing.

'I was going to give you this.'

I passed it over to Goddard, who took it instinctively from me.

He started to unfold it. 'What's this?'

Ward stopped scribbling and watched.

'A letter addressed to Lindsey,' I replied. 'I've never seen it before, but it may well give you an answer. I found it this afternoon deep inside a drawer in her bedside table.'

SIX

I think I should admit here to something that I would never have told my late parents.

Lindsey and I had met some eighteen months before, in early March, through an Internet dating site I advertised on. You know, one of those you see on TV where, in the thirty second slot that the company can afford to buy, a beauty queen and a smiling Adonis fall deeply in love. Why those perfect human specimens need a dating site, I've no idea. I'd tried Internet dating for several months looking for the ideal woman. I'd been out for an initial drink with a handful, but they didn't go anywhere, although I did get a kiss on the lips once. Made me feel I was with the virginal sixteen-year-old Juliet all over again.

I recall very clearly the first telephone conversation I had with Lindsey. I suspected from the start that she had all the attributes I was seeking.

'You look great in your photo,' I'd said.

'Entirely genuine. I don't even *own* an airbrush.'

She told me she'd trained as a nurse at Great Ormond Street and then worked at the Royal Devon and Exeter Hospital. 'After Dad died, I gave it all up to look after Mum. Best to keep carers in the family, isn't it? She's not wheelchair-bound, but she uses one off and on. I feel I make a real difference in her life, which is great.'

I didn't initially say anything about wheelchairs, but after a few telephone conversations, I took the gamble and told her that I used one. Her reaction was encouraging and a few days later we met for a drink at her local pub in Tiverton. We hit it off big time. She was a true sanguine and loved to talk and have fun. There were never any concerns about conversation running dry or being dull, as she always had something interesting or humorous to say. Her voice was filled with excitement and kindness and laughter that all twinkled with her crystal blue eyes. She made me feel alive.

After, I admit, no little persistence on my part, the times between our meetings gradually shortened and we were soon following, with my guidance, the traditional path of pub drinks, meals out, cinema and theatre. I was extremely hopeful that Lindsey was just the person I'd been looking for and, from every sign she gave me, that the relationship was going somewhere. I cannot say how happy that made me. And if you think I'm an emotional softie, I'm not going to argue here.

In the light of this background, you'll perhaps believe me if I told you I was shocked at the letter I gave Goddard.

SEVEN

I knew that Lindsey had admirers in the past because she'd told me, but the idea that someone was absolutely besotted with her was new to me.

Goddard had all but finished reading the letter. I watched his eyes dart along the tidy lines. He then lowered the piece of paper, replaced his glasses and, as an afterthought, passed the sheet over to Ward, who almost snatched it. He didn't need to pass it to me. I'd read it so many times that afternoon that I virtually knew it by heart. There was no address on the letter; indeed, there were no contact details of any kind for the sender, as if the writer had thought such details unnecessary. The letter was typed and was at least dated—last Monday. It read like this.

> *My darling Lindsey,*
>
> *You've ignored my letters, but at last I've just received one from you. Why didn't you write before when it would have been so easy? There's no electronic trail.*
>
> *I've missed being with you so much. I know our times together were only brief, but their brevity and clandestine nature makes them all the more special. You used to say how much you loved me and how good we were together, and, every single day that passes, I regret that I drove you away. I didn't mean to hurt you. I repeat, I am so sorry. I was perhaps damaged, and not fully in control of my actions. I'm much better now and wish I could prove that to you.*
>
> *Lindsey, I desperately want you back. Just seeing you*

now and then is not enough. I want us to be as we were before the incident. I appreciate that you're married to Mike, but nothing need stop us being together if we can rekindle the passion that we had. It would be so simple.

Leave him, Lindsey, and let us be openly together. I yearn for you, want you and need you. I can't stop thinking about you.

Call or speak to me – please! Even if we can meet and chat for just one last time. I promise you, promise you with all my heart, that I will be good. Please trust me.

You are still my world, and I love you.

C xxx

The final handwritten flourish of the letter C and the attached kisses were flamboyant, no holding back.

Goddard looked across the table at me. 'So, who's "C", Mr Miller?'

I shrugged. 'I haven't the foggiest. You'll appreciate this is a bolt out of the blue. I knew she'd had a stable partner in the past, but he was a Peter, which is well off a C, and that finished a while back anyway and was hardly clandestine. She told me she'd had a couple of short flings before we met, but never mentioned anyone with a name beginning with C or that she'd been pestered by someone.'

'The C might stand for a nickname.'

'I still can't help, I'm afraid.'

I wondered if Goddard could read anything into the letter, maybe something I hadn't seen. If she'd been the victim of oppressive attempts by an ex-lover to get back together, I was certain she would have mentioned it, especially if we'd been married at the time.

Goddard almost read my mind. 'So if Lindsey never mentioned a C or a harassing ex-boyfriend to you, why do think that was? Why didn't she bring you in on this?'

I thumped both arms of my wheelchair. 'I *really* don't know, Chief Inspector. Maybe she was embarrassed. Maybe she felt I would worry, what with the wheelchair and everything. Maybe she thought she could handle it herself. How should I know?'

Goddard looked pensive. 'Maybe she was getting back together with the mystery C? It seems from this letter that she'd started to communicate with him again.' He paused and waited for me to speak.

I exhaled loudly. 'Look, I've never seen this letter before, Chief Inspector. It was hidden, right? If *I* don't know who this guy is, I'm not sure anyone else would either.' I was conscious that I sounded aggressive, but I didn't care. I was getting tired. How could it be acceptable, on the day you're told your wife has been murdered, to get such a grilling as if you were some kind of criminal? Whatever happened to understanding the impact of shock? To giving empathetic space to reflect and mourn?

'Friends? Maybe some friends of hers would know?' Goddard persisted.

That was easy. 'Okay. Her closest friend is Grace, Grace Atkins. She lives in Tiverton. Lindsey had lots of friends, but I reckon the only people she's likely to have talked to about this kind of thing are her manager at the hospice, Bronia Field, and, of course, Julie Wycliffe in London.'

'Thank you. Could you give me each of their contact details, please?' Goddard said.

'Very well. I'll get them now.'

I took myself off to the office where Lindsey and I had 'his and her' desks. I looked at her desk and the filing cabinet and bundles of files on her side of the shelving and wondered what secrets might be lurking within. I would need to look later. I picked up our shared address book and returned to the kitchen, pushing the wheels hard.

Back at the table I looked up the three names and gave the mobile numbers to Ward, who wrote them down, no doubt with perfect accuracy, in his notebook.

Goddard said, 'I'd very much like to speak to this "C" guy, whoever or wherever he is, Mr Miller. If you come across any information or remember anything else Lindsey may have said, then contact me immediately. Indeed, I want you to report anything unusual to me from now on. Okay? Here's my card.'

He took a business card out of the pocket of his tired jacket and placed it on the table.

'Thanks, I will.' I looked Goddard in the eye, feeling a little calmer. 'I should tell you that Grace Atkins felt something was troubling Lindsey over the last few months, and certainly since we got married.'

Goddard raised an eyebrow. 'What do you mean, "troubling"?'

'It's only what Grace told me earlier today when she dropped by. I rang and told her about Lindsey although I haven't told anyone else yet, by the way. She said she couldn't get any more information out of Lindsey about what was troubling her. It may have nothing to do with this C person, but it may have everything to do with him. I just don't know.'

Goddard seemed to make a decision. 'I'll speak to Mrs Atkins and the other two,' he said.

There was a question I wanted to ask him. In all the circumstances, it was an obvious one. I'd thought about asking DS Johnson, but had backed off. In reality it was probably better to ask Goddard as the officer in charge of the investigation. I braced myself. Hoped I could handle it.

'Chief Inspector,' I began, and then paused. They both looked at me. 'No one has yet told me how... how Lindsey died.'

They glanced at each other.

'Lindsey's body has been taken to the mortuary at the hospital in Exeter,' Goddard said. 'We'll need to wait for the results of the post-mortem to be absolutely certain, and that will be undertaken as soon as practical. The pathologist, Dr Richard Milton, has carried out an initial inspection at the scene in the woods, so I could give you some general indication if you want me to.'

'Yes please,' I said, my hands tightening on the arms of my wheelchair.

'It's not pleasant,' he said.

'I understand. I guess I'll find out sometime or other, so I'd prefer to know now rather than... than imagine.'

'Fair enough,' Goddard said, clearing his throat. He shifted slightly on his chair and continued in gentle, but matter-of-fact, tones. 'Mrs Miller sustained quite a brutal attack. It looks like her hands were bound behind her back and she was dragged through the undergrowth whilst still alive. She then had her throat cut. Death would have been instantaneous at that point, absolutely instant. She wouldn't have suffered, believe me, other than the fear.'

I brought my right hand up to my mouth and bit on a finger as I started to shake. I closed my eyes and tried to resist the images that were forming. I failed. I opened my eyes again and looked at Goddard. 'Do you think this C is responsible, Chief Inspector?'

Goddard studied me. 'Too early to say, sir. Prior to this information, my inclination would have gone in a very different direction.'

'Which was?'

'Littleworth Wood is a beautiful place,' Goddard said. 'But it does have a dark side.'

I leant forward. 'Meaning?'

Goddard crossed his arms. 'Meaning this is not the first murder there, Mr Miller. A woman was killed in similar circumstances in the wood in July last year.'

EIGHT

Grace's promised call came shortly after nine o'clock that evening. I took it in the office, where I'd started to go through some of Lindsey's paperwork. The papers and files were not in the best of states since, as a sanguine, she never made order and tidiness a priority. She just had occasional and spur-of-the-moment bursts of activity, when her desk surface once more re-emerged into daylight, and unobtrusive piles appeared simultaneously in sheltered corners of the carpeted floor. But she never successfully completed such efforts, as something more interesting would distract her before her task had reached its proper and tidy conclusion.

'How was Barney?' I asked Grace.

'Fine thanks. He was desperate to do what a chocolate Labrador has to do. More to the point, how are you?'

I sighed and started rotating a pencil round my fingers of my left hand, but dropped it on the floor. More practice required.

'I'm struggling to get my head round it all, Grace,' I said. 'I still can't believe she's gone. Just like that. A wave to me yesterday, drives off and that's that. All the plans we had, the life together we'd hoped for, all gone. Not even a proper goodbye.' I paused, and then added, 'I had a visit from Chief Inspector Goddard this afternoon. They had a look round the house before they left, you know, Lindsey's things. He confirmed to me that they want me to go and formally identify her tomorrow and make a statement in the afternoon.'

'Sounds right. You'll have to do that, but it won't be easy for you.'

I knew it wouldn't be easy. I wondered how I'd feel seeing her again like this, in a mortuary.

'I knew it was coming,' I said. 'Guess I'm just a pawn in the game now. My car should be back by lunchtime so I can go then. I can go any time, apparently. I just need to let DS Johnson know so that an officer can be present with me.' I wasn't exactly sure why that was necessary. I was hardly going to make it up. We all wanted to know the same thing, surely: was it Lindsey lying there?

'Tell you what, I'll give you a lift to the mortuary. We could go in the morning rather than waiting for your car.'

Typical of Grace to take control. I welcomed the offer of her company and support, and she said she would collect me at ten o'clock.

'I'll let the police know. Just watch out for Lawrence, our postman, though—drives his little van like a true maniac and always delivers around that time. Villagers have learnt to stay off the road and cower behind curtains—they take no chances, as he takes no prisoners.'

She laughed. A good sound to hear in all the circumstances, especially after such a grim day. 'I can handle that,' she said confidently. She paused before she asked, 'What else did the Chief Inspector have to say?'

'I'll fill you in tomorrow, but it sounds like the killer was pretty rough and brutal. He said there'd been a similar murder in the wood last year, which I vaguely remember.' I picked up the pencil from its resting place on the floor and placed it back on Lindsey's desk.

'You know, Mike, I've been thinking. Wouldn't it be great, worthwhile, if we made our own enquiries, followed up leads, and did our bit for Lindsey? Ultimately, try and find out who did this, and what it's all about. Fight her corner for her as she can't do it herself. We've got the time after all.'

She sounded really determined, and I was loath to dampen her logic and enthusiasm. 'That's a little tricky for me, Grace, isn't it, what with this bloody wheelchair and everything? I suppose I could direct in the background. Ultimately we're just going to have to rely on Goddard and his team. He seems to know what he's doing, which is at least something.'

'I thought there was more to you than that, Mike. "Just direct in the background?" Is that it? I wanted a comrade in arms, not a director. I can direct myself pretty well, thank you very much. Where's your get up and go?'

'Frankly? Got up and gone. Come on, Grace, let's stay away from flights of fantasy. Obviously I would love to do something more, and I'm more than willing to support you. It would be great to play a part in giving Lindsey justice, but I couldn't actively investigate it, could I? '

'Might give you a story for your novel…'

That made me pause. My close friends knew that I would hunt and peck on my laptop as I struggled without true hope or discipline to create a crime novel worthy of the name and concept.

'You may be right,' I said. 'But let's leave it for now and chat about it another time, huh? It's been quite a day.'

'Poor you. I do understand. I would like to speak to this detective, though' She sounded as if she relished the prospect.

'That shouldn't be a problem—he said he wants to speak to you—and Bronia and Julie. I gave him all your contact details. He'll want to know if Lindsey ever went out with someone beginning with the letter C?'

'That's a curious question. C? Is that it?'

'I'll explain when I see you next.'

From the moment's silence down the phone, I could picture her making a thoughtful expression. I'd noticed her habit of pinching her bottom lip and pulling it gently downwards when she was concentrating on an issue. 'Off the top of my head the only "C" I know is a Charles, in fact I know two of them. One's a cousin of mine, the other's a member of the royal family. I can introduce you to one, but not the other. Why will he want to know that?'

I rested my head in my hand. 'Did Lindsey know your cousin? Did they ever meet?' As soon as I said it I realised I was being dragged in, riding on Grace's own decision to investigate.

Grace was silent again for a moment. 'I've no idea, Mike. Possibly. I didn't keep tabs on her too closely—I was a friend, not a minder or her mother. Maybe they met at some do or other, I simply don't remember. Chances are they did, as he only lives in Exeter after all, but then I don't see much of him despite the proximity. At fifty, he's the permanent bachelor. He's a heterosexual, though, as he's had girlfriends in the past, quite a few as I recall. I've met a couple of them in days gone by. Why's this all relevant, anyway?'

'It's not for me to deal with this, Grace. I'd better leave that to Goddard to explain else I'll get myself into hot water... Hang on,' I said and paused. 'I think that was someone knocking on the door. I'll call you back if you like unless you want to hold on? Won't be long.'

'I'll hold,' she said.

'In which case I'll put you in my lap, so to speak.'

'Naughty,' she said and gave a short laugh. She had a lovely little laugh. I'm not sure I'd noticed it that much before.

I left the room and made my way across the hallway to the front door, turning the wheels of the wheelchair as hard as I could to propel myself forward with the cordless phone resting in my lap. I stretched up to the latch and opened the door, but no one was there.

And then I looked down, gasped and cried out

NINE

'So who would have done that?' Grace asked.

She glanced across at me from the driver's seat of her BMW 7 series, which was indeed roomier than her Mercedes, as we headed towards the mortuary in Exeter the following morning. I continued to stare out of the windscreen, hardly taking in the fast-moving rural scenery on this sunny September morning. We followed the main road and headed south, keeping pace with the River Exe.

'Are you in there, Mike?' she said glancing across at me. 'Tell me again what happened.'

I remained silent for a moment longer and then stretched in my seat.

'I heard someone knock at the door,' I repeated. 'But no one was there. Then I looked down on the doorstep. It honestly made me jump—I just wasn't expecting it. I'm sorry if I frightened you.' I gave her a weak smile.

She extended her left hand and gave me a reassuring pat on my thigh.

'Well, yes, you did make me jump. Not easy to do that, believe me.' She gave me a wink and indicated to overtake a white van that was slowing in front of us. 'But, as I said, who would have done that, and why? It seems so macabre.'

'I don't think I've ever been that close to a real human skull before, and certainly not one so small and drizzled with red paint. Reminded me a bit of those shrunken heads in some glossy geographical magazine. It looked like blood, which doesn't make anatomical sense of course, but then none of it actually makes sense, does it? What's it all mean?'

'Have you actually measured it?'

'The circumference was about forty centimetres. I looked on the Internet and a skull that size would appear to be a baby or a toddler, which is really weird.'

'So where's it come from?'

I shrugged. 'No idea.'

'So there are no skeletons in your cupboard?'

'This is serious, Grace.' But then I couldn't help twitch a smile, as I failed to resist her humour. It seemed wrong to see humour in such a situation, but I was on my way to see Lindsey in difficult circumstances. I would need all my instincts and natural optimism to see everything through.

We were quiet for a moment.

'I think you should tell the inspector so he can check it out,' she said.

'About the skull?'

She nodded. 'Uh huh.'

'Do you think I should? Maybe it was just a prank, you know, kids messing around or something.'

'Hardly. Come on, Mike, you must admit it's a bit odd for this to happen the day after Lindsey died—unless you have a regular delivery of such things?'

'No, you're right,' I said. 'I'll mention it to Goddard when I next speak to him. Weird, isn't it? This is Westland for heaven's sake, not Amityville.'

We drove on in silence for a while. Grace seemed lost in thought too. She had been one of the first friends Lindsey had introduced me to. We'd met up with Martin and her at a restaurant in Exeter. I'd taken to her straight away and, although she was a few years younger than Lindsey, I could see they were both on the same wavelength. They had the same humour and enjoyed each other's company.

Martin, however, was not someone I related to at all. He was five years older than Grace, dark-haired and overweight. A strong ex-rugby player who could probably handle himself if he had to. I suspected his physique, and his money, had given him the arrogance that I found obnoxious. He would bore me silly with tales of his motorbike and what he'd fixed on it, or where he'd been on it and how fast he'd gone. Lindsey told me she had similar feelings, but since he and Grace came as a package, we were obliged to tolerate him. Lindsey did arrange 'girl only' weekends to spend time with just Grace, which gave me time to myself too.

As she slowed the car towards a roundabout, Grace said, 'What do you make of the previous murder in Littleworth Wood over a year ago? You said Goddard mentioned it yesterday evening. I'd forgotten about it.'

I did recall it and I'd read something about it. 'It does ring a vague bell,' I said. 'Wasn't it on Crimewatch? I seem to recall someone saying something about it, maybe Edith who runs the village shop. Do you remember what happened?'

Grace honked the horn to frighten a pheasant from imminent death on the road ahead. It ran bewilderedly for the verge. 'It was obviously a big thing locally last year, but I'd forgotten the detail if I'm honest. I looked it up on the Internet last night. The woman's name was Sandra—Sandra Roberts, I think. She was forty-one and divorced. Had one son and lived on her own in a decent house in Tiverton. There was a photo of it. She was found by a couple out for an early morning walk with their dog—well, the dog found the body I gather and they called the police. Must have been a shock for them.'

I nodded. 'Did it say how she died?'

'Her hands had been tied behind her back and her throat had been cut.'

'Same as Lindsey,' I said almost to myself and closed my eyes briefly.

She'd heard me. 'Oh my God, really? That's pretty interesting, isn't it?'

We eventually reached Exeter and the satnav advised that our destination was approaching. I broke the further silence and said, 'Did they find out what happened—you know, who did it last year?' I had the impression the subject was still very much on her mind, too.

'I couldn't see anything about that. The police were making enquiries, but then the Web trail went cold. No updates, no reported trial retelling the story. I presume it remains unsolved, which is a bit scary if you think about it.'

'Guess so. Still it's just another story, not relevant here.'

Grace turned to look at me. 'Not relevant? Are you joking?'

'Okay, okay, they have similarities, but this is Lindsey we're talking about.'

'I appreciate that, Mike, but come on. I don't want to sound harsh or insensitive, but the—what do they call it?— the *modus operandi* was the same. Seems a bit of a coincidence, don't you think? Like that nutter who murdered prostitutes in East Anglia a while back. Didn't Goddard seem to be thinking along these lines from what he said to you?'

'He didn't spell it out.'

'Well, maybe he didn't want to, or need to, but it seems perfectly possible to me,' Grace said. 'The reports on the murder last year didn't mention a series, obviously. There was just the one murder. Things are different now.' As she turned into a small car park next to the mortuary complex, she continued. 'But the reports did take another angle on it, and on Littleworth Wood.'

'What was that?' I asked.

She killed the engine and applied the handbrake. 'They talked about the occult, Mike, saying some sort of witches' coven was operating in the wood.'

TEN

DS Johnson had already arrived and was standing patiently in the reception area. We greeted each other quite formally and I introduced him to Grace. An orderly guided Johnson and me to a 'viewing room', while Grace took herself off to wait for me.

Lindsey was lying on a mortuary table under a large white cloth. I was immediately drawn to the square hole over her head. As soon as I saw the pale, silent face, I knew it was her. A few strands of her short brunette hair and grey roots at the scalp were also visible.

I turned away. The whole experience felt curiously unreal and brought home to me that we wouldn't be growing old together, or sitting on the warm veranda of our ivy-clad Italian villa with crystal glasses of chilled Pinot Grigio in our wrinkly, aged hands while we watched the sun set over the wooded hills of Umbria.

I closed my eyes. 'Yes, yes, it's her,' I said, as if not addressing anyone in particular even though Johnson was right by me. 'There's no need for me to look further.'

I turned, opened my eyes and made for the door as fast as I could. Johnson followed respectfully and silently behind, leaving the orderly with Lindsey. Once back in the reception area, he said goodbye accompanied by reassuring and comforting words.

Grace stood up from a padded bench when I entered the waiting room. She took a couple of steps towards me, knelt down on the carpet-tiled floor in front of me and hugged me. I held her for several minutes. I could feel her warmth and joined in with her gentle, rhythmic breathing.

Once we were out in the tarmacked car park again, she helped me clamber into the car and folded my wheelchair back into the sizeable boot.

She climbed into the driver's seat. 'Home time.'

There were things I needed to do, not least to look further into Lindsey's personal things, but it was also a warm, sunny morning. I pined for some friendly company. 'Are you in a rush?' I asked, looking across at her.

She shook her head. 'Tennis lesson later this afternoon, that's all. Save you were going to tell me why the inspector wants to know about someone Lindsey knew beginning with C.'

'I can tell you that now. I thought it might be a good idea to go and see Bronia at the hospice,' I said. 'You know, before the choleric Goddard lands on her with all his pleasant bedside manner. I would rather she heard the news personally from us, not least as Lindsey's manager. Lindsey wasn't due there until Wednesday afternoon. What do you think?'

'I had thought about that,' she said, 'but I didn't suggest it as I didn't think you always hit it off with her.'

'There's sometimes an edge in her voice, but I think we're okay—certainly will be if you're there.'

She clicked her safety belt decisively into its lock before starting the car. 'Is she working today?'

I shrugged. 'Dunno. I could ring her?'

'Let's live dangerously and just drop by. It's not much out of the way, is it? It can't do any harm, I'm sure.'

ELEVEN

'I don't believe it—I really don't believe it,' Bronia said. Tears welled up in her hazel eyes and she took a white tissue out of her navy and white uniform and dabbed them carefully.

Grace and I arrived at St Chad's Hospice on the edge of Tiverton late morning. The modern building was made of glass and treated wood and stood by a small copse so that established trees gave it a restful and rural existence, especially in the warm sunshine.

Bronia had looked surprised at seeing us both there and had immediately showed concern. She took us to her drear, minimally furnished office, a room only enlivened by the dramatic splurge of yellow in the cheap 'Sunflowers' print on the magnolia-painted wall near the door.

'So how are you, Mike?' Bronia asked, as she gave her nose a final wipe with her tissue, after listening in silence before her tears had flowed.

I sighed. 'Me? Completely devastated, if I'm honest,' I replied. 'I'm finding it difficult to come to terms with everything—not only that she's gone, but also that someone, for some godforsaken reason, has actually done harm to her. I'd like to know who that is, and why.'

Bronia studied me, her eyes still damp. 'That's what I would expect of a husband,' she said, and returned the tissue to a pocket of her uniform.

'You'll get a visit sometime soon from DCI Goddard,' I said. 'Please just tell him all you can.'

'I'm not sure if there's anything worthwhile I can tell him,' she said as she continued to look at me. 'The biggest thing I don't understand is what she was doing in Littleworth Wood anyway, especially when she said she was in London with Julie. You must have some idea, Mike, surely. She was your wife after all. And what's Julie say about it?'

I shrugged. 'I've not spoken to her,' I said.

'Why ever not?' Bronia said, giving me a colder look. 'I'd have been on to her like a shot.'

I stared at her. 'That's easy for you to say, Bronia.'

'Well, why wouldn't you?'

I said nothing.

'Well?' Bronia pressed.

'Because that's for the police, not me,' I said, wagging a finger at her. But even as I said it, I could see myself giving way.

'Oh, come on,' Bronia said. 'Let's get real. When will they ever get round to that? Besides, don't you want to know?'

I remained silent and looked at my fingers, picked a nail.

Grace touched me gently on the knee. 'You're going to have to find out sometime, Mike.'

I nodded. 'Sure, I guess so.'

'So let's go for it,' Grace said.

I sighed. 'Okay, I'll ring her.' I took my mobile out of my pocket and flicked it to the contacts directory.

Bronia snapped up the telephone on her desk. 'Don't bother with that. Remind me of her number, Mike. We can call her on this phone and put the speaker on. It'll be clearer than that thing.'

I dictated the mobile number and Bronia dialled it as I

spoke. As the response signal rang out round the small office, we all as one, like Pavlov's dogs, rested our arms on Bronia's desk.

A bubbly voice suddenly answered.

'Julie,' I said, directing my voice to the phone. 'This is Mike Miller, Lindsey's husband.'

She paused momentarily and then replied cheerfully. 'Hi, Mike. How things?'

She hadn't already been told—no word from Goddard, which frustrated me slightly. Julie sounded shocked and upset. Through long periods of silence, the three of us sat staring at Bronia's phone.

'Julie,' I said, 'Lindsey told me she was meeting up with you on Saturday. Did she arrive?'

'*What!*' Julie exclaimed. 'She said *what*?'

I reiterated what I'd said, adding the detail I'd given the detectives.

'But that never happened,' she said. 'Lindsey and I didn't meet up this weekend. I was in Norwich for a start.'

'But the Italian in Putney? The hotel?'

'I'm sorry, Mike, none of it's true. I didn't see Lindsey this weekend—didn't even speak to her come to that.'

I was conscious of Grace and Bronia exchanging glances.

'So why did she tell me what she did? And where the hell did she go if not to Putney?'

Bronia said sarcastically, 'To the wood, obviously.'

'But she left home at about two fifteen or so,' Grace said. 'She wouldn't have been in Littleworth Wood for over eight hours.'

We were all silent for a moment.

'Julie,' I said, addressing Bronia's phone, 'how did

Lindsey seem when you last saw her? Grace said she'd detected some sort of concern or worry about her. Did you pick that up as well?'

'I can't honestly remember when I last saw her, Mike.'

'Well, I can help you there. Either that weekend in early June, or even the visit last Christmas?'

'June? I didn't see her in June. Or Christmas come to that.' She paused. 'Mike, I haven't met up with her for almost two years.'

TWELVE

Several years ago, I was on holiday on a Greek island in the western Aegean. Might have been Skopelos, maybe Skiathos. My then girlfriend and I were outside a taverna by the calm sea drinking a bottle of pretty decent wine and basking in that warm evening glow after a lazy day on a sunny Mediterranean beach. Peaceful, serene, secure. Then I'd felt it. A gentle tremor, but enough to register on the Richter scale. Suddenly rooftops seemed to float and the firm land beneath my feet turned soft and spongy. The quake lasted for no more than two or three seconds and then was gone. No damage, no casualties, no harm. But all of the customary and natural rules of existence seemed broken, and life became, just in that extraordinary moment, a new game with new rules, new standards, and new norms.

Anyone told that facts they'd always taken to be true were in fact utterly false was, in my opinion, going to feel like I did that day in Greece.

'Are you absolutely sure?' I asked Julie.

'Of course I'm sure, Mike,' she replied. 'We've talked on Skype and texted each other frequently. I can very easily recall the last time I met up with Lindsey. It was a Christmas holiday, but not last year—the year before. She hadn't even met you then. I even missed your wedding, of course, as I was abroad.'

'Did she go up to London that time, Julie?' Grace asked.

'Sure. Stayed with me here in Putney. She slept on my

apology for a sofa bed in the siting room.'

'Was she with anyone, then?' I asked. 'A boyfriend?'

'You should know that, Mike,' she said.

'I'm not sure what I know now.'

No one said anything for a moment.

'Well, as I remember it,' Julie said through the speaker, 'she had no one in tow. I recall she was looking for someone because she told me that she'd been trying some Internet dating sites. I warned her to be careful—'

'Thanks,' I said in a jocular tone.

'Nothing personal, Mike. It's just that you hear about some right nutters using those sites, don't you? Anyhow, I warned her to be careful, meet in public, take precautions like that—and she seemed to take it all on board.'

'She did,' I added.

'I did have the impression that she'd got an admirer, but she didn't say anything about him. No real mention. Couldn't have been you, Mike, could it? When did you meet up with her?'

'The following March.'

'So, no, it couldn't have been you then.'

'No other clues?' Grace asked.

Julie paused. 'No. But it couldn't have been anyone she wanted, as she said she was still on the lookout for Mr Right.'

Grace said, 'Do you think there was someone pursuing her? Advances she didn't want?'

'It's possible, I guess,' Julie said. 'Why do you ask?'

I said, 'I had the impression she had an unwelcome admirer who'd finally broken her down at some point.'

'As I say,' Julie said, 'that's entirely possible, but I don't know. All I know is that she was single and looking for a partner and seemed to have something in the back of her mind.'

Grace had obviously been thinking about what I told her on the way over about the letter, as she said, 'Julie, are you aware of anyone she knew whose name starts with C? A friend, or even a boyfriend?'

'The letter C?'

'Yeah.'

'I don't recall anyone. There was a Peter of course, but that hardly helps. Why do you ask?'

'It's just that Mike found a recent letter in her things from some sort of ex—' Grace said.

'*Recent*? How recent is "recent"?'

'Try beginning of this week,' I said.

'Bloody hell. You're joking, Mike, aren't you?'

I noticed the surprised look on Bronia's face.

'Sadly not. I found it in her personal stuff yesterday. It seems she got together with him before I met her, I presume, possibly before we married. She dated him for a short while, but apparently in a clandestine sort of way.' I paused and took a deep breath. 'I have the impression from the letter that he did something, there was some kind of an event, an occurrence, an incident that caused her to end their brief, and intimate, relationship. This C guy has pestered her with letters—'

'Pestered?' Julie interrupted. 'How many letters? What did they say?'

'No idea,' I said. 'I haven't found them yet, even if they still exist. He refers to them in the recent letter.' I picked my fingers again as I stared at the phone and added, 'So this all means nothing to you, Julie?'

'No, none of it. I'm sorry.'

'Nor me,' Bronia chipped in.

'You will tell Goddard about this admirer, Julie, won't you?' I asked. 'He must understand that this letter has such roots in the past. It might help the police track the guy down. You can help Goddard with that.'

'Goddard?'

'The chief inspector on the case,' Grace said.

'Yeah, sure. Of course I will,' Julie replied. 'If you think it'll help.'

'It will, Julie. I'm sure it will.'

Julie said, 'Please tell me when the funeral is, won't you? Any idea on timescale?'

I hadn't really given it any thought. I said I'd keep her posted and we closed the telephone call at that point, each promising to keep in touch.

The three of us seemed to relax back into our chairs. Grace looked at me caringly and said, 'You okay, Mike? You look a bit a pale.'

I shook my head. 'What's going on, Grace? If Lindsey didn't go to see Julie over those few days in December and June, where the hell *did* she go?'

Grace and Bronia exchanged further glances.

'You'll be telling me next, Bronia,' I said, 'that Lindsey never volunteered on the nightshift here.'

Bronia looked at me hard. Somehow I knew what was coming. 'Nightshifts?' she said with a puzzled tone. 'Lindsey never worked any nightshifts here, Mike.'

THIRTEEN

At first Grace and I said very little to each other as she drove me back the four miles to my bungalow in Westland. As she accelerated away from a rural crossroad, she said, 'I'm sorry to say it, Mike, but it seems that Lindsey was leading some kind of double life—and that just sounds crazy knowing her as I do.'

'Knew her,' I said. 'I thought she was away seeing Julie over two weekends—she wasn't. I thought she was out volunteering at the hospice over several nights—she wasn't. I thought on Saturday she'd gone up to London—she hadn't. So, as I said earlier, where the hell *did* she go?' I listened to the car tyres caressing the road below us. 'She gave me no indication whatsoever there was anything wrong in our marriage, in our relationship. She seemed happy and content. Busy, yes, but she didn't need to work following her inheritance. Anything she did was down to her. She could have spent each day in bed if she'd chosen. It wasn't as if I was the burden to her that her Mum had been.'

Grace glanced at me. 'Really?' she said, and then refocused on her driving, eyes ahead. 'She never gave me the impression her Mum was a burden. Her Mum was a sweet old widow, eighty if a day, frail and tiny.'

I reflected on how to put my point across. Lindsey had introduced me to 'mother' in early April the previous year after we'd been dating for about a month. Mary was lovely that day with an evident love of life.

'Lindsey felt that she was doing something worthwhile

looking after her Mum, but she increasingly found caring for her more than a little frustrating.'

'Gosh, I never knew that. But then I guess she never did talk much about her Mum, especially her death, and I was away for the inquest.'

'Really? She talked a lot about her to me, but I guess that's logical enough. It's true though, Mary could be quite challenging,' I continued. 'Well, you met her, didn't you? Delightful, but with a determined streak.'

'That was for sure.' Grace smiled to herself as if remembering some past incident. 'So, now I have you to myself, tell me more about it, you know, the July accident,' she said, pulling past a slow-moving removals lorry.

This was another day I wouldn't forget.

'The accident?' I said. 'That was tough all round. I really don't want to repeat it all now, especially today.'

'Go on, tell me. Don't do a Lindsey on me.'

I sighed and crossed my arms in resignation. 'Well, you'll recall that Mary was pretty reclusive, and that afternoon Lindsey had to collect a prescription for her from the doctors' surgery. She was only away from the house for about twenty minutes. She returned home and found her in the en suite of her downstairs bedroom. She was fully dressed, slumped into the bath, her waist on its edge, drowned.'

'Dreadful. Lindsey shouldn't have left her like that.'

'That's hardly fair, Grace. Lindsey had her life too.'

'Of course she did, although that's looking increasingly curious-'

'Grace…'

'Well, it is, isn't it?'

I paused. 'Come on, Grace, we're talking just twenty

73

minutes. Twenty minutes.'

'It took just that time for Mary to lose her life, Mike.'

'I really don't think that's fair. Lindsey was her full time carer out of love—she did her best, right?'

'Sure, but she could have got someone else to run the errand, couldn't she? Or someone to sit with Mary while she went for the pills.'

I stared at her. 'Lindsey couldn't provide total cover, could she?'

She nodded. 'So why couldn't you have helped? She could have waited until you came over.'

Ironically, I'd been in the bath at my old Taunton flat when Lindsey rang me. I'd dressed as quickly as I could and drove the thirty-five minutes that it took in my car to comfort her.

'She never asked me or mentioned the errand to me. It was nothing unusual after all. When I eventually arrived, Lindsey was in a right state. Obviously I wish I'd been there—it wouldn't have happened, I agree. But that's hindsight, huh?' I took a deep breath and tried to relax as I watched the hedges and the countryside pass by. 'The police established that the doors were locked at the time, with the back door key on its hook and the front door's Yale lock operative. Lindsey always locked them whenever she left her mother for a short trip. The coroner concluded death by misadventure, and that Mary, in one of her determined moods and in defiance of strongly given advice, had gone to run herself a bath and then slipped, banged her head and drowned.'

'Poor woman,' Grace said, still looking agitated. 'What a tragic way to go. What a waste when it could have been so different.'

'I suppose. However it came about, and whoever was to blame.' I took a breath. 'Anyhow, the sad case was closed and I was left to comfort Lindsey.'

As she turned the BMW into my close, she said, 'And here you are having to face all these sorts of issues again. At least you have some experience now.'

'I guess so,' I said as she halted on my drive.

Grace turned to look at me. 'Mike, you know how I mentioned before about us investigating Lindsey's murder? About doing our bit in case the police get bogged down, like they have over Sandra Roberts? I am really serious about it.'

'As you said, I suppose we do have the time.'

'More than Lindsey's got. We should do it for her.'

I undid my seat belt. 'And no little self-interest on my part.'

'Because she was your wife?'

'That for sure. But you know, Grace, it's almost as if someone's got it in for me.'

FOURTEEN

After a snack lunch at home, I wheeled myself down to the village shop, passing my recently returned Ford Focus on the driveway as I left.

Edith Riley was, as usual, behind her counter. Despite being in her late seventies and recently having had a minor heart attack, she still ran the Westland post office and village store, a role she'd performed religiously for almost forty-five years. On her short, petite frame, she wore a simple but dated cotton skirt, blouse, and pale pink cardigan that she had on whatever the weather. Her white hair moved in unison in its old-style bob, and she looked at me through her thick glasses.

'Mike,' she exclaimed. 'I've just heard on the local news and I was going to come and see you. It's so horrible. Unbelievable. Is it really true?'

Goddard had told me that they would be releasing Lindsey's name as soon as I'd confirmed the identification. I'd agreed. Do anything that helps, I'd said. I eased my wheelchair a little nearer the counter and looked at her kindly. 'I regret it's true, Edith, but, if you don't mind, I don't really want to talk about it. I only came in for a pint of milk, that's all.'

Edith looked quite shocked. She offered her condolences and said with a look of pure sincerity, 'If there is anything I can do, Mike, anything at all, please do ask, won't you?'

I smiled and gave her a casual nod of gratitude and

acknowledgement. 'Thanks, Edith, that's very kind.'

'And don't worry about the shop,' she added. 'We can manage without you until you want to come back.'

I volunteered a couple of times a week just to help out, but the job also got me out of the house to meet some people. Edith was always a generous soul. Popular in the village. The small shop probably made little if any money for her.

'That's great. Thanks, Edith.'

I bought the milk and left. As I powered my wheel chair down the close to my home, I saw the large figure of my bungalow neighbour, Craig, doing some gardening near the low wall that bordered the pavement. I guessed he was heading towards his fortieth birthday and, despite the stubbled chin and slightly greasy, dark hair, he had quite a classic, handsome appearance. He was the picture of someone who had rather let himself go. Although Lindsey and I had tried to be sociable after he moved in, it was never reciprocated, which confirmed Edith's straw poll view that he was someone who liked to keep himself to himself.

He glanced up as I approached but didn't react to my cheerful greeting. Some would say that was rude. Some would have let it go. For some reason that morning, I didn't.

As I came to a stop a couple of metres from him, I said, 'Sorry, Craig, it's usual to at least say "good afternoon" back.'

He leant on his hoe and stared at me. Said nothing.

'Didn't you hear me?' I persisted, feeling increasingly aggravated under his stare.

'Oh yes, I heard you,' he said with a dry, measured pace. 'But I have nothing to say to you.'

'Not even "good afternoon"?'

'Aye, not even good afternoon.'

I could have let it go at that. Given up, but I didn't. Something rankled me and I went further than perhaps was warranted or called for. 'You know, Craig, I've had a few neighbours over my time, but you have to be the least neighbourly person I've ever met. Whatever issues are winding you up or holding you back, it takes nothing, no effort at all, just to say good afternoon to someone, particularly the guy living next to you.'

He just continued to stare at me.

'You're unbelievable,' I said and made to wheel myself on.

'I'll talk to you when I'm ready,' he said, turned and made towards his side gate.

I stopped. 'What do you mean by that?' I called after him, but he just strode away through his gate, which closed behind him. I waited for a few moments looking at the white-painted side gate, half-wondering whether he would come striding back. But I was confident that he wouldn't, and the stillness of the place confirmed that. 'Idiot,' I muttered to myself, more for my own satisfaction than for any communicative reason, and carried on up the pavement to my own home.

For the next couple of hours, I went through Lindsey's desk, although the exchange with Craig kept re-occurring in my mind and I felt increasingly annoyed with myself for reacting as I did. The last thing I needed was some public scene. Everyone's different and I knew deep down he was who he was, and good luck to him. With regard to Lindsey's papers, I felt that I shouldn't throw anything out in case Goddard had a go at me, even though they'd looked round once already. I took the view that I was helping, as my tidying would save the police from going through a mess.

The phone in the office rang and made me jump. It was Goddard. He wanted to see me the next day, and he took up my suggestion of calling round at about nine thirty in the morning.

I made a couple of calls and did some paperwork with the intention of popping out on an errand or two later. Before I did so, the house phone rang again. The caller just launched at me, so I slammed the phone down. Before it could ring again, I scrambled down with some difficulty under my desk and wrenched the line out of its socket. And there I stayed, lying under the desk breathing heavily.

First there was the story about the bloodied skull on the doorstep, now I had something else to say to Goddard in the morning.

FIFTEEN

The woman inserted the key in the lock and gently turned it. Glancing quickly round at the empty garden and open wicket gate, she pulled the handle down with her gloved hand and eased the back door open. As she entered the quarry-tiled kitchen, she paused and listened. From the corridor beyond the kitchen door came the sound of a television – or was it just music? Silent footfalls took her into the corridor and past the sitting room and what clearly was now a loud television. Someone coughed in there, harsh and chesty. She glided on.

The bedroom door at the end of the corridor was ajar. She went through, closing it quietly behind her. A few short steps took her into the still of the en suite where she closed the door, not even disturbing the large white towel that hung on its hook. Leaning over the old Victorian bath, she quickly inserted the plug and, holding her breath and with glances at the door, turned on both taps to their full. The pressure was good, as she knew it would be, and the bath started to fill rapidly. Habit made her dip in her right hand to test the water, although she realised that temperature was irrelevant. She didn't even notice that the glove, which had been on her hand, was no longer there.

It took a couple of minutes to fill the bath to just over half way. She turned off the taps, and silence descended over the settling water. She returned to the sitting room door.

An old lady appeared in front of her in a wheelchair and looked surprised. 'Would you like a nice cup of tea?' the old lady asked.

The woman didn't reply, but just grabbed the wheelchair's handles and pushed it at some speed through to the en suite, leaving tracks down the corridor and across the bedroom carpet. Then the frail old lady was draped over the edge of the bath. The woman banged the wrinkled forehead on the rim of the bath and then pushed the weak head under the water, the lady's white hair fighting to breach the surface. Bubbles drifted upwards, and the frail old lady was still.

There was now a man in the bath, lying under the water. He sat up fully dressed. The old lady suddenly raised her dripping head, turned slowly towards the man, and said, 'Would you like a nice cup of tea?'

'It's my fault,' the man said. 'I should have been here.'

A telephone rang next to the bath.

And I woke up with a start. I sat up in my marital bed and looked around my bedroom. The doorbell rang a second time. I turned to my alarm clock. Nine twenty-five. I'd overslept, and now Goddard was here. I manoeuvred myself out of bed and grabbed my dressing gown, still fighting the dream's images in my head. The doorbell rang a third time.

'Coming! I'm coming!' I shouted, and pushed my wheelchair to the front door, opening it with all the apologies I could muster.

SIXTEEN

Goddard and Ward allowed me a few minutes to dress and then we reassembled around the kitchen table each with a mug of tea, which Ward had made, with varying degrees of sugar. Once again, Goddard sat in Lindsey's chair opposite me with Ward on his left, notebook and pen at the ready, tongue poised. Goddard said he wanted a preliminary chat and then a formal statement.

I nodded. 'Sure, Chief Inspector, that's fine. But first, there've been a couple of incidents since we met that are causing me a lot of concern. If I can be frank, I'm seriously worried about my safety.'

Goddard looked quizzical. 'Go on,' he said in a serious tone.

I told him exactly what I had related to Grace: the sudden knock on the door, the absence of anyone there, and the shock of finding a red-painted skull on the doorstep.

'What did you do with it?' he asked without any great show of interest.

'I put it in the garage ready for you.'

Goddard relaxed in his chair and crossed his arms in an almost sub-conscious manner. He probably related the event to one of those idiots who telephone the emergency services because they've dropped their ice cream cornet. 'Why do you think it's important, Mr Miller?'

'Well, you told me to report anything abnormal, and it's not exactly normal, is it?' I said with a touch of exasperation. Did he really need me to explain? 'It didn't get there on its own, did it? Someone must have deliberately put it there. So why do that? Is someone trying to scare me, give me a sign, a warning? You're the detective, what do you think?'

Goddard remained still, thoughtful. Kept looking at me. Then he uncrossed his arms and sat up straight. 'You said there were a couple of incidents. What was the other one?'

'I was in the office yesterday afternoon when the phone rang. I noticed the number was withheld. It was a man's voice. Kind of stilted as if he was trying to disguise it.'

'What did he say?' Goddard asked.

'He came out with a torrent of vitriolic abuse. Said I was a pile of shit. Said he was pleased that Lindsey was dead and that she deserved it. I was shocked, angry, upset—all at once.'

'What did you say?'

'Nothing. I just slammed the phone down and yanked the wire out of the wall. And so it stays. I'm not reconnecting it. I'm going to just use my mobile from now on, and hope that remains off limits.'

Goddard tapped his fingers rhythmically on the table. Ward was scribbling. Goddard then asked me some questions for more detail, but I said there was little I could add other than he sounded like a middle-aged man with no distinctive accent.

'It was all very brief, very sudden,' I added. 'Can you trace the call, Chief Inspector?'

'Not if the number was withheld.'

'That's what I thought.' I paused. 'So how would you be feeling if one moment there's a frigging daubed skull on your doorstep and the next you get an abusive and threatening phone call like that?'

'We'll note it as a line of enquiry of course, Mr Miller,

but if the number was withheld, and the caller disguised his voice, then there's a limited amount that we can do. Most likely to be some nutter rather than the murderer himself. These things happen, I'm afraid.'

'So another line of enquiry, huh?' I said staring at him.

'I said we would look into it, okay?' he said in a conclusive tone. Slightly more than a sop for my concern, but not a great deal more. 'Stick with your mobile for the time being then or go ex-directory to keep any new landline number private, secure. We'll inspect and photograph the skull before we go.' He paused and then summed up the developments, although he stressed no one was presently in their sights, as it was early days. Lindsey's car was still being analysed, and he was waiting for the report. He then moved on to the post-mortem and asked me if I would like to know what had been established.

'I presume there's not a lot more to add?' I asked.

Goddard nodded. 'Save for one issue, that's right. Dr Milton confirmed that time of death was about eleven o'clock on Saturday night. Lindsey died where she was lying. As you know, her wrists were bound behind her back when she was found. The only surprise was cuts and welts on her wrists, which indicated they'd been tied for a while or that she'd struggled hard to free herself—or both. Her legs had also been tied, but later released. Do you want me to continue?' He stared at me with a raised eyebrow.

It was difficult to listen to him. The description was all very vivid, but I needed to hear it. I nodded firmly, slowly.

Goddard leant back and continued. 'There's also some clear evidence that she had duct tape over her mouth, which had been removed after death. Various cuts and bruises consistent with a general assault and with her being dragged some distance through the undergrowth prior to being killed. There's no logical motive for that, other than the specific spot was selected for some particular reason. The cause of death has not changed from what I previously told you,' he added with tactful brevity.

'You said there was one new issue?' I looked at him expectantly. To my surprise, Goddard held back. I braced myself.

'That's right, there was one further discovery.'

'Yes?'

He paused a beat. 'Lindsey Miller was about three months pregnant.'

SEVENTEEN

I sat in silence for a few moments.

Lindsey pregnant?

This was an utter bolt out of the blue. It was of course entirely possible, but why hadn't Lindsey said anything to me? She would have known by that stage surely? The image of a small fair-haired baby floated through my mind. I pulled out my ever-present hankie.

'I'm sorry if this has come as a shock to you, Mr Miller. Obviously it's proper that I should let you know, you have that right.'

I nodded and twisted my handkerchief and fingers together in a mindless pattern of agitation in my lap. I felt I had to move. I pushed my wheelchair back and guided it round to the patio doors and looked out at the garden. Goddard and Ward left me in silence for several minutes as I reflected on the enormity of what I'd just been told. There was a lot to take in.

Then it struck me.

Of course there was no proof that I *was* actually the father. The name Karl revisited with a vengeance. After a while I returned to the table. I knew I had to focus on the other aspects of the post-mortem. On Dr Milton's other findings and the evidence he'd thrown up. Goddard had given me bare facts, but no explanations as to why this had all happened. I respected the fact that it was indeed 'early days' and I knew they wouldn't make any real progress in such a short time. There were no pictures of someone standing over her with a smoking gun or any CCTV to analyse.

I suddenly recalled what Grace had told me about the unsolved murder in Littleworth Wood last year. 'Chief Inspector, you mentioned when we met on Sunday that there'd been another murder in the wood, last year, I believe. Grace, one of Lindsey's three friends I mentioned to you, told me about some research she'd done on it.'

'You mean Sandra Roberts?'

'Uh huh. Is it really still unsolved?'

'I'm afraid so,' he said. 'We recently regenerated some interest following a repeat of the reconstruction on the BBC's "Crimewatch" programme. But it remains, as you say, unsolved.'

'Who's in charge of that investigation? Can't you liaise with him, or her?'

'I do every day,' Goddard said. 'It's me.'

'Oh.' I paused, then said, 'So will the Roberts' case help us find out who killed Lindsey?'

Goddard eased his hands in his trouser pockets. 'Possibly. But I have to keep a sterile corridor between the two cases.'

'What do you mean by that?'

'I have to look at them as if they were two independent cases, which of course they are. My superintendent keeps a watch over both.'

I felt exasperated. 'But that's crazy, isn't it? The connection between the two cases is obvious.'

Goddard said firmly, 'I grant you that there are similarities in how they both died and the location, but procedurally they must be treated independently until circumstances change, if they ever do.'

'Doesn't sound logical to me.' I paused and thought. 'By "location" you mean Littleworth Wood, I presume?'

'No, I mean the *exact* location within Littleworth Wood. They were both killed literally within a few yards of each other just fourteen or so months apart.'

'Would that have been why Lindsey was dragged through undergrowth to a particular spot?'

Goddard nodded. 'It has occurred to us of course,' he said.

'Anything special or significant about this spot?'

I noted that Goddard hesitated momentarily. He took his eyes off me and glanced up at the small window to my right. When he turned back, I couldn't read his face, which frustrated me. He said, 'It's just a small clearing in the wood. There are others similar to it, of course.'

'Surely it must be unusual to have two people killed at the exact same place, in the exact same way?'

'It is, in my experience,' Goddard said. 'Could be coincidence, but it's more likely that either the same person was involved or a copycat did some pretty detailed research on the Roberts' case.'

'And your inclination?'

'Too early to say,' he said without hesitation.

I sighed.

Goddard removed his hands from his pockets and sat up straight again. 'If you're feeling frustrated, Mr Miller, I can assure you that I am too. But we will solve this, believe me.'

Ward gave a supportive nod as he paused in his writing to look up at me.

I said, 'I hope so. I really do.'

Goddard leant forward on the table with his forearms

and looked at me through his silver-rimmed spectacles. 'I've been able to speak to Julie Wycliffe in London.'

'And?'

'And I think you know what's coming,' Goddard said. 'She told me you rang her yesterday morning.'

'Yes, I felt that she should be told what's happened. Is that okay?'

'In a sense I agree with you, Mr Miller. But I gather you asked her about Lindsey's movements and established, as we'd all suspected, that she didn't go up to London on Saturday afternoon. It seems that for some reason she misled you about that—and indeed where she was when she rang you late at night.'

'She did ring me,' I said. 'She rang me from her mobile so can't you track where the call was made from? I thought that kind of technology was available now. This is an occasion when surely Big Brother could be helpful?'

'We've done all that,' Goddard said. 'The records show she rang your home number here at ten thirty—'

'Ten twenty-nine, sir,' Ward interrupted.

Goddard turned and glared at him, and Ward looked back down at his notebook like a chastised child.

Goddard looked back at me. 'Yes, as Detective Sergeant Ward thoughtfully pointed out, at ten twenty-nine to be exact. The call was made from Littleworth Wood and lasted about three minutes.' He glanced round at Ward and then back to me. 'Two minutes forty seconds to be precise... The call was likely to have been made from close to where she died.' He took his glasses off, twiddled them about slowly in his hand and looked at me again. 'Tell me again about this call. How did she seem?'

'Perfectly normal. She said she was tired. It was

perhaps shorter than our normal chats—considerably shorter now that I think about it. Almost as if she was checking in, you know, telling me all was okay.'

'So how does someone with bound hands call you on their mobile? Thirty minutes later she was dead and yet she had a "normal" conversation with you. How do you explain that?'

It was a fair point. 'With respect, Chief Inspector, it isn't really up to me to explain it, is it? You're the one investigating this. All I know is that my Lindsey called me to say that she had had a good evening out with her friend. Don't you think that if I suspected she was in some kind of trouble, I'd have called the police? There was no indication of anything so terrible, nothing at all. I went to bed that evening at peace with the world, knowing my wife was tucked up safely in a London hotel. I had no idea she was about to be murdered in a wood a few miles away from where I was lying.'

'So you think she was coerced into making the call? Forced? Threatened?'

'Chief Inspector, I don't know what to think. She used to do amateur dramatics, but acting all normal with a knife to your throat seems a few notches up on that standard of acting, don't you think? More Hollywood than Westland village hall.'

'You're sure it was her—not someone imitating her?'

'I'd think I'd recognise my own wife…'

'So why did she make the call?'

I shrugged. 'She always rings me before she goes to sleep if she's away. It would have been curious if she hadn't.'

'And what would you have done if there'd been no

call?'

'Worried of course. Would have called her at midnight or something like that.'

'And if she hadn't answered?'

'Would have rung Julie. She'd have known what was going on. Ultimately I'd have rung you lot, I certainly wouldn't have left it. Lindsey would have known that. I'm... was her husband, right? That's what caring husbands do, don't they?'

Goddard leant back and appeared to reflect.

'So a brief call would have reassured you and would have sent you quietly to bed?'

'Exactly. And that's what happened after all. I can only surmise she told someone that, or they worked it out for themselves—it's not exactly rocket science, is it?'

Goddard nodded, giving me the impression he was working it through. 'We found her mobile in her handbag, along with her purse, car keys and the usual feminine clutter. Incidentally, did Mrs Miller usually carry cash?'

I pictured her purse and saw the small wad of notes traditionally stuffed into it, never ordered.

'Of course, as most people do,' I said. 'Why do you ask?'

'Because there was no cash in her purse—even the coin section was empty. All her debit, credit and store cards were in there though. Someone was obviously either fussy or cautious. I suspect the latter.'

'But greedy...'

'Oh yes, greedy, definitely greedy.' He nodded in an exaggerated way.

There was a sudden noise in the hallway and I recognised the sound of the letter flap falling back into place.

I glanced at Goddard. 'Just the post,' I said, cocking my head towards the door. 'I'd quite like to get it, if I may.'

Ward made to stand up. 'I could fetch it for you, Mr Miller. No hassle.'

'That's kind,' I said. 'Thanks.'

Ward left the room at a rapid pace and returned a few moments later with four envelopes of differing sizes, two white, two brown, which he passed to me. I flicked through them quickly. Bank statement for me, bill for Lindsey, bill for us both and an A5 white envelope neatly typed for me. Exeter postmark. Ward sat down and, as Goddard started to talk again, I absent-mindedly eased my finger under the sealed flap.

'It seems to me, Mr Miller...'

My finger moved along under the flap.

'...that we need to establish Lindsey's exact movements from early Saturday afternoon until about ten thirty.'

I nodded. The flap lifted. I glanced down. There was a single sheet of paper in the envelope. I tugged on it gently. Eyes back on Goddard, trying to be polite.

'We'll need to find out where she went in that time. There were no other phone calls either to or from her mobile. Who saw her? Who was she with? Where did she go? And so on,' Goddard continued. 'We've started that process, of course.'

The sheet of paper slid out.

'We're going to have to appeal for witnesses.'

I glanced down and read the few lines of large print. I gasped and, as the paper hit the floor, I shouted, 'Shit – they're after *me* now!'

EIGHTEEN

At the very moment I made that exclamation, a figure appeared on the patio outside the closed glass doors. It was Grace. She gave an exaggerated wave and pointed at the door handle.

I pushed myself away from the table and let her in. She was carrying a cake tin and seemed unfazed about interrupting. 'The garden gate was unlocked,' she said. 'I thought I would sneak in and just leave this—just a chocolate cake I've made for you. But you're in here, not the sitting room, so that hasn't worked.' With a quick shrug of her shoulders and a flashed "well I did try" smile, she placed the tin firmly on the side.

I thanked her, handled the introductions, and told her that a threatening letter had just arrived in the post.

If Goddard was put out about Grace's arrival, he didn't show it. He told her to stay where she was, which she initially bristled at, while he directed the operation to secure the letter. He asked me to pick the paper up very carefully and place it on the table next to the envelope. At Goddard's instigation, I directed Grace to some freezer bags in a kitchen drawer to use as makeshift evidence bags. Goddard felt the sender would have taken care though and used gloves, probably surgical.

As the letter lay upwards on the table, Goddard read the words out loud whilst sitting in his chair. Ward had stood up and was looking over his shoulder.

'Miller, your time is nearly up. Sell your little house and move right away. If there's no "For Sale" board within a week of today, you'll share accommodation with your pathetic wife. I can hurt you, too.'

Thirty-seven words composed into a chilling threat. I faced the three of them with a look of alarm. They stared at me as if I'd been handed a death sentence, black cloth on the judge's wig and everything. Grace came round and stood behind me, placing a hand on my shoulder.

After I'd carefully placed the envelope and letter in separate clear freezer bags, Goddard studied the envelope. 'Exeter postmark,' he observed. 'Posted early yesterday evening with a standard first-class stamp.' After flicking the envelope over, he cast a quick look at its empty back and handed it to Ward. 'Have them both tested,' he added to his junior.

'What do I do?' I asked, conscious of a slight tremble in my voice.

'Do? You do nothing,' Goddard said as he settled forward on to the table. 'At least not immediately.'

'*Nothing?*' Grace chipped in. 'What do you mean *nothing?*'

'It's okay, Grace,' I said. 'The Chief Inspector is pretty harassed already at the moment. He's just told me that he's also investigating the Sandra Roberts' murder.'

'Really?' Grace said. 'That's still unsolved after well over a year.'

Goddard stood up giving himself some physical height over us. 'We can give you limited protection in due course,' he said, as Ward watched him with intense interest, 'but according to this threat, nothing's going to be attempted for a week.'

'If they're being honest,' I said. 'But, for some reason, I have limited faith in the moral calibre of the person who's just murdered my wife. Tell me if I'm being a bit picky, Chief Inspector.'

'I understand where you're coming from, Mr Miller,' he said, trying to eyeball me, 'but we'll make all efforts to progress this over the next few days, and then you and I will review the position.'

'That's all very well,' I said, feeling my blood pressure rising, 'but, with respect, Sandra Roberts was murdered in similar circumstances some fourteen months ago and you're still no nearer an arrest—'

'Mr Miller—'

'Well are you?' I continued despite his exasperated look.

A flicker of resignation crossed his face, and his body seemed to deflate. 'No, I guess there's still some way to go.'

Grace said, 'So progress "over the next few days" isn't exactly likely, I guess, Chief Inspector?'

'Agreed,' I said, staring at him. 'Hardly encouraging, is it?'

Goddard said nothing. Ward checked his notes and avoided all eye contact.

'Mike needs your support here,' Grace said.

'I appreciate that,' Goddard said.

I said, 'So we're agreed that I'm not exactly in the best position to resist an assault. Too bloody right,' I thumped both wheels of my chair angrily. 'You might say I'm somewhat vulnerable. You've told me that whoever killed my wife did so brutally. That she was dragged. That her throat was ruthlessly cut. Unless I'm mishearing you, Chief Inspector, that sounds like a pretty fit sort of bloke to me and one I wouldn't want to have assaulting me. Is that so unreasonable?'

'Well, no—'

'So waiting here like a sitting, fucking duck is hardly an option, is it?' I glared at him.

'What I suggest, Mr—' he began, but I hadn't finished with my rant.

'What *I* suggest, Chief Inspector, is that your uniformed guys increase their patrols in this frigging village, and I'll contact a friend of mine in Tiverton who runs an estate agency.'

'So you're going to sell and move?' Goddard asked.

Ward scribbled a note in his book. Grace moved into my field of vision and watched the exchange with an appearance of growing concern.

With a withering stare, I said slowly, almost through gritted teeth, 'No, I said I was going to contact an estate agent.' I leant forward in my wheelchair. 'I'm going to ask him to erect a "For Sale" board in front of my house within the next two or three days. We are at the end of the close. With the bend in the service road, no other house has a clear view of my drive and no one travels down our close for a Sunday tootle. No one sane, anyway. So no one's going to know much about the board, are they? Except me, perhaps that weirdo Craig what's-his-name in the nearest bungalow, and the killer who comes to check? Should buy us some time, don't you think?'

'And should he ring the agents to double check—false name and all that?'

'Then they confirm it's for sale but do no more. I'm sure Jonathan Rosford, can sort that. He's been a friend since we bought this place and has been an estate agent a good few years.'

'Well, I'm not sure if—' Goddard started to say.

'"Not sure, not sure",' I mimicked, my knuckles turning white as I grasped the handles of my wheelchair. 'All I've heard is negative, Chief Inspector. Fucking negative. Nothing seems to be happening to catch the guy that killed my Lindsey and, for all we know, killed Sandra too. And now *my* life is under threat.'

'Calm down, Mike,' Grace said. 'This isn't helping. We're all on the same side here—all want the same thing.' She turned to Goddard. 'Look, Mike's right, Chief Inspector,' she said calmly, 'absolutely right. It looks like he's under a serious threat now, and a very real one at that. What concerns me is whether Mike sells up or not, he's never going to be safe while this maniac is on the loose. We have no idea why he murdered Lindsey—or indeed if that is linked to poor Sandra—but it seems the only way Mike is going to have peace and feel safe is to catch the killer, whether he moves or not.'

'And that's why we will do all we can to catch him, Mrs Atkins.'

I started to speak, but Grace said, 'I for one certainly can't just sit here and do nothing while the murderer of my best friend and Mike's wife can threaten Mike at will. That can't be right, can it?'

Goddard said nothing.

'Well, can it?' Grace persisted.

Goddard looked disheartened.

Grace said, 'We're going to have to do what we can to protect Mike and get justice for Lindsey. Mike and I are going to have to get involved, really involved in tracking this madman down, aren't we, Mike?' She shot me a glance.

'And frankly, Chief Inspector, we'll do it whether you like it or not.'

'I don't like it. This is our job.'

'Well, do your job then,' I said. 'And do it a damn sight better than you're doing with Sandra Roberts. We don't want a similar year to go by in the search for Lindsey's killer. Grace is quite right and I'm with her.' I looked at Grace, 'Together we're certainly going to do our bit to solve this— aren't we?'

NINETEEN

Grace left for some urgent appointment. It was all so quick, all so tense that I didn't even have the chance to tell her about Lindsey's pregnancy. Goddard and Ward took their statement from me in an icy atmosphere and left.

I made the decision that I needed some space, some time to myself, and that I would travel south to Sidmouth. I sorted a few things and then rang the station shortly after one fifteen to speak to Goddard. He wasn't there, but DS Ward was—which, after that uncomfortable meeting, was a bit of a relief. Ward took a message, including the address, and no doubt noted it all down both carefully and verbatim in his black pocket book.

Taking myself off on my own would indeed give me time to think of Lindsey and all that she'd given me in our short overlap of life together. That tiny union in the Venn diagram of our respective circles of life had meant so much to me. I wanted to think about how her death now left me and to plan the subsequent steps. And, of course, time on my own to consider the letter and its consequences. What did I *need* to do next to work alongside Grace?

I telephoned Jonathan Rosford, told him what he needed to know, and sorted the erection of a 'For Sale' board. I told him I was relying on him more than I could say.

Having set the house alarm, I drove my newly serviced car to Exeter and parked in my usual spot, which, yet again, was available. I bought some basic provisions for my stay, and headed out of the city towards Sidmouth, just another automaton on the tarmacked road of life.

On reaching Sidmouth some forty minutes later, I passed the office of my late father's solicitors' practice, which had kept him away so often from his only son and stay-at-home wife, who I always felt wanted to see more of him and less of his briefcase. A Lowry-like image sprung to mind of people trudging to work, spending their lives toiling for the best they could do—always wanting more, but in reality just existing. Hardly a life. I wound my way up Peak Hill to Cliff House, which I'd retained after my parents' death. It was a substantial brick property constructed in the early 1900s that had been extended and modernised at no little cost by my parents.

After closing the electric door of the separate garage, I made my way across the brick pavior driveway to the side door. This had been ramped—indeed the house had been adapted for wheelchair use where it was required. The irony was that it hadn't been done by me, or indeed for me. My grandma, my mother's own mother, had spent the final three wheelchair-bound years of her life living with my parents. A hidden benefit of this arrangement was that she had spoilt me rotten behind my parents' back, and so funding dates with Juliet and the subsequent early girlfriends was never an issue for me.

The side door took me into a small lobby giving the option of a left turn into the original kitchen or straight ahead through one of the solid internal doors into grandma's modern extension. Now the house had an abandoned stillness, despite being furnished just as my parents had left it. I'd kept on Mrs Burrows, my mother's trustworthy 'daily help', to look after the house in my absence, and her husband tended the garden. I entered grandma's old sitting room with its wheelchair-friendly patio doors, which gave great views of the garden. I opened the doors to allow the fresh afternoon air to enter. A door at the rear led into a sizeable en-suite bedroom, which was spacious even with her original marital bed and its amazing feather mattress. Yes, it was good to be home.

I returned to the lobby, unlocked the dividing door and entered the kitchen with its hand-painted units and Bethel white granite worktops and made myself a late sandwich lunch.

Leaving the kitchen, there was a short passageway, which ran off to my left. The downstairs cloakroom was to my right. 'The room at the end of the passage,' as my mother would euphemistically call it, as she was unable to bring herself to call it the 'toilet' or even the 'cloakroom'. I crossed the end of the passage with the cloakroom on my right and entered the study opposite the kitchen door. This was now messier than when my father had been in occupation. I found a pad of paper and pen, returned to the kitchen and settled down with my lunch.

I jotted down a number of random words: *Lindsey. Littleworth Wood. Where had she been? Coven. Last year's murder – identical?*

I glanced out of the window in time to see a grey squirrel bound effortlessly up the large sycamore in the middle of the lawn. I returned to the pad: *Martin? Charles? KARL??* I underlined Karl twice. *Red-painted skull. Telephone and letter threats. Sale of bungalow.* Then another flurry. *Not with Julie Wycliffe. Not at the hospice on nights. Not with Julie since before we met?? Pregnant!* (Underlined twice again). I doodled and drew lines on the paper. I looked up at the casual photograph of my parents hanging on the wall opposite me. Mother smiling, father impassive. It was as if he were frowning at me as he had in days gone by. A distant voice from my childhood, 'Get on with it, boy. The Millers don't come second.'

'Sure, Dad,' I said out loud. 'This is my game to win, and I'll give it my best shot.' I started to get my mind in gear. There was no alternative.

And then my mobile rang.

TWENTY

I read the caller identification on my mobile and answered.

'Mr Miller, Goddard here. I'm on speakerphone so DS Ward can hear. I received your message, you're back in three or four days, I gather?'

As brisk and to the point as ever.

'That's right, Chief Inspector. Is that okay?'

'Yes, yes of course,' he said. 'I've interviewed...' The signal faded.

'Sorry, Chief Inspector, I've lost you. Can you hear me?'

Crackling sounds and his voice again. 'What's that? Can you hear me?'

'Yes, got you now,' I said. 'Not the best area for reception down here. You were saying you've interviewed someone. I didn't catch who... Chief Inspector?'

His tone was impatient. 'I said I'd interviewed *Bronia Field* this afternoon at St Chad's Hospice.'

'Anything of interest?' I asked, pressing my mobile a little firmer to my ear.

'She said she saw you yesterday. That you and... and Grace Atkins called by unannounced. Two things arise from this, Mr Miller. Firstly, it seems that you thought Mrs Miller was working there some nights when in fact she wasn't according to Ms Field. And, secondly, following on from your outburst this morning, you both seem to have already started to conduct your own investigation. Is that right?'

I heard a sharp tone of disapproval in his voice.

'Well if asking a couple of questions amounts to an investigation—'

'Mr Miller, please allow me to conduct this enquiry. Any input by Mrs Atkins and yourself could be damaging and it's certainly not helpful to what I'm doing. Is that clear?'

I was very tempted to give him both barrels and reply that there was no law against us trying to find out who'd murdered my wife if it led to protecting myself, but I shied away from any further confrontation on the point. We'd said enough that morning.

'Yes, that's clear,' was all I said. But it stuck in my craw.

'Good. Now what's this about Mrs Miller working nights?'

I told him that although Lindsey had primarily worked daytime shifts when she was a volunteer at the hospice, she would also on occasions undertake a night shift. Not frequently, not regularly, just every now and then to suit the demands of the place.

'But you now know she never did that?' Goddard asked.

'Exactly.'

'What do you make of that?'

'What do I make of anything? My whole life has been turned upside down, Chief Inspector. Black is white and white is black. Nothing's making sense anymore.'

Goddard persisted as if he hadn't heard me. 'With respect, Mr Miller, what do you make of this discovery?'

'Well, it's a bit of a shock of course. How could it be anything else? She said she was at the hospice, but she clearly wasn't.'

'So where was she if she wasn't at the hospice?'

'How the hell should I know?' I said with growing exasperation as the emotional and physical distance between Sidmouth and Westland started to disappear. 'There has to be trust in a marriage, Chief Inspector. In *any* relationship in fact. I trusted her when she left to go to the hospice and it never occurred to me that she wasn't going there, why would it?' I paused. 'I can't add anything else, okay?'

'Okay for now.' I could imagine him characteristically leaning on his desk and spinning his glasses slowly round in his left hand. 'We'll speak again. Good afternoon, Mr Miller.'

'Goodbye, Chief Inspector.'

He rang off.

I took a beer from the fridge, settled back at the kitchen table and opened a scrapbook that I'd collected from its shelf in the study. I'd kept a scrapbook ever since I was a teenager and had several volumes now of articles and pieces from newspapers and magazines. This volume was the one I revisited most often; its thumbed pages bore witness to that. It covered the period when I was at university and the six months or so after I left midway through my second year.

I flicked through the pages until they readily fell open on the most emotional weekend of my life. I looked at these tatty and yellowing pieces of newsprint each time I visited Cliff House. I may have been spurred on to do this when I looked at the large, empty area of hard-standing next to the garage where my parents' treasured caravan had stood when not on one of its regular outings.

My mother and father fell in love with caravanning before I was born. Wherever they took their caravan—across the English Channel to mainland Europe for a couple of weeks on a busy campsite or spent a night at their favourite isolated spot on Dartmoor—they were happy on their childish adventures. As a lad, I'd enjoyed the travellers' life, too, especially the freedom of exploring different places as a family. There was something almost hunter-gatherer-like to set up in a remote spot by a quiet brook—far away, as my father would say, from 'the madding crowd'.

That weekend had started normally enough for me. Although Rosemary made this one different. Just eighteen, she was a cute little first-year student studying law like me. Not the prettiest of girls, but she had the most gorgeous petite body. One of my friends told me that Rosemary had 'the hots' for me and so I chatted her up and arranged to collect her from her university hall of residence for an early evening dinner at a local French restaurant. As grandma had passed away by then, I was obliged to fund the evening from just the grant my father gave me each month. I wasn't in university accommodation myself in my second year. Together with my two friends from Sidmouth school days, Jonty and Mark, and three girls we'd become friendly with in the first year, we'd rented a large six-bedroom house in suburban Exeter. My room was at the top of the house up a creaking staircase that caused consistent complaints when used at night-time. Large, with a double bed, the room itself gave a decent view of the untidy, secluded rear garden.

The restaurant was good and the wine better. An early nightcap at the Bull and Butcher pub and then back up the noisy staircase to my garret. A further glass or two of some cocktail each, and the eagle had landed. I don't know what her memories are now of that single night we had together, as I haven't seen her for years. She's probably a part-time lawyer somewhere with two-point-four children and a husband who commutes to the city. But I know what *my* memories are of: a high degree of satisfaction; boundless, hedonistic pleasure; and, ultimately, a well-planned and executed mission.

But the morning put a damper on my conquest and brought news that no son should have to bear. The police had tracked me down and came knocking on our door, disturbing the whole student household on that overcast Sunday dawn. In their own way, each of my friends tried to comfort me, but I was not in touch with them. I said something that really hurt Rosemary. I hoped she forgave me, but we never met up or talked again. My mind was an electric storm, but at least my friends understood that I was not myself. Who would be?

I glanced down at one of the well-read newspaper cuttings in my folder and read it yet again.

Local couple die in caravan blaze tragedy

Friends paid tribute to local solicitor David Miller and his wife, Margaret, who died on Saturday night in their caravan parked in a remote area of Dartmoor near Bovey Tracey.

Early investigation has suggested the couple, aged 49 and 45, died when a fire started in the caravan's kitchenette and they became trapped. Experts today warned about the need for both smoke detectors and firefighting equipment to be properly maintained and available.

The alarm was raised just before 6 a.m. on Sunday morning by a local man who was out jogging on the moor and saw the burnt remains of the large luxury caravan.

Devon and Cornwall Police detectives are now trying to establish the cause of the fire, although a faulty cooker appears to be at the heart of the enquiry. A post-mortem examination into what caused the deaths is due to be conducted later. The incident is not being treated as suspicious, and a police spokesman indicated that death was likely to have been caused by smoke inhalation.

Today, the curtains at the couple's home on Peak Hill in Sidmouth were closed as neighbours and friends came to terms with the tragic discovery.

David was a partner in the local firm of Miller & Dewsbury. The firm's three offices closed today as a mark of respect.

The couple leave an adult son.

At the later inquest, the coroner agreed with the experts that the fire had started because of a fault with the cooker. I gave evidence that my father religiously replaced the smoke alarm batteries every three months and had the caravan and its fittings regularly serviced. Some unanswered questions were thrown towards the local company who had serviced the caravan, but they obviously denied any negligence. The coroner finally concluded death by misadventure, that they had been trapped and burnt alive, something that I find hard to write even after all this time.

TWENTY-ONE

Cliff House was somewhere I always felt safe and secure. It had a homely atmosphere and was a haven for me, especially at this time. I relaxed in the garden and woke later in the afternoon when a solitary cloud masked the warmth of the sun. I caught up with paperwork in the study, made myself some beans on toast for supper and settled in front of the television to watch some old Western.

As I nodded off later in the evening, my mobile on the table next to me burst into life and I answered it.

Grace said, 'Hi Mike, are you in the house? The light's on, but there's no one home, so to speak.'

I realised that with everything that had happened that morning, I hadn't been in touch with her nor told her of my brief sojourn to the coast.

'Are you outside, Grace?'

'Sure am,' she said briskly 'And I've found your bell, which appears to be working. So answer the door before I trip over another lonely skull.'

I smiled. 'Sorry, Grace, no can do as I'm not there you see. I'm taking a couple of days away on the coast for a bit of self time.'

'Oh, right,' she said slowly as the signal faded. Did I detect some disappointment? 'It was just that I was passing the village and thought I'd pop by, you know, make sure you're okay and all that. So, are you?'

'Am I what?'

'Okay.'

'Yeah, sure. Well, as much as I can be with the news I received this morning. Didn't have a chance to tell you earlier.'

'What was that?' she asked, with a sudden note of concern in her voice.

'Lindsey was pregnant.'

'Oh Mike, I'm so, so sorry. You didn't know? Can it get any worse?'

'I'm still reflecting on this Grace. We'll talk about it when we next get together.'

She was quiet for a moment. Then she said, 'Do you know anyone with a...?' And she faded as the signal messed us about.

'Say that again, Grace, I lost you.'

'I said, do you know anyone with a motorbike?'

The question made me think for a moment. 'Your darling ex for one,' I said. 'Why d'you ask?'

'It's only that when I came into the close right now, a motorbike shot past me. Took me by surprise.'

'Can't think what that was doing there. Any kind of description? Part of the registration number perhaps?'

'No. I tried, but it all happened so quickly. There one moment, gone the next. A flashing headlight and a burst of engine. Could have been a bloke or a girl, more likely a bloke as the rider looked quite big. The best I can do is dark clothing, probably leathers. It's almost impossible to recognise anyone on a motorbike with the helmet and everything.'

'Not the skull delivery man, then?' I asked, more jovially than I actually felt. What the hell was a motorbike doing in my quiet close at this time of night? I was grateful that I'd set the alarm and carried out all my usual security checks.

'I'd better give the bungalow the once over, Mike—just check there are no broken windows or anything.'

'Are you sure?'

'No problem. They did teach us reservists a thing or two, you know.'

'Okay, but keep talking to me as you go round, I want to know you're safe.'

'If you want, but I'm all grown up now, Mike.'

And so she gave my house the once over. I had a running commentary as she circled round the house and then told me off for leaving the side gate unlocked yet again. I didn't admit it to her, but that time was my fault. My weekly fight of putting the bin out flashed before me. I locked it when I wasn't there for obvious reasons, but left it unlocked to feel free when I was there. In the background I could detect the familiar sounds of my property, such as the latch on the garden gate and the sound of her heels on the paved path to the side of the house.

Grace found nothing out of order, nothing of concern. However, I suddenly felt I should return. If people were coming to my bungalow, invited or otherwise, I needed to be there to keep control. I would leave the following afternoon, earlier than I'd originally planned. I knew there were tasks to do, however disapproving Goddard might become.

TWENTY-TWO

The man was dressed completely in black, head to toe, as he descended the high metal staircase. Stretched out below him was wild moorland that he could still see even though the night was still young and deep and forbidding.

At the bottom of the staircase, he jumped about a metre or so onto wet, cold grass. There was no one about, and just the sound of a motorbike could be heard on the distant road. Ahead of him stood a silent caravan parked by a brook that still babbled and ran with no respect or interest in the all-prevailing night. He moved towards it, almost gliding over the soft terrain. He paused by the caravan door and then slowly tried the handle. It gave under his touch, and the door swung gently out towards him. He climbed the couple of steps into the kitchen where he once again stopped still and listened. No sound at all save for occasional snoring from the principal bedroom at the far end of the luxury caravan.

He placed his bag on the floor and extracted a small bottle. He fiddled with the cooker, and, after unscrewing the bottle's top, poured out some of the precious liquid, allowing some of it to spread in a wavy line across the length of the floor. He'd been shown how to do this and had practised it well. He dipped his hand into his pocket and took out a cheap cigarette lighter. He clicked it several times but it didn't light. He shook it again, violently. More clicks, but still no flame. He threw it into his open bag and stared at the cooker. A single flame suddenly hovered over it, dancing with no apparent source, until, with a sudden rush, the flame erupted.

The man leapt back towards the door. The fire dutifully and predictably followed the trail, and the sitting room became a blaze. By then, the man had jumped out of the door and closed it behind him, feeling the strong heat on his face as he did so. The top-of-the-range caravan was becoming a top-of-the-range inferno.

The man ran clear of the caravan until he could dip down behind a grassy knoll some hundred metres away. And there he watched. It was awesome. The speed and intensity of the fire was immense and lit up the surrounding moorland, casting violent and fast-moving shadows. Debris, embers and ashes shot high into the air above the towering flames. The man could still feel the heat, like by a garden bonfire. He tried to ignore the screams.

The screams were still there as I woke to daylight and realised that two neighbourhood cats were having a significant set-to on the patio beyond grandma's open bedroom window. I was soaked in sweat. Drenched. I threw the covers off and manoeuvred myself out of bed, and hurled the open scrapbook across the room—worse than cheese at bedtime.

I opened the patio doors and stared out at the garden as one of the cats, a tabby, decided not to push its luck any more and ran for the holly hedge. The sky was already blue and bright, and the warmth was so unseasonal that I actually took my breakfast out onto the patio and enjoyed the garden again. Signs of autumn, but still lush and leafy and inviting.

Taking advantage of my time in Sidmouth, I took myself down into the town and spent a couple of hours on the front, where the slight sea breeze with all its salty freshness washed over me, bringing back countless childhood memories. I lunched in a local pub, rightly well known for its real ale, and afterwards returned to Cliff House, where I relaxed in the garden to the point that I actually fell asleep, maybe due to the beer, the warm sunshine, my poor night's sleep, or a combination of each. I awoke with a hint of a cricked neck and took myself back into the house where I packed what little possessions I'd brought. I tended to keep what I needed at the house rather than transport stuff to and from Westland. I eventually departed late afternoon and left a note for Mrs Burrows reassuring her that I was indeed the one who'd been tramping about the house and asking her to sort the bed.

After a leisurely journey, in the early evening I reached Exeter, where I undertook a couple of tasks, including refuelling my Ford Focus. My mobile rang. It was Grace.

'Where are you, Mike? You back yet?' she asked.

'Well, I'm in Exeter. Heading back. Why?'

'I thought I would give you an address to visit on your way back. Sounds like I've just caught you.'

'Sure, whose?'

'Martin's.'

'*Martin's*? As in your Martin? Your ex?'

'The very same.'

'Is this to do with last night, Grace, you know, the motorbike?'

'Might be,' she said. 'I thought there'd be no harm in calling round, Mike.' She paused a beat then added, 'I'd like to come with you, but that might not work so well. I'm not saying I couldn't deal with him, but I don't exactly know where he is in all this. No point in spoiling the main performance because of a sideshow, so best if I'm not there.'

'I understand that,' I said, 'but I'm not sure this sounds like a particularly sensible plan.'

'Now, bear with me. I've been doing some thinking…'

'And?'

'Well, I know this may sound crazy, but Martin wasn't exactly a fan of Lindsey's, was he? You know, not after all the support she gave me with the divorce and everything.'

'I suppose not.'

'Whatever their relationship, Mike, you have to agree that Martin had to give me large piles of his cash because of Lindsey.'

'Mm, I suppose so,' I said carefully. 'But I can't imagine for a second Martin doing anything dreadful to Lindsey because of all that. He hasn't got it in him.'

'Really?' she said pointedly. 'Sometimes it's hard to know what people are capable of.'

'Sure, but—'

'Did you think he would cheat on me with Sally?'

'No, I suppose not. Nor with anyone come to that. He might have been obnoxious and self-centred at times, but to cheat on you and do what he did, never…'

'So, if you didn't think he was capable of that, why are you so sure he wouldn't harm Lindsey out of revenge?' she said.

'Well, having an affair is in a somewhat different league than committing a brutal murder—or any murder come to that.'

'Yeah, but then again, as someone once said, who are you when no one's looking?'

'Point taken,' I said.

'And remember that the threatening letter you received on Monday morning was posted in Exeter where he lives. A coincidence?'

I was quiet for a moment. 'I don't know, Grace. I just don't know. My world's been turned upside down recently, just like yours earlier this year.'

I wondered if maybe I should stop resisting the suggestion for the sake of Grace's logic, but part of me had no wish to have a confrontation with Martin. He wasn't exactly going to see me as a friend—even less so if I turned up unexpected, firing questions and accusing him of murder.

After a moment, Grace's argument won the day. 'Okay,' I said, 'whether he's just a deceitful bastard or a full-blown axe murderer, I could go and see him, I suppose. Especially if it keeps you happy.'

'Me happy? My happiness is nothing to do with this, Mike. Don't you get it yet? We can't just sit around and wait to see whether Goddard does his job. And although he's a bossy chap, he doesn't strike me as the best detective around here, and that's hugely disappointing if we want justice for Lindsey and safety for you, isn't it?'

'In that order?' I said lightly.

'You know what I mean. Well?'

'Okay, okay,' I said, waving a virtual white flag down the phone. 'I'll go and talk to dear Martin now as I'm down here. So, where's the love nest?'

She gave me the address.

'Ring me later, Mike, and let me know how you get on. And confirm to me he's not buried you in the garden.'

I smiled and we rang off. Time to visit Martin.

TWENTY-THREE

On that dry Wednesday evening with the warm sun starting its nocturnal descent in a clear blue sky, I carefully followed the satnav to where an expanding new estate of upmarket Exeter houses met the Devon countryside.

'The Willows' was a substantial modern brick house that stood behind a high wooden fence on the curve of the estate road and backed onto the open countryside. No doubt Jonathan Rosford would have described it as a 'tranquil location'. I expected electric gates, but the entrance was open and unguarded save for the lone CCTV camera aimed at the gateway from the side of a conveniently located oak tree. As I paused on the point of entry, my eyes tracked along the short, curving gravel drive up to a closed front door some forty metres away. I eased forward and felt quite dwarfed as I followed the approach up to the meticulously maintained house where I parked. I could smell the money.

By the time I'd manoeuvred myself out of the car and into my wheelchair, the front door had opened, and a young woman stepped out towards me. I settled into my chair and watched her cover the few metres to my car. If I were honest, I would have to admit that Martin had an eye for women. She could not have been more than twenty-three, her tall model's figure accentuated by a pair of skinny jeans and simple t-shirt cut away to reveal a stunningly flat abdomen and tiny waist. As she stopped near to me, she swept her long brunette hair back behind her ear, possibly as a nervous gesture, possibly because it was simply getting in her way. Whatever the reason, it was damn sexy.

She gave me a polite smile. 'Can I help you?' she asked, her dark hazel eyes flicking over me. A man in a wheelchair presumably gave her a sense of safety.

I returned my best smile. 'You must be Sally,' I said. 'Is Martin home?'

She stood her ground and gave me a slightly guarded look. 'I'm sorry,' she said slowly. 'Do I know you? I... I don't recall—'

I kept smiling and shook my head. 'No, no, no,' I said. 'It's me that should be apologising, not you, so please forgive me. I'm Mike, Mike Miller, a friend of Martin's ex, Grace.'

I held out my hand, but she didn't move. A look of slight concern raced across her face before she recovered. I returned my hand to the wheel rim of my chair and smiled again at her as if it were no big deal, as if I understood.

'Oh, oh I see,' she said. She swept her hair back behind her ear again. It evidently was a nervous gesture. 'Well, if it's Martin you're after, you're in luck. He's only popped out to collect some Chinese and will be back shortly, any second in fact. I'm not sure however... Oh, here he is now...'

I turned my head towards a yellow Maserati that powered its way flamboyantly down the drive and skidded dramatically to a halt, scattering loose gravel over the immediate area. The door flung open, and Martin stepped out carrying a large brown carrier bag filled with silver takeaway containers. He bore down on me with a face that displayed a curious mixture of both surprise and indignation. He was bigger than I recalled, had put on weight. He looked every inch the ex-rugby man that he was. He had an air of extreme confidence, a man who was winning in life—and who was on home turf.

'What the hell do you want, Mike?' He gave me a scowl and then turned to his girl. 'Get inside, Sal, and take this.' He swung the carrier bag towards her.

'I was just—'

'I said inside, Sally. Now.' He was sharp, succinct, and angry.

In a simple and calm act of obedience, she stretched out a long, thin arm for the food, spun round and walked back elegantly towards the front door.

'Well?' Martin asked. 'What the hell do you want?'

I turned my head to face him again. 'I wanted to ask you a couple of things, Martin. You may already have some idea what they might be.'

He stood firmly upright, towered over me and crossed his arms tightly. 'I haven't a bloody clue, Mike. Besides, you can see it's my suppertime and I'm going to eat it while it's hot.'

'Have you heard about Lindsey?' I asked giving him an intense stare.

'Heard what? What's the bitch done now?'

'She's dead.'

My bare statement appeared to have thrown him. Tipped him off balance. Or had it?

He looked at me with one of the coldest stares I'd ever received. 'Shame,' he said slowly and sarcastically.

'She was my wife,' I said quietly, although as I spoke the words I realised that the emotion would be lost on him.

'She was my pain in the arse,' he said in a mocking tone.

He headed towards his door. I felt an intense hatred of

the man shiver through me. I wanted desperately to rise from my wheelchair and hit him, but that wasn't an option.

'You still got your motorbike, Martin?' I called after him, forcing myself to keep calm.

He twisted back towards me. 'My what?'

'Your motorbike—you still got it?' I repeated.

He placed his hands on his hips like a truculent teenager. 'What the hell's that got to do with you?'

Imagining that Grace was standing beside me cheering me on, I persisted. 'Were you up at my house last night?'

He moved swiftly back towards me, placed his large hands on the arms of my wheelchair and brought his face close to mine. I could smell wine on his breath as he hissed, 'What the fuck are you on, Mike? Why the hell would I be on my motorbike at your house? Last night or any bloody night come to that? Huh? Why?'

I wasn't going to be intimidated and I stared back at him. 'So you still have your motorbike, then?'

'Yeah, so what? Now why don't you just piss off out of here, right? And if I see you here again, I'm not going to hold back from showing you how unwelcome you are. So scram. Go on, fuck off.'

And with that he released his hold of my chair and walked swiftly up towards his front step.

Just before he went inside and slammed the oak-panelled door, he turned to give me a curious look I just couldn't interpret.

TWENTY-FOUR

The following morning, shortly after ten o'clock, Grace called round to the bungalow. We'd arranged the visit by text the previous evening on my return from Martin's. Lawrence the postman had just tumbled a load of envelopes through the front door and I was sorting them out when I heard her car pull up on the drive. It occurred to me that the last time she'd called by, an apparently escaping motorcyclist had met her, and, on this occasion, she'd have narrowly missed a crazily driven post van.

I opened the door, and she entered wearing a colourful summer dress and white cashmere cardigan.

'I see what you mean about your postman,' she exclaimed with a smile. 'Nearly had my wing mirror.'

As I closed the door I replied, 'A major hazard in the village this time of the morning. Usually by the time he starts his rounds on a Thursday, I'm in Edith's sanctuary helping her out. I should have reminded you.'

She leant down and gave me a kiss on the cheek. 'No matter,' she said with a smile that flashed briefly and was gone. 'I'll get us some coffee.' She stood up straight again, walked round behind me and pushed me down to the kitchen. She was evidently distracted as she ambled about fixing our drinks, dropping the teaspoon on the floor and fumbling for it.

We settled in the sitting room on the sofa and I noticed her eyes were watery, something I'd rarely seen before. She picked up the wedding photo, studied it and, like me, seemed to be drawn back into that March day six months ago. 'Happy days,' she said, almost to herself.

'Indeed,' I replied. 'So recent, yet feels like a decade. You okay? You don't look a hundred percent.'

She tenderly replaced the picture on its small table and slowly turned to look at me, taking my hand. 'Mike, your baby. I haven't been able to stop thinking about it. She must have known, surely? She always wanted a child, she often talked about it. She'd have made a great Mum—and you a great Dad.' She flashed a smile. 'I know it's difficult but please tell me more about it so I can understand it better.'

I sensitively repeated my conversation with Goddard.

'As far as I'm concerned, that was my baby,' I said. 'I believe, and have always believed, that Lindsey was faithful to me.'

Grace paused for a brief moment and released my hand. 'I'm sure you're right, Mike.'

But I picked up that merest hesitation and filed it away.

We sat in silence for a few moments. Then she shook her head, as if willing herself to move on, and became light, frivolous, her delicate hands now clasped together, like a kid on Christmas morning. 'Right,' she said, looking at me with a refreshed, positive air, 'I want to hear all about your encounter with the cheat. What happened? You said in your text that you'd had a 'run-in' with the boy. Was he rude? Did you meet the slut?'

I placed my coffee mug on a drinks mat and smiled, enjoying her enthusiasm and reinvigorated attitude. A light relief to the earlier painful discussion. 'Yes and yes,' I said.

'Excellent. What did you make of her? All skin and bone, isn't she? Just a thin, anorexic little girl.'

'Absolutely. I'm not sure what he sees in her. A slight wind and she'd be over the horizon, like a leaf in a gale. Can't work out what he's playing at, but there we are.'

I've learnt that there are times when you can't afford to be honest in what you say. Maybe you understand that. The fact that I thought Sally was sex on legs was not something to be shared with her boyfriend's ex-wife. It would hardly have been helpful.

'So what happened?' she asked.

As we drank our coffee, I gave her a quick summary of my encounter with the 'weedy Sally' and the bullying Martin. She was shocked at his coldness about Lindsey. She kept muttering 'I don't believe it' over and over again, lost in thought.

When I finished, she settled back into the sofa with her hands on her lap and said, 'So, what do you think?'

I sighed. 'Think? I really don't know, Grace. On the one hand he appeared ignorant of issues, surprised at my presence, but on the other hand...'

'Yes?'

'Well, on the other hand he appeared so unbothered about Lindsey that I wonder if there was more to it than he cared to admit.'

'You think he was acting?'

I shrugged. 'I don't know. I just don't know. It's possible. He was pretty good if he was. Save one thing.'

'What was that?' She asked as she leant forward towards me.

'The look he gave me just before he entered the house. It was... was kind of weird. I couldn't work out if he was thinking I was mad... or... or...'

'Or what?'

'Assessing whether he'd taken me in.'

'But it's such a long shot, Mike, you know, whether he's involved or not. Sure, Lindsey cost him a lot of money—'

'And his pride,' I interjected.

'Yes,' she said. 'And that. But it's not as if he's broke or anything, as he was left with more than he could reasonably spend in a lifetime and his income is outrageous. The love nest cost into seven figures.'

'You've seen it?'

'Of course. Who doesn't sneak a look at the ex's new place?' She looked at me as if I was naive.

'I guess so,' I said. I'd never actually been in that position, but it made sense that curiosity would take the upper hand. I took a drink of my coffee. 'So what now, huh?'

'Well, in reality Martin is just one idea,' she said looking thoughtful, 'but unless there's any DNA evidence, or he slips up, there's no way of tying him in. Why don't you push the blessed Goddard to speak to him and tell him what happened yesterday evening?'

'Is that wise bearing in mind his attitude to us getting involved?'

'Stuff that,' she said. 'I'm more concerned about finding out who killed Lindsey than police etiquette. We've already made the decision to involve ourselves in this investigation come what may. He can throw whatever book he likes at us, we have no choice and we can't back down on it.'

'Look, Grace, I've been thinking.' I paused knowing I was about to sail into choppy waters. 'I'm not sure this is actually a good idea. In any event this is my fight, not yours.'

'Excuse me, Lindsey was my best friend,' she said trumping my firmness.

'Absolutely, but this isn't a game, Grace.'

She sat forward on the sofa. 'Of course it isn't, Mike, but I'm as passionate about getting justice for poor Lindsey as you are. My late father always regretted not doing more for his brother when he was wrongly convicted of stealing from his employer—I'm not repeating that mistake here, okay?'

I raised my choleric side. 'I appreciate that, of course I do, but I'm concerned about you. There's a killer lurking out there, Grace, and a merciless one at that. We don't know why he's killed Lindsey—but we do know he has me in his sights now. I know we've tried to be relaxed to maintain our sanity, but in reality we are facing a genuinely serious threat.'

'All the more reason for me to be involved, then. Two is better than none if you would otherwise pull out,' she persisted.

'No, it's all the more reason for you to distance yourself from me. Standing near me when I'm a target means that the grapeshot could hit you too. I wouldn't want that—for you or my conscience.'

We were both silent for a moment. I guessed she was reflecting. But I knew she was a tough woman.

She raised her choleric side too and no doubt recycled the old gatekeeper's habits she had once used when she'd been PA to a top insurance executive. 'Mike, we both know that despite his bark, this Goddard is all but useless. The killer of Sandra Roberts is still not caught and may well be the same guy that murdered Lindsey. I can't simply sit back here, whether you do something or not. How could I? I appreciate your concerns, really I do, but I'm going to do this with or without you, whatever the risks. Ideally we do it together as a team. We'll be stronger and think better.'

I stared at our empty coffee cups taking in the fact that she was going to do this in any event. I couldn't let her do it on her own. I came to the inevitable conclusion that not only did I have to carry on our wild goose chase, but Grace would inescapably be alongside me. And if that were the conclusion, better for me to have some input, some direction. Talking things through together would, I concluded, be better than sole analysis—even Poirot had his Captain Hastings, Holmes his Watson.

'You're not afraid of the danger?' I asked, as my stance started to crumble.

'I could do with some excitement in my life, if I'm honest. I've even thought about re-enlisting as a reservist, but I think I'm past all that now. Not being good at taking orders any more doesn't help either.' She gave me one of her winks.

'As I said, Grace, this isn't a game. This is serious stuff.'

I will always remember how she leant right forward, looked me straight in the eyes and said, 'I know.'

TWENTY-FIVE

I discovered that working 'as a team' didn't mean we'd be free of arguments.

'Okay, so Martin's on the "possible" list,' Grace said, looking across at me as we continued our sitting room chat. 'But there are others: the C from the letter and the Karl I heard Lindsey speaking to surreptitiously on her mobile.'

'So that makes three so far…'

'We need to add to the list and strike off the innocents. I mentioned my cousin Charles, the Exeter-based Casanova. I thought you might pay him a visit, like you did with Martin, to test the water there. But I'm still absolutely stuck on this Karl. Have you had any further thoughts on him?'

I shook my head. 'No, nothing.' I'd racked my brains, scrutinised the address book and searched more of Lindsey's personal papers and letters. But I hadn't found any reference whatsoever to a Karl. I had no more letters to hand over to Goddard either.

We moved on to the threatening letter that had arrived in the post on Tuesday morning. 'As you saw,' I said, 'Goddard wasn't overly hopeful about finding helpful prints or DNA, but, when I think about it, he's not overly hopeful about anything.'

She nodded. 'It's shocking, if not really worrying, that he hasn't solved last year's murder of Sandra Roberts. If Sandra's killer had been caught by now, Mike, do you think Lindsey might be alive today? Is there a link?'

'I've wondered about that,' I said. 'But if the same person killed both Lindsey and Sandra, then Martin, plus Mr C and Karl, whoever they are, cannot be involved in Lindsey's death, can they?'

'Because they didn't know Sandra?'

'Quite. Take Martin, for example, had he known her? You were still with him when she was murdered, so did he act suspiciously?' I paused. 'What am I saying? This is all a bit pie in the sky, isn't it? Real amateur stuff.'

Grace didn't seem to hear my doubt. 'Maybe she was a mistress of his and for some reason he needed her dead.'

I smiled. 'My word, your imagination is really working overtime. Do you actually think you were married to a serial killer, Grace? Come on.'

'Okay, it's far-fetched, I'll give you that. But remember two people are dead.' She paused a beat and said, 'What about a copycat? Nothing to do with Martin, Mr C or Karl, but someone else who has simply copied Sandra's murder to confuse the police. Mind you, that option would have been open to all three of them as well, I guess.'

'Which brings us back to those three men being possibly in the frame again. No connection with Sandra, one of them just imitated the murder, a sort of cover as you say.'

'And it's personal because of the threat to you—you know, the letter telling you to sell and move. The killer wrote that surely?'

I said nothing. But she was right. I just knew the killer wrote the letter. Could have been by a crank, sure, but who would have done that so promptly? But the identity of the killer was the issue we were discussing. Where next?

'There's one more thing,' she said, bringing me out of my thoughts. 'Let's not forget the skull. When I did that research on Littleworth Wood and discovered stories about a coven, I wondered if that was what this was all about.'

'You mean three weird sisters committing annual sacrifices? This is the twenty-first century, Grace, not the Middle Ages. Let's keep it real.'

She frowned. 'I am keeping it real, Mike. These covens do exist whether you acknowledge them or not. Why wouldn't they? Paganism is effectively a religion. It all means something to someone, whatever the date, whatever the year.'

'Not all religions survive.'

'Name one that hasn't.'

'Well, you don't see as many druids about—and how many people worship Zeus anymore?'

She crossed her arms. 'You know what I mean.'

I didn't want a fight over this. I acknowledged inwardly that she had a point. We were both quiet for a moment. The meander through possible scenarios was also quite taxing. Lindsey had only died four and a half days ago after all. There's only so much one can take.

In the end she broke the heavy silence. 'I know what we'll do next.' She stood up and started to pace the room. 'As I think there might be something in this coven thing, I'll do further research on it. Should be interesting and might help.'

'Sure. And what shall I do?'

She stopped and looked at me. 'You? You do as I suggested earlier and go visit my cousin Charles in Exeter. See if he's the C who knew Lindsey more than he should have done. Knowing Charles, a man-to-man talk might be more fruitful, and it allows me to get on with the coven research. We can double up our efforts and save time. I'll give you his address.'

TWENTY-SIX

Grace asked me to ring her as soon as I was able to about my upcoming encounter with Charles and left late morning. She was obviously focused on doing her research as she said she would even cancel a lunch with her sister, Helen. They tended to meet quite regularly since their mother had died and had left them, as Grace would say, 'as orphans'.

I drove into Exeter at about six o'clock, conscious that this was the second encounter in as many evenings. Grace had said that her cousin was a creature of habit, and I was trusting that he would be home when I called. If not, I would have to come up with another plan. We had agreed that it would be best not to ring him and thereby give him the chance to avoid meeting me.

Fifteen Meadow Road was a modern detached house identical to the other homes on a small estate developed towards the centre of the city that was probably a transformed brown field site. Smart, but nothing flash. Several steps down the property ladder to Martin's place. I pulled up by the kerb in the quiet suburban road and manoeuvred myself into my wheelchair. I saw no movement from the house.

I pressed the doorbell and waited. No reply. After some thirty seconds, I pressed it again, feeling self-conscious for doing so. It always struck me as odd that I felt that way. If the occupier hadn't heard it the first time, it made sense to repeat the call. If the occupier was out, I could keep the wretched thing pressed for an hour and no one would care. Anyhow, the second attempt provoked a response, as a few moments later the red-painted front door opened, and Charles stepped out onto the porch.

'Hello, can I help?'

Although he was fifty, he looked at least five years younger than that milestone. Thick, wavy, brown hair, light blue eyes, and a handsome face. Dressed in slacks and a blue blazer with silver buttons, he was tall and athletic. Would have given some guys in Hollywood a run for their money. In a funny sort of way, I warmed to him straight away. Might have been his broad smile and friendly manner.

I looked up at him and said, 'My name's Mike, Mike Miller, I'm a friend of your cousin, Grace. Have you got a few minutes, Charles? I have a couple of queries to run by you. Sorry to crash in on you like this.'

'Mike,' he exclaimed, thrusting out his hand to shake mine. 'How the hell are you? It's been a while, hasn't it?'

I continued to look up at him and tried not to let my face betray the fact that I was struggling. 'How long?' I managed in a non-committal way.

'Well, Grace and Martin's New Year bash, wasn't it? Their last do before everything blew up and the shit hit the fan.'

The party came flooding back to me. Lindsey and I had turned up quite late at Grace and Martin's, as we'd been enjoying our own company under the covers earlier that evening and reluctantly went out of a sense of duty. For the life of me I couldn't remember Charles being there, but he looked confident enough about the events of that night.

'Of course,' I said with a smile. 'Over eight months ago. Is it convenient to have a quick chat, Charles? I would have rung, but…' I let my voice trail away.

'Well, I'm due out any minute. Is it urgent?'

I looked a little deflated. 'No,' I said. 'But it would be helpful as I'm here. Can you give me five minutes?'

He paused and looked at me. His eyes flicked over my wheelchair. It seemed to win me the sympathy vote, not for the first time.

'Hang on,' he said, appearing to make a decision. He dipped his left hand into his jacket pocket and pulled out his mobile. He dialled a number and turned away from me, bending his head towards the floor as if that would somehow give him some privacy.

'Hi, doll,' he said when the call was evidently answered. 'Got a slight situation here. Going to be about ten minutes late… I said *ten minutes late*. Can you hear me?' He eased a bit further from me. 'It can't be helped, okay?' he continued and then paused. 'Hey, that's not fair, babe. When was the last time?' He scratched his ear and almost spat out his words, 'Look, ten minutes, okay? If you keep rattling on like this, I'll make it fifteen. Now go get yourself ready for me and stop messing me about.'

He rang off abruptly and turned to face me. His smile returned to his face.

'Sorry about that,' he said, slipping his phone back into his jacket pocket.

'Look, I don't mean to cause any bother—'

'No bother,' he said stepping towards me. 'Women, huh? Always a hassle. Can't live with them, can't live without them. They need to know their place, that's all. Right, why don't you come on in, Mike, and let's have that chat you wanted. Can I help you up the step?'

We talked in his lounge, a large room decorated in an

oriental theme. There were two white leather sofas, a scattering of Chinese silk rugs and plenty of Eastern rosewood furniture, including a rather fine hand-carved Chinese writing bureau in one corner.

Charles left me in my wheelchair at the end of one of the sofas and walked back to the door to close it.

I didn't know where to start so relied on what he exhibited for his guests. 'You seem to like Chinese stuff?' I asked as I twisted round to watch him return from the door.

He laughed. 'Spot on, but it doesn't exactly take Sherlock Holmes to work that one out, does it?' He stood by the sofa opposite me and looked round the room as if observing it for the first time. 'I spent almost ten years out in Hong Kong back in the days when it really was British—you know, before the lease fell through. Loved it. A real powerhouse for commerce. Entrepreneurial, exciting, little tax. And Chinese girls are something else—perhaps you know that? I was younger in those days, of course—cities are for the young, aren't they?'

'I suppose so,' I said. 'What were you doing out there?'

'I'm an accountant by trade,' he said as he sat down on the sofa to face me. 'Unusually, I specialised in high tech manufacturers—you know, guys who make things which you can't drop on your foot. I'm not a very good accountant, mind, but I get by.'

I smiled and wondered whether he was pulling my leg, being modest.

'I worked for one of the big firms in the day,' he continued, 'but now I'm a salaried partner with a small crowd in Exeter. Not too much commitment, which suits me and it's only a short drive to the office—a touch easier than commuting in Hong Kong or London.'

'I guess so,' I said.

'So, what can I do for you?' he asked in a friendly tone.

I thought for a moment and abruptly realised how much I was out on a limb here, how complex in truth this was. Seemed easy when talking about it with Grace, a touch harder now in reality. *Well, Charles, nice guy as you are, did you ever have an intimate relationship, even an affair, with my Lindsey? Did you treat her badly? Did you hurt her in some incident or other? Did you murder her last weekend?*

I smiled. 'As I said outside, Charles, I wanted to ask you a couple of quick questions if I may.'

'About?'

'About Lindsey. You met her at Grace's party as my fiancée. We married in March.'

Charles leant back and crossed his arms over his chest. 'Congratulations,' he said with a smile. 'I'd heard something about it through Grace. Should have sent you both a card or something.'

I raised my hand in a half-hearted protest. 'That's a lovely thought,' I said, 'but there would have been no need. It was a very quiet do, only four of us in fact, including Grace.'

Charles said, 'Never done this marriage thing myself. Seen too many of my friends come a cropper. Can be pretty ruinous. One of my pals said the process was pretty simple. Meet a girl, bed her, marry her, divorce her and give her your house. Then start again. Too much hassle from my angle. Leave out the "marry" bit and you retain your house, which seems to make total financial sense to me. Maybe I'm not such a crap accountant after all.'

I smiled. 'Always the bachelor boy, right?'

He nodded. 'That's it, not that my mother approves. She

135

turned eighty last week and she's still nagging me about settling down.' He paused and rubbed his eye. 'So, what do you want to know about Lindsey? And why ask me? You're married to her after all.'

I smiled again to keep him on side and kept crucial facts close to my chest, like a cross-examining lawyer. 'It's a bit more complicated than that, but I'll come back to that in a minute or two. I was wondering if you knew Lindsey before?'

'Before what?'

'Before that New Year party? Had you ever met her before?'

He looked bemused. 'No, I think I'd have remembered that. If you don't mind me saying, she's a good-looking girl as I recall her. Short-cropped, brunette hair, right? Slim, pretty?' He looked at me as if awaiting marks for his powers of recollection.

'You have a good memory.'

He seemed to relax. 'I have so far as the fairer sex goes. I take a real interest so to speak. I like them and, fortunately, they seem to like me.'

'Do you treat them well?' I asked.

'What do you mean, spoil them?'

'If you like. Some guys can't treat women well at all. You know, can be violent.'

He looked at me. Seemed to be taking in what I'd said. A darker look crossed his face. 'What are you saying?'

'Nothing, it's—'

'Are you insinuating something? What *is* this all about?' He moved right to the edge of the sofa and placed his hands on the seat as if to rise.

'Look, it's a simple enough matter, Charles. I believe

someone had a fling with Lindsey before she met me, possibly after she met me—'

'Well, she's hardly a teenager, is she? How old is she, thirty-three, thirty-four?'

'She was thirty-nine on her last birthday.'

'Well, there you are,' he said with the attitude of someone who had evidently proved his point. 'I should think she'd have had quite a few "flings" as you call it before she met you. So why ask me about it? Just ask her.'

'Because I've found a very personal letter she'd hidden, signed off by a bloke using nothing but the letter C, and a handful of kisses. Posted in Exeter.'

'And you think it was from me?'

I said nothing.

'Not exactly a rare initial, is it, huh?' He said, staring at me as if I were stupid. 'Hardly a Z, is it? There must be quite a few of us C's around, even in Exeter.' He paused and seemed to take a breath, take stock of what was happening in his sitting room. His tone softened to become almost conciliatory. 'Anyhow, not me Mike. Sure, she's a nice girl, but she's your girl. If you've recently got married then she must be your girl. I don't touch them when they're married—too complicated. Fancy my health if they have a big husband.' He glanced at his watch. 'Look, sorry, Mike, but I've got a date and I really must go. Is there anything else? If you really do think I'm her ex or whatever, why not ask her direct?'

'I can't'

'Embarrassed? I thought you marrying types were meant to be able to talk about anything with each other.'

'We did, but we can't now. She's dead.'

'*Dead*?' he exclaimed. 'Christ, I'm sorry, mate. I... I

137

didn't know…' He flopped back into the sofa staring at me. He looked genuinely surprised to me. 'Why didn't you say? How… what happened? Cancer?'

'Murder.'

He looked as if I'd thumped him.

'Fucking hell. Are you serious?'

My face showed no expression. 'Not exactly material for jokes.'

I found it was my turn to observe him closely. He looked bemused, but I've learnt that people can disguise their thoughts and feelings, and not everything can be as it appears. He suddenly seemed to comprehend, as if some electrician had twisted two wires together in his brain and they were sparking. It shot across his face and he stood up.

'You're not suggesting I know anything about this, are you? I see where you're coming from now. If you really think—'

'Look, Charles, I don't know what I think, okay? The police are obviously looking into her death, but I can't sit here and wait for them, can I? I want to find out what's happened to her, who's responsible. We were only married a few months for heaven's sake. And now I'm getting threats.'

'Really? What sort of threats?'

'Long story.'

My response seemed to prompt him to glance at his watch again.

'Look, Mike, I've got to shoot. She's not a bad girl and I shouldn't mess her about. I'm very sorry to hear about Lindsey, honest I am. For what it's worth I can assure you that I only ever met her at that party, not before, not after and I certainly never wrote to her. Don't even know where she lives… lived.' He smiled weakly.

'No hassle, Charles,' I said. 'Let's leave it like that, shall we? I'll get out your way and sorry again for crashing in on you like this.'

He said nothing. Just nodded and walked over to behind my chair. 'I'll push you out.' He left me by my car after I'd declined his offer to help me get into it. His three-year-old blue Mondeo had already left the drive by the time I too hit the road and turned for home. I was hungry, but my mind was focused more on my encounter with Charles, wondering what Grace would make of it all.

There was one thing, however, that I was sure about—if we wanted to make progress, we had to raise the stakes.

TWENTY-SEVEN

I'd just come back from taking my Barney for a walk that Thursday evening when Mike rang me.

My house is off the main tourist beat of Tiverton, and a footpath joins my road about fifty metres from my house and leads up to some fields. Barney loves the walk, as all chocolate Labradors would, and we go most days. I left him in the large laundry room to dry off and hurried into the kitchen to get the call.

'Hi Mike,' I said. 'Did you see Charles?'

'Just got back, Grace' he said.

'And?'

'And I'm not sure what to make of him,' he said. 'Seems like a bog standard accountant. He's had some pretty high-flying jobs in the past though.'

'That's right,' I said. 'I stayed with him while he was in Hong Kong. Helen and I went with our parents. I must have been about, what, ten or twelve? Christmas eighty-eight anyway. I remember because of that Pan Am plane being blown up mid-flight. I recall kicking up a right fuss with my parents about flying home. Charles' girlfriend helped calm me down.'

'Chinese was she?'

'Yes, how did you know?'

'An inspired guess. He was on his way out when I got there, but he gave me a few minutes. Seems a nice bloke, but he has one penetrating stare. Made me feel quite uncomfortable. He claims he met Lindsey and me at your New Year bash. Was he there? I don't remember him if I'm honest.'

It flooded back to me. 'Of course, yes he was. Arrived quite late and left not long after midnight. Brought a Helen with him—I remember that because she had the same name as my sister. That was probably the last time we met up. Other than my sister and me, our family aren't much cop at keeping up with each other.' I paused, and then asked, 'So, do you think he's the C who wrote the letters?'

'I don't think so,' Mike said. 'It was always very speculative, of course. Might as well have gone to see your other Charles.'

'Yeah, right,' I said. 'He may have had an affair in the past, but he wouldn't be writing to Lindsey. No, at least my cousin Charles had met Lindsey, however briefly—'

'Might have been brief, but he certainly remembered her. A lot of accurate detail.'

'Really?' I said. 'He's always been a womaniser.'

'I certainly have that impression, although he says he doesn't get involved with married women.'

'Lindsey wasn't married when she first had a fling with the mystery C.'

'But she was later, and when he wrote that letter,' he said.

'Maybe he sees becoming involved before any marriage as an exception. Prior rights, so to speak.'

'Mm, possibly.' Mike was quiet for a moment. 'But I think we're wasting our time,' he continued. 'Although I did see a flash of another side of him.'

'Really? What was that?' I asked.

'Well, when I arrived, he agreed to give me a few

minutes, you know, delay his evening. He rang some girl he was going to see. Can't remember her name, but she was evidently a bit hacked off with him going to be late and all that. He was quite abrupt back at her.'

'Overly abrupt?'

'Well, I thought so. He could have been politer.'

'Doesn't mean he's violent though,' I said.

'No, I guess not. It's just…'

'Just what?'

'No, forget it.'

'No, go on, Mike. Just what?'

'Well, if someone can be so abrupt, change so quickly, it makes me think that's all.'

'You mean it reflects what the C put in his letter? You know, he regretted doing something and was then promising to behave?'

'Yeah, I guess,' Mike said.

It was my turn to reflect. It seemed extremely unlikely that we had hit on the right person so quickly. What were the chances of that? There had to be many guys whose name began with C and who could have taken a shine to Lindsey. True, the letter had an Exeter postmark, but even Exeter itself must be well stocked with such men, even discounting a C passing through the town and simply posting a letter there.

'So what are we going to do now?' Mike asked.

'I've been thinking about that,' I replied. 'I think we should get in touch with Goddard tomorrow morning. See what he's been doing, and tell him about your visits to Martin and Charles.'

'Is that wise?' he asked. 'He wanted us to keep our noses out, didn't he?'

'But we told him we can't, didn't we?' I said. 'And what's he going to do about it? He can hardly stop us.'

'I don't know about that,' Mike said. 'He must have some powers to stop us messing up his enquiries.'

'Is that what you think we're doing?'

Mike seemed to try to douse the flames. 'No, of course I don't, Grace, but Goddard won't share that view, will he?'

'Well, he's not going to stop me. I'm on Lindsey's side.'

At the time this occurred, I was pleased we were going to press on. Looking back a little later, however, I wish Goddard *had* stopped us.

TWENTY-EIGHT

As agreed with Mike, I set about my idea of research into the coven that purportedly used Littleworth Wood, crazy as it sounded. I explored the Internet and intended to spend some time in the Tiverton library the next day, but I could also ring someone locally who might know some answers: Judith Podmore.

Judith had lived in Tiverton for all her seventy-five years and had been involved in every element of the community. She'd been a close friend of my late mother's, and I visited her in her small cottage on an irregular basis. I guessed that if anyone knew local folklore, it would be Judith.

I settled in my sitting room and rang her. She answered quite promptly, and I dealt with the small talk before taking the conversation in my required direction.

'Judith, how well do you know Littleworth Wood?'

'There's a curious question, Grace. I know it very well. I used to play there with my brother and sister when we were children, and it's been my friend ever since. Joe and I used to take the dogs up there regular, some good walks. Why d'you ask?'

'That's lovely. Mum and Dad used to walk up there too. Did you hear about this awful murder?'

'Yes indeed. It was on the wireless. Poor woman.'

'Lindsey, Lindsey Miller. She was my best friend, Judith.'

'Lindsey, of course. I'm so sorry, Grace, I didn't make the connection. Well, you wouldn't, would you? These things always involve someone you don't know, don't they? Oh dear, dear, dear. So, how are you?'

'Coping, thanks. She was such a nice person. I've been comforting her husband, Mike. He's in a bit of an emotional mess as you can imagine.'

'Yes, he must be. Poor man.'

'Judith, may I tap into your local knowledge?'

'Of course, ask away.'

'I read somewhere that some sort of local coven may have a connection with Littleworth Wood. Do you know anything about it?'

There was a long silence on the phone. Then Judith said, 'Why do you ask?'

'Well, I was talking to Mike, and we are concerned about what the police have said. Apparently Lindsey was killed at the exact same location as another woman, Sandra Roberts, who was murdered there last summer. It just seems a bit odd, that's all.'

'Grace, these are matters for the police, not you and… and Mike. Leave it to the professionals. You don't want to be digging where you shouldn't.'

'But there's no harm in trying to help, is there?'

'Normally I'd agree with you, but this is slightly different.'

'What do you mean?'

'I mean there are some things better left alone. Take my advice, Grace, leave it alone.'

'Why, Judith? What's the problem?'

There was a pause, and then she spoke more sharply than I'd ever heard her speak before. She almost sounded like a different person.

'Grace,' she said, 'do *not* ask me anymore. I will talk no more on this subject. Leave it all well alone.'

TWENTY-NINE

I'd found it helpful updating Grace in my telephone call that Thursday evening and bouncing ideas around. As we finished our conversation she said that she'd made some good progress exploring the issue of the occult in Littleworth Wood. She was well into it and wanted to get on with it further. I thought it would be pretty harmless for her to surf the Internet or thumb through books in the library.

On her suggestion I rang Goddard and was able to get through to DS Ward. He told me that Goddard had gone home, and he wasn't prepared to contact him unless it was an emergency. I wasn't comfortable putting it in that category, and I guess the guy was entitled to some home time.

'Okay,' I said, 'but I need to get together with you both.' I thought it would be tactful, perhaps manipulative, to openly treat Ward as part of Goddard's team, and an essential member at that.

'That's going to be tricky, Mr Miller. The Chief Inspector's very busy.'

'I appreciate that, but I have what I consider to be helpful information which might make him less busy.'

'Well, I'm not sure…' Ward muttered.

'Look, I'll come to you if that helps. That'll save him travelling out to the sticks, huh? I can come down to Exeter any time tomorrow. When's he free, even for just ten minutes?'

I'm sure Ward knew Goddard's diary off the top of his head. He eventually backed off and we arranged that I'd be there for eleven o'clock. No doubt this would now be in the diary and Ward would expect me to be there on the stroke of eleven. I just felt that a change of scene would be good for me, and there was something interesting about going into Goddard's lair.

I was about to make myself some supper when the front door bell rang. Long and hard. My first thought was that it was Grace. I left the kitchen and trundled across the hallway in my wheelchair to find a giant of a guy standing on the doorstep. He was about six and a half feet tall, very stocky wearing baggy jeans and a t-shirt that disclosed some thick, muscular arms. Would have made an intimidating professional wrestler. He was holding a cheap black leather jacket and a motorcycle helmet. But his most striking feature was his untidy, long black hair and greying, unkempt beard that gave every impression of having grown wild for years. He looked about ten years older than me and he reminded me of a traditional Hells Angel.

'Are you Michael Miller?' he said in what seemed to be an American accent.

'Who's asking?'

'The name's Frank. Frank Mackenzie. I'm Lindsey's cousin.'

THIRTY

I didn't invite Frank in. There was no need. He simply stepped past me into the hallway clipping my wheelchair with his solid foot as he did so.

'This the way to the kitchen?' he said, moving purposefully in that direction in any event.

'Sure,' I said, pushing the door shut and hastening down the hallway after him.

When I reached the doorway, I saw him settle back against a work surface with his thick arms crossed and glance around. He'd placed his leather jacket and helmet on the side next to him. I noticed a blue and red tattoo on his forearm that said 'Rosie'.

As I stopped the wheelchair just inside the room, he gave me a thorough looking over.

'So, what happened to Lindsey?' he said.

'You've heard then? She—'

'Of course I've heard. It was on the radio.'

'In Canada?'

'No asshole, on the moon. Jeez, what do you think? On the BBC here in England.'

'So you've been over here for a few days?'

'Yeah. Didn't know at first Lindsey had moved.'

I wasn't sure whether I should be offering him a drink or anything. I was certainly feeling uncomfortable in his presence. His manner was unrelentingly aggressive.

'Can I offer you anything?' I started.

'No, I'm fine. I've just had a couple of beers.'

'Do you want to sit?' I floundered, gesturing towards the kitchen table.

'No, I won't be here long. We need to talk money.'

My throat suddenly felt dry. I looked at him carefully, trying to ignore his persistent gaze.

'Money? What do you mean "money"?'

He pushed himself away from the work surface edge and started to pace. I twisted to watch him walk, concerned not to let him out of my sight.

'Dollars, pounds, dinero. Money. I need some and you have some. Or you will soon.'

'I... I don't follow you.'

He suddenly stopped pacing and stood less than a metre directly in front of me. He crossed his arms again and stared coldly down at me. I felt like a piece of dog turd he'd trodden in.

'Rosie has gotten really bad this summer.'

'Rosie?'

He frowned and ran his large hand roughly through his hair. 'Rosie, my sister. Lindsey's only other cousin,' he said. 'She's got MS, as you probably know. I've given up my military career to look after her. We're broke now, spent what little savings we had. I spoke to Lindsey last autumn, shortly after her mother died in that bath accident. She said if things got worse, I should let her know. Her side of the family has the money.'

I tried to take it all in. Lindsey had said nothing to me about this. I knew about the Canadian cousins, although their names had escaped me at that moment. I knew there was reference to them in Lindsey's will, since she'd told me about it. But I hadn't expected to hear from them, let alone receive a visit from this brute of a man.

I shrugged and said, 'I don't know what you expect me to do.'

'*Do*? Isn't that obvious? This is family money, and you're hardly family.'

I bristled. 'Excuse me, Lindsey was my wife—and I've only recently lost her.'

'So what you can *do,* asshole, is help her family, then. You *can* do that, right?'

'For heaven's sake, Frank, I can't be expected to get my head round any of that at this time. I loved Lindsey. She was my world.'

'But the money will be yours? Or might be.'

'What you on about, Frank?' I paused and stared up at him. He said nothing. I swallowed and said, 'I think this conversation has gone as far as it can. Please leave. If you want to come back tomorrow, before the beers, then let's fix when.'

'You sayin' I'm drunk?'

'I'm saying this conversation is closed for today.'

He stood still, looking at me. I felt he was weighing things up, thinking things through. I had the impression his brawn far outstripped his brain. A potentially dangerous combination. It made him unpredictable, perhaps illogical.

After a moment or two he started to move slowly towards the kitchen door. 'You haven't seen the last of me, Michael. You won't get rid of me so easily,' he said slowly, glancing round at me.

'We're through for this evening,' I said.

He pulled a couple of pieces of paper out of his trouser pocket. He deliberately unfolded them and waved them at me.

'You know what this is?'

'Haven't a clue.'

'It's a copy of Lindsey's will. She emailed it to me in January. Before your wedding or something. You know what it says?'

As it happened I did know what it said. Lindsey had told me at the time when she came back from seeing her solicitor in Exeter.

'What's it say, Frank?'

'It leaves all her money to you. But a lawyer friend of mine says there's something called a "survival clause" in it, to save on tax or something.'

'So?'

'So the money is yours if you survive Lindsey by twenty-eight days. If you don't live that long, it comes to Rosie and me, less what she's given to that hospice she helped at.'

'Yeah, that's right,' I said. My hands felt clammy.

He replaced the papers into his pocket and picked up his coat and helmet. As he stepped into the hallway he said, 'Think about the money, Michael. Think about it carefully. I'll be back this time tomorrow to talk money. Be ready.'

He smiled sarcastically and left.

THIRTY-ONE

I arrived at the police station in Exeter before eleven o'clock the following morning and was shown into a small windowless interview room painted in an unsettling institutional lime green. The constable thoughtfully moved one of the basic metal chairs to make room for my wheelchair. I declined a coffee in anticipation of a paper cup of brown water from some ancient vending machine.

Goddard came into the room after some five minutes. The draught through the door diluted slightly the room's stale fug that reminded me of my school changing room. There was no sign of DS Ward. He was probably busy sharpening his pencil somewhere. Goddard sat opposite me in one of the metal chairs and looked at me across the chipped laminated table.

'Well?' he said, with his body in an open posture. 'How can I help, Mr Miller?'

'I was rather hoping for an update, Chief Inspector. Have you anything of interest to report?'

He shuffled in his chair, glanced briefly away and then looked back at me.

'Nothing of significance yet.' He held my stare.

'Anything of insignificance?'

'Well, I guess not, but then—'

'So here we are on Friday morning. My wife was murdered almost a week ago and you have nothing from your enquiries to date?'

'These investigations are not quick, Mr Miller.'

'Then how come you hear of murders with arrests within days?'

He took a deep breath. 'With respect, Mr Miller, those are usually domestic murders. You know, when the victim is killed by a close relative, often in his or her own home. This is obviously not the case here, or with Sandra Roberts come to that. You must be patient.'

'How on earth can I be patient when there's some nutter out there threatening me as well? So what *have* you done so far?'

'I've done what I can with the resources and time I have available. A week may seem long to you, I understand that, but to me, for an investigation like this one, it's not long at all. I've got a report from the pathologist, I've spoken to Julie Wycliff and Bronia Field, I've inspected the site in Littleworth Wood, I've considered various forensic issues and I am looking into other lines of enquiry.'

'Such as?'

'I'm not at liberty to say.'

'*Not at liberty?* Chief Inspector, I'm the victim's husband. Surely that means something around here? Well, doesn't it?'

'Of course it does. In a way.'

'*In a way?*'

'Look, Mr Miller. I have certain procedures to follow. I will tell you what I can, but you're going to have to be patient...'

'Like Sandra Roberts' husband?'

'She wasn't married—divorced.'

'You know what I mean.' I said sharply. I paused. Decided I would tell him now about our own enquiries. Sod the reaction. He could surely see my expressed anger by now. 'While you have been going through your procedures, Chief Inspector, we've been making a few enquiries of our own.'

'I thought I said—'

'That I should sit on my bloody backside doing bugger all? It sounds like with your lack of time and resources, let alone your "certain procedures", we're best placed to progress matters whether you like it or not.'

'I don't like it, and I thought I'd made that plain to both you and Mrs… Mrs Atkins.'

'And I thought I'd made it plain that I wanted a result, not another Sandra Roberts case with an open file over a year on.'

He took his glasses off and rubbed his hand across his eyes before resetting them on his face. He stared at me. He seemed to be taking a deep internal breath as he fought with the pressures.

'Go on, tell me what you've been up to.'

I rubbed my chin and looked at him. Maybe it was time.

'I've been to see a couple of suspects,' I said.

'*Suspects*?' It was his turn to look bemused. 'Who the hell have you been talking to now?'

And so I told him. In detail. About the motorbike Grace had seen at night in the close. About my visit to Martin. Our exchange, his motorbike and his final look. My concerns about what that curious look had meant. And I told him about Charles, and about the fact that he seemed okay, but how I was concerned about his harsh reaction to his girlfriend on the phone. His apparent swings of mood. I went through it all, setting it out precisely as I saw it from my angle and from my experience.

To be fair, Goddard listened. He was a good listener. All the right positive body language. Almost encouraged me. Not that I needed any encouragement. I wanted to give him further lines of investigation. Move him out of the apparent malaise he appeared to be languishing in. I brought him slap bang right up to date. Save for what I then regarded as an irrelevant visit from Frank, he had it all.

When I'd finished, I sat back in my wheelchair. I was truly fascinated by how he'd react. At first there was nothing. He then put his elbows on the apology for a table and brought his hands together in front of his mouth, fingers straight up towards the gloomy ceiling, in a classic pose of prayer. He studied me through his silver-framed glasses for a few seconds before speaking.

'Mr Miller, I do of course understand your anxiety and I do of course understand your desire to find out what happened last Saturday night, and who was responsible. Further, I do understand your frustrations at how long it is apparently taking for me and my team to move matters forward. However, I am deeply—and I mean deeply—disconcerted by your actions. I cannot stress enough the need to leave this matter to the police. You may be causing us a real problem.'

'But—' I started, but he thrust out a flat right hand in a firm signal to stop me.

'There are no "buts". Put simply, you are treading where you should not be treading. Unless you agree right now to stop this unnecessary and, frankly, disruptive approach, I will have to take action.'

I made to start speaking, but he once again signalled me to be quiet.

'I am serious, Mr Miller. There are ways for such a

serious investigation to be done. Since you're not a trained detective, I don't expect you to know that. What I do expect is for you to do as I am asking. Not just for your sake, but for Lindsey's too.'

I didn't say anything this time. I did of course understand what he was saying. I guess I just wanted him to see that I was desperate to get to the bottom of the matter, that I wanted him to follow up on both Martin and Charles alongside any other "line of enquiry" his team was pursuing. I nodded slowly and looked up at him. He was now resting his chin on his hands, which were clasped together at the apex of the triangle formed by his forearms. He'd removed his glasses, which now swung freely from his fingers.

'Okay, Chief Inspector. I understand what you're saying. But can I ask you this?'

'What?'

'Will you at least visit Martin and Charles just to see what you make of them? I've explained my theories to you and here are their addresses.' I took a piece of paper out of my jeans and passed it over to him. He glanced at it and put it in his jacket pocket. A good sign.

'Alright,' he said. 'And you'll stop playing Poirot?'

I nodded.

He rose from his seat. 'We seem to be through then. And we have a clear agreement going forward.'

I eased the wheelchair slowly back from the table.

'Thank you, Chief Inspector,' was all I said.

As I made my way towards the door, which Goddard opened for me, I knew I'd not even mentioned that Grace was looking into the alleged coven of Littleworth Wood. But then that was Grace playing Poirot, not me.

THIRTY-TWO

'There is certainly some evidence about a coven operating in Littleworth Wood in the past,' said Grace. 'Look at this.'

It was shortly after five o'clock that Friday evening, and we were sitting alone by the fireside in the snug of the Chequers in Westland. The pub was a favourite of mine, as it couldn't get more traditionally English: white-painted stone, thatched roof, low doorways and beams, and small hideaway rooms. There was even a thatched bar in the lounge. A permanent seductive smell of long-gone fires mixed subtlety with aromas of real ale and home-cooked food. Perfection. The snug was the cosiest of the rooms and, save during the true summer months, there was always a gentle log fire snuffling away in the hearth. Yes, getting the wheelchair over steps and through narrow red quarry-tiled passages was a challenge, but worth the effort. The beer, locally brewed, was pretty damn good too.

I took the small bundle of papers from Grace. I studied them but found it difficult to concentrate, as she wanted to tell me about her day's work. I gave up, took a decent swig of beer and listened to her. She was confident in her new specialist subject.

'It really is a whole new world to me, Mike,' she said. 'I'd heard of witches and covens—Macbeth and all that as well as some creepy Hollywood films—but it never dawned on me that these cults still lived on in modern times in the Western world.'

'You mean you could have been standing next to a high priest in the checkout queue at Asda?' I said with a smile and placed my pint glass on the small oak table between us.

Grace frowned. 'Mike, this is serious stuff.' She was silent for a moment or two and then smiled. 'But yes, I suppose you do have a point. Anyhow, the thing is I've been on Wikipedia and various sites as well as into the small library in Tiverton. I've typed up what I've learnt and also done some copying and pasting from my Internet research. What you have in your lap is everything I've pulled together.'

'Can you summarise it?' I asked, knowing from her level of motivation that she was going to give it a go anyway, come what may.

'I'll try,' she said. She leant back in her chair and placed her hands at the end of the two wooden arms, almost stretched. 'I've learnt a lot though. Did you know there used to be a village called Littleworth? Well, more of a hamlet really. About two miles from Tiverton.'

'News to me, but then I'm not exactly a local to here.'

'True. Anyhow, it was mentioned in the Domesday Book in the eleventh century, but was effectively destroyed by the Black Death that ravaged England in the mid fourteenth century. In the early Middle Ages, the hamlet was known for witchcraft. A pagan group of local witches were known as the Coven of the Grey Moon. Their creed was based on Wicca, a belief system and way of life that follows Celtic pre-Christian traditions. Or something like that. It's fascinating stuff, Mike.'

'Makes you sound quite the academic,' I said with a smile.

'It's still in me somewhere. Long time since I was at

uni, but I did learn some life skills if little else. Anyhow, I evidently made the right decision in not coming with you to see Charles and Goddard.' She took a sip of her Prosecco. 'The coven was destroyed in the Middle Ages during the infamous witch hunts in both this country and mainland Europe. You know, ducking chairs and burnings at the stake and all that. Must have been pretty gruesome, and not much fairness or rule of law.'

'So if the coven was destroyed centuries ago, how come it's still part of local folklore?' I took a drink of beer.

'Well, that's where it all starts getting rather juicy,' she said. 'It seems that sometime in the nineteen thirties, the coven was recreated from scratch by a guy called Edward Denning. Made a lot of money in the city and bought some manorial property not far from here. He took more than a passing interest in witchcraft and was deeply involved while working as a stockbroker in London. He was made a high priest of his city coven and effectively took the chance to set up his own coven when he moved out here. Apparently in Wicca, it's normal to do that.'

'So the Coven of the Grey Moon came back to life?'

'Absolutely,' Grace said, her eyes alive with her newfound knowledge. 'It was well funded by Denning, too. Even after his death.'

'Old age would have claimed him years ago, wouldn't it? Unless he used magic powers to give him eternal life.'

'Mike, that's hardly respectful.'

'Respectful? He was a witch or wizard or whatever, not someone who has my respect. Sacrificing goats at full moon while completely starkers is hardly mainstream religion.'

'Each to their own,' Grace said and crossed her arms. 'Anyhow, old age didn't get him in the end.'

'No? What did?'

'Fire.'

A shudder ran through me and I fought memories.

'What happened?' I asked quietly.

'His big manor house went up in flames in 1967, or 1968, something like that. Late sixties. His young son and his nanny escaped, but Edward, then a widower, died.'

'Did the coven survive?'

'Yes. Mainly because of his money'

'So, is it still going?'

'That's where the trail goes cold,' Grace said. 'It was certainly going in the early eighties because one of its inner circle, a Dean Wilson, did the unthinkable and broke ranks. He was the summoner, one of the most senior and influential members. There was some major fallout at the top level, and Dean took his revenge by going to the national press. One of the Sundays did a massive exposé. Talked about all that Denning had done.'

'Wouldn't have made Dean popular in the area, not even with the tourist board.'

'That's where the plot thickens,' Grace said. 'Dean was dead within the week. Found hanging from an oak tree in Littleworth Wood. An open verdict was recorded by the coroner due to insufficient evidence about either foul play or suicide.'

'Timing's a bit of a coincidence.'

'Exactly.'

'What was the great exposé, then?'

'A copy of the newspaper article's in that bundle, but in essence, it seems the coven had started to move away from strict Wicca teaching, and therefore away from Denning's principles, even though he was funding it from beyond the grave, so to speak.'

'And since I've never heard of Wicca, save in the context of woven baskets, what exactly does it teach?'

Grace rolled her eyes. 'Mike, behave.' She took another drink of her wine. 'Right, in really simple terms, from what little I've read, Wicca is a peaceful and tranquil way of life that inspires harmony with their divine and the whole of nature. Followers believe that the spirit of their "One", their God or Goddess if you like, exists in all natural things, and so they have to treat all of nature, everything like that, with true love and respect.'

'Not sure I follow all that,' I said. 'So basically they take their clothes off to get close to nature, like naturalists— or swingers?'

'Mike, please stop it. Take it seriously. Yes, I've read that those in the inner circle of a coven, those initiated, will hold secret rites with nudity.'

'Is that what Dean exposed, so to speak?'

She gave me a friendly glare. 'Yes, but he went further. He said that the Littleworth witches had moved away from this peaceful respect of nature to a darker side. He claimed that they had made animal sacrifices and this, of course, flies in the face of Wicca teachings, indeed in the face of traditional witchcraft, believe it or not. They shouldn't harm nature.'

'Okay, so a few sheep and goats had a sudden and unexpected end. Sad for them, but hardly a crime,' I said.

'Possibly. But Dean hinted that they'd gone beyond animals.'

'You mean people?'

She nodded. 'He didn't say it expressly, but, as you'll see when you read the article, it was—how shall I put it?—

more than implied.'

I stared into the fire and we both sat in silence for a few minutes. I was conscious of someone putting their head round the door and withdrawing. The fire popped and I was reminded of its comfort. 'Anything else of interest, Grace?' I asked eventually in a subdued voice. 'Not that what you've said so far isn't plenty to be getting on with. Thanks for spending so much time on this wild goose chase.'

'Don't think there's anything else,' she said, turning from the fire to look at me. 'I don't know how far it takes us though, Mike. I've really no idea if the Coven of the Grey Moon is still operating or not. And even if it is, there's a major problem.'

'Which is?'

'Witches?'

'No, *which is*?'

She laughed. 'Sorry, I get you.' The smile fell from her face again and she suddenly looked quite concerned. 'The major problem is that the coven is extremely secretive, possibly even more so than normal. Dean Wilson may have exposed some barbaric practices, but even he didn't dare name any of the other of the thirteen members. At least they never made the newspaper report.'

'The press was probably wary of a libel action,' I said. 'So, there are thirteen in a coven?'

'Not necessarily. It's a traditional maximum, if anything. But the Littleworth witches did decide on thirteen. No more, no less. Dean would have been "replaced" unless they packed the whole thing up.'

'Which means that if the coven does still exist, there are thirteen ordinary looking people in this area who are not what they seem and who are fully conversant with what's been going on in the wood.'

Grace looked thoughtful. 'And not only conversant but active participants.'

'Active participants in murder, if Dean's evidence is correct.'

Grace sat back in her chair and drank the last of her wine. She placed the empty glass gently on the small table and shifted towards me, almost conspiratorially. 'Dean may have made the whole thing up of course, Mike,' she said in a low voice. 'You know, was upset at the fallout and wanted to do some damage to his former friends. Decided to get his own back. Who, after all, could challenge him if the coven members protect their identity? They don't exactly have a spokesman or a chief executive who could make a public statement, do they?'

I nodded and thought about what she'd said as I finished my beer. 'You do realise, Grace' I said slowly, 'that *anyone*, and I mean *anyone*, we speak to locally—or even slightly further afield—could be one of the thirteen? And would know far more about all this than we do. They might even know what Dean was hinting at to the reporter, or even what happened to poor Lindsey.'

Grace nodded as if she could only agree. 'I guess,' she said. 'So how *do* we find out who's a member?'

I shrugged. 'Dunno. Someone who is sometimes out at night or absent from home every now and then, I guess.'

And we looked at each other as if the same awful thought dawned on us simultaneously.

THIRTY-THREE

This time I was ready for him.

The hired motorcycle turned up on the drive just before eight o'clock that Friday evening. Grace and I left the pub at about six thirty to go our separate ways for supper. I hadn't told her about Frank, just as I hadn't told Goddard. I guess I was still working out what his unexpected arrival meant and how I was going to handle it. I knew my rights. He was unwelcome, but not too much of a challenge. That's how it seemed.

I watched him slowly twist his bulk off the victim of a motorcycle and stabilise it. The machine was red and black, and I could make out the manufacturer as Lexmoto with the legend 'Street 125' towards the rear, whatever that meant. He removed his helmet, left it on the seat this time, and stomped his way like an angry troll towards the house. I pulled away from the sitting room nets and wheeled myself to the front door just as he pressed the bell heavily. I opened the door and he stepped inside, acknowledging my presence with the merest of grunts.

'Kitchen?' he asked, and paused for my response. I detected a different demeanour, a more conciliatory air. No uninvited invasion this time.

'Sitting room's more comfortable,' I said. 'In here.'

I led the way into the sitting room and motioned him towards an armchair. He settled on the edge of its seat as if he were wearing dirty clothes and didn't want to mess it up, all of which was probably the case. I felt safer in my wheelchair and stayed about three metres from him. His beard looked even bushier, and he gave me a penetrating stare.

'Well?' he said. 'Have you thought about it?'

'Thought about what?'

A black cloud crossed his face. 'What I said yesterday—the family money. You've got all the family money and my Rosie needs it.'

'And *you* don't?'

'Yeah, but to look after her. She's sick, man, really sick, and could be for years. We have no money. Everything we had is gone. Normally we do things together, like travel together. This is the first time I've flown on my own. I don't like it, but I'm here. So I need to make the effort and expense worthwhile, don't I?' He continued to watch me carefully.

'So how much do you want?'

'Half.'

'*Half?* You've got to be kidding, aren't you? You and Rosie aren't the only ones with health issues you know.' I patted the wheel rims hard.

'If she hadn't married you, we'd have all of it, right?'

'But she did, so you haven't, have you?'

He said nothing.

'Look, Frank. I'm not cold-hearted, and I'm willing to help, but I've just lost her, okay? I'm not really focused enough to talk about stuff such as this.'

'It's really simple, Michael. Lindsey said she'd help. We're her last and only relatives. Neither of us even have children. She must have left a few million, eh? I'm pretty sure you can spare some for us.'

'I said it's all too early to raise, Frank. I'll help, but I'm saying no more for now.'

He stood up. 'Not good enough, Michael. We need some now. I'm not going back to Toronto without at least half, okay? It's family money, our money.'

'It's no one's money at the moment, Frank. Me and her solicitor are the executors, but I've not even thought about sorting it all out.'

'Well, get it sorted. And Rosie and I are getting our half. She needs so much care, and I can't look after her by myself.'

'I'm sorry, Frank, but it's just not going to happen.'

Crossing his bulky arms and staring at me, he said with a chill in his voice, 'Oh yes, it's gonna happen, Michael. That's why I'm here. It sure is gonna happen, and you can take that to the bank.'

'You threatening me?'

'Just telling you how it's gonna be, that's all.'

'Don't threaten me, Frank.'

He stepped a little closer. I noticed his hands had tightened into two chunky, twitching fists. 'Then give us our fair share and I'll back off.'

'Wrong approach, Frank.'

'You know what? You're an asshole.'

'Time to leave, Frank.'

'A fucking asshole. Lindsey couldn't have known what she was doing.'

'Leave,' I commanded to little effect.

'We don't know who you are, Michael. For all we know, you killed her for the family money.'

I suddenly felt very angry. 'Get out Frank or I'll call the police.'

'Did you kill her, Michael?'

'You're insane. *Get out.*' I reached out for the phone, dialled three numbers and put the receiver up to my ear.

'How much did you pay someone to kill her, huh? Go on, how much? You would have gotten away with a pretty decent profit…'

'Police, please,' I spoke clearly into the phone.

'Fuck you,' Frank said, moving towards the door. 'I'm outta here. But I'll be back. You can take that to the bank too.' He stormed off into the passage.

I apologised to the woman on the phone and replaced the phone in its holder. The front door slammed. I slumped back into my wheelchair trying to come to terms with the nonsense that I'd had my darling Lindsey killed, and how I could ensure Frank returned to Canada with what I wanted to give him. Time to talk it all through with Grace.

THIRTY-FOUR

I was later to learn that my Friday morning rant at Detective Chief Inspector Goddard at Exeter police station had the effect that I'd wanted. I of course appreciated that he was a man under pressure. Lindsey's murder wasn't the only case on his desk, and somehow he had to juggle his time between each one and spread his budget-hit resources the best he could. I didn't envy him. I wouldn't want his job, believe me. Especially having to deal with people like me on top of everything else. But at the time I don't think I really saw it that way. In fact, I know I didn't. All I wanted was for him to up the investigation in line with what Grace had instigated.

I anticipated a solitary weekend, but then to some extent I was used to being on my own in the bungalow, even when married to Lindsey. It was late morning, just as I was finishing off another good session of sorting Lindsey's papers in the office, when Grace rang. We'd curtailed our discussion in the pub the evening before as a small group had entered the snug, robbing us of our privacy.

'Do you really think it's possible, Mike?'

Together with Frank's second visit, I'd thought a lot about our conversation through the early hours of the morning, trying hard to piece the wider scenario together. It wasn't easy.

'I don't know,' I said. 'Are we just jumping to conclusions? Adding two and two, and making even more

169

than five? I woke at about three and couldn't get back to sleep thinking about everything.'

'It's curious though, isn't it? A coven seems to be operating around here with its focus on Littleworth Wood. A coven that, by a whistle-blower's report, might have made human sacrifices. Lindsey told you she was at the hospice doing nights, and yet Bronia is adamant that she never did. And I don't think Bronia's lying about that. Why should she? Besides, she seemed surprised. And then her absences at weekends, you know, when she said she was visiting Julie in London. What's that all about?'

I said nothing. Just listened.

Grace continued as if my silence hadn't registered. Her questions were evidently rhetorical. 'And so we come to the weekend when she said she was going to London, yet is murdered in Littleworth Wood. In an identical way, and in a deliberately identical place, as Sandra Roberts. Do you think she was a member of the coven? Was Sandra Roberts? Or were they just victims? What's this all about, Mike?'

'I wish I had some answers.' I stared at Lindsey's empty desk. Grace stayed quiet. I could hear her gentle breathing, so I carried on. 'Look, Grace. We may be totally off track here. This may have nothing to do with anything. I don't think we should get carried away.'

'Why ever not? It all seems a bit odd, don't you think? And don't forget the skull, Mike. Coincidence or witchcraft?'

'Well, some things certainly require explanation,' I said. 'But can you really see Lindsey playing witches? How on earth could she have kept that from me? I've been through her most intimate things, and nothing sends me in this direction. Not even a pointy hat. Nothing. I think we're just becoming paranoid.'

Grace gave a little sigh. 'Maybe you're right,' she said. 'It's so fanciful, so unreal.'

'Yet unproven either way,' I encouraged.

'Mm, guess so. So that needs to be sorted once and for all, right? I've an idea,'

'What is it?' I asked.

'Well, we've just made the link again between Lindsey and Sandra Roberts, haven't we?'

'Yeah, I suppose so…'

'Okay then, so what if they *were* both members of this coven and then, for some macabre reason, both became its victims?'

'I guess Lindsey's unexplained absences do point to more of an involvement.'

'Was there a pattern?' Grace asked. 'I don't want to appear flippant, but was she away every full moon or something like that?'

'I don't know,' I said. 'I could try and recollect, but I'm not optimistic.'

'Don't you have a joint calendar or a diary or something like that? Is there some history on it?'

'We did keep an appointments calendar,' I said. 'I'll check it. So what's your idea?'

'Well, if they *were* both members, then someone in Sandra Roberts' family might just know something.'

'But surely Goddard's made these enquiries, Grace? After all, he told me that the wood had sinister goings-on—a "dark side", I think he said. At the very least he would have seen Dean's newspaper exposé.'

'Yet he hasn't said anything.'

'Maybe it's one of his famous "lines of enquiry"?'

'Possibly. You going to ask him?'

I laughed. 'Not at the moment,' I said. 'I don't think he's my greatest fan.'

'So let's speak to one of Sandra's relatives. Goddard said she was a divorcee, didn't you say? The ex-husband, or children, may be around still.'

'Bound to be. She was quite young, early forties or something.'

'Yes, that sounds about right,' she said. 'Okay then, let's work out how we can track down someone to ask, shall we? Get their views on Goddard, too. And if the coven comes into the story, it could just link the two cases together.'

'Meaning?'

'Meaning we're going to investigate this further.'

'And my promise to Goddard?'

'I recall you saying you wouldn't play Poirot. I don't remember you saying you wouldn't go on a witch hunt.'

THIRTY-FIVE

It's probably fair to say that my telephone conversation with Grace was the highlight of my weekend. She said she'd get the ball rolling, and we'd talk again on Monday. That suited me. I half expected a further knock on the door from Frank, but whatever he was doing, he wasn't doing it at Field View. I wondered whether I should in fact have reported his appearance to Goddard. I concluded I would leave it for the time being, see what direction it took.

By the Sunday evening, I'd just about completed tidying up Lindsey's things. As you may imagine, this took quite a long time. The higher shelves of her wardrobe were not an option. I kept meaning to ask Grace to help with those but forgot every time she called. But I'd managed to reach what I could from a wheelchair and, when I went to bed at well past my usual hour, a small pile of black bin liners in the hallway held paper waste, miscellaneous rubbish and some respectable clothes for charity. I thought the best place for the clothing, somewhat ironically, was the St Chad's Hospice charity shop in Tiverton, and I hoped that Grace might help me with that task too.

If my telephone conversation with Grace was my highlight of the weekend, then my dream that Sunday night was the low point. I don't recall all the detail, but I do recall running through a dark wood at night-time. Yes, I was running; no wheelchair. Free to run everywhere and anywhere, as I could before. I was running and I was

173

frightened. Something or someone was chasing me. I had to run, but the undergrowth tore at me and fought my every stride. I tried to look back but couldn't twist round. Just kept looking ahead, ducking branches, scanning the uneven ground, panting and tired.

I eventually stumbled into a clearing lit up by the brightest of full moons and a large bonfire twenty metres high that shot smoke, debris and flames up into the clear, star-covered sky with crackles and pops. Standing by the fire was a man dressed in a grey monk's habit with the large hood pulled low over his face. He beckoned me to approach him. As I drew near, he lowered his hood and, although he had a magnificent white beard, I recognised him to be Goddard.

He looked right through me and ordered firmly: 'Do it now.'

I turned round, and a dozen monk-like men were standing in an arc close behind me, their faces hardly visible in the shadows of their hoods and flickering light from the bonfire. From the little I could see, each one was solemn and literally oozed evil intent. They started to move as one towards me, like a battle line, one slow step after another. I realised they intended to drive me into the heat of the flames. I looked for a way out, but I was trapped. There was little I could do, and I realised I needed to wake up, to save myself from the agony.

My mobile rang next to me and it was Monday morning.

My first thought was that it was Grace, but the number said differently. I picked it up and a man's voice said, 'Mike? I hope I haven't called too early. It's Jonathan here.'

I glanced at my bedside clock. It was twenty past nine. I

sat up. I hadn't been expecting to hear from Jonathan Rosford at the estate agents.

'No, it's fine, Jonathan. I've been up for a bit. How can I help?'

'Well, Mike, I thought you might want to hear about a call I had this morning.'

'About the house?' I asked with some surprise.

'Yes. The guy rang off a minute ago.'

'What guy?'

'Well, I left instructions with our reception to put any enquiry about your bungalow through to me. The call I've just taken was from a bloke. He asked about the house, you know, the price, whether there was a sale chain and so on. He said he'd seen the 'For Sale' sign in the garden and queried why he couldn't find it on our website. I explained that we'd only very recently been instructed and that the vendor wanted a board up quickly, but that we were still processing the website notice and printed literature.'

'Nice one. What did he say to all that?' I asked.

'He asked again for the price and I told him what we'd agreed. Six hundred and seventy-five thousand pounds which is slightly, but not unrealistically, above the market value taking account of house and location.'

'Did you get his name and details?'

'He said his name was Adrian Smith, but he declined to give me his address or phone number. He said he'd keep an eye on our website and asked when I hoped to put the details on. I said there were some technical hitches, but, if all went well, by the end of the week.'

'Was that it?'

'Yes.'

'How would you describe him, you know, from his

voice?'

'I'm not much cop at this sort of thing, Mike, but if I had to take a guess, I'd say he was middle-aged, say forty to fifty. Maybe more. Hard to tell really. He was certainly well spoken, educated. Professional sort of guy. I don't think I can add much more.'

'Did he say where he was from? Did he mention family?'

'No, Mike. As I said, nothing more.'

'Okay. Thanks, Jonathan.'

'What do you want me to do, Mike?'

'Do?'

'You know, about the website? Shall I put up some details?'

I thought about it. No details would make it evident that the property was not really for sale. A technical hitch had a limited life span as an excuse. But if the details were there...

'Jonathan, let's get some detail on the website. Send one of your surveyors around later today or tomorrow, whatever suits, and you can do the photos and so forth. No need to measure anything as I can give you the original brochure we had from the builder. Describes everything.'

And so it was that some youngster named Darren called round shortly after lunch. Although I gave him the builder's glossy brochure with colourful diagrams of the rooms, each festooned with precise measurements, he still insisted on tramping round the bungalow to record measurements with some red-lighted ray gun. He never said if they were in fact the same as in the brochure. Frankly, I didn't really care. But according to Darren it had to be accurate so as to avoid 'some sharp bastard from suing us for misdescription', or something like that anyway.

As Darren was leaving, Grace turned up in her BMW. I waited by the open front door as she walked into the house and bent down to give me a kiss on the cheek.

'Who was that just leaving?' she asked, as she closed the door.

'That was Mr Darren Pedantic from the estate agents.'

We moved down to the kitchen and I told her about the call from Jonathan.

'Could have been anyone,' she said. 'Including either Charles or Martin. Odd that they didn't leave contact details though. And they must have been into your close to have seen it.'

'I agree,' I said. 'Unless someone reported it to them. But why no details? And visiting the close—doesn't make me feel overly safe, I have to say. And I've yet to see a police car patrolling round here either despite my request to Goddard.'

'I'm sure it'll be okay,' Grace said, although she didn't sound very convinced.

'Anyhow,' I said, leaning back and stretching my arms, 'what are you doing popping round here. It's good to see you of course, but what brings you?'

'I tried ringing you, but there was no answer.'

I pulled my mobile out of my pocket and saw the missed call symbol. I realised I'd put it on silent when Darren arrived. 'Sorry,' I said. 'So what did you want?'

'To let you know I've made some progress.' She looked quite pleased with herself.

'Progress? With the coven?'

She nodded with a slight grin. 'Exactly that, Mike. So now we're off out.'

'*Now*? Where to?'

'Yes now. I've managed to track down Sandra Roberts' ex. He's willing to talk to us this afternoon.'

'Blast. I can't do that, Grace. I'm due at the doctors for three fifteen.'

'Well change it. This is important.'

'So's my appointment, Grace. Took forever to get it.'

She crossed her arms and stared at me. 'Mike, rearrange it. We can't let this opportunity with Sandra's ex go.'

'Can't we change that?'

She said nothing, just kept staring at me.

'Okay, okay, I'll ring the doctors.'

'I could always see the ex on my own…'

'No, I said I would sort the doctor. I'll come with you.'

She uncrossed her arms and smiled. 'Good, that's sorted then because, Mike, it sounds like he has some interesting things to say.'

THIRTY-SIX

Gary Roberts was very willing to talk about his murdered wife.

He lived on the edge of Exeter on the Tiverton side. As Grace drove us there, she told me she'd tracked down Sandra Roberts' twenty-year-old son Jason, who still lived in Tiverton and worked on a local farm.

'A very fit young man,' she commented in a matter-of-fact way. 'Good-looking, too.'

'Grace,' I said in a mock admonishing tone, 'he's half your age. You shouldn't be having such thoughts, Mrs Robinson.'

'Just an observation, Mike' she said, keeping her eyes on the road. 'Girls can dream too, you know.'

'Fair enough,' I said as the tyres squealed through a roundabout. 'So you spoke to Gary Roberts, then?'

'Yup. Jason gave me his number. He's still in touch with his dad despite the divorce.'

Grace's satnav took us to a modest house on a ten-year-old estate. Gary Roberts welcomed us in, and, after the usual manoeuvring of my wheelchair, we were all seated in his small lounge with mugs of tea.

Gary's short-cropped, fading blond hair was thinning on his head, and he wore gold-framed glasses that were quite trendy for his age. I guessed him to be late forties, possibly fifty. He had a kind and intelligent look and a healthy physique. He obviously kept himself in shape.

'I'm so sorry to learn of your recent loss, Mike,' Gary said after we'd completed introductions and small talk about the weather and the ease of finding his house. 'I read about the murder in the paper—it caught my attention for obvious reasons. I know it'll be a very difficult time for you.'

'Thank you,' I said sincerely. 'As Grace explained, we hoped to exchange some thoughts and information, as we both seem to be in the same position to some degree. When did you move to this house, Gary?'

'Just over three years ago when we separated. Sandy and I were divorced some six months later. She kept the Tiverton house—and Jason come to that. My father had recently died, and we agreed I'd use my inheritance to buy my own place. Seemed to make sense. Looking back, there was no one else involved. Well, certainly not on my part anyway, and I believe that was the same for Sandy. Anyhow, enough of all that, don't want to bore you.'

Grace looked eager to discuss the matter in hand, but said. 'It's not boring at all, Gary. We're really sorry about Sandra. Really awful.'

Gary nodded slowly, thoughtfully. 'Thanks, Grace.' He paused for a moment. 'Wasn't easy. Still isn't come to that. You see, Sandy and I never really fell out, if you know what I mean. Rarely argued. We decided we were better off on our own, that's all. You know, thought we'd be happier. The challenge was that I was deputy head of our school in Tiverton, and she was head of the history department. Sort of couldn't get away from each other even in the daytime. Then I went for my present headship at St Cuthbert's here in Exeter and I suppose the break up and the move was inevitable. Mind you, I'm off with stress at the moment. It came on towards the end of last term. One theory is that the anniversary of Sandy's death might have triggered it. The governors are very understanding, but I do feel I'm letting them and the school down. I hate that.'

'Key thing is to get yourself fully better,' Grace said.

'True,' Gary said with a gentle nod. 'But somehow it isn't easy when there's no closure on Sandy. Sure we were eventually allowed to bury her after a second independent post-mortem. We all said our goodbyes, gave a eulogy, but I just want to know what happened. Find out who was responsible. The police are doing their best I suppose, but they seem no further forward. And now there's your wife, Mike. Forgive me, I've forgotten her name...'

'Lindsey.'

'Yes, that's it, Lindsey. Makes you wonder what's going on, doesn't it?' He took a sip of tea.

'It certainly does,' I said and glanced quickly at Grace. 'Gary, have you got any kind of theories about Sandra's death? Anything at all? As Grace explained on the phone, we thought it was worth comparing notes, exchanging ideas.'

Gary looked serious. 'Isn't that something for the police to do? Mind you, I don't have any real faith in this Chief Inspector Goddard, but he and his team should be doing the leg work and the investigating here, shouldn't they?'

'Agreed,' Grace said. 'But no harm if there are more hands to the pump though, huh?'

'No, I guess not,' Gary said slowly as if warming to the idea.

'Are you willing to tell us what actually happened, Gary?' I said.

'Sure. It's easier now than it was. In essence Sandy told Jason she was going shopping. She left home mid-afternoon on the Saturday. Nothing unusual about that. She said she was going into Exeter and was then going to see an aunt of hers for tea. She never made it for the tea, and indeed the police have never found any evidence that her car actually came into Exeter that afternoon. What is known is that the car was found in Littleworth Wood, as indeed was poor Sandy.'

'When was she found?' I asked quietly.

Gary took another sip of his tea. 'Sometime on Sunday morning. Jason raised the alarm when he returned late from a party and found the house empty. The police took her absence seriously, but walkers found her. I went over to the house to collect Jason and he stayed here for several months. We sold the house, and the trustees have bought him a small place in the town. He was Sandy's sole beneficiary, you see, which is how it should have been.'

Grace said, 'So why do you think someone killed her? Had she fallen out with someone? Or was it just a case of being in the wrong place at the wrong time with the wrong person?'

Gary shrugged. 'I don't know, despite all the thought I've given it,' he said. 'It was all so sudden, so unexpected. So shocking. I have no explanation, not then, not now. And as if that wasn't bad enough, in a sense, it got worse.' He looked down and wiped an imaginary speck of lint off his trousers with a couple of brush strokes of his hand. 'The post-mortem showed that she was almost four months pregnant.'

THIRTY-SEVEN

No one said anything. Nothing. Grace turned and looked at me. I looked at her. My mind was a maelstrom.

Gary couldn't have helped but pick up the unspoken, rapid communication between Grace and me. 'Have I said something?' he asked with a confused expression, looking at us both in turn as if following a tennis match.

I looked at him and quietly said, 'Lindsey was three months pregnant, Gary.'

'*Christ.* Really? That's incredible. I'm really sorry, Mike, but that's a real coincidence, isn't it?'

'Seems so,' I said.

'I don't do coincidences,' Grace said, 'but it is really strange though, isn't it? Quite amazing. What did Sandra's boyfriend have to say about everything?'

'That's another mystery to me. The thing is, Jason wasn't aware of any boyfriend. Sandy had never brought back anyone to the house or talked of them. There were no signs of any relationship, at least nothing that a nineteen-year-old could spot.' He paused as if taking a mental deep breath. 'I find that really quite odd,' he added.

We were all silent a further moment.

'Gary,' Grace said, 'what does Goddard make of all this? When he told Mike that Lindsey was pregnant, he didn't mention that Sandra was pregnant too. What are his theories to date?'

'That's right,' I said. 'He goes on about some

procedural "sterile corridor" between the two cases. Indeed he won't even tell me some of the "lines of enquiry" he's making in Lindsey's case.'

We looked at him expectantly.

Gary gave a wry smile and scratched his ear. 'The honest answer?' he asked. 'Frankly, I don't think he's got a bloody clue. Sorry,' he added glancing at Grace. 'In the early days, they did a "Crimewatch" reconstruction on the BBC about where she'd been that Saturday afternoon, but that only threw up hopeless do-gooders and deluded nutters. If every reported sighting had been true, she'd have surpassed David Blane as an illusionist. They did a further appeal not so long back, but still nothing helpful. I think Goddard has settled on the theory of a deranged opportunist who has gone to ground or who, like what's-his-name, the Yorkshire Ripper, has started a series of killings and will make a mistake one day soon. With respect, maybe Lindsey is the next in a sequence.'

'Goddard told Mike that Littleworth Wood had "a dark side". Do you know what he meant by that?'

I was about to chip in further, but she subtly signalled to me to be quiet. I guessed she wanted Gary to speak without any leading.

'A dark side? Is he referring to the rumours of witches?'

'Witches?' I said with a tone of surprise. 'What do you mean by that?'

'Well, one of the angles Goddard poked at was whether Sandy had got involved with, or fallen foul of, a… a—what do you call it?—a *coven* of witches. Talk about clutching at straws. According to local gossip, a coven meets in the wood and has done for quite a while. Presumably when there's a full moon or something like that. Hardly sounds twenty-first century, does it? They're probably just a group of doggers. Utter nonsense in my view.'

'Sandra never got involved in anything like that, then?' Grace asked, glancing at me.

'Like heck. What do you think? I'd have run a mile if the house had become filled with cauldrons and potions. I've no doubt my darling ex-mother-in-law could have handled a broomstick pretty well, but that's an entirely different story.' He smiled weakly.

I flashed a polite smile back. 'But are there any theories as to why Sandra ended up in the wood that evening?'

He shook his head firmly. 'None, none at all. She knew the woods, obviously, as they are so close to Tiverton. We used to walk our dog there in times gone by. What I find difficult is that she was there by herself. There's no way she'd have gone out for a walk on her own. She was too nervous. I believe she was taken there.'

'Against her will?' Grace asked.

'I just don't know. I'm guessing, so the whole nightmare makes more sense.' Gary said, running his hand through his hair. 'Her car was found not far from where she was. There was evidence that she'd been bound and that duct tape had been placed over her mouth. So she was mistreated at some point. It was all detailed publicly at the inquest. I found it all very challenging. She may have been my ex, but she was still the mother of our son and my wife for over twenty years. No one deserves what she suffered, however quick the end.'

I nodded and glanced at Grace.

'I think we've covered all we can,' she said. 'We'll leave you in peace. Thanks for your time, Gary.'

He smiled. 'No problem.'

'Let's keep in touch,' I said. 'We have something unique in common, however unfortunate it is. Having chatted this through with you, it seems even more unique than I'd realised. We'll keep you posted of any significant developments.'

'Thanks. I'll do like-wise.'

As Grace pushed me towards the sitting room door, which Gary held open, she said, 'Gary, could I ask you one more thing?'

'Of course.'

'Do you know if Sandra went away at weekends on her own? Or was away late at night? Did Jason ever say?'

'When we were together, she did have occasional weekends away,' Gary said. 'Either with a group of girlfriends or on her own for some self time. Not often of course—just now and then. Why do you ask?'

I joined in, 'Don't take this the wrong way, but did she always go where she said she was going?'

Gary said, 'As far as I know. What you suggesting?'

'Nothing. It was nothing, really.'

He frowned. 'I thought we were going to share information, Mike. You suggesting she was having an affair or something?'

'No, not at all. It's just that my Lindsey told me she was going places, and I've now found out that she didn't go to them. For example, she said she was going out some nights to volunteer at St Chad's Hospice, but the manager tells me she never did.'

'That's odd,' Gary said.

'Too right it's odd,' I said. 'So, do you see why we asked the question? Where *did* she go? Sandra and Lindsey seem to have so much in common, I was just wondering if

186

this was another trait they shared.'

Gary looked thoughtful. 'Let me reflect on it further.'

'Thanks,' Grace said. 'We just felt we should consider all possible angles.'

Gary looked distant, and Grace pushed me out of the door, easing the wheelchair over the mild obstacle course.

'There is one thing…' Gary started.

'What's that?'

'No, it's nothing.'

'Could be something, Gary.' Grace said.

'Well, I sometimes wonder whether, with such slow progress, Goddard actually wants to solve the case.'

THIRTY-EIGHT

Mike was very quiet as I drove him home after our visit to
Gary Roberts. The biggest issue for me was that both Sandra
and poor Lindsey were about three or four months pregnant
when they were murdered. I found the whole thing
fascinating. Another intellectual challenge to tackle. Not
only had I lost my best friend, but also a possible godchild.
Martin and I had never had children, which had been an
issue between us. After a variety of medical tests, we found
out the trouble lay with yours truly and not the self-
proclaimed stud. I knew Mike and I were thinking on the
same wavelength when, about five minutes into the wordless
journey, he suddenly spoke up.

'I could have been a dad,' he said quietly.

'I know,' I said. 'Lindsey would have made a great
mum. No doubt.'

'She was one of life's carers. Had to be a nurse, I
guess,' he said.

We were silent for a few more minutes as I drove us
steadily back towards Westland. My heart went out to Mike.
No one asks to spend the rest of their life in a wheelchair.
One day you can be fit and strong, athletically mounting a
seriously sized horse, the next you're in hospital being told
that you'll never walk again. I wasn't sure how I'd have
coped in that situation, or how he coped, particularly in the
long night hours, and especially now without Lindsey.

'So what you doing now?' I asked, as we turned off the

main road into a modest tree-lined lane signposted to Westland.

After a pause, Mike said, 'Now? Now I'm going to start to plan my supper. Are you in later?'

'Sure. I want to have some serious thinking time.'

He smiled. He had a sincere, friendly smile. 'Good,' he said. 'I'll call you when I've given it more thought myself.'

'Great, we can keep moving it forward then, even if it's not what Goddard wants.'

'But I'm certain it's what Lindsey would have encouraged.'

I guessed he was right.

After I'd dropped Mike back at his bungalow, I returned home to my house in Tiverton. It was around six o'clock when I entered my beamed kitchen and made myself a cup of tea. I settled in front of the computer and undertook some further research on the Sandra Roberts' murder. I located more information from the inquest, including details of where, how and when she was killed, but the report made no reference to the fact that she was pregnant. It would no doubt have been deep in the autopsy report, but I didn't bother looking for that. I didn't see the point. Gary had given us the fact.

I then tried to learn more about the coven of the Grey Moon and Littleworth Wood itself, but found nothing that I hadn't already read in my earlier research. As the light started to fail, I glanced at my watch and realised it was already early evening.

I decided I'd spoil myself. Although the weather didn't really require it, I made up a fire in the wood-burning stove in the sitting room. In the kitchen, I started preparing a fillet steak and salad. After a guilty hesitation, I threw a small portion of oven chips into the Agar as well.

Relying on the electric light from the hall, I walked upstairs and into my bedroom to close the curtains before turning the light on. As I stretched out to pull the left curtain, I glanced out onto the quiet village street below. My house has a small front garden that opens to the pavement and allows unobstructed views of the whole street from both the downstairs and upstairs windows. Dusk was gathering and the street lamps had come on, giving the scene an almost Christmas-card feel, such was the softness of the light, the cosiness of the shadows, and the quaintness of the houses. I looked across at the short row of traditional white-terraced cottages opposite and followed their line to the corner of Cowgate Street. That's when I first saw him.

I almost did a double take, but down at that street corner was a man wearing what looked like a motorcycle helmet. He was a long way off but seemed to be looking in my direction. He was just standing there on the pavement, half hidden by the corner of the cottage wall. As I watched him, he suddenly turned round back into Cowgate Street and became hidden from my sight by the row of cottages. Slowly closing the curtains, I continued to look at the now empty street. I peeped through the overlapped curtains again, but there was no one there. Had I imagined it? No, he had been there.

I moved away from the window into the darkened room, turned my bedside lamp on. As I stripped naked and got into the hot shower, I thought about what I'd seen. Who was he? Or was he a she? And why had they been standing there? Maybe it had all been innocent: someone pausing to look at their mobile phone or check the time and having to remove motorcycle gloves to do so. I dried myself off after my shower and regretted not going out into the street to tackle the guy.

I ambled down to the kitchen in my pink dressing gown and matching slippers and finished off making my steak and salad. The chips were perfect. Mike telephoned me for a quick chat, but, since my supper was ready, I said I'd call him later. A decent fillet steak requires an equally decent bottle of red wine, and so I settled on the sofa with a classic Argentinian Malbec. I turned on the TV and ended up watching one of those American romantic comedies that I've always loved. The wood stove gave off dancing light and occasional crackles as it filled the room with homely and comforting scents. Eventually, and I guess inevitably, I nodded off.

I was awoken by the sound of the front door bell out in the hallway. I took a few moments to realise what I'd heard and sat up on the soft sofa and stretched my legs across the floor. The clock on the mantelpiece said ten past eleven. Who the heck was visiting at this time of night? I eased myself out of the sofa and put on my slippers. I half expected to hear the bell for a second time as I presumed it was something urgent.

I walked out of the room into the relative chill of the hallway. I'd left the outside light on as usual, but there was no window in the hallway and the door was solid. Martin and I had discussed having a window or some kind of frosted porthole put in the front door to see the silhouette of anyone standing outside. I took my customary precaution of sliding the security chain across before I eased the door slightly ajar. No one was there. I pulled the door open a fraction more until it shuddered once it reached the full length of the chain. I continued to peer out, but saw nothing.

Until I glanced down. Something small and dark on the edge of the path was just catching the main light from the outside lamp. I looked until the object finally took shape, and I found myself staring into the unseeing eyes of a small, red human skull.

THIRTY-NINE

I released the door from its chain and stepped out on to the front step. The skull looked back at me. I glanced around. There was no one about, not even standing at the end of Cowgate Street. I moved forward onto the path and squatted down to study it. It was similar to the one Mike had shown me at his house, but with much more red paint. I glanced round again, like a trapper. The street remained silent.

I recalled how Goddard had taken charge of protecting the evidential quality of Mike's threatening letter. I returned to the kitchen, took an old supermarket carrier bag out of a drawer and tore off a couple of sheets of paper kitchen roll. I picked up my mobile and took everything back to the front path. All was quiet and still. I photographed the skull and its setting and then picked it up using the paper sheets, placing it in the carrier bag.

As I closed and re-locked the door, my mind continued to work it out. What the hell was going on? Despite the hour, I had to talk it through with Mike. I picked up the phone and dialled, and the line rang several times before a sleepy voice answered. 'Grace?'

'Sorry, Mike, did I wake you?'

'Yeah…what time is it? What's up?'

'It's about eleven fifteen. Sorry to wake you, but I didn't know what to do'

'What is it? What's happened?' Mike asked with genuine concern in his voice.

I told him how I had fallen asleep on the sofa after supper. 'The doorbell woke me about five minutes ago. I looked out, couldn't see anyone. And then I saw it.'

'Saw what?'

'Another painted skull. It was lying on the front path. It's just like yours.'

'*Bloody hell*,' he exclaimed. He certainly sounded awake now and I could picture him sitting up in bed, putting his bedside lamp on.

'And there's more. I'm absolutely positive there was a bloke watching my house earlier.'

'You're joking?'

'Straight up. Sounds crazy, but how about getting together to talk this through. I've had some thoughts. I could pop over now if you're awake.'

He paused then said, 'No, I've a better idea. I'll come to you, and then I can see where it was.'

'Good thinking,' I said. 'That way I won't need to bring it over either which should protect it more for forensic tests.'

'I'm on my way'

We rang off. I truly appreciated his willingness to be so involved. Good friends are hard to find.

*

It had gone midnight by the time I parked on the street in front of Grace's house. Some downstairs lights were on. As I manoeuvred myself out of my car and into my wheelchair, I glanced around. Didn't see anyone. The street was empty, just me.

Grace answered the door promptly. She was wearing casual slacks and a turtleneck jersey and looked tired under the outside light. I leant back as she manoeuvred my wheelchair into the house with some effort. In the kitchen she picked up a carrier bag that was lying on the table and opened it up wide enough to show me the skull.

I declined a drink and we went through into her sitting room. She poked the remnants of the fire in the wood-burning stove and tossed another couple of logs inside as I transferred myself untidily into an armchair.

'This is all really curious, Mike.' She closed the stove door and sat down on the edge of the sofa.

I looked across at her. 'Absolutely. You can think of numerous explanations for a one-off skull at my house, but one at your house as well limits the options somewhat, doesn't it?'

She nodded and stared through the blackened window on the front of the stove at the flames taking hold of their new victims. 'That's what I thought.'

'Did you hear anything other than the doorbell?' I asked. 'Anything at all?'

'No, nothing,' she said. 'Mind you, this is an old house. They made house walls pretty solid back in the day. Double-glazing and a thick front door complete the soundproofing.'

'What about when you'd opened the door?'

She thought for a moment. 'It was all quiet. Usually is round here at that hour. Very little, if any, traffic on this twisting back street. You just get the odd local resident walking home from the pub or returning from somewhere in a car.'

'Tell me more about this person you saw earlier, you know, the one you thought was watching the house.'

She told me in detail about the man or woman she'd seen at a distance on the corner of Cowgate Street, half hidden by the cottage wall, standing as if looking at her house. She paused in her recollecting and added, 'I think I'll ask some of my neighbours in the morning if they saw anything. You know, about the motorcyclist and the skull.'

'Doesn't sound likely,' I said.

'I'll give it a try anyway. Would you ring Goddard in the morning and tell him what's happened? Let me know what he says.'

She sat silently as if putting together what she was going to say. 'I just don't know what to make of this, Mike. I've been thinking about little else since it all happened. Why target me? Someone painted the skull and brought it to my house under cover of darkness. They left it where it could be easily seen from the front door. They got my attention by ringing the doorbell and running away. This was quite deliberate, wasn't it?'

'So what are they trying to achieve?' I asked. 'And who are "they"?'

Grace shrugged. 'That's the big one, of course. To *warn* us? To *scare* us?'

'But if they were warning or scaring us, they must have an ultimate motive. Warn us about what? Scare us away from what? If you're going to warn or scare, surely there's little point unless you spell it out? Look at that letter I received about selling up. That was pretty plain, wasn't it?'

Grace nodded. 'I agree,' she said. 'And of course there's something else.'

'What's that?'

'Whoever's done this, they've linked some things together.'

'What?' I asked.

'Us.'

FORTY

I had my breakfast with Grace.

We'd talked into the early hours of the morning and, since I was extremely tired, she offered me her sofa for the night, which was kind. What else could I have done but accept? I was conscious that my car was parked outside her house for the night, but I was beyond thinking about local gossip. I was sure that if someone had noted the overnight stay and had actually known the true circumstances, they'd have understood.

I'd lain watching the last two logs gradually disintegrate through the blackened glass and heard Grace upstairs moving about methodically as she completed her night-time ritual. A slight creaking of her bed told me that she'd settled. I didn't get the most comfortable sleep on the sofa, but it was adequate.

'More toast?' she asked as she rose from the table and started to clear it.

'No more for me, thanks,' I said, stretching flamboyantly in my wheelchair. 'That was perfect.'

'I was worried whether you were comfortable?' she enquired. 'It would be better if I had a downstairs bedroom.'

'Honestly, I was fine, Grace. Slept like one of your logs.'

Seizing a cloth to wipe the table, she smiled and said, 'So, in the cold light of day, do you still agree that we should report this new incident to Goddard?'

'Absolutely. A dead cert,' I said. 'Nothing to do with me "playing Poirot", was it?'

'No. Well, let me know what he says.'

'I will.'

*

I telephoned Goddard not long after I arrived home shortly before ten o'clock that Tuesday morning. He said he would be 'up in my area' later on in the day and his arrival with DS Ward soon after three o'clock woke me from my catch-up nap. This time, we sat in the sitting room.

I started by telling them about the previous day's call from Jonathan about the mysterious enquiry on the house. Goddard listened and Ward made notes. In reply to Goddard's question, I said that I hadn't seen anyone around save for the person on a motorbike late at night that Grace had seen. He said he would talk to Jonathan further.

With Ward scribbling in his notebook, I then told him about the skull at Grace's house and 'the watcher', as Grace and I started calling him the previous evening.

But the greater coincidence I raised was the two pregnancies, giving him the impression I'd learnt about Sandra's from the Internet.

'So what do you make of that?' I said with a degree of agitation. 'Why didn't you mention it before? Is it relevant?'

'Mr Miller, please relax. It's not my role to keep you informed of every piece of information nor draw such connections between the two cases. The fact that both Mrs Roberts and Mrs Miller were pregnant is a curious coincidence and a line of enquiry that the superintendent wishes to pursue, of course. But it could just turn out to be mere coincidence.'

I threw in what I knew about the coven.

'When you tie all that together with the mutual pregnancies and painted skulls, it stacks up to something quite alarming, doesn't it?' I said. 'What's your take on all that? Is it a "line of enquiry"?' I tried not to be too sarcastic, but there was a sufficient edge in my voice to make Goddard understand that I was unhappy.

'This is all very fanciful, Mr Miller. Obviously I'm aware of what you're talking about. A group of people meet together now and then in the wood who call themselves that name. There's nothing illegal about that, and nothing they do which can be seen as illegal either. Some would describe them as cranks, but I couldn't possibly comment on that.' He looked at me meaningfully.

'Cranks or not, according to Wilson's exposé, they've committed serious crimes under the guise of cult worship.'

'Those reports were fully investigated and no evidence of any wrongdoing was ever found.'

'A lack of evidence of wrongdoing is not the same as *no* wrongdoing,' I said.

'True. But as policemen, we can do nothing without evidence, as I'm sure you understand.'

I nodded. I knew he was right. 'So do you know who's involved?'

'We did at the time of the enquiry, but membership changes, like with any club so to speak.'

'So, the ten-million-dollar question: were either or both Sandra and Lindsey involved? Or were they its victims?'

'I do not believe they were either of those—'

'*Do not believe*. You mean you don't know?'

'It's very difficult to be certain of anything, Mr Miller,

199

but that is my current belief.'

I sat back forcefully and crossed my arms to signal disapproval and frustration. 'Okay, and so who are the ringleaders of this bloody coven?'

'I'm not at liberty to say, Mr Miller.'

'*Not at liberty*? Not again. We're still talking about my wife's murder, aren't we?'

'Which I presently believe has nothing to do with a private club, and there I must leave the topic. I have warned you about interfering, and you agreed to back off. I have no wish to put temptation in your way.'

I started to speak, but he cut across me and carried on. 'And talking of agreements, I have kept mine. I saw Charles Fairfax over the weekend and Martin Atkins at lunchtime today. Neither was happy about being brought into this— particularly, I should say, Mr Atkins. Nevertheless, they were both cooperative but had nothing helpful to add. I have no intention of talking to them again.'

'Unless something significant happens that might require such a further conversation?' I said.

'Well, obviously. If circumstances change, that would be different.'

I didn't know it at the time, but circumstances were about to change.

FORTY-ONE

If I'd thought Frank was aggressive, my late afternoon visitor put him in the shade.

I was in the kitchen making a cup of tea when the doorbell rang. It wasn't a normal ring but sounded rather like someone leaning on it. The sound abruptly stopped and was followed by a series of thumps on the door. The kitchen clock said a quarter past five, so Goddard had been gone well over an hour. As a precaution, I picked up and checked my mobile phone and made my way into the hallway. I prepared myself and eased over to the front door. Looking back, I should have followed Grace's example, but I didn't. I simply opened the door without the security chain.

Martin was standing on the front step. I could see his motorbike in the driveway behind him, his black helmet resting on the seat. He was wearing his black leathers, which made him appear even bigger than usual. He looked livid. He pushed his way past me into the hall and, as I moved away from the door, he slammed it shut so hard, a small piece of plaster fell from round the edge of the door frame and clattered to the wooden floor. He towered over me with his hands on his hips, his angry stare intimidating.

'What the fuck are you playing at, Miller?' His voice was venomous and loud.

I decided that the best policy was to keep calm. There was little he could do in these circumstances that wouldn't rebound on him once the police were involved.

'Martin, I don't know what the problem is, but I must ask you to leave, please.' My voice was quiet, but I suspected he detected a slight tremble. Despite the legal position, I knew I was extremely vulnerable. He was a strong, heavy man and emotionally charged. He had the strength and obvious will to do me harm. I may have been sitting in a wheelchair, but the morals of that situation were clearly lost on him.

'What's the problem?' he sneered. 'So getting some pompous detective to come round to my sodding house with his fawning sidekick asking whether I murdered your fucking wife is not a bloody problem? Are you thick or what? What the hell have you been saying, Miller?'

I said calmly, 'Chief Inspector Goddard is investigating the murder of my wife, Martin. What action he takes to that end, or what enquiries he makes, are nothing to do with me. I'm not his boss. If you have a problem with what he's done, make a formal complaint about it.'

'Shut it. You know exactly what I mean, you self-righteous bastard. Why the fuck would he come round to my house unless you'd put him up to it? Well?'

'With respect, I haven't "put him up" to anything. I've just answered his questions and told it as it was.'

'Told what?'

'Well, in case you've forgotten, we all used to socialise together, before your affair that is. If you—'

'"My affair", as you put it, has fuck all to do with any of this, right?' he interrupted. 'The fact that Grace is a boring, frigid cow has nothing to do with Goddard, has it? Lindsey may have found herself killed in a wood, but the simple fact is that I had nothing to do with the bitch's death, okay? You're just taking this opportunity to do some warped stirring for your own ends, Miller. Well, aren't you?'

I smiled, couldn't help myself. Some people can be so much wider of the mark than others. In all the circumstances, smiling was probably the wrong thing to do, but sometimes things just happen. His face reddened, and he stepped towards me.

'Stay away from me please, Martin. Don't come any closer. You asked me a question, let me answer it.' He started to speak, but I just launched. 'Chief Inspector Goddard quite properly asked me about Lindsey's friends. How could I have not mentioned you and Grace, huh? It's surely common ground that Grace was going to let you off the hook financially, and Lindsey gave her the backbone to get what she was entitled to have, since you weren't offering it.'

'You bastard...'

I remained calm. 'Well, I'm right, aren't I? That's not going to make you Lindsey's greatest fan, is it? Calling her "a bitch" rather confirms that, doesn't it? Especially in the present circumstances.'

'I'd have given Grace something fair. There's enough to go round...'

I smiled again. 'Easy to say now a court's ordered it, isn't it? I'd believe you if you'd done it voluntarily rather than make Grace leap through the hoops.'

'I was following my solicitor's advice...' He paused. 'Why the hell am I explaining myself to you? You're nothing, Miller. Just a creepy little sod who can't stay on a fucking horse.'

I managed to remain calm even in the face of that. I simply said in a quiet voice, 'That was below the belt, Martin. You threatened me when I came round to your house, are you going to threaten me again?'

He looked livid and glared at me. 'You're a piece of shit, Miller. No, I'm not going to threaten you again. I only ever do that once and then I carry it out.'

And with that he stepped right up to me and swung his fist in my face. I tried to move but couldn't avoid it. My head cracked backwards, and I felt pain in my face and strain on my neck. I spun back round like an owl and raised my arm defensively to look at him. But he was moving again. He placed both hands on the left arm of my wheel chair and, placing his left foot against the right wheel at the front, pulled the arm upwards. I suddenly, and very quickly, found myself rising in the seat. I started to tip to my right until the equilibrium was breached and the chair crashed down throwing me out of it in the process. My right elbow took the brunt of the impact and I was somehow able to prevent my head from hitting the hard wooden floor. I sprawled about and attempted to push myself up.

Martin placed his motorbike boot on my chest and shoved me firmly back to the floor. I looked up at him. He would have seen fear.

'Next time you piss me off, Miller, I'll be back and you'll get a damn sight worse, okay?'

'Feels good throwing a cripple out of his wheelchair, does it?' I said loudly.

He bent over me, bringing his face quite close. 'Certainly feels good when it's a tosser like you, Miller.'

'I wonder what Goddard will make of this incident?' I asked clearly. 'You seem to have a violent streak, Martin.'

'If you've tipped yourself out of your sodding wheelchair, Miller, that has nothing to do with me, has it? Make up whatever pretty story you like, I'll deny it. Who's going to believe a little nobody like you? I'm through with you.'

And with that he walked over to the door.

As he opened it, he turned to me and said, 'Just watch it, Miller. Don't cause me any more hassle, right?'

'Aren't you even going to at least help me up?' I shouted.

But he left and slammed the door behind him. I lay back down on the floor, catching my breath until I heard his motorbike burst into life and noisily depart. I stirred, lifted the wheelchair back up onto its wheels, and picked up my mobile, which had fallen on the floor nearby. I was relieved it didn't seem broken by the fall. I looked at the phone and eagerly double-checked it. It was unbroken; not even a scratch from its experience.

While still sitting on the floor, I pressed various options on the mobile. In the back of my mind I could still hear Martin yelling at me that no one was going to believe me that he'd assaulted me. With one final push the mobile sprung into life and with some relief I heard it all clearly: the sound of a door opening, the sound of a door slamming, and then an angry voice, "What the fuck are you playing at, Miller?"

FORTY-TWO

'So what are you going to do with it?' Grace asked.

She'd responded as reliably as ever to my call after Martin left. She arrived at almost half past six that Tuesday, and we were once more in my sitting room. I played the recording of Martin's visit a second time and she listened to it again just as incredulously. Personally, I was pleased that the tiny microphone had picked up so much, particularly when the phone had been thrown to the floor.

'What do *you* think I should do with it?' I asked, placing the mobile gently down on a side table.

'You must report all this to Chief Inspector Goddard. We can't let the bully get away with such aggressive behaviour. He has no excuse, none whatsoever. Tell Goddard.'

'Maybe,' I said. 'But where's that actually going to take us? It's like a sideshow to the main event. And can you imagine Martin's reaction with me if he gets arrested for assault?'

Grace stood up and walked to the window and its view of the cul-de-sac. Her hair was now free of the scrunchie or clip that she usually wore and reached just shy of her shoulders. 'It would be no more than he deserves,' she said. 'Report it. It's his fault. He'll think the police won't be interested or have enough evidence to bring any charges. Your word against his.' She paused and turned to me. 'And who says it's a sideshow to the main event anyway, Mike?

We've both witnessed for the very first time an extremely ugly side to his character. And what's that tell us? Personally if I were told that he'd murdered poor old Lindsey in that wood, I'd believe it now.'

I nodded. Martin clearly had a quick temper and a violent streak.

'I'll reflect on what I'll do with the recording,' I said. I'd already thought about some options, but I didn't want to act hastily. I knew the recording was valuable and wanted to extract its full worth.

'Now,' she said, 'I mentioned earlier that I had something else to tell you. It's not as dramatic as Martin's visit, but worth reporting.'

'Oh yes,' I said as I recalled her brief comment. 'What is it?'

'Well, I had a call this afternoon from Charles, my cousin. He told me that he'd had a visit from Goddard over the weekend and it was clear that he wasn't overly chuffed about it.'

'I can understand that.'

'I think he was just looking for some background information as well as some reassurance. He was calm— rather matter-of-fact if you like. I had the impression that he just accepted his "name started with the wrong initial", as he put it, and that your conclusion was miles out. I had some sympathy for his argument, if I'm honest. I told him that you'd seen it as a long shot and that you'd accepted what he'd told you. Goddard had become involved simply because the police wanted to ensure that all reasonable enquiries had been made in what is, after all, a serious investigation.'

'Fair enough,' I said. 'So where's all this leave us, then?'

'Not very far at the end of the day,' Grace said, 'But further than we were. I think a key sticking point is where Lindsey actually went when she said she was working on the late shift at the hospice or seeing Julie in Putney.'

'From what Goddard has said, they're trying to retrace her steps on that Saturday afternoon, but it's not been easy.'

'So do you really think she's been mixed up in some way or other with the coven? It just seems so unlikely.'

'I just don't know, Grace. I agree with you that it doesn't fit our image of Lindsey. But then lying about where she was going, secretive correspondence with a lover, and a clandestine telephone liaison with a Karl don't fit the old image either, do they? And then there are the skulls, of course. What's that all about? There must be a reason for them. Someone around here must be responsible for those, huh? At least the thirteen members of the coven must surely be in the frame, don't you think? Whoever *they* are.'

'I guess so,' she said slowly. 'So why don't we have one final push on this coven issue? We know it exists because Goddard confirmed it, but I've thought of an angle.'

'What's that?' I said.

'We know of one former member. Someone who no doubt kept a lot of written detail—a diary at least—sufficient to convince a national journalist.'

'Dean Wilson?'

'The same.'

I said, 'We won't get much out of him. He hung himself in the wood after the Sunday paper exposé remember. I paused for a beat and added, 'Or was hung…'

'That's not the official version.'

'I know,' I said. 'But it all makes you think, doesn't it?'

'Well, however he died, he must have, like Sandra, left family behind. Presumably they won't be overly disposed to the coven. Why don't we track them down, Mike, and see what they have to say?'

FORTY-THREE

Jack Hendon was a non-descript little man of about fifty years of age. It suited him to be non-descript. He was a private detective and, by all accounts, a pretty good one. He had a small office tucked away in a run-down building in Exeter. I was told that Jack could prioritise jobs, especially when cash was involved. It was Jack who tracked down Dean Wilson's sister for me.

After our get-together on that early Tuesday evening in my sitting room, Grace went off to see if she could locate any relatives of the late Dean Wilson on her own. I hadn't heard from her by Thursday evening, so I telephoned her at about seven o'clock. I clutched a printed email in my hand. It was to me from Jack Hendon and proved to me that he was good, very good. And cash indeed made him quick.

'Hi Grace, any news?' I asked.

'Nothing yet, Mike,' she said. 'I've been on the Internet and also made some local enquiries. Not been easy as we're going back over thirty years. Best I can do so far is that Dean was not originally from here but from Bristol direction, possibly Weston-super-Mare. Doesn't seem to have been married, so probably no children. I've concluded that the quickest way to track any relatives is to hire some kind of private detective and I'm just looking for a decent one now. Hang the expense, it has to be done. How about you?'

'The estate agents have my bungalow fully marketed now. I spoke to Jonathan there this afternoon. Nothing further from the mysterious enquirer, Adrian Smith, though.'

'If that was his real name…'

'Sure. That's a slow boil. No more threats though. I'd half expected something by now, but all's quiet on the Western Front.'

'That's good news.'

'Absolutely. Oh yes, I've found Dean Wilson's sister,' I added casually. I let my words hang to see what reaction I'd get. I was right with my guess.

'*What*?' she exclaimed. 'Are you joking? How did you do that?'

'Well, to be honest, I didn't do much, save be inspired by you. And like you I concluded that a private detective was the real answer, and someone in Exeter was recommended to me. I contacted him first thing yesterday morning, and he's already come up with the information: name, address and telephone number.'

'Right, okay.' I had the impression she felt I'd stolen a march on her, which wasn't far off the truth, I guess.

'He knows he's up for a decent tip from me,' I said.

'So is she living locally or further north?'

'You were getting warm. The family do come from Weston-super-Mare and his sister still lives there. It was Dean who moved away.'

'I guess my detective would have done as well.'

'Oh, that last bit wasn't from him. I spoke to her about twenty minutes ago.'

'*Already*?' she exclaimed. 'You're not hanging about, Mike, are you? What did she say?'

'Her name's Ada Hoyle. And she's willing to meet us. Just a matter of fixing it up. Fancy an hour's trip up north to the seaside?'

FORTY-FOUR

I'd never previously met someone who could see the future.

Two days later, Grace and I drove north towards Weston-super-Mare on the M5. It was mid-afternoon on a slightly overcast Saturday. The traffic was quite heavy, but fortunately most of it was heading south. A hint of spray remained on the road from the morning's rain, and the occasional splash came from under our determined tyres. Grace's slender hands gripped the steering wheel tighter than usual as she concentrated on the task.

'Let's analyse your conversation with Ada,' she said glancing at me and then quickly back to the road ahead.

'You think there's more to it?' I said. 'It was really very straightforward. I explained that Lindsey had been murdered in Littleworth Wood and that I was undertaking some research into the wood itself. I said I'd come across references to her brother, Dean, and the Sunday paper article and I wanted to discuss it further with her. I made it clear that I was open-minded, just an ordinary guy looking for ordinary answers. She seemed to understand.'

'So she wasn't surprised to hear from you?'

'Didn't seem to be.'

'So other than fixing up the visit, she didn't say much?'

'Correct.'

Grace nodded slowly as she indicated to overtake a red oil tanker. 'How old is she? The article said that Dean was fifty-one when he spoke out, so he would have been that age when he died a few days later. And that was over thirty years ago. She must be in her—what?—seventies or even her eighties?'

'She's seventy-nine. She did say that and that she was two years younger than Dean. She said she was willing to help as much as she could, as long as we weren't from the press.'

We followed the motorway north before winding our way into Weston-super-Mare. The sense of being by the coast was strong, and I was reminded of my recent trip back to Sidmouth. Severn Close was in a maze of former council properties now mainly privately owned. Ada Hoyle's property was a tired terraced town house standing behind a fore-garden, which had been block-paved and on which was parked a well-maintained, ten-year-old red Ford fiesta.

We rang the bell. A few moments later the door opened slowly to reveal a short, very plump woman with neat grey hair. She had a prominent mole on her right cheek and was dressed in a calf-length flowery dress and a light blue cardigan with buttons that strained to stay in place. She looked a little unsteady on her slippered feet, and I wasn't entirely sure whether she held the door to close it quickly or because she needed it for support. From her face, she thought she knew who we were but was waiting for confirmation.

'Mrs Hoyle?' I asked in a positive tone giving her my best smile.

She nodded. 'You must be Mike Miller,' she said and, turning to look at Grace, added with a polite smile, 'and you're Grace? Mike told me all about you.'

Grace smiled back and stepped forward. 'Positive things, I trust. Nice to meet you, Mrs Hoyle.' They shook hands gently.

'Oh, please call me Ada. Now, come on in,' she said as she stepped backwards and opened the glazed door. 'I've put the kettle on. You must need some tea after all that driving.' She seemed to take in the wheelchair for the first time. 'Can you manage all right with that, dear? I'm afraid there's not much room.'

Grace said, 'We'll be fine thanks.' She gently tipped the chair back and eased it up through the door into a narrow hallway.

We followed Ada into her small, cluttered sitting room with two tired armchairs and a small sofa covered with a throw of colourful knitted squares. Photographs of family were everywhere: on side tables, bookcases, and the tiled mantelpiece over an ancient electric fire that looked more like a safety hazard than a source of heat. The room was musty, but nothing that a good blast of fresh air couldn't have sorted.

Ada stood by what was obviously her favourite chair and started to fret. 'Oh dear, there really isn't much room for your wheelchair. I'm sorry about this. I hadn't realised, you see...'

We were eventually all sitting down with tea and biscuits. Ada looked at me expectantly, silently inviting me to start.

'Thank you ever so much for seeing us, Ada,' I said, taking my cue. 'As I explained on the phone, I'm trying to find out what happened to my wife in Littleworth Wood. The place seems to have a grim history and I'm so sorry to ask you to drag up some sad memories.'

Ada settled back slightly into her chair and straightened her dress self-consciously. 'Thank you, dear. It's over thirty years ago now, but it seems like only yesterday. I was quite a young woman then. I'm seventy-nine now, you know.'

I smiled. 'You don't look a day over fifty.'

She laughed. 'Oh, get away with you. I've been a widow for over ten years. That's my Bert there.' She pointed an arthritic finger at the photograph of a cheerful old man clutching a trumpet that took pride of place on the mantelpiece next to a brass carriage clock. 'A musician he was. Played in a band that used to tour all round here, if you know what I mean. He did all the working men's clubs and the piers, he did. I could listen to him play for hours...'

Grace said, 'I'm pleased you were so happy together. You must have some lovely memories. Rather better ones than those of thirty years ago, I guess.'

The gentle smile faded from her lined face. 'Yes, poor Dean.'

'Was he your only brother?' Grace asked.

'No, dear, no he wasn't. Dean was the oldest. Two years older than me he was. Robert was the youngest. He was almost five years younger than me. He emigrated to Australia when he was thirty-one. Died in Sydney last year. I was in the middle, so to speak, and now the last one left. Dean would have been eighty-two this October, you know?'

I said, 'I was so sorry to learn of his terrible death, Ada. It must have been awful news for you and the family to hear.' I paused to let my sympathies sink in. 'Did you know he was involved with the coven?'

She shook her head gently. 'No, no I didn't. It was a real surprise to me, Mike. If I'm honest, Dean and I weren't that close—well, not since he moved away to Tiverton, anyways. Took a job there, he did. He never said anything about being involved in any witchcraft or anything. I guess

215

he knew I wouldn't approve. By all accounts he was quite an important person in their group.'

Grace asked, 'When did you hear about it all? From the paper or before?'

Ada relaxed a bit more into her chair. 'Oh before, dear. But only just. Dean drove up to visit me, you see, on the Saturday of the weekend it was all published. He told me what he'd been doing and that he'd gone to the papers to tell them all about it. There'd been a fallout apparently between him and some of the other leading people in the group— quite a big one by all accounts. It prompted Dean to ring the newspaper, and a journalist had been round to see him.'

'How did he seem?' Grace asked.

'Dean?' She clarified, removing her glasses and placing them on the table next to her. 'Well, he seemed almost relieved that the story was to be made public. Yes, relieved he was. It was the last time I saw him, other than at his funeral, of course.' She rubbed her hand down her face and let it rest on her chin. 'He left no will, no instructions at all. He was single, never married. Had girlfriends, but never found anyone he wanted to settle down with. Not like me and my Bert. It all fell to me to sort it out, of course, what with Robert being in Australia and everything. He didn't come back for the funeral. Too far it was. I had him cremated. No fuss. It's all such a long time ago now, isn't it?' She placed her hands together in her lap.

I nodded again. I had the strong impression that this lovely old lady knew her life was so very much in the past. She'd been left behind by her two brothers, and indeed by her Bert, to manage the best she could. Memories, photographs and the occasional highlight of a visitor. I didn't want to grow old.

'Why was there a fallout?' Grace asked.

'Now that's a long story. It's summed up quite well in the article.' She pointed to a faded newspaper on the table next to her. 'As I understand it, Dean didn't approve of things the leaders wanted to do, and they wanted him to leave. He stood his ground, but it was very unpleasant I heard.'

I said, 'What happened to Dean's possessions?'

'How do you mean?'

'Well, I guess I was wondering whether he left anything about the coven. You know, something in writing.'

Ada was silent for a moment and her eyes flicked over us both. After a bit, she said softly, 'It's curious, you know.'

'What is?' Grace asked gently.

'Well, there was all this hoo-ha over thirty years ago about what Dean told that journalist and then it all died down after Dean's death. Nothing there was after that. Nothing at all. Until now.'

'Now?' I said. 'You mean us?'

'Oh no, dear. No, I don't mean you two. I was referring to the gentleman who rang me earlier this year and asked me questions about Dean—just like you're doing now.'

FORTY-FIVE

Life can be curious at times, can't it? Just when you think you're making progress, something springs up to knock you off course. I wondered if Grace was having that same experience.

Ada's gaze flicked between us, her left eyebrow quizzically raised. 'You both look surprised by that.'

I don't know how I looked, but Grace certainly looked very surprised to me. 'Who rang you?' I asked. 'Was it a journalist or someone like that?'

'I don't know. He never said why he wanted to know. He did tell me his name, but I can't for the life of me remember it.'

'What sort of person was he?' I asked. 'How did he sound? Was he young, old? Did he have an accent of any kind? Professional?'

Ada looked thoughtful. 'Oh dear, now you're asking,' she said. 'He didn't really sound young, but then he wasn't old either, if you know what I mean. I think he was quite well spoken, but he kept losing that at times. Yes, that's right. I remember thinking his accent sounded a bit odd. I couldn't fully work it out.'

Grace said, 'Do you think he was trying to disguise his voice?'

'Why on earth would he want to do that, dear?' Ada paused and seemed to mull it over. 'Mind you, maybe that was it. I don't really know. It wasn't like when you rang me,

Mike. You made more sense, you did.'

I smiled at her. 'So what did he want?' I asked.

'I think at first he wanted to find out if I knew any more about the coven than had been reported in the papers. Well, I told him really what I've told you. Then he asked me exactly what you asked me, Mike. Had I got any notebook or anything like that of Dean's?'

'And what did you tell him?' Grace enquired.

'I never gave him a straight answer and then I started to feel very uncomfortable.'

I said, 'Couldn't you just have told him you had to go? You were busy or something.'

'Oh, I couldn't have done that, Mike. It wouldn't have been true, would it?' she said, turning towards me with mild surprise. 'I didn't have to go anywhere. I did try to get him off the phone, but he was very persistent.'

'How did it finish?' Grace asked.

'Well, believe it or not he just hung up on me. How rude was that?'

I nodded. 'It must have been a very unpleasant experience. Did he ring again?'

She shook her head subtly. 'No, no he didn't. He never rang back. I've not heard any more about this whole thing until you rang yesterday.'

'I hope I didn't worry you. Now that I know about the earlier nasty call, it was very good of you to hear me out.'

'Your call was very different, Mike. You were very polite and thoughtful. Not pushy like that other gentleman. I feel very comfortable sitting here with you both.'

I thanked her and then said, 'So, *did* Dean leave a notebook?'

She smiled. 'In truth, I'm old and I'm tired. The doctors

say my heart's not good. And I've my own reasons to believe I'll be joining Dean and Robert and Bert soon.'

I was quite taken aback by this. She looked like someone with plenty of life left in her. 'May I ask why you say that?' I asked.

'My mother was a medium,' she said. 'She could speak to the spirit world. I know that's sometimes seen as controversial, but believe me she could. Maybe that's where Dean got his interests from, but of course it's nothing to do with witchcraft or covens. That's fantasy, escapism if you like. My mother's gift was real. I know that.'

'How?' Grace enquired gently.

'Because she passed the gift on to me.' On the wall, she pointed to a sepia photograph of a Sioux Indian chief dressed in traditional costume with a full-length feather headdress. 'That's my guide. All mediums have a guide. I used to do readings for people, but I gave that up when Bert died. You see, I knew he was going to die. I knew before the doctors had even diagnosed his cancer. It's a gift you see. I didn't ask for it and, to be honest, didn't really want it, but I had no choice in that. I try and turn it off, so to speak, but sometimes I just get told things. The spirits can be very persistent when it's important.'

As Grace and I exchanged glances, Ada stood up stiffly and walked slowly over to a small bookshelf in the corner of the room. She placed one hand on a waist-height shelf for support before leaning down to pick out a small red A5 notebook with a hard back. She looked at it momentarily as if making a decision and came back to us. She sat down carefully and passed the book over to me with an outstretched arm as if it were a precious offering.

'This is Dean's notebook—he left it with me on that

Saturday. My Bert used to say that if you want to hide something, leave it somewhere obvious. "In plain sight" I think was his phrase.'

I smiled politely at her. 'Good advice. Thank you, Ada, we'll look after it—and Dean's reputation.'

'Bless you,' she said

I took the book and immediately studied it. The cover was frayed at the corners, and the page edges were slightly thumbed and grubby. 'GREY MOON' had been roughly written in capitals with a firm biro, and the words were almost engraved into the cardboard. I opened it up and flicked through the pages. A lot of handwriting. Neat, in blue ink, sometimes black. The occasional drawing, some childishly coloured with crayons. About a third of the pages at the back were blank.

After some concluding small talk and commenting on the time, we made to leave. As we entered the hallway, Ada opened the front door for us. I shook her hand and Grace manoeuvred me down the small step onto the paved front garden. She released her grip on the wheelchair handle and turned to Ada, who'd moved into the doorway.

'Thank you again, Ada,' Grace said with her best smile and shook her hand. 'You've been very kind.'

'Thank you, dear. Look after that book now.' She then leant forward towards Grace and in a quieter, anxious voice said, 'and look after *yourself*, dear. I have grave concerns about you.'

And before Grace could say anything, Ada closed the door quickly.

FORTY-SIX

"It's a gift you see. I try and turn it off, so to speak, but sometimes I just get told things. The spirits can be very persistent when it's important."

I switched the television off, lay back on the sofa in the sitting room of my Tiverton home, and looked at the beamed ceiling. Another Saturday evening on my own. I was getting used to it. Yet somehow it didn't bother me anymore. It used to, of course, which annoyed me. Why had I allowed myself such weakness with Martin? Thinking of them together in the early days after the destruction of my illusionary life, when Martin had abruptly and cruelly shattered our comfortable and relaxed routine, had made me physically hurt. One moment he was my husband and all was good; the next he was sitting up in the spare room bed next to that deceitful girl. Both naked. Both resigned on hearing me enter the house, knowing that the breach of trust, the lies and the acting had reached their final conclusion. Discovered. The affair had run its natural, ugly course.

He'd packed a bag that night as I'd shouted and screamed and thrown God knows what at him. She'd just quietly done his bidding, pulled skimpy clothes over her skinny body, and sat downstairs in the kitchen waiting for him like some faithful old dog. And then he was gone to answer the siren call of his spindly bit of rough. If I sat now in silence, I could still hear their shriek of embarrassed laughter as they collided in the hallway. I could still hear him slam the front door as he left our marital home for the final time, leaving me sobbing on our bed. That was the worst day of my life.

As we neared the end of our journey back, Mike suggested a drink together at the Chequers pub in Westland. The busy and noisy bar was filled with locals, regulars, the inevitable tourists and weekenders, and my cousin Charles. I did a double take. He was there with a woman, probably about ten years younger than him. She had dyed-blond hair and a pretty face and was obviously displaying her cleavage. I tapped him on the shoulder, and he turned with instant recognition. He kissed me on the cheek and gave a perfunctory nod to Mike, who was trying to ease his way through the throng behind me, which was parting slower than the Red Sea.

I leant over towards Charles' ear and said loudly above the din, 'Months without seeing you, dear cousin, and now contact twice in a few days.'

He smiled at me. 'Once more tomorrow and I'll consider myself a bus.'

He introduced me to Miss Cleavage. A Caroline. She seemed pleasant enough. I was jostled as someone pushed past me. No apology, but then the bar was so busy, you'd spend your whole time apologising during the simple act of making a five-metre journey. After craning in turn towards my ear, he explained that Caroline lived in Tiverton and that this was her favourite local pub. Not so favourite, I thought, as I didn't recognise her—and she was the sort of girl you'd remember. Charles said that they hadn't expected the pub to be quite so crowded, but at least there was an atmosphere. With mutual signs and body language, we both gave up at that point and allowed the deafening conversations, laughter and shouts towards the bar to win the day. We made vague and polite promises to get in touch to arrange some catch-up time and with exaggerated nods, we parted.

I bought a pint of bitter and a glass of white wine and turned back to see that Mike had grabbed a chair and a small table from a departing couple. The spare chair was soon taken, but we were able to chat together, despite the hustle and bustle that swarmed all around us as people came, hovered and moved on. The convivial environment prompted us to talk more than we'd managed in the car. We remained focused on ourselves as if we were in some kind of bubble. Mike was obviously excited about Dean's notebook and speculated what was in it, even though he was clutching it in his hand and could have read it there and then. He said he didn't want to risk leaving it in the car, which made sense.

With the wine and beer gone, Mike admitted to fatigue and wanted to go home. I glanced about in time to see Charles heading for the toilets and so had given up on the idea of a further quick goodbye. There was no sign of Miss Cleavage. We left the busy hostelry through the rear door to the small car park. I dropped Mike off at his bungalow. He said he'd get on with looking at the notebook and would ring me sometime soon with an update. This all suited me, as I wanted some time by myself.

I made my way home and crashed out in front of the television. I thought about heating up the leftovers of a shepherd's pie, but couldn't be bothered. Feeding Barney was the limit of my early evening endeavours. I turned on my side and stared at the unlit log-burning stove, or Mike's view when he stayed over the other night. That had been good of him. To rise from bed at such a late hour and drive over to talk it through with me. He was a good friend. Lindsey had been lucky. Mr Right indeed. And I'd ended up with slag Martin. I would do better next time.

And look after yourself, dear. I have grave concerns about you. Poor Mike had tried to make light of her comment, but, truthfully, it had made me really curious. What did Ada mean by it? After she closed the door, I rang the bell again, but she didn't answer. The door stayed firmly shut. I rang her from Mike's mobile, but the call hadn't been answered. What had that comment been about? She said that she had grave concerns about me. How grave? What concerns? Was it my health, like she knew about her failing heart and Bert's sudden cancer? Was some accident waiting for me round the corner? Would some natural disaster befall me? Or was it all wrapped up in the current mystery of Lindsey's death, Littleworth Wood, and covens and painted skulls?

At times like this, I missed my soul-mate husband the most. Not the dishonest Martin now living near Exeter with his mistress, but the devoted Martin I'd married, the one with whom I'd exchanged promises of eternal love and a solemn and public vow in front of our friends and family to forsake all others. The man who'd courted me, pursued me, took my hand, won my heart and—if I were forced to admit it to myself—still had part of it.

I wandered into the kitchen and made some toast with peanut butter, one of my traditional comfort foods. Sod the diet. I recalled with a smile that Lindsey had always gone for a decent bowl of custard as her priority on such occasions.

Barney sat and watched me transfixed, not missing a single movement. In response to his pleading brown eyes, I tossed him a couple of dog biscuits, which he devoured noisily in seconds before fixing his stare on me again. The adoring eyes were now even more intense and bewitching, so I patted him on the head and headed out into the hallway. The kitchen and the laundry room were the extent of his domain, so I knew he wouldn't follow me. No point in making the dog fat—it was easy, after all, to impose a diet on your dog even if one struggled with one's own.

*

It was almost quarter past one the following day, Sunday, and I was making myself a sandwich when my telephone rang. It was Mike. He just launched, loudly and earnestly. 'Grace, I've been burgled.'

It took me a few moments to focus.

'Sorry? What do you mean "burgled"?'

'As in a person or persons unknown have broken into my house and have nicked something.'

I thought for a second he was messing around, but his light response had a dark tone.

'What you on about, Mike? Nicked what?'

'Dean's notebook.'

FORTY-SEVEN

Some would say it was all my fault.

In my defence, I did think long and hard about helping in the shop. Working there would at least get me out of the house, meet people, and be helpful. The gossip about Lindsey's death had done the village rounds—several laps, I gather. As the widower, I was no longer the focus of the community's collective words and vision. Other stories now topped the gossip chart, with the number one being that our elderly vicar, the Reverend John Furnival, had slid his white Fiat Punto neatly into a ditch. He didn't sustain any injuries, fortunately—other than his pride—and it was said that he would still take the ten-thirty service that Sunday morning.

I learnt of the vicar's adventures from old Edith Riley, with whom I'd discussed my idea of an early return. She warned me that the shop wouldn't be particularly busy, which came as no surprise, as I knew it rarely was except at the height of the tourist season. However, she said I would be very welcome if I felt up to volunteering until lunchtime.

'It might even do you some good, Mike,' she said to me on the phone when I'd rung at nine o'clock that morning. 'It'll get you out the house a bit. I found it was helpful doing that after my George passed away. I'll see you shortly then.'

I'd locked the house up as usual, although, as I was to later admit, I evidently failed to set the alarm. Maybe because I was in a hurry, maybe because I was a bit blasé about the threats that had come my way. What I did know was that it felt good to go into the heart of the village again and take my familiar place behind the ancient till that sat precariously on the store's crowded counter.

A steady stream of shoppers passed through, most from the village. Some I knew by name, some I sort of recognised. A handful of visitors, too: couples renting holiday cottages in the area or simply driving through to enjoy a day out in the glorious countryside. I'd helped before on a Sunday, but only rarely.

At about one o'clock, Edith persuaded me to call it a day. I finished my third cup of tea, said my goodbyes, and retraced my route back home. As I entered the drive, the bungalow looked fine. All normal. I unlocked the door and entered, noting that the alarm had not gone off—usually I go straight to the small wall-mounted box to enter the four-digit code to stop its irritable bleeping.

After I closed the front door, I noticed the draught. Not much of one, as it was quite a still day, but you notice when your house has a different feel about it. I went straight down to the kitchen. The patio door was slightly ajar, just wide enough for an adult to slip through. On the floor below the window and near the kitchen table was broken glass, some of which was crudely stuck to a foot-square piece of cardboard, and the rest was scattered quite widely. The window had been unlocked and remained swung open, although only just. It didn't take a forensic expert to work out all the signs. I took my mobile out of my pocket and rang the local police station. They said they'd send someone over and gave me an incident number, which I took to be a piece of red tape.

I looked round the kitchen, but could see nothing out of place. I took a forty-centimetre tall metal jar labelled 'Flour' off a shelf below the work surface and opened it. The cash was still inside. I placed it on the central breakfast island.

I moved into the sitting room. Nothing was normal. Drawers were open, things were overturned on the floor, and chair and sofa cushions were wildly strewn about. I hastened over to the sofa and stared at its cushionless base. Dean's notebook wasn't there. I looked round the rest of the bungalow. Everywhere else was undisturbed. I rang Grace at about quarter past one. Other than a couple of biscuits with my tea, I'd had nothing to eat since an early breakfast, but I wasn't hungry. Stressful circumstances seem to negate hunger. And I felt stressed.

'How do you know it's gone?' Grace asked.

'Because I was reading it on the sofa last night and left it hidden under a base cushion when I went to bed. I haven't touched it since, and yet it's not there now.'

'How've they broken in? When was this? What else have they taken? I don't understand how they can break in and take this book from right under your nose.'

'It wasn't from under my nose. I volunteered at the shop this morning. You know, simply to get out. Try and get some normality back into my life. Ironic, isn't it? While I was there, someone thoughtfully broke in through the small kitchen window and then took the easy route out through the patio doors. That's how I read it.'

'And presumably legged it across the field?'

'Exactly. Our rear garden isn't overlooked, as you know. No one would have seen anything. That privacy is a key reason why I liked this house.'

'Has a downside though, doesn't it?'

'So it seems. I'll have to consider having it properly fenced. That hedge will take years to grow into a deterrent. CCTV might not go amiss either.'

'Sounds a good plan. Have you rung the police yet?'

'Yeah, they're on the way. Apparently.'

'Mike, I'm not getting good vibes about this. Please tell me something else was taken.'

I paused. I had to tell her. 'Grace,' I said. 'Nothing else seems to have been taken. Nothing else was even touched or moved, other than the sitting room where they evidently started. Even the cash was in its tin.'

'This opens up a mass of questions, doesn't it? What's so important about the book? Who wants it, and why? The top one, I guess, is who the hell knew we had the book in the first place? Did you tell anyone we had it?'

'No, of course not.'

'So how did they know? And why's the book so important enough for someone to break into your house and steal it?'

'I have some idea about that,' I said. 'I read quite a bit of it and I've jotted down some stuff—not much, mind. Can you come over later?'

'Sure. I'll be with you at eight.' She paused. 'Shit, Mike … someone must have been staking out your house...'

'Or followed us yesterday. Or saw me in the shop.'

'Was it busy? Did anyone stand out?'

'No.'

'Did you tell what's-her-name… you know, Edith, about the book?'

'I don't think so—'

'You don't *think* so?'

'Well, I'm sure I didn't. I did talk about Littleworth Wood though. She'd obviously heard about the coven but said it was all a load of "journalistic twaddle". Told me not to worry about it. I may have gone on about it quite a bit, but

230

I'm sure I didn't mention the book. And even if I did, Edith isn't exactly the burglar type, and I was with her all morning in any event...'

'But someone may have overheard you.'

'Look, Grace. Firstly, I'm sure I didn't tell Edith and, secondly, no one overheard me.'

'Mike, I've had a rather nasty thought.'

'What is it?'

'If anyone overheard, it was last night in the pub. And you had the book with you.'

'Bloody hell. I never thought it was going to be of such significance.'

'And Mike...'

'Yes?'

'Charles was in the pub last night.'

FORTY-EIGHT

Save for the uniforms, the visit to my house by two police officers to investigate a crime was almost a déjà vu.

A fortnight and a handful of hours had passed since the visit by DS Johnson and DC Williams. Shortly after four o'clock that Sunday afternoon, I opened my front door again to two police constables. They introduced themselves as PC Derek Gosling, a stocky man in his late thirties, and PC Andy Webster, a tall, gangly lad some ten years younger than his colleague. PC Gosling explained that they'd been on patrol on my side of Tiverton and had answered the call for attendance at my bungalow following the report of the burglary.

I led them into the kitchen and showed them the broken window and the open patio door. One of my wheels crunched on a piece of glass.

'Have you touched anything?' PC Gosling asked.

'No, well, nothing around the points of entry and departure. That's how I see it anyway, but you're the experts. In through the window and out through the door, I reckon.'

PC Gosling nodded and pointed at the cardboard on the floor amidst the glass. 'Pretty crude and amateur. Looks like someone's been reading the Ladybird Book of House Breaking. Sticking cardboard on the pane to reduce the showering of glass. Helps keep the noise down.'

I said, 'Well, no cavalry from the neighbourhood watch scheme in any event. They were probably all in church.'

Peering at the window frame, Gosling said, 'Might be amateurish, but I've no doubt they wore gloves, whoever it was. We'll get forensics in anyway. Can we look outside?'

I directed them outside through the garage while I stayed in the kitchen. They were gone several minutes, and I watched them moving about the garden, leaning over the borders, and peering at the patio whilst their quiet, indistinct chatter floated now and then through the marginally open patio door.

Gosling went over to the straggly hedge and looked out across the field. They then stood together on the lawn, chatted and pointed before making their way back to the house. I heard the back door in the garage close, and they re-entered the kitchen.

'Find anything?' I asked.

'No,' Gosling said. 'They may have come across the field from the woods, but there's been so little rain, it's hard to identify any footprints. It looks like the grass is kept pretty short by those sheep. Peaceful and private out there, isn't it, Mr Miller? Lovely. Doesn't help us here, mind. Whoever it was may have done the field route or used the side gate.'

'I keep that locked.'

'Not today you didn't. Closed, but unlocked.'

'Really? I could have sworn I locked it.'

After they took a look at the sitting room mess, Gosling said, 'Let me make some notes.'

While PC Webster took a few photographs, Gosling and I sat at the kitchen table, and I related my Sunday morning. He asked me all the obvious questions about my movements, who knew where I was, and the fact that I lived alone. After a few minutes he turned to what had actually been stolen.

'*A notebook.* Is that it? With respect, unless it was the

early thoughts of Leonardo da Vinci, what value was there in that?'

I ignored the lack of tact. 'I didn't notice it at first.' I said and then pointed to the flour tin on the breakfast island. 'I checked my cash which I keep in there, but it's not been touched. I went into the sitting room and immediately saw the mess and noticed that the book had been taken from the sofa where I'd left it last night.' I tried to summarise the background and significance of Dean's book, but I think I lost him.

'It seems to me, Mr Miller, that this is something for Chief Inspector Goddard rather than me and PC Webster. I'll file a report and get forensics out here as soon as I can. In the light of the murder case, you're likely to get some prompt attention.'

'Thank you. And don't worry about DCI Goddard, I can let him know. I need to speak to him in connection with the murder investigation soon anyway.'

As Webster re-joined us, Gosling said, 'Okay, if you wish. I'll need to ensure he knows about it through my report, but that's likely to take a bit of time so he'll hear it quicker coming from you. I'll leave a message for DS Ward in any event.'

They said their goodbyes with vague promises of action and optimistic wishes that the CID would find out who'd broken in. As I closed the door, I knew I was a few minutes nearer to telling Grace about my notes—notes that would significantly change her views about the coven and its activities. It would not take her long to conclude why the book had been stolen. Yes, everything was starting to fall into place.

FORTY-NINE

Grace joined me for supper in the end. I cheated: ready-made lasagne tossed into the oven in its foil tray and a green salad shaken out of a plastic bag. Instant, quick and actually not too bad. I wasn't sure of the meal's dietary value, but I always thought that anything with salad wouldn't be too unhealthy.

We sat at the kitchen table that Grace had laid for us, complete with a reasonable bottle of Shiraz. I momentarily thought about Lindsey, since it was one of her favourite wines.

Grace asked, 'Were they here long?'

'Forensics? No, not too long. I gather I've done pretty well to get them here so soon, especially on a Sunday, but being the centre of a murder investigation has some hidden benefits. They had a good peer at the window, door, and outside. No eureka moments though. I got the impression it was all pretty standard and that whoever broke in wore gloves—no surprise there.' I took a sip of wine. 'I've got a glazier coming in the morning so, in the meantime, that classy piece of cardboard is my Heath-Robinson attempt to cover the hole. At least I can shut the patio door now. Although, to be honest, I did slide it mostly shut using a tea towel. Opened it again to where I'd found it when they arrived.' As Grace looked jokingly aghast, I added, 'Well, I was right, wasn't I? Gloves and all that. And they're going to find my dabs all over it anyway, aren't they? Stands to reason.'

Grace nodded as she finished a mouthful of food. 'Fair enough. When will you hear?'

'Not sure. Forgot to ask that. I guess it's all academic anyway since they're unlikely to come up with anything.'

'That's a bit negative.'

I smiled. 'Try "realistic".'

'Okay, time will tell.' With her elbow on the table, she picked up her wine glass and looked at me. 'So, we need an agenda. First item, who broke in and why? But main item, what was in the notebook?'

'In terms of the main item, I'll come back to that in a moment, although I just wish I'd read it all,' I said. 'As to the first item, who, let's run through it. Has to be someone with an interest in the coven, right? Someone then who wants to protect it?'

Grace nodded. 'Or attack it—you know, in the same way Dean tried.'

'Mm, alright, I can run with that. Okay then, what if it was someone without an interest—positive or negative—in the coven, but concerned with Lindsey's death?'

Grace smiled, 'You mean the murderer?'

I grinned. 'Yes... yes, I suppose I do.'

'Why would the murderer, with no connection with the coven, go to all that trouble of waiting until you were out, break in and then make off with Dean's book? Why would he be interested in the book?'

'Why do you say "he"? Might be a woman.'

'Only if she was an accomplice. Lindsey's murderer had the strength of a man.'

'Okay, I'll accept that.' I said.

'Of course, the theft of the book, and the whole coven

thing, might have nothing to do with Lindsey's death.'

'You mean a coincidence?' I said.

'I don't do coincidences, Grace said.

'But the facts as we know them just don't add up to that, do they?'

'Well…'

'Same modus operandi, the pregnancies, Dean's death—even the painted skulls. I could go on.'

Grace leant forward in her chair. 'This is quite a challenge, huh? What's good is that there has to be an answer. Maybe I should train to be a detective.'

I smiled. 'You have the tenacity and determination—and good luck to the villains if you do is all I can say'

'So, what *did* you read in Dean's notebook? Did you get through much?'

As I pushed myself back from the table, I said, 'I'll show you.' I manoeuvred to one of the kitchen units and opened a low drawer. After taking out a pad of paper, I returned to join her. I placed the pad on the table in front of me and flicked it open. I cast my eye over my handwriting that ran on to three pages. Rough notes and jottings made the night before when I had Dean's notebook with me on the sofa.

'Are those notes from Dean's book?'

I nodded. 'Uh huh. Let me pick out some highlights.' I continued to glance at what I'd written and then looked up at Grace, my finger marking a couple of places on the first page. 'There were a lot of random thoughts and entries. Nothing really ordered. It wasn't like a diary or something.'

Grace leaned forward and looked at my notes, which would have been upside down for her. 'So what *are* the highlights?'

'Firstly, he recorded that the coven met in two locations in Littleworth Wood one towards the north, in the summer, and the other towards the south-west in the winter—'

'What about autumn and spring?' Grace interrupted.

I shrugged. 'Dunno. Didn't say. He made a couple of sketches of the locations. I looked them up on my ordinance survey map, and the summer one is where Lindsey was killed, if Goddard told me right.'

'Well that tells us something.'

'Possibly. But let's not jump to conclusions. He makes it quite clear that the coven was persuaded to start making animal sacrifices and this had actually happened…'

'This was a principal feature in the newspaper article, wasn't it?'

'That's right.'

'Is there anything more about that?'

'Dean wrote that a number of the coven's thirteen were opposed to such practices, but the pressure was coming from a recently recruited young novice clearly pushing to be fast tracked to the inner circle. And he was not without influence. This newcomer also argued that they were required to perform human sacrifice.'

Grace stared at me. 'You're kidding, aren't you? That's murder, not anything religious. Surely they could see that?'

I nodded. 'Some of them, including Dean of course, could. Dean argued that any sacrifice, including animals, violated Wicca's basic tenet of "Harm None". Hence the big bust up it seems. You'll recall that Dean was in the inner circle as the coven's summoner. He stepped down and this youngster was appointed. That's when Dean quit altogether.'

'Because of the appointment?'

'Mm… sort of…'

I was aware of Grace studying my face as I looked down at the notes. I found it a challenge to look at her, but eventually I looked up. Her face was full of concern and anxiety—the look of someone wanting answers but apprehensive about what she might hear.

'Mike, what are you holding back? Why did he quit? Because of the animal thing?'

'He does record why there was a fallout, and I guess to some degree it was related to this animal thing. But worse.'

'Worse? Am I thinking right here?'

'Grace, let's leave it shall we.'

'Leave it? No way. Tell me, Mike.'

'Another time, Grace.'

She looked quite angry. 'What the hell is it, Mike? You look quite rattled. Come on, we're in this together, I thought.'

I paused, and then said, 'Well, you know that the article hinted at human sacrifice?'

'Uh huh.'

'Well, he doesn't just hint about it in the book.'

'You mean they killed someone?'

'Look, it's not exactly easy to talk about, Grace.'

She stared at me hard. I guessed she was weighing everything up in her mind—calculating how to get more from me.

'Tell me, Mike. We've come this far together after all. I can't let you cut me out at this point.'

I paused and wondered how to put it. I knew she was tough, but what I was going to say was not easy to hear. I studied her face and looked into her blue eyes, which flicked across my face disclosing a curious mixture of curiosity, anger and apprehension. She was looking for clues from my own face.

It had to be said.

'They killed a two-week-old baby, Grace.'

FIFTY

I watched Grace. Her eyes turned steely and a hardness set into her face. She shook her head very slowly. 'But that's… that's…'

'Awful?' I suggested.

'No, murder,' she said. 'Straightforward murder, Mike. The callous bastards.'

The silence that followed was disturbed by the fridge clicking on and starting a gentle hum.

'But whose baby, for heaven's sake?' she said. 'And how come the police were not involved?'

'I guess not every murder is investigated, Grace. If no one reports what happened.'

'But a baby went missing. Someone must have reported that surely? What did Dean say about it?' She craned her neck forward to look at my notes.

'He didn't say anything—well, at least not in the part I read. Maybe he did later in his notebook. Guess we'll never find out.'

'No wonder someone wanted the notebook.'

'That's what I thought. But it could all have been fiction, Grace,' I said. 'There is no evidence other than what Dean wrote.'

'But what about everything else? The press report, his death in the wood? And now this notebook, preserved by his sister for some thirty years? Surely together they all add up to something.'

'Mm, it's all a bit circumstantial, though, isn't it?' But I had to admit she had a point. When all these issues were strung together, you couldn't help but be taken down a certain path. The question for me now was: did I let the path take us, or did I explore a different route? Was it time to report all this to Goddard? Or would the fact that he'd see me delving into his case again create greater problems?

Grace stood up and walked over to the patio doors and stared out. She took a tissue out of her tight jeans pocket and, as surreptitiously as she could, dabbed her eyes. Only fourteen days before, we'd sat in the garden after DS Johnson and DC Williams had called to tell me about Lindsey. I felt a tremendous urge to stand up, walk over, wrap my arms around her and comfort her. But it was not a practical idea. Nor did I think she would thank me for identifying her vulnerability.

'Tell you something,' I said. 'The more I think about it, the more upset I feel. Innocents at the hands of brutes.' I took my handkerchief out of my pocket as she turned round.

'Want a hug?' she asked.

'That would be nice,' I said.

She crossed the room and, as I pushed myself back from the table, she knelt on the floor in front of me and we embraced, her arms wrapping over my shoulders, my hands resting flat on her lower back and waist. Her blond hair flickered in my face as she snuggled into my neck. Her scent was so feminine, I felt I was going to burst. I could feel her warmth through her blouse, and, through still fingers, I was aware of the slimness of her body, the gentle furrows of her rib cage.

'Better?' she asked softly in my ear.

'It's evil, pure evil, Grace Who could do such a thing?'

'I know, I know.'

She pulled slowly back and knelt in front of me..

'We've got to do something to stop them getting away with this, Mike.'

'But what? That's what's bugging me. Goddard's not exactly going to go a bundle on what we've been doing, is he? There's so little evidence and even what we did have has now been stolen. And this death was about thirty years ago. How easy will that be to investigate? Goddard's having enough of a challenge with one that's little more than a year old.'

She stood up,. 'I'm not going to give it up, Mike. Not now. I couldn't before for Lindsey's sake, but no way now in the light of what Dean recorded. I couldn't live with myself—could you?'

I nodded.

She stepped back and paced the kitchen floor. 'Besides, you say that poor baby died thirty years ago. True. But who has died since? Have you thought about that? Dean wasn't around to record anything else. How can people get away with murder for so long? I'm trying to get my head around it. And, of course, is the fact that Sandra and Lindsey were both pregnant relevant to all this? It just gets worse and worse, doesn't it?' She suddenly stopped pacing, crossed her arms and stood in front of me. 'Who is involved with the coven? We need to find someone and talk to them.'

'Goddard seemed to know something, but wouldn't let on. Data protection and all that kind of bloody rubbish,' I said.

'What does Dean say? You mention this novice who joined the coven. Does he give any identities?'

'Not really…'

'What do you mean, "not really"? Black or white, isn't it, Mike?'

'I'm afraid not. Near the start of his notebook he listed thirteen names, starting with "Me". Just single names, no surnames and, as I recall, some pretty wacky ones.'

'Wacky?'

'Well, not your standard John or George or Jane. I'm kicking myself that I didn't jot them down. I just never expected to lose the book. Besides, they didn't exactly help to identify anyone.'

'Do you remember any?'

'No, sorry—save for two. They were both on the list. The first one was Lucinda.'

'And the second one?'

'Ah yes, the second one. He was mentioned several times, and I know who he was by the context.'

'Go on.'

'He was referred to as Guy the Grey Wolf. I said it was all pretty wacky. And he was the novice, then about twenty years old. The one who led to Dean leaving the cult. The one who became the newly appointed summoner. The one who just escaped the fire tragedy with his nanny. The financier Edward Denning's only son: Clifford.'

FIFTY-ONE

I heard the car enter the drive and its engine cut. A slam of a
driver's door and the sounds of someone approaching the
house. Confident, firm steps of expensive leather shoes. The
slight pause as the area was scanned for a bell, which then
rang, echoing in the stillness of the hallway. I pushed myself
away from the sitting room window, where I'd watched my
visitor's arrival.

Jonathan Rosford had rung me shortly after my
breakfast that bright Monday morning and had told me that
Adrian Smith had telephoned again. He wanted to visit that
morning. Just him. I agreed, and the arrangements were duly
made.

I opened the door. He'd taken a step or two back and
was surveying the front of the house. He turned towards me
as the door swung open and moved back onto the step.

'Mr Miller? I'm Adrian Smith. Come to look round? I
presume Rosford's told you?'

I nodded and smiled. 'Yes, of course, Mr Smith. Come
on in.' I held out my hand and we shook as he stepped past
me into the hallway. For some reason I left the door ajar—it
was a warm day after all.

As I manoeuvred the wheelchair round, I studied him
briefly. A serious-looking man of above-average height who
I guessed was in his mid-fifties judging by his thin grey hair
brushed where he could with a traditional side parting.
Frameless glasses and a minimalist white moustache gave

him every appearance of ex-military. The straight posture and stocky but trim figure helped this impression, although the rigid back may have been due to his consciously making the most of every centimetre of height he'd been blessed with. He was dressed in a tweed jacket with patterned shirt and tie, light trousers and the well-polished brown brogues that had announced his approach to the house.

Rubbing his hands enthusiastically together, he turned towards me and asked, 'So, where do we begin?' He was well spoken. Clipped, but not rude or unpleasant. In control of himself.

'Sorry?' I said.

'The tour? Where's the tour begin?' he repeated with a slight smile although his brown eyes appeared bereft of any humour. 'I presume you've shown others round?'

'There has been some interest,' I said, suddenly feeling like a salesman. 'No well-worn route yet, but there no doubt will be one soon. Let's start with the sitting room, shall we?'

And so I gave him the tour as he put it. I wheeled myself around the house as much as I could, pointing out features, answering his questions in the most positive way I could and allowing him to peer and poke into every corner. I established that there was in fact a Mrs Smith, but she was away for a few days, and they agreed that he'd do some initial viewings to move their house-seeking project forward.

We eventually reached the kitchen for the final stop. He noticed the window with my sticking plaster cardboard. The glazier, Billy Collins, had been due early morning but had rung me to say he was delayed and would arrive when he could. Billy was a local man I'd used before who was a regular in the village shop and the pub, so I wasn't hard on him. I know I'd told Jonathan Rosford that I was going through the motions about selling, but I still had my reputation to think about. And the preservation of options is never a bad strategy.

'What's happened here?' he asked as he walked over to the window for a closer look.

'Break-in. Yesterday morning in fact. Not the best advert, I guess, but exceptional.'

'Oh,' he said with apparent surprise. He turned to look at me. 'Take much?'

'Very little,' I said, watching him carefully. 'Police have been—you know, all the usual stuff.'

Smith nodded. 'Don't get many break-ins round here though. It's a good area.'

'You live locally then, Mr Smith?'

'Adrian, please,' he said with a polite smile. He walked to the patio doors. 'Lived round here all my life,' he continued as he surveyed the garden. 'Near Westland for over twenty-five years—live two and a half miles out on the Exeter side. How long have you lived here, Michael?'

'I prefer Mike,' I said as I wheeled my way slowly across the kitchen. I paused by the table.

He looked round at me. 'Sorry—*Mike*,' he said in a friendly tone.

'Not long. I'm very new in fact. We bought it last November.'

'We?'

'My wife and I.'

'Oh, I see. Why the sudden change in plan—you've hardly been here a year, have you? Nothing wrong with the place is there?'

'Change in circumstances,' I said in a non-committal way.

He turned back to look out of the patio doors again and said slowly, 'Shouldn't really be talking to you, of course.'

'Sorry…?' I said with surprise.

He looked back at me and grinned. 'You need to have lived here for at least fifteen years before we locals regard you as one of us—twenty's safer. Until then, you're a stranger. It's nothing personal. May I look outside?' He was already stepping forward as he asked.

I smiled back as I recalled village tradition of old. 'Be my guest.'

He opened the glazed door and stepped out onto the large patio. I moved past the kitchen table and watched him as he slowly wandered round the garden and took in the view across the fields.

He turned and strode back towards the house.

'A lovely spot,' he said as he re-entered through the patio doors. 'Super views. I always thought this development would have good qualities. This bungalow seems to have the prime position.'

I nodded. 'I like to think so,' I said. 'Why didn't you buy it last year—you know, when it was first built?'

'Timing wasn't right,' he said. 'What are your plans, then? Have you found somewhere else?'

'Not yet.'

'Will there be a chain?'

I shook my head slowly. 'No, needn't be. I have a place in Sidmouth—Cliff House near the golf course—which I use as a retreat. I can always move there until I find what I want.'

Adrian nodded and looked pensive. 'Well,' he said eventually, 'I think I've seen all I need to see for now. I'll let Rosford know what I think.'

'You mean what you and Mrs Smith think?'

'Yes, yes indeed,' he said looking slightly flustered. 'Exactly that.'

I followed him through to the hallway, where we shook hands and parted.

I remained in the open doorway and watched him turn his black Porsche 911 around in the driveway. As he drove off into the cul-de-sac, the glazier's white van pulled up and parked where the Porsche had been standing moments before. Billy Collins approached the door with his toolbox swinging lazily and rhythmically in his strong left arm. He was a tall, friendly-looking man with a fine head of unruly grey curls and a lined and crinkled face that spoke of experience and hard work.

'Sorry about the delay, Mike,' he said as he paused on the front step. 'Couldn't be helped. Your "For Sale" board is attracting some attention then?'

'You mean the Porsche?'

'Aye, I do.'

'To be honest that was the first prospective buyer. I'm hoping it'll pick up.'

He smiled. 'I wish you luck with it. Never a fun time.' He paused and looked at me with a serious expression. 'As I said to you in the shop yesterday, I was so sorry to hear about Lindsey. Dreadful thing. Can I ask, any developments? You know, are the police making progress and all that?'

I shook my head. 'Sadly no. I'm told these things can take a while. We can but hope though, can't we?'

Billy nodded. 'Sure. All the best with it.' He suddenly seemed to remember the reason for his visit and stepped into the house. 'Right, where's this pesky window? Kitchen wasn't it?'

I followed his strides down the hallway and into the kitchen where he removed the piece of cardboard and reckoned it wouldn't take long to fix. He was true to his word and, while I undertook some paperwork in the office, the window was soon repaired. He appeared in the office doorway.

'Right, all done. I've vacuumed and everything. All as good as new.'

I thanked him and followed him into the hallway.

As he walked towards the front door, Billy said, 'I'll drop a bill off some time soon.'

I knew from experience that meant at least a month, but it was his business, not mine. He paused in the doorway and looked back at me. 'And good luck with the house sale.'

'Thanks,' I said.

'Moving far?'

'No plans yet. Thought I'd see how the sale went first. I can always rent locally or move back to my late parents' place, Cliff House in Sidmouth.'

Billy stepped outside and turned back to face me. 'Yeah, guess so. Still, a promising first prospective buyer, huh? I'd be getting my hopes up if it was me.'

'What do you mean? Do you know him?'

'Yeah, done some work for him in the past. Comes from money and has bought a few properties locally. Needs a glazier every now and then.'

'Looked ex-army to me.'

Billy shook his head, his curls moving in unison. 'No. Always lived around here, even after the tragedy.'

'Tragedy? Adrian Smith didn't look like a victim of a tragedy to me.'

'Smith? Is that what he called himself?' Billy smiled as

if admiring someone's gall. 'That was no Adrian Smith, Mike. That was Mr Denning himself. Clifford Denning.'

FIFTY-TWO

After Billy had gone, I sat in my wheelchair on the patio with a lunchtime sandwich and cup of tea and stared out across the narrow field to the wood. I noticed for the first time how autumn was starting to touch the leaves, but summer still held sway. The contented sheep continued to graze mindlessly on the short grass, although I struggled to see what was left for them to eat. As the sun gently warmed my face from its blue sky, I rolled my sleeves untidily up to my elbows and closed my eyes. A few minutes to calm down and reflect before Grace arrived.

Clifford Denning. The man himself had ventured out into my home. Billy had been pretty forthcoming about what he knew about the man and his background. Clifford and his thirty-year-old nanny had managed to escape a blaze that had ripped through the manorial home when he was but a small child. The fire took the life of Edward Denning, his wealthy father, a former stockbroker who had abandoned London for a quieter existence in the Devon countryside. There was something ironic about that. Apart from the manor's smouldering ruins, all Edward Denning had left behind, Billy had said, was an orphaned son and a 'shitload of investments and insurance money'.

But I knew there was more and asked Billy about what he knew.

'The coven?' he clarified. 'Sure everyone around here knows about that. We all read newspapers and the Internet.

Clifford's father was into all that. The history of the coven goes back centuries, but it had ceased to exist. Times and people change, I suppose. Anyhow, Edward Denning started it up again and it's still going to this day. Clifford Denning's involved now, according to all local gossip—indeed he's the main man I gather.'

'Didn't look like a witch to me,' I said.

'Know what you mean, but there's stuff in his house about it. I saw it when I was doing a job there once. Couldn't miss it. I understand that's why his wife divorced him.'

'So who else is involved locally, Billy?' I asked.

'No idea,' he said dismissively with a shrug. 'I've no interest in that sort of thing myself. You hear bits, that's all. I'm not one for gossip, me, I get on with my business. Mind you, not the sort of thing you want to be talking about round here,' he added seriously.

And with that he left.

Before I rang Grace, I had gone into the bedroom and opened the disguised floor safe where Lindsey had kept her best jewellery and I kept some important, original papers to save the cost of a bank safety deposit box. I also kept something else. I lifted out the Glock 17. I accept it was an illegal weapon, but it was also illegal to break into houses and to rob, threaten, and assault. I suspect most people are fearful of some sort of violent crime against them, and I was no different. Perhaps it was the visit from Denning that made me check it over and hold the unopened box of ammunition. I had never fired it. Indeed, to my knowledge it had never been fired; at least that's what the guy had told me when I bought it cheaply for cash in a pub.

I took out my mobile and rang Grace to tell her how the High Priest himself had brazenly come to my house using a false name. Grace was at the hairdresser's when I called and promised to come over as soon as the process permitted.

I opened my eyes. A couple of sheep had wandered quite close to the young hedge, only the ragged wire fence holding them off. What could this visit mean? I spent the next half hour trying to get my head round this sudden development. It was definitely hard to relax.

My thoughts were disturbed by the hurrying click of female heels on the paved path leading from the side gate. I turned to see Grace walking determinedly round the corner of the bungalow towards me.

'Hiya,' I said as she came up to me and gave me a kiss on the cheek. 'I left the gate open for you as promised.'

'You mean you've still not taken my advice then,' she said.

She settled on the seat and straightened out her knee-length, plain, white cotton skirt. She was barelegged and dressed for summer, and it struck me again what a good-looking woman she was. Her blond hair had obviously just been under the dedicated labours of a skilled hairdresser.

'You had lunch?' I asked.

'Yes, thanks,' she said with a smile. She was quiet for a moment before she looked at me. 'So what's this visit mean, Mike?'

'I'm still trying to work it out,' I replied, shifting round a hint in my wheelchair to face her. 'He gave no clues at all. He acted like a regular guy looking round a house as a prospective buyer. It was only because Billy recognised him as Clifford Denning that I am any the wiser.' This was entirely true. 'Adrian Smith' could have wandered into my home and out again without my understanding who he really was. I recalled my comment to Grace a few days before about how you wouldn't know that you were standing next to the High Priest in the Asda checkout queue.

Grace sat and thought for a moment. I watched her fingers move to her mouth and tug gently on her bottom lip as she stared across the field. She suddenly let it go and turned to me. 'Well, if he came here incognito, it must have been on some kind of reconnaissance, as he could hardly put pressure on you if you didn't know who he was.'

'Unless he was just looking to buy the house…'

'Yeah, right. And the Pope's a Muslim. Come on Mike, what the hell would the wealthy Clifford Denning want buying *this* house? With all respect to you, this is a guy who comes from a manor house.'

'Maybe he's looking to downsize, retire?'

She shook her head gently. 'I don't think so. There's some other reason. It can't be a coincidence—and, besides, I don't do coincidences.'

I nodded. 'True.'

'You could talk to your estate agent friend, Jonathan, about it, couldn't you?' she suggested. 'I guess it really is that easy to pretend to be someone else when you're looking at houses. No identification required. Give a name, any address, turn up and you're in.'

'Good idea, I'll do that.'

'You say he acted as if he didn't know you. You've never met him before, but surely he would know about Lindsey? If Lindsey were involved in the coven, and I say *if*, or *if* she were a victim of them, then he would know her that way. And even if the coven has nothing to do with her at all, then he must surely have heard about her on the news and recognised her from one of her photos—there are enough pictures of her round here.'

'In the latter case, he may have recognised her from the papers, if he'd even heard about Lindsey's death. I can't say I usually take much notice of local news and I doubt I'd remember someone's face even if I did see it once in the local rag.'

'Mm, possibly. How about local gossip?' Grace asked.

'He's probably above all that.'

'No one's above all that. I bet even royalty read OK magazine.'

I smiled. She was probably right. I watched her tugging gently on her lower lip.

'Mike, it could be that this really has nothing to do with the coven.'

'What do you mean?' I asked.

'Well, what if this is personal between Denning and yourself? That he wrote the letter to force you to sell, that he was responsible for Lindsey's death. This visit was a cover to assess your progress.'

'Sorry,' I said, giving her a bewildered look. 'Am I missing something here? What about Dean's notebook, the similarity with Sandra Roberts?'

She stood up smartly and looked down at me. 'Mike, I've just realised. We've said it enough times, but we've overlooked the obvious. We're talking here about *Clifford* Denning. What if he's the "C" who wrote that letter, who had a fling with Lindsey, who tempted her back for a final meeting? Not as the High Priest, but as her former lover?'

FIFTY-THREE

Grace wheeled me back into the house. She went into the kitchen to make us both a cup of tea, and I pushed myself into the office away from the clatter of mugs and the labouring kettle to call Jonathan Rosford from my mobile.

'How did the viewing go, Mike?' he asked.

'Okay. He turned up on his own at the agreed time, made all the right noises and disappeared off. Have you heard anything?'

'No, not yet. But it's still early.'

'Did you meet him when it was fixed up, Jonathan?'

'No. It was arranged by phone. Why d'you ask?'

'What if I told you his name wasn't Adrian Smith?'

'Go on…'

'It's Clifford Denning.'

'You're kidding. *The* Clifford Denning—how do you know that?'

'Depends who you mean by *the* Clifford Denning? There's probably more than one.'

'Not from round here there's not,' Jonathan said. 'The Clifford Denning everyone knows inherited a fortune from his father when he was a kid. Was brought up by some aunt. Is that the one you mean?'

'Yes, absolutely. So why the alias?'

Jonathan was quiet for a moment. 'He has an interest in investment properties, Mike.' he said. 'Bought quite a few properties locally. Perhaps he thought we'd increase the price if we knew he was interested.'

Grace appeared in the office doorway carrying two mugs of tea. She placed one carefully on a coaster on my desk in front of me. I caught her eye and nodded a thanks. She settled into Lindsey's desk chair, sipped her tea and listened in. I pressed the speaker button on my mobile so she could hear.

'So you think he's a genuine buyer?'

Jonathan laughed. 'Why else would he have been there, Mike? He's hardly checking the place out for a burglary— you've got nothing he can't buy. Drives a Roller for God's sake.'

I caught Grace's eye. 'Let it go,' she whispered. I thanked Jonathan, who promised to contact me should he hear further from 'Adrian Smith' and agreed with my request to go along with Denning's alias for the time being.

'Well, that sounds like the answer then,' I said. 'Keeping a low profile for an investment purchase. Makes sense, I guess.'

'Maybe,' Grace said slowly. 'But I'm not convinced, Mike.

'Sure, it's really odd,' I said. 'But why would he visit without any obvious threat if someone connected with the coven broke in yesterday and stole Dean's notebook? I'm not sure what Denning would gain by such a visit if one of his minions reported back yesterday.'

Grace fiddled absentmindedly with a pencil on the desk. 'Okay,' she said eventually, tossing the pencil gently to the back of the desk. 'Let's say this has nothing to do with the coven and that Clifford Denning did have a fling with Lindsey and is now looking to buy you out.'

'But that doesn't add up, Grace, does it? He has nothing

against me if I'm just the cuckold, even less so now Lindsey's gone. And further, if he did in fact meet up with her and kill her, or even if the coven killed her, then I'm still nothing to him—or them come to that.'

Grace shook her head. 'You're forgetting that letter, Mike. For whatever reason the killer wants you out of this house. Wants you to sell it. You must mean something else why go to all that hassle to write to you?'

I shrugged.

'They must have a reason,' she said. 'Okay we can't see it, don't understand it, but it's obvious, isn't it, that someone, somewhere must have it in for you personally?'

'Come on, I'm just the widower. The guy left behind— and a bewildered one at that.'

She paused for a moment and then her face lit up. 'Hey, maybe that's the point,' she said enthusiastically, placing her hands on her knees. 'Maybe that's *exactly* the point.'

I looked at her quizzically. 'What d'you mean?'

'Don't you see? You're so bewildered, Mike, so passionate about Lindsey, that you've started making enquiries, started to turn over stones.'

'But the police are doing that. What's so special about our enquiry?'

'We are dealing with Chief Inspector Goddard remember, the great detective who has spent over a year getting exactly nowhere with finding the person who murdered Sandra Roberts. Now, amateurs like us, filled with determination and brazen gall, could make quicker progress than the money-strapped, over-worked detective meandering down various "lines of enquiry".'

I thought for a moment as she beamed at me. 'Okay,' I said slowly, 'but no one knows I'm doing that, least of all

Denning.'

'Really? Think about it. You've already engaged with Charles and Martin—and Jonathan Rosford in a way. And Ada Hoyle and Gary Roberts. There's even Edith from the shop and Billy the glazier. And I talked to Jason—you know, Gary and Sandra's son—as well as my parents' old friend, Judith Podmore. And there's even your private detective, Jack what's-his-name. That's quite a cast of characters, and one of them may have a link to Mr Influential Denning, even through another third party. If you think about it, Mike, there are thirteen members in that coven. We only know one— Denning. Who are the other twelve? And even if, in the most unlikely scenarios, Lindsey was another, that still leaves eleven other locals who might be involved. All of whom have connections.'

I reflected for a moment.

Grace said, 'And that's not the whole cast, either.'

I looked up at her. 'Isn't it? Who else?'

'At least six members of the local police force.'

FIFTY-FOUR

After Grace had left for her weekly tennis lesson with her coach, Rob, I spent the rest of the Monday at home. Other than agree to a couple more viewings with Jonathan, I didn't do much—not until the visitor turned up anyway. I was in the office at about eight o'clock when I heard the motorbike. I paused what I was doing and listened carefully. I thought I recognised the sound from the last time. As I wheeled my way across the hallway, the bell rang. I opened the door. Mistake. Smelling like he'd spent his afternoon knocking back beers, Frank stormed into the hallway, almost tripping on the doorstep as he did so. He regained his posture and, breathing heavily, he glared down at me.

'You're having an affair, aren't you, Michael?'

'Get out, Frank.'

'Screwing that Grace woman, eh? You married Lindsey for the family money, didn't you? *Didn't you?*'

'I'm going to ring the police, Frank.' I started to push myself backwards, but he stepped forward and placed one of his large feet against a wheel.

'Out the way, Frank.' I said, although I realised he was hardly going to listen.

'Tell the truth. You had her killed, didn't you?' His face was red, and I genuinely felt threatened. I started to regret not telling Goddard about this brute, and realised my folly in thinking that I could handle the situation. I had to keep calm.

'I loved her Frank. That might be hard for you to

understand, but it's true, okay? And I'm not having an affair—not with Grace nor with anyone else come to that. I was happily married, Frank, and I'd planned to be that way all my life. So please back off, okay?'

'You must have been seeing this Grace skank while you were married.' He stepped back from the wheelchair and placed his large right hand on the wall for support. 'You simply don't sleep with someone just like that.'

'Just like what? I'm not sleeping with Grace, Frank—not that it's any of your business.'

'It sure is my business, and don't you forget that. Anything to do with the family money's my business, okay?' He tried to move away from the wall, but rapidly replaced his hand for evident support. 'I haven't just been sitting on my ass. I've been making enquiries about you, Michael, making friends. Your neighbour Craig's been mighty helpful.' He belched loudly. 'You stayed overnight at her place on Monday night, didn't you?'

His accurate assertion took me by surprise. 'I've nothing to say to you, Frank, other than to repeat that I'm not sleeping with Grace, so please leave.'

'Fuck you.'

'I was going to give you and Rosie some money, Frank, but I've changed my mind. I won't be bullied by you nor sit here listening to your stupid accusations.'

He finally pushed himself away from the wall and edged towards the open door. 'You told the police about me, Michael?'

I studied him. 'Why would I, Frank? You're just a scrounging relative come round with a begging bowl.'

'Sure was, but you've kicked me when I'm down, Michael. Kicked Lindsey's own fucking cousin and his sick sister. Bastard. It's no more mister nice guy now.'

'You can't touch me. You might be able to get away with shit like that in Canada, but not here, believe me.'

'Oh, I can hurt you, Michael. You believe me, I can hurt you. And not only you, but your girlfriend too.'

'Leave her out of this, Frank.'

'Are you gonna make me?'

'Don't tempt me.'

He laughed loudly and sarcastically. 'You're a fucking cripple, Michael. I dunno how you can screw anything, but you sure can, eh? And you can pay for someone to kill poor Lindsey—'

'Get out, Frank,' I shouted. *'Get out of here now.'*

He hesitated, wavered in the doorway, and then seemed to make a decision. 'I'm going, Michael,' he said, 'but things are gonna start happening round here. I've got nothin' to lose now. Nothin'. And if you do say *anything* about me to the police, your girlfriend will get it. Got me?'

With that he left the house, and I moved quickly to slam the door after him. I slumped back into my wheelchair, gripped the arms and listened to him kick-start his motorbike and ride away.

FIFTY-FIVE

I'm not one for argumentative confrontations, but Frank really wound me up. I festered on his ridiculous accusation and the unreasonableness of his brash approach until it was starting to eat me up. On reflection I should have rung Grace to help me calm down, but I didn't. Instead I went out into the darkened evening and trundled down the close to Craig's bungalow. The fact that he appeared to be riding shotgun for Frank seemed, in some curious sort of way, a treacherous move on his part even though there was no logical rationale in reaching such an emotional conclusion.

Craig's bungalow was all but in darkness save for a bright porch lamp and a hall light visible through the frosted narrow windows in the front door. I stretched up and rang the loud doorbell, long and hard. Nothing happened. I sat for a moment or two and then stretched up a second time. I'd hardly settled back in my wheelchair when I saw movement in the hallway and Craig opened the door a short way and peered out.

He looked down at me with an impassive stare. 'Yeah?'

'I gather you've been making buddies with Canadians,' I said.

'What if I have?'

'Well back off, Craig. Mind your own business, and get out of mine.'

'My business is my business, now sod off and get off my property.'

I remained where I was. 'What is it with you? Why you interfering where you shouldn't, helping out a drunk living in a fantasy world?'

I thought he was going to raise the stakes. He took a short step towards me, but then seemed to change his mind. He just stared down at me.

'I have my reasons. Now piss off.' And he closed the door deliberately and quietly. The hall light went out.

I sat staring at the door. I was tempted to ring the doorbell again, but I realised it would be a futile exercise, whether Craig answered it or not.

I returned home and lay down on my bed. That's when I rang Grace.

'You okay, Mike? You sound out of breath.'

'Just had a run-in with Craig—you know, the miserable git next door.'

'What about?'

It was time to tell her. 'Do you remember Lindsey had a couple of Canadian cousins? Her mum's sister's children? Frank and Rosie.'

'Vaguely. Why?'

'Frank turned up here the other evening.'

'Really? When was this? Why didn't you tell me?'

'Didn't think it was relevant.'

'Not relevant? Come on, Mike. Of course it's relevant. What did he want?'

'Money. Came with a large begging bowl wanting a lot of Lindsey's money.'

'What did you say?'

'That I'd think about it. They are relatives after all. She's got MS and they're as broke as church mice. But he's a brute of a man, Grace. He was back this evening and told me he's involved this Craig to help him spy on me. It's all pretty unpleasant. That's why I visited Craig to give him my view on life.'

'I see.' She was quiet for a moment as no doubt her brain had started to work on the new information.

'I should tell you something else,' I continued.

'What?'

'According to dear Frank, we're having an affair...'

'*What*?'

'He knew I'd stayed over at your house the other night.'

'But that's rubbish. I'd like to give him a piece of my mind. Have you told Goddard about Frank?'

'No. Didn't see the point until now. And Frank's threatened us if I tell the police.'

'Threatened? Us?'

'Yeah. He sees us as an item. I said he was a brute.'

'What's going on, Mike? I feel this is rather unfairly running away from me.'

'I understand that. I'm sorry you're in the middle of all this. So it seems we're both being spied on—might explain "the watcher" you saw in Cowgate Street, though.'

'That's interesting,' she said, and paused for a moment. 'So what's this Craig got against you then? He seems to have some real issues.'

'Dunno. I know nothing about him. He's definitely off piste though.' A large spider scuttled across the bedroom floor. 'Grace,' I continued, 'how about some supper on Wednesday night to discuss all this further?'

'Love to, Mike, but a guy's invited me out to dinner. We could meet tomorrow though so we can get on with it. I was in two minds whether to accept, what with our investigation and everything, but life goes on and a couple hours of normality might even sharpen me up—especially now I've heard about Frank and his accusations.'

I was silent for a moment as I reflected on how much a part of my everyday life Grace had become.

'Who's the date with?'

'It's not a date, just dinner.'

'That sounds like a date to me. Boy takes girl out, what else is it?'

'You sound angry?'

'Who's the boy?'

'My tennis coach. He asked me this afternoon.'

'Rob Barker?' I said. 'He used to give Lindsey lessons. Hell of a lot younger than you, isn't he?'

'About the same age as you, actually. Single, fit, with nice legs.' She stopped suddenly. 'Sorry, Mike, I didn't mean…'

I let it hang there.

'Mike?'

'That hurt.'

'I said I'm sorry.'

I held the phone tighter and looked across at the pillow next to me. 'You know he has a reputation as a bit of a womaniser, don't you? If you must go, be careful.'

'It's just a dinner.'

'I'll get on with the investigation then. You play.'

'I said we can meet tomorrow. It's just a couple of hours on Wednesday evening, Mike.'

'Depends what type of date…'

'It's *dinner*, Mike—now drop it.'

'Okay,' I said, and stretched my arm across Lindsey's pillow. 'We'll meet tomorrow then. What are we going to cover?'

She paused as if regrouping her thoughts. 'Right. I think we'd better tell Goddard about these threats by Frank, as well as Craig's involvement. It's really troubling me. Perhaps throw in the visit by High Priest Denning—there's surely something going on there, isn't there?'

'Agreed. I'll fix a meeting.' I paused. 'I've decided I'm going to report Martin now, too. Thumping me in the face and tipping me out of my wheelchair in a fit of rage is hardly normal is it? Rather shows the character of the man, doesn't it?'

'We're going to have to do that, I guess.' Grace replied. 'I said so at the time, but you wanted to reflect on it. Some water has passed under the bridge now and I don't want to start a war with him. I've been through all that. But I suppose there's really little choice if we are going to progress this.'

'*He* started this war, Grace,' I said in a sharper tone than I'd intended. '*Both* of the wars if we're counting. Your acrimonious divorce and now this.'

'I know.'

'So we can't let him get away with it, can we?' I said firmly. 'He may have wormed his way into your heart, but you're not thinking it's okay for him to assault me, are you? You seem hesitant. Seems like fit Rob has diverted your attention…'

'That's not fair. I'm not at all hesitant, Mike. I know what we must do. It's not like that.'

'So what is it like?'

She paused and said in a quieter tone, 'Look, let's not fall out over this. I treasure our friendship. Of course he shouldn't get away with it, I've said that, I just know what he's like, that's all. But we can cope with whatever he might throw at us, I'm sure of that.'

I said nothing.

'You there, Mike?'

'Yeah.'

'Look, ring Goddard in the morning and fix an urgent visit. I can drive us.' She took a breath. 'We're going for this. Always have been, always will, whether it upsets Martin or not, huh?'

'I'll fix it,' I said. 'Martin's hardly going to repeat it, is he? He can't be that stupid.'

We closed the call on a slightly more upbeat note, but something made me feel quite low.

FIFTY-SIX

Rob Barker stepped out of the shower, careful to avoid putting his wet feet on the tennis kit that was strewn all over the floor. He dried himself off with a white towel before spraying expensive eau de toilette over his athletic body. He entered the dark bedroom, lit only by the light from the en suite behind him. The large double bed disclosed a shape.

Grace emerged naked from under the duvet and looked at him. 'Nice legs,' she said. 'Come here, I need you.'

He strutted to the bedside and stared down at her. 'You look pretty good yourself, Mrs Robinson.'

Then he was on her and in her until she was lying on her side, looking at his sleeping back in the rays of the en suite.

'Again?' she asked.

Rob stirred and slowly turned over to face her. His hair was suddenly bushy, his beard grey and immense. Frank said to her, 'I'm going to hurt you.'

He started to push her towards the edge of the bed. She fought back, but then she was falling, falling towards a rocky shore far below.

I woke up.

The macabre visions of my Monday night dream were still real in my memory as we drove down that Tuesday afternoon to Exeter. We sat together in the same miserable, green interview room with both DCI Goddard and DS Ward as Goddard had been too busy to call on us at my home. Personally, I was pretty certain that a long interview had taken place in that room earlier from its oppressive atmosphere of warm air and stale body odour. I don't think it escaped Grace's attention either, from the look she gave me. There was no window to throw open. A long burst of air freshener would have worked wonders.

With Grace's prompt, I'd started with Martin's visit, which was an easy one in terms of my breach of promise to Goddard about playing Poirot. My injuries were fortunately minor—just a couple of bruises which I could exhibit to him. Goddard looked sceptical until I produced my mobile and backed up my official complaint, as I deemed it, by playing the recording of the incident and he consequently agreed to interview Martin.

The next phase of our conversation was a little trickier in terms of my involvement. Grace told him that she'd visited Ada, which was true, and about Dean's notebook. I chipped in every now and then, mentioning the theft of the book in particular. He seemed resigned to hear us out until I mentioned the death of the baby.

'Hang on, hang on,' Goddard said, leaning back in his chair and folding his arms. 'Are you saying that Dean Wilson actually wrote a statement to that effect?'

'Not to that effect,' I said. 'It's what he *actually* wrote. In some detail.'

'That sounds complete nonsense. Do you seriously believe that a random group of local men and women have been killing babies in Littleworth Wood for over thirty years?'

'Look, Chief Inspector, all I can say is that Dean wrote this in his notebook.'

'Anything in more recent times is obviously speculative,' Grace said. 'But it's also curious, is it not, that both Sandra Roberts and Lindsey were several months pregnant—and both Mike and I have had the skulls of babies left on our respective doorsteps? Well?'

I have to admit Goddard looked flustered as if his mind were spinning, not helped when DS Ward confirmed my statement that the notebook had indeed been stolen in the reported burglary.

Goddard at first said nothing. Just stared at us. Then he removed his glasses and said, 'Well, this is all very interesting, but I'm not sure how much further it takes us. I find the references to this coven in Littleworth Wood a touch fanciful, if I'm honest.'

'*Fanciful*. Well, explain this then.' And I told them both about Clifford Denning's visit to my home, ostensibly to view it. I stressed the deception of 'Adrian Smith' and the emergence of another individual with a name beginning with the letter C. I reminded them of the letter I'd shown them several days before.

I was however stumped when Goddard queried how someone could intimidate if he was both unknown to me and said nothing threatening. Even Grace looked stuck for an answer.

'So if he wasn't there to intimidate Mike, what was he there for?' Grace asked.

'That's for him to answer, not me.'

'Are you going to then?' I said.

'Am I going to what?' Goddard said.

'Ask him about his visit. Ask him why he came to my home.'

'I will. But I suspect he'll say he was viewing it with

an eye to buying it,' Goddard said in a matter-of-fact tone.

'He may say that—bound to say that, I guess. But whether he's being honest...' I allowed my voice to drift away.

'Nothing else, I presume, both of you?' Goddard said, making to stand up.

'Actually, yes,' Grace said. 'We've been threatened.'

Goddard's face looked weary. 'Threatened?' he said calmly. 'By who now?'

'Tell him, Mike,' Grace said.

So I told Goddard about Frank and his threats, both against Grace and myself, and how he wanted 'half the family money' for his terminally ill sister and himself. I threw in the involvement of Craig for good measure. 'What you going to do about it, Chief Inspector?'

'Nothing until we can find him. If he shows up again either ask him where he's staying or give us a ring, okay' Goddard said.

'It always seems to be nothing,' I said, glaring at him. 'I told you he's accusing us of having an affair. He's a brute of a man and quite irrational in my view. I am concerned for our safety, especially for Grace.'

'We can only do so much, Mr Miller.'

'That's not overly encouraging from my point of view,' Grace said.

I started to sound off but realised he was right to some degree—not that I admitted that. After Goddard took yet another glance at his watch, Grace and I were obliged to wrap up our meeting.

As Grace pushed me to her waiting BMW, she said, 'I'm fascinated to see how Martin reacts.'

Having a mutual enemy seemed to be the best focus to

273

heal our previous evening's disagreement. 'I agree,' I said, and inwardly reflected whether the war would in fact escalate—and, if so, how.

FIFTY-SEVEN

After returning from Exeter police station, I spent the balance of Tuesday at home and volunteered in the shop on Wednesday morning and for part of that afternoon too. There seemed little else that Grace and I could actively do pending Goddard's further enquiries. Since returning to the shop after Lindsey's death, I'd been more erratic with my attendance. Edith didn't mind. I think she just welcomed some company in the shop—she could make tea for two, which no doubt reminded her of when her much-missed George had been alive and they'd run the dinky store and post office together as a harmonious couple.

In the stillness of the house later that afternoon, I did some Internet research and scribbled diagrams and doodles on sheets of paper in a further effort to connect all events and make something meaningful that would explain the various threads and occurrences. My mind kept returning to Grace and I missed her input. I was on the point of calling her once, but on reflection, I placed my mobile back down on my desk. I reasoned that it would be better to come up with something universally credible first.

It was then that my mobile rang. I'd selected the classic ringtone of the black dial-faced telephones of my childhood, which my parents had retained at Cliff House well past their 'use by' date. Indeed, they still stood in their original locations, useless and silent now since I'd had the line disconnected. My mobile described the ringtone as 'old phone'. Couldn't argue with that.

I answered it on the fourth ring. 'Yes, Chief Inspector.'

Goddard reported confidently that he'd interviewed both Clifford Denning and Martin Atkins. The former at his home, the latter that morning under caution at Exeter police station. Neither had been amused by his intervention.

'Martin Atkins was calm and had a lawyer with him. Some hot shot who'd trekked west from London. No expense spared, it seemed. Especially at such short notice. On hearing the recording, Martin admitted the assault and has been cautioned.'

'*Cautioned*? You mean that's the end of it?'

'Yes, as long as he behaves.'

'Terrific,' I said with strong sarcasm. 'British justice, huh? Sounds more like some kind of cost-saving measure to me. Where's the fairness in that? Whack a paraplegic in the face and tip them out of their wheelchair in their very own home and get a tap on the back of the hand. Pathetic.'

'Mr Miller, it's standard procedure in such cases. He has no previous record. The police are well within their rights to caution—'

'And what about *my rights*, huh?' I asked angrily. 'What about *my right* not to have some hooligan crashing into my own home? What about *my right* not to be thumped at will in the bloody face? What about *my right* as a paraplegic not to be thrown out of my sodding wheelchair by some fully fit, sadistic madman? Well?'

'I understand how you might feel, Mr Miller,' was the calm, measured response.

'Do you? Do you really? I find that somewhat surprising, Chief Inspector. What incentive is there for

Atkins not to do this to me again, huh?'

Still calm and measured, Goddard said, 'Because he knows he'll be arrested.'

'And slapped on the hand again...'

'No, it would be more serious the next time. This original offence would be back on the agenda.' He paused a beat. 'But it seemed to me that Mr Atkins blames your intervention more on his ex than on you. Thinks she's behind it all and put you up to it.'

'So he's going to take it out on her now is he? She's not "behind it" as you say. Not at all. I trust you warned him to keep away from her?'

'Of course.'

'Why "*of course*"? Not seen much initiative from the police around here.'

'Mr Miller—' Goddard said firmly.

'Okay, okay,' I said with a degree of concession. 'I'm sorry, Chief Inspector. I just find this all very frustrating. And so what about Denning—what did he have to say?'

'Mr Denning was more than surprised by my visit, Mr Miller. I faced a lot of sarcasm along the lines of "what's this country coming to if a gentleman can't legitimately view a property without having the CID call round". He remained calm, but he was undoubtedly put out.'

'Well, if it was so legitimate, why the alias? Did you ask him that?'

'Of course. As Jonathan Rosford surmised, Denning chalked it up to a discreet reconnaissance by a well-known property investor not wanting to stimulate a price hike.'

'There's a surprise. I guess it's difficult to disprove that.'

'Agreed.'

'And did he know my wife before I met her? Is he the "C" who wrote to her?'

'He said he knew neither you nor your late wife, Mr Miller. He said that the first time he met you was at your bungalow when he viewed the property. I have every impression that the man is well connected and was being straight with me. Although it's true that he played his cards very close to his chest. Frankly, there's not much else I can do so far as Mr Denning is concerned.'

I raised my voice. 'But what about the coven? Dean's notebook? Everyone knows Denning is the main guy. One of his lot must have nicked the book—you know, broken into my home. What did he have to say about that?'

'Mr Miller, I have no evidence whatsoever that your burglary had anything to do with this coven, let alone Mr Denning.'

'Unbelievable,' I said with frustration and sarcasm. 'Unbelievable. What will it take to get you to do something about this coven, Chief Inspector? It's staring you right in the face. If only I was in your position—I'd do your job properly.'

As soon as I said it I realised it was a little harsh. But I couldn't rewind and delete.

There was silence down the phone.

Goddard then spoke calmly. 'Mr Miller, I am an experienced and trained detective. I have ways of doing things. The police have ways of doing things. I appreciate you may see things differently, but I am the professional here. The judgement call is mine.'

'I could be forgiven for thinking that you don't want to investigate Clifford Denning and the coven.'

'What do you mean by that?' he said sharply.

'Well, tell me why you haven't made such enquiries. The murder of at least one small baby, however many decades ago, surely warrants a police investigation? Well, doesn't it?'

'Mr Miller, I'm not at liberty to tell you what the police have or have not investigated in the course of your wife's murder, or indeed what we have investigated in connection with any other serious allegation of a crime—'

'Oh forget it,' I said with frustration and anger in my voice. 'Just forget it. I'm just going to have to sell up and get the hell out of here. Good afternoon, Chief Inspector.'

I clicked off the phone with venom and slammed it down before staring out of the window in the silence that enveloped me.

FIFTY-EIGHT

I hardly had a chance to reflect on my run-in with Goddard before my mobile rang again. I'd reached the door of my study on my way to grab a beer from the kitchen when the old phone ringtone summoned me back. My immediate reaction was that it was Goddard calling back, but the number was withheld.

I pressed the answer button. 'Mike Miller.'

'Mr Miller, this is Clifford Denning.' Firm, positive—even more choleric than Goddard himself. Must have been quite a meeting between them. I'd have paid good money for a ringside seat.

It was arguably fortunate that Denning rang when I'd recently been in full flow with Goddard. My conversation with him had put me in a mood where I was not going to be walked on. I was ready for a no-nonsense approach with all comers. Bring them on. At least that's how I thought.

'Are you sure you're Clifford Denning?' I said. 'So not Adrian Smith today? How the hell did you get my number, Denning?'

'I have connections, Mr Miller. I know quite a lot about you. I've made it my business.'

'I'm certainly not your business.'

'You'd be surprised. Anyone who crosses me becomes my business. Be very aware of that. For example, I don't appreciate a police visit. You may be in a wheelchair, but that makes no difference to me, okay? I suggest you make

280

amends by accepting my offer on your house. It's under the high asking price, but not unreasonably so. It's time to move, Mr Miller. Talk it through with Grace.'

'How the—'

'I'm going to keep this very short, Mr Miller. I don't expect to hear that you've been stirring things up with the police again. On anything. Is that clear? I'm not a happy man, Mr Miller. That's not good news for you to hear, believe me. So, accept the offer by noon tomorrow and we'll call it quits. I can assure you, in the clearest possible of terms, that you shouldn't mess with me. Understand? Goodbye.'

And he rang off. Just like that.

I went into the kitchen and looked out of the patio doors. It was drizzling and looked pretty miserable outside. I was going to need the heating on at this rate. Who the hell did Denning think he was? He might, as he said, have connections. He certainly had the money to research me in any event—he only needed someone like my cash-hungry investigator, Jack Hendon, I guess. Wouldn't take long. Or was there more to it than that?

As I watched the sheep in the adjacent field, I dialled Jonathan Rosford. The receptionist put me straight through.

'Jonathan? Mike Miller here.'

'Mike, I was about to call you.'

'About the offer?'

That surprised him. 'How did you know? Just had it.'

'From Denning…'

'Sure—and literally Denning. None of that Adrian Smith stuff anymore. I'm not sure exactly what's happening here, Mike. I know you said originally that you didn't intend to sell, and we set the asking price too high. But this is actually a great offer though—merely twenty-five under. If you're going to change your mind after all and sell, this is the offer. I should take it. Might be worth a slight haggle, but, knowing Denning, I doubt it. I know there are a couple more viewings, but there's no chain here. Straight cash purchase. Quick sale—and no finance either. Good to go. Shall I accept? What do you want me to do, Mike?'

I rubbed my chin slowly and watched a rain drop snake leisurely down the patio door glass. Despite everything, in my mind there was only one direction I could go bearing in mind Denning's approach.

'I hear what you say, Jonathan. It's a good offer. Call him back. Thank him for the offer. Tell him Mr Miller has taken everything into account and has no wish to sell to him at any price.'

FIFTY-NINE

Passionate as I was to investigate Lindsey's murder, I realised having an evening out with Rob was a helpful break and, just like any holiday, I felt it would refresh me, perhaps even inspire me. And it didn't take me long to identify the secret of Rob Barker's success with women.

The tall handsome tennis coach, with his wavy blond hair, designer stubble and athletic physique, had honed his gentlemanly charms and manners to a fine art. Every minute I was in his company, be it travelling in his car or dining at the exquisite French restaurant, I felt as if no one were more important in the world than me. In his day, Martin had been lovely—polite, attentive, amusing, if a little brash—but beside Rob, he was a clumsy oaf, a blathering buffoon. Maybe I should have chosen someone more Rob-like when I was younger.

It was dark when we finally emerged from the candlelit oasis and he drove me home in his metallic blue, Audi A3. As we entered Tiverton, I thanked him and said, 'I can't believe I've never found that place before.'

'Probably too romantic for Martin,' he said with a smile. 'His loss is my gain—taking you there for the first time, I mean,' he added quickly. For the first time that evening he looked slightly flustered.

I patted him on the knee. 'I know what you mean,' I said.

He parked up on the road outside my house and

walked round the bonnet to my car door. As he took my hand to help me out, he said, 'Thanks, Grace. That was a great evening. Really enjoyed it.' He paused momentarily and then added, 'Shame to end it.'

I smiled at him and kissed him on the cheek. 'I agree. It's been great—maybe make it longer next time…'

He seemed to relax, as if he knew where he stood after a period of uncertainty. 'Sure. Of course. I'll ring you.' He kissed me on my cheek and returned to the car.

As I walked down the path, I turned to give him a brief wave as he sped away. Not sure if he saw it.

If I was being honest, I'd been more than tempted to respond positively to his final advance. Not only did I find Rob overwhelmingly attractive physically, but also his manners and his humour had sent his appeal into the stratosphere. But despite my rekindled desires, I wanted to focus my thoughts back on finding Lindsey's killer—the evening out had inevitably exceeded the two hours after all.

As I approached the front door, I dipped into my handbag for my house keys. And it was then that I noticed the more than obvious fact that I'd forgotten to leave the porch light on. That surprised me. I was well and truly into the habit of leaving that light on when I went out. As my fingers searched inside my small bag, I glanced around. I hadn't left *any* lights on. The whole house was in darkness. I could have sworn I'd left the hall light on, and possibly my bedroom light. Nothing. None of the usual light around the edges of the front door. Just dark windows reflecting guardian streetlights. Even the moon was buried in ever-thickening cloud. I felt a couple of gentle raindrops fall on my face, one on my hand.

My searching fingers suddenly touched metal and with

a sense of relief I plucked out the small bunch of keys. I turned towards the remote street light in a desperate bid to see what I needed and squinted at them, turning them round gingerly and methodically in my hand. I selected what I thought was the small Yale key and approached the door. For some reason I shivered. Maybe it was because it was cooler. Maybe it was because I sensed something wasn't quite right

I heard a distant, old female voice in my head saying, '*I have grave concerns about you.*'

All was still. I glanced round. No sign of life from any of my neighbours' houses at this late hour. No movement in the street. All quiet.

I faced the door. I thought I heard a slight noise from around the corner of the house to my right.

'Hello?' I called. 'Who's there?'

I stood still, staring into the gloom. But I neither saw nor heard anything further.

I shrugged and stepped up to the door, key poised. I could feel the soft give of the doormat under my feet and the increasing pace of the raindrops on the porch's narrow roof above my head.

I thought I heard the noise again.

'Hello?' I called, peering into the darkness.

No response. Nothing.

I shivered and fumbled with my key. And dropped them. The small bunch clattered on the stone step and was quiet.

'Shit.'

I crouched down on my haunches and felt for the step with my hand. I grew more and more agitated as my fingers ran randomly over the step's rough stone and the coarseness of the mat. There was a torch in my car, but the car keys were in the house. If Rob had hung on I could have used a torch from his car, if he had one, but that wasn't an option. I hated being outmanoeuvred. The step was cold and slightly damp. I was torn between looking down into the darkness and keeping an eye on the corner of the house. I tried to pull myself together and was making good progress until the vision of the painted skull returned to my memory. Despite all logic, and because of tiredness, I suddenly thought the damp step was fresh red paint, or even blood, and I recoiled, whisking my hand away. With my eyes on the corner of the house, I carefully sniffed my fingers in the darkness, like some Wild West tracker. Water, not gloss.

'This is so annoying,' I said out loud. Glancing back to the gate and then once more towards the corner of the house, I resumed the search for the keys. A methodical approach was necessary and so my hand now made orderly runs, like a farmer's harrow, across the step and mat and then down into the adjoining lawn.

They weren't on the step but had fallen into the edge of the lawn. With huge relief that the waste of time was over, I grasped them and, holding them firmly as if they'd been messing me about, stood up. Once more I attempted to select the right key. Once more I thought I'd located the Yale. I scratched around the key casement until the key slid reluctantly into the hole. And turned. With one final glance at the corner of the house, I pushed the door open and reached for the light switch on the wall to my right.

I found it straight away and clicked it down. Nothing happened. Just a click, no light. I turned it off and on with increasing speed. What was wrong now? But in discordance with all logic, nothing happened. Just clicks. The hall remained in deep, impenetrable darkness. There must have been a power cut—so why were the streetlights on? I could have sworn I heard a further noise behind me outside, so I entered quickly, shutting the door firmly behind me with a curious mixture of safety and fear.

The blackness was all around me. As I mentioned before, there was no hall window to allow even the streetlights to enter. I decided I would try the kitchen light, since, if that too was out, I could get the torch fixed into its charger on the wall. Even though I was very familiar with the layout of the hall and the clear route to the kitchen door, I took slow, minute steps in what I thought was the correct direction. I held my arms in front of me like a steady sleepwalker and tipped my head ever so slightly to my right and downwards with my eyes half-closed, using the stronger peripheral vision.

I edged across the hall floor, my hands caressing the darkness. I guess I'd travelled a couple of metres when I felt it. My outstretched right hand touched something soft yet firm in front of me at my shoulder height. I recoiled. 'What the... ?' All was still. I slowly eased my hand forward again. It was still there. I brought my left hand forward and touched it. I couldn't fathom it out. The object was tall, quite narrow and moved under my touch. I eased round it and stepped towards the kitchen.

I reached the kitchen door. It was closed. I ran my right hand down the wood until it reached the handle. I turned it and pushed it open into the room. The kitchen was brighter with what little light there was breaking in through the two small windows whose curtains stood to attention either side. I flicked the switch, but the bulb remained off. I crossed more speedily to the near work surface and with some relief found the torch in its rightful place. My fingers curled round its plastic handle and I snapped it from its grounding and turned it on. A strong beam pierced the darkness across the kitchen to the closed laundry room door where it seemed to shatter and diffuse.

I crossed to the fuse box on the far wall. I saw that the main red switch had sprung and turned the whole system off. I leant upwards and pressed it down. The kitchen exploded with light.

As my eyes adjusted, I noticed my right hand was covered with blood, which was also smeared in random streaks on the plastic handle of the torch. I recoiled and dropped the torch, which fell with a noisy clatter to the kitchen floor and bounced on the quarry tiles before coming to rest, its light extinguished. The bulb or some essential mechanism had broken.

I looked at my hand, twisted it round. The amount of blood was minimal but enough to make me rush over to the sink. I turned on the taps and watched the blood swirl into the water and spin round down the plughole. I rapidly dispensed an excessive amount of hand soap as if my life depended on it and vigorously washed my hands like a surgeon scrubbing up for an urgent operation.

My mind was racing, but I couldn't help but conclude that the liquid on the outside doorstep was in fact blood. I would have to take a look. I dried my hands and hurried back through the kitchen door. I moved more purposefully than I felt. I guess the adrenaline was pumping overtime, giving me a deceptive bout of confidence and courage. I found the light switch at the kitchen end of the hall. I briskly turned it on and the room was fully lit.

And I stared in utter confusion and disbelief.

There, hanging from a black beam across the ceiling and gently rocking from the impetus I'd given it, was the bloodied body of my poor Labrador, Barney.

SIXTY

After I'd rung the police, I rang Rob as I calculated that he'd be still driving home. I needed physical help to take Barney down, the sort of assistance that would have been beyond Mike. If it had been earlier in the evening, I might have rung a neighbour or a friend, but it was in my view too late at night and too macabre a request. Rob was the only choice. He answered on his hands-free and I could tell that he was surprised to receive my call. I told him what had happened. There was a period of long silence down the phone.

'Rob, are you still there?'

'Sure. Sorry. Is this for real?'

'Yes, it really is, Rob. Can you turn round? I'll tell you more when I see you.'

'Bloody hell. This is all pretty grim, Grace.'

'So, can you come back?'

There was a moment's hesitation before he said, 'Of course.'

I asked him to use the back door so I could avoid the hall.

We rang off, and I paced up and down the kitchen staring at the closed door into the hall every time I neared it. The image of poor Barney was burnt into my mind in all its gruesome detail: the slit on his throat, the small pool of blood on the floor, the red-stained matted fur on so much of his stiffening body. Then it occurred to me. He was tied to a beam with a rope around his rear legs and stretched out with his head towards the floor like the carcass of a pig in an abattoir. Yet there was limited blood. In my stunned confusion, my initial thought was that he'd been hung up and killed, but that made no sense. Such a manoeuvre would have been nigh impossible. The resistance, the weight, the noise, the mess…

And then I realised there were drops of blood on the kitchen floor and some slightly larger patches. I looked at the closed laundry room door and moved slowly towards it. Barney's basket was in there surrounded by his toys and the favourite of the day: a small stone from the garden, now wet with saliva, to which he'd taken a child-like penchant. As I neared the door, I stretched out to take the round brass handle firmly. I turned the knob slowly while easing the door towards me.

The room was dark, but the light flooded in and I needed no more. The floor was covered in blood. Shiny and dark. A great stain on the pale lino. I reached inside the room and flicked the light switch. As I gazed round the room, two things struck me. The first was the knife. It was one of my black-handled steel kitchen knives, one of a set that Martin's aunt gave to us on our wedding day. The knife lay on the floor by the red lake, stained, silent and still after its murderous assignment. And then there was the mop leaning upright against the wall just by the doorway. Its spongy head was covered in blood, and a small amount had oozed from its porous grip onto the floor around it. After a brief moment of thought, I connected it to the smears of blood along the floor towards the door. Whoever was responsible for Barney's awful death had obviously roughly wiped the floor to remove any traces of footprints from bloodstained shoes.

I flicked off the light and slammed the door shut.

Leaning against it, I looked down at the tiled floor and looked again at the splashes and spots of blood that ran in a rough trail across to the hall door. I walked over to the kitchen table where I dragged out a wooden chair and sat down heavily onto it.

My mind turned again to Mike. I'd wanted to call him first because he, of anyone, would understand what was happening. I'd told Rob about the divorce and Martin's antics over that, but I'd not told him about Mike and everything that had been happening over the last couple of weeks.

As I sat there, I twisted my mobile round in my hand and glanced up at the wall clock. Eleven fifty. I'd rung the police at this late hour—that was easy and they were on the way. But it really was too late to call Mike. However, I felt this new drama was so closely entwined with what had been happening that I almost felt duty-bound to call him. I recalled how I'd felt when he belatedly told me about Frank. I summoned his mobile number and pressed the button. As I raised it tentatively to my ear, I convinced myself that Mike, with all the time he wanted, could always have a lie in if indeed I was now waking him up.

'Grace. You okay?' His voice was alert, not sleepy.

'Not really. How did you know?'

'Come on,' he said kindly. 'It's nearly midnight. Must be important. What's up?'

They say women are intuitive. I'd come to realise how intuitive and really reassuring Mike was. I told him what had happened on arriving home.

Mike's voice was full of empathy and understanding. 'I'm so sorry, Grace,' he said. 'After all you went through in the divorce, too, so you could keep him… I'm not sure what

I can do though. There's no way I can deal with something hanging from the ceiling.'

'Oh, don't worry about getting Barney down,' I said. 'I've rung Rob and he's coming back to help.'

'Back?'

'Yes, he dropped me off after our dinner.' I paused. This wasn't the time to tell him all about my evening, or even think about it. 'No, Mike, the reason for ringing is that this just seems to be the next chapter in our own story, what with the skull and now... now this. Have you heard from Goddard about Martin's assault on you?'

'Yes, and everything else, this afternoon. He was interviewed this morning, admitted it and was just cautioned, believe it or not.'

'And within a few hours Barney is dead.'

'Are you blaming me?' Mike said rather sharply.

'No, no, of course not. Not at all, Mike. But someone's stirred up about something, and I seem to be bearing the brunt of it.' For some reason I felt I was on the cusp of falling out with Mike, which seemed all wrong and not at all what I wanted. I tried to pull it back. 'Look, Mike. I wanted you to know what happened. I would welcome your insight as to who's responsible. I know it's late, but I'm a desperate person turning to a reliable friend for some support.'

'Okay. Sorry, it's late. Forgive me,' Mike said. 'Leave it with me. I'll give it some thought and call you tomorrow. Okay?'

'Okay.'

'And Grace...' he added.

'Yes?'

'I'm sorry again about Barney.'

SIXTY-ONE

I tossed my mobile next to me on the bed, placed my hands behind my head and stared up at the ceiling. Barney deliberately and brutally killed, strung up and positioned in some awful trap to scare and frighten her on her return home. How cruel was that? I wanted to go to her, but had to accept she'd summoned Rob. I consoled myself with the irrelevant fact that I was ready for bed from my warm bath and nightcap of a more than decent-sized Glenmorangie.

Her call re-ignited me back into action. I tried to place this development and its consequences into the overall scheme. I needed my paper.

I rose from my bed and went across the hallway to the office. Earlier that evening I'd been working on this particular flow chart, plotting people and movements, drawing arrows and writing large question marks. Barney was connected to Grace by a small line. I picked up a ballpoint pen—an appropriate red one—and put a large cross over his name and wrote the date next to it. I circled Martin and, using the same red ballpoint, jotted down a number of words and phrases: '*Ex-spouse; fought over Barney on divorce; new war; revenge for my actions.*' I paused and then added, '*Where was he this evening?*' and circled the sentence twice. Next I circled Clifford Denning. I drew an arrow from his name to an empty space on the paper and wrote, '*Controls the coven; witchcraft; animal sacrifice and murder; hacked off with me; knows about Grace—has connected us.*' Again I added, '*Where has he been this evening? Who might he have instructed?*' And then, for some reason, I wrote, '*Why has Goddard refused to investigate him and the coven*?' and underlined it.

The clock in the sitting room chimed, reminding me of the lateness of the hour.

Frank was now linked to Craig and I wrote similar whereabouts thoughts against them, reflecting that Frank was staying somewhere that remained a mystery to me. For the sake of completeness, I then circled Charles Fairfax. He was connected by a line to Grace on which I had written in neat capitals the word '*cousin*'. A line ran off Charles in another direction. A shorter line led to his girlfriend, Caroline. As far as I could see, Charles would not have anything against Grace—no reason to kill her dog. I could in fact only think of one reason why Charles might have undertaken such an action and that was surely fanciful— because he was in some way connected to the coven, that he'd been instructed to do it by or through Denning. Then I wrote something else: '*Met them both in the pub the evening before Dean's notebook was stolen.*'

I sat back in the chair and rubbed my hand on my face. I was beginning to feel tired—but I was also thinking of a number of questions to ask Grace. Questions about Barney. She'd told me he'd been killed and hung up from a high beam in the hallway, but what had led up to that? What evidence was there about entry to the house? Had entry been forced? Had she called Goddard or the police? And had there been a struggle with Barney? Or had he gone quietly— because he recognised the intruder…?

SIXTY-TWO

As I made my way through the hallway to the stairs, I averted my eyes. I felt guilty that I wasn't able to release Barney from his undignified position, but it was a difficult task for me physically and, besides, the police needed to witness his plight and extract any available clues.

I sat by my bedroom window with the light out, but a sufficiently comforting glow came through the room's half-open door from the hallway downstairs. I looked across to the corner of Cowgate Street, but there was no one in the shadows. No one I could see, anyway. I couldn't help but peer in that direction automatically every time I was at the window.

A few months ago I was in this very room making love to Martin. Now I was divorced, watching out for some stalker on the street and waiting for a potential boyfriend to arrive while my pet dog swung dead from the ceiling below me. How had this all come about? And then there were the many questions surrounding this evening's events.

Dancing headlights appeared below me as Rob's cabriolet pulled up outside, followed almost instantaneously by a police patrol car, all official and shiny under the street lights. Rob stepped out of his car and the orange indicator lights flashed twice as he locked it remotely. He walked over to the two officers getting out of their patrol car. They had a quick chat and walked as a group on to my driveway.

I left my vantage point and hurried downstairs, past the

hallway violence, and into the kitchen. I glanced at the closed laundry room door and rushed towards the back of the kitchen. I inserted the door key and turned it. I flung the door open and peered out into the night, and then heard voices and footsteps as Rob led the officers round the corner of the house on the footpath. I stepped back inside and held the door for the three people to enter, immediately feeling that a touch of normality had returned and that sanity was prevailing.

The officers introduced themselves as PC Weaver, a solidly built man in his late thirties, and PC Flynn, a dark-haired, portly woman of about thirty. They both smiled and seemed friendly with a professional air. Rob, in his chinos and open patterned shirt, gave me a slightly awkward kiss on the cheek. I thanked them all for coming and directed them to the laundry room, standing well back as they each peered in. I then walked over to the kitchen door, opened it and explained that Barney was in the hallway. The officers led the way and while I left them to study Barney, I walked on through into the sitting room telling them to join me when they'd seen enough. That took them about three minutes.

Rob entered the sitting room first. I wasn't sure if that was because he'd seen enough or because he felt it was tactful to let the police continue their subdued discussion in private. I was standing by the fireplace. The privacy of the moment, coupled no doubt with the reality of what he'd just witnessed, must have made him walk over to me and give me a strong hug. I responded and wrapped my arms around him. I finally realised that the dying scent of Eau Sauvage that drifted gently into my senses had been one of Martin's favourites. As he pulled away from me, Rob planted a more positive kiss on my lips and stepped back towards a chair.

The officers entered and perched together self-consciously on the three-seater sofa. PC Flynn extracted a black notebook from some discreet pocket in her uniform and prepared to take a few notes. In answer to PC Weaver's questions, I recounted what Rob and I had done that evening, with Rob chipping in every now and then with additional detail. I explained that I was divorced, lived alone in the former matrimonial home, and that Barney had been a treasured companion from my marriage.

'There are no signs of forced entry then, Mrs Atkins?' PC Weaver queried with his Devonshire lilt. 'Did you lock the doors when you left the house this evening? Any windows left open?' He looked at me expectantly.

'The front door is a Yale lock, officer. It does have a deadlock but, to be honest, I've rarely used it. Probably the last time was when Martin—my ex—and I had a week's holiday in Tenerife last October. It's been as infrequent as that.' PC Flynn was making a couple of notes. 'As for the back door, I'm sure I locked that. It's a habit of mine. The key is kept on a hook near the door so no one can break a pane in the door, reach in and turn it. That was Martin's idea.'

Images of our October holiday flashed through my mind. I refocused when I realised Weaver was asking me a question.

'No bolts?'

'Sorry?' I said.

'No bolts on the back door?' he repeated.

'No. We never bothered. I will now though.'

Weaver said, 'To confirm, no sign of a break-in, then? I had a quick look in the dining room. All seems in order. Nothing upstairs?'

'I haven't actually checked that other than my bedroom,' I said. 'I didn't think they were practical options.'

Weaver said, 'No problem, but we should investigate.'

'I'll pop up if that's okay with you, Mrs Atkins?' said PC Flynn.

I nodded. 'Of course. Be my guest.'

PC Flynn left the room. I heard her footsteps on the staircase and the sounds of her walking across the floors upstairs, a couple of doors opening and closing.

With the sounds above us, Weaver asked me, 'So who has a key to the house, Mrs Atkins?'

'Only me—oh, and Katherine. Katherine Meadows is my cleaner who comes in twice a week. She lives in Tiverton—maybe you know her?'

Weaver shook his head slowly.

'And then there's the spare.'

'The spare?'

'Yes, the spare. I keep it under a plant pot near the backdoor. It was Martin's idea just in case between us we locked ourselves out. For an emergency so to speak.'

'Is it there now?' Weaver asked.

'I'll go check.' I walked out of the room, and headed to the back door in the kitchen. Outside it was now raining gently and steadily. I stepped over to the third plant pot from the house and tipped it on its round bottom. At first I couldn't see anything, but then the light from the rear spot and from the kitchen door showed me a flash of brass. I bent down further and picked up the key. As I carried it back into the kitchen, I studied it in the palm of my hand. It was dirty, grubby, and damp, and I was unable to decide whether it had been recently used or not. In any event, it had been in its proper place.

Back in the sitting room, I handed it to PC Weaver and sat back down in my armchair. I glanced at him expectantly as he held it between two fingers and looked closely at it.

'Who else knew it was there?' he asked, still looking at the key.

'Martin, Katherine and probably a handful of friends, I think. You know, those who would find it helpful at some time or other,' I added defensively.

Weaver nodded and placed the key on an oak occasional table. 'Well, that limits it to some degree, although it sounds as though you don't take your security overly seriously.' His comment sent me spinning back to my old maths teacher handing back a particularly shoddy piece of homework. He went on, 'So, who do *you* think is responsible for this?'

I'd been thinking of little else since I'd discovered the atrocity. It had to be someone who knew about the key; someone who knew Barney since he evidently went without a fight; someone who had a grudge against me; someone who knew how important Barney was to me and that to kill him would be like a dagger in my heart. There could only be one candidate. The war was turning very, very nasty.

'I reckon the prime candidate is my ex,' I said, almost reluctantly. Had it really come to this?

'Has he got his own key still?'

That stopped me in my tracks. I'd never thought about that. All the time and money sorting out the transfer of the legal title to me, yet the means to physical entry had been completely overlooked. Weaver had another question before I could reply, 'Could he have copied it even? Or did you simply change the locks on divorce?'

I felt a complete mug. 'I know it sounds stupid,' I said

quietly, 'but believe it or not I don't think he ever returned his keys. And I know for certain I didn't change the locks. Why would I have bothered? He wanted out of my life and there was no reason to think he'd be coming back. It was agreed right at the start that I'd keep the house and all its contents save for some personal items that I had delivered to him. So he had no need to enter the house, did he? The only possession, other than finances, that we fell out about was poor Barney. We both wanted "custody" of Barney, but the judge ruled in my favour as, technically, Martin had given him to me when he was a puppy and this had been his home all his life. Martin was not at all happy about that, of course.'

'So why do you think it was your ex? Has something happened recently? You said earlier that you separated months ago, beginning of the year, wasn't it?'

I nodded. 'Yes, that's right. And yes, something has happened recently. It's a long story, but I'll try to give you some understanding as to why I think it's him.'

And so I summarised the last couple of weeks. Lindsey's murder, my investigation with Mike, Clifford Denning and the coven, Martin's run-ins with Mike including the assault and the subsequent caution when Martin had told Goddard that he thought I was behind all that Mike had done—possibly the blue touch paper of war. I was conscious throughout while I was painting this picture that Rob was listening intently and in silence. He said not a word.

'Anything else?' Weaver enquired when I'd finished.

'I don't think so,' I said. 'What about Barney? Can we cut him down now?'

It was agreed that PC Flynn would take a photograph and, when she returned, PC Weaver and Rob went out into the hallway to sort him out. I heard the scraping of a chair and, after a few moments the sound of the laundry room door closing. The taps ran in the kitchen and the cloakroom. As they returned to the room, PC Flynn rose from her seat and I stood up as well.

'I don't think there's much more we can do here now,' Weaver said. 'We'll notify CID and no doubt they and forensics will be in touch. I'm very sorry about your dog, Mrs Atkins. We've laid him out in the laundry room for now.'

I thanked them both for attending and showed them to the front door. In my mind's eye, Barney was still hanging there. Silent, staring, twisting ever so gently in his macabre and unnatural position. I realised it would take some time to shift the image and bring the hallway back to its old self. As I closed the door, I leaned back onto it and felt an overwhelming sense of grief for such a wonderful dog, such a perfect companion, and, frustratingly, my eyes filled with belated tears.

Rob stepped slowly out of the sitting room into the hallway. He gave me a tired, weak smile. I walked unhurriedly over to him and put my arms around him. His arms slowly lifted and he held me delicately. We remained in that position for a few moments.

I lifted my head and looked into his handsome face. 'You can stay if you like,' I said with a slight smile.

He said nothing and studied my face. Gently wiped a tear from my cheek with his left thumb. He brought up his right hand and ran it through the side of my hair. Straightened it, caressed it ever so briefly. My mind was already a few steps ahead and had us both naked together in my neglected marital bed.

He placed both his hands on my shoulders and looked into my eyes. He spoke softly. 'You're a lovely, attractive woman, Grace,' he said, 'but this whole scenario, well... it's... it's kind of heavy, isn't it? Sort of unreal. It's not what I anticipated, and I feel I'm a touch out of my depth here. I appreciate the offer, really I do. I've had a wonderful evening—well, the first part that is—but let's just leave it as tennis coach and pupil, huh? Is that okay?'

I felt deflated, embarrassed. I said quietly with what little strength and dignity I could muster, 'Sure, Rob. That's cool. No problem. I'll... I'll see you next Monday, yeah?'

He nodded, and kissed me on the cheek. He pulled away slowly, slipped past me and opened the door. As he left he simply said, 'Bye then, Grace,' and the door clicked shut. Stillness and silence flooded into the house broken only by the sound of Rob's cabriolet starting up and departing into the night.

I wandered back into the sitting room where I lay down heavily on the sofa. Men. Even the handsome ones didn't always have a backbone. There was, however, no way that I was going to let Martin get away with this. If he wanted a war, he could have a war and, I have to admit, that with some relief I felt a coldness towards him flow into my heart to drown the debilitating emotion that had bound me to him for far too long.

SIXTY-THREE

As I recall it, the idea of Grace going to Lyme Regis was mine.

My mobile rang a little after eight fifteen that Thursday morning. I was still in bed but had been up late the night before with my various diagrams and calculations following Grace's midnight call. I wasn't due in the village shop until nine o'clock. Grace gave me a very quick summary of the events following her return home from her date with Rob. The police forensics were due that morning, and she'd been in touch with a professional cleaning company as well as her daily, Katherine, who were all on stand-by. She'd also arranged with a pet cremation service to call to collect Barney's body. She was still in control, but noticeably quieter than usual.

'Look,' I said decisively, 'it sounds like your home is going to be Piccadilly Circus all day. Why don't we just leave them to it? There's no need for you to be there if you put Katherine in charge. How about it? Let's go and look at the sea or something—unless you've got plans with Rob?'

'No plans,' she said quietly. 'I'd have liked plans with him, but all these recent events have scared him off. If I'm honest, Mike, and this is confidential between us, I wanted him to stay last night after he returned to help with Barney, but that's when he ran. Maybe the suggestion was the last straw. Maybe he wasn't the man I thought he was.'

I paused a beat and then said, 'All the more reason to

get out and about then, huh?'

So I cancelled my morning stint in the shop and we travelled to Lyme Regis down on the Dorset coast. Grace pushed me along the front. Fortunately, the clouds had cleared and the sun was shining from a generally blue sky. I put on my sunglasses and enjoyed the Polaroid view. It was warm enough, in fact very pleasant for the time of year.

At lunchtime we bought fish and chips and sat on the beach wall gazing out to sea. It was at that point Grace turned to me with a slightly sheepish expression and said, 'Mike, I think I did something rather silly.'

I looked up from my chips. 'Tell me,' I said with a friendly smile.

She put her can of Coke down on the wall and crossed her arms. After a moment's pause, she said, 'I rang Martin.'

I nearly dropped my food. '*Martin*? What, this morning? About last night?'

She nodded. Said nothing, just looked at me.

'What did you say? What did *he* say?' I asked as I struggled to get my head round it.

'Well, I thought that as Barney was our dog—'

'Was *your* dog, Grace. You fought hard enough for him.'

'Sure. But in quiet moments, he was still our dog. I just ended up looking after him. Martin was very fond of him at the end of the day. If Barney had been our son—'

'He was your *dog*,' I interrupted.

'Yeah, I know, but *if* he'd been our son, then we'd have come to some different arrangement or something so our son didn't miss out on either of us. Wouldn't have been fair on our son to have limited access, would it?'

'Where's this all going, Grace? I thought Martin was

your prime suspect, bordering on a dead cert?'

'I know. You see, Mike, I reckoned that if it wasn't Martin, then I wanted to let him know about Barney. And if it was Martin, then I thought I might get some kind of clue— you know, in the way he reacted.'

'So how did he react?'

'It might well have been because he was busy when I rang—'

'*What* did he say, Grace?' I said with jokey firmness.

She paused and then said, 'I told him that Barney had died last night. I was going to say a little more, but all he said was "Tough" and put the phone down on me. I wasn't expecting that. He's changed, Mike. Changed big time.'

'Or you're seeing him for who he really is…'

She said nothing.

We finished our lunch in silence. Would a guy who has just sneaked into his ex's home and killed the ex-family dog react in that way? Here Martin was, on a scale of one to ten in the pissed off stakes, at about eight or nine, I reckoned. The dog probably meant nothing to him anymore. May never have meant anything but became a matter of principle in the divorce or simply a weapon to get his own back at what he saw as a money-hungry, bitch of a wife.

But could someone else have been responsible? What other angles were there? Clifford Denning was also pretty hacked off, and he'd made the link between Grace and me. But how would he, or a minion, have obtained access? He was 'well-connected' Goddard had said. He evidently found out stuff pretty quickly. And I'd already read out my notes and what they said about the brutal actions of the coven. If those acts had happened, then it would be nothing for a coven member, just one of the thirteen, to kill Barney in the way that he died. And then, of course, there was Frank. He had threatened to harm Grace if I told the police about him when he'd visited last Monday evening. And I *had* told the police. But surely he wouldn't have known that, as the police didn't know where he was staying and therefore couldn't have interviewed him yet. But he knew about Grace. Grace had seen someone outside her house. Was there sufficient link to show that Frank was responsible for Barney's demise?

Yet by all accounts Barney hadn't put up a struggle. Grace reckoned he'd recognised his killer. Maybe he had. Maybe he hadn't. My own experience of Labradors was that, if push came to shove, they'd lick any intruder rather than bite him—especially if food was offered. A couple of dog biscuits and they were your friend for life.

We rescued the afternoon with a laze on the beach in the warm sunshine, aided by a cup of tea in a seafront café and, later, a drink in a modest pub with a light supper. I thought Grace looked decidedly more relaxed as dusk was falling and we reclaimed her car. Clipping on my seat belt, I said, 'I've got an idea, Grace. Why don't we drive home via Sidmouth and I can show you my old family home, Cliff House? It's not too far out of our way.'

'Cliff House? I never knew you had another place.'

'Really?' I said with a puzzled look. 'Lindsey and I came down here quite often for a break. Sometimes she came on her own. I thought you knew. Didn't she ever say?'

'I recall you both were away at times, but she never mentioned a Cliff House.'

'Well, there's a thing. I wonder why she never said anything? Anyhow, I inherited it from my parents and couldn't bring myself to sell it—nor even let it, come to that, so we could use the place whenever it suited.'

'I'm learning something every day,' she said.

We reached Cliff House at about nine o'clock.

'I guess you're not seeing it in all its daytime glory,' I said as Grace helped me into my wheelchair in the drive, 'but it's a favourite house for me. I lived here all my life, I guess, until I went to university in Exeter. I wanted to show you.'

I let us in through the ramped side door and I showed her first my grandma's annex.

'This is where I stay when I come down here. She used a wheelchair so it's all set up which is kind of convenient, huh? The bedroom's through there,' I said, pointing at the doorway. 'Grandma's bed is the most comfortable one I've ever slept in.'

'Really?' Grace said and she flicked on the light and went in. I followed her to the doorway. She stood at the foot of the bed, turned to face me and then, with a wide grin, let herself fall backwards, as straight as a diver on a high board, back onto the bed. She bounced rigidly and settled, laughing as she went.

'You're right,' she said. 'Gloriously comfortable.'

We entered the main house through the connecting door with Grace pushing me as we went. She loudly admired everything she saw. Turning into the short passage from the kitchen, we passed the cloakroom and the office and into the hallway.

'Gosh, there's even a fireplace in the hall,' Grace said looking at the brick hearth with its mounted tapestry fire screen.

'Not had a fire in there for years,' I said.

'You've got a set of irons though?'

'Just for show now, I guess. Probably used at some time or another, but central heating does the job now—somewhat easier.'

'And I love the stairs, Mike. Quite grand.'

'They've always been a favourite of mine.'

Grace let go of my wheelchair and looked up the stairs which turned on two small half landings to double back on themselves to the upper floor. A wide oak bannister completed the opulent effect.

She glanced back at me and said, 'May I?'

'Of course,' I replied with a grin. 'I'll stay here if I may.'

She smiled, turned and walked up the stairs two at a time. The depth of carpet meant that I lost her footfall.

'You okay,' I called up the stairs.

'Sure am,' came the distant reply.

A few minutes later she came back down the stairs flamboyantly acting as if she were some film star walking elegantly downwards to meet her legion of fans or the press. 'It's all rather grand, darling' she said in a classic diva voice. 'I simply adore it.'

I laughed and we went through to the drawing room where I pointed out what I could of the garden and did my best to describe it.

'It's just lovely, Mike. It truly is,' she said as we headed back down the short passage to the kitchen. 'A perfect sanctuary away from the world. You're so lucky.'

I turned my neck to look back up at her. 'Lucky? I wouldn't say I was lucky, Grace. We should be visiting my wonderful parents now, not an inherited house. They were too young to go—I was too young to lose them, especially as an only child. This house has too many precious memories.'

I felt Grace's hand gently caress my head. 'You're such a lovely man, Mike,' she said.

We locked up and headed home. Grace dropped me at the bungalow, which suddenly felt quite small after the expanse of Cliff House.

'Thanks for such a great day, Mike,' she said after she'd pushed me into the hallway. 'That was such a good idea to get away and have a change of scene. The fresh air has helped me cope with what's happened to poor Barney.'

I smiled and took her hand, squeezed it gently. 'That's good to hear. It won't be easy and will inevitably take time. He was such a good and loyal friend to you. Anyhow, I'm delighted you enjoyed the outing. I do hope all is now tidy and sorted at home. Time to mourn and move on, huh?'

She nodded. 'Guess so,' she said and gave me a parting kiss on the cheek. 'Things can hardly get worse, can they?'

How wrong she was.

SIXTY-FOUR

The visitor to my Tiverton home was totally unexpected—and early.

The doorbell went as I was finishing off a piece of toast whilst standing by the Aga in the kitchen. I couldn't sleep and had awoken early. I decided to get up and start the day. I glanced at my watch. Seven thirty. Who was calling round so early this Friday morning, and unannounced? I stuffed the last corner of toast into my mouth and walked into the hallway and across to the front door, wiping my hands on a piece of kitchen towel as I went.

'*Charles*,' I said with surprise as I saw my dapper cousin standing in the sunlight on the doorstep. 'You really have turned into that bus this time—three times in not so many more days.' I grinned at him.

He stepped towards me and gave me a kiss on the cheek. 'I'm heading up north for a long weekend, Grace, and thought I'd pop in, see how you are. I appreciate its hopelessly early, but I trusted it wouldn't be too early for you, what with the dog walk and everything. Looks like you're in your jeans already, and no sign of a nightie. Is it convenient?'

'Of course. Come in.'

'Sure?'

I nodded and stepped back, opening the door wider as I went.

'Coffee?' I asked cheerily.

'Sounds good,' he said, 'if that's not too much trouble.'

I led the way back into the kitchen while he closed the door.

As I took a packet of fresh coffee out of the cupboard and opened it, he crossed to one of the windows and then glanced around.

'So where's your kid?' he asked, turning to me with a friendly grin.

I stopped putting the ground coffee into the percolator and looked up at him.

'You okay, Grace?' he said with a note of concern.

'Barney's dead, Charles. He died yesterday.'

'Oh, I'm so sorry, Grace, I had no idea. That's really sad. I know he meant an awful lot to you.' He crossed the room towards me, 'Accident? He wasn't very old, was he?'

And so, as I sorted the coffee and we settled at the kitchen table, I told him about the events of Wednesday evening. He listened intently, chipping in with brief questions and making empathetic comments.

'So you think Martin was behind it, Grace?'

I shrugged. 'Maybe. Maybe not. It just doesn't seem like anything he'd do that's all. I know he's hacked off with me at the moment—possibly always has been—but I truly don't think he has such violence in him. I really don't.'

A picture of a bellowing Martin flinging poor Mike out of his wheelchair flashed through my mind like one of those brainwashing movies with subliminal images. I chose to ignore it, rightly or wrongly.

'Is it anything to do with your friend Mike? Sounds to me he's been stirring things up while investigating—if that's the right word—his wife's murder. He's even managed to drag me into that, as I told you on the phone. Hacked me off, too, if I'm honest.'

'Yes, sorry about that Charles. The honest answer is that it is all rather my fault. The police were so rubbish, I just wanted some prompt justice for Lindsey, so I rather egged Mike on to help me find who was responsible. All sounds pretty fanciful when I say it like that, I guess, but that's how it was, you see. In a way I suppose I've been trying to help him, poor man. You can't help but want to do something for someone in such dreadful circumstances, can you? To lose your wife, your partner, so suddenly and in such an awful way is really grim. I suspect he has ruffled a few feathers, but then again I rather think I have done so as well. So, you can blame me, especially for Goddard's visit.'

Charles took a swig of coffee and said, 'I have to say he struck me as a bit of a buffoon. Self-confident, but a buffoon.'

I said, 'He seems to be struggling with Lindsey's murder—and the one in Littleworth Wood last year.'

'Sandra Roberts?'

His knowledge surprised me. 'Yeah, Sandra Roberts. How did you know that?'

He seemed to pause, looked a little ruffled. 'Oh, it's no mystery,' he said in an off-hand way. 'I knew Sandy. Met her a while back—she was getting a divorce then as I recall it. Nice woman. Had a son—Jason, I think. Well-mannered lad and interesting to talk to.' He paused, and then added, 'So you've been helping Mike Miller?'

I have to say that I was fascinated by the fact that Charles had known Sandra Roberts. He seemed ready to move on promptly from the topic.

'How did you meet Sandra?' I watched him carefully. His eyes flicked away across the room before returning briefly to meet my gaze.

'Long story,' he said. 'Met her through a mutual friend who introduced us. Met a lot of women in my time. She was pleasant enough, but not really my type if I'm honest. Anyhow, enough of her. I only wish the idiot Goddard could catch whoever did it. Doesn't seem right to think someone's wandering around at liberty having done something so appalling, does it?'

I nodded thoughtfully. 'I agree with that,' I said.

'So what have the police got to say about Barney? You said there was no sign of a break-in so someone must have had a key then?'

'I'm pretty sure Martin has a key, as he never returned his after he left, and I never bothered changing the locks, believe it or not. Well, he'd gone hadn't he? The forensic guys were here yesterday and looked at a key I keep hidden outside. They examined it and the back door lock. I got the impression that they thought it had been used—you know, fresh bits of dirt and soil were in the lock as well as some signs on the key itself.'

'That would tend to rule out Martin, then. He would have used his own key.'

'Would you have used your own key if you'd been Martin? Surely that would have been a bit of a giveaway. The best approach would have been to use the key from a location that he knows is well publicised. He knows I'm a creature of habit. Might have brought his own key as back up—relying on the fact that I hadn't changed the locks. That makes sense, doesn't it?'

Charles shrugged. 'Yeah, guess you're right. So the field's still wide open then?'

I nodded. 'Reckon.'

'Neighbours?'

'Didn't hear anything unusual, not even any barking, although they aren't in the first flush of youth, and I doubt their hearing is what it was.'

Charles finished his coffee. 'So, how are you after all this?' There was a note of genuine concern in his voice. 'Here you are with something as terrible as this and no one close to share it with.'

'I'm okay, thanks. I spent the day yesterday with Mike while the house was cleaned and sorted. That was his idea and it was a good one—got me away from here. We went down to Lyme Regis for the day and then to his old family house in Sidmouth. He owns that—quite impressive. A brilliant bolt-hole, and he said I could go whenever I wanted, especially if times got tough. I might take him up on that one day.'

'Whereabouts in Sidmouth? I was there a couple of days ago.'

'Up near the golf course. It's called Cliff House. Having seen it, I can understand why he doesn't want to sell it.'

Charles nodded. 'Sounds like you're getting pretty close to Mike,' he said.

I shook my head. 'Oh no, it's nothing like that, Charles. He's just the widower of someone who was my best mate, that's all. We've seen a lot of each other and he's really sweet, but I've no designs on him. On others, sure, but not him. He understands that. Besides, I couldn't do that to Lindsey and she's only been gone just on three weeks at the end of the day.' I paused, and then asked the question we singletons hate, but I realised I was asking it too late to stop. 'How's your love life, by the way? Still with Catherine?'

'Caroline,' he corrected. 'No, she's history now. Too

demanding. Got my eye on a woman called Suzanne who's a couple of years younger than me. Divorced of course, as they all seem to be at that age when I meet them. One eighteen-year-old daughter who's off to uni this year, so not too much baggage to cope with. Watch this space.'

I smiled.

'Well,' he said, making to stand up. 'I'd better be off. Almost eight o'clock. A bit of a drive ahead of me.'

'Going far then?'

'Shrewsbury, so yes. Meeting up with some friends. What you doing this coming weekend anyway, if you ladies of leisure still call them that?'

As we walked to the front door, I said, 'Of course they're still weekends for me, too. Not sure exactly what I'm doing mind. Something will come up.'

And it certainly did, although it was far from what I'd anticipated.

SIXTY-FIVE

Looking back, I reckon this Friday was the day when everything started to go seriously wrong.

Grace later told me about Charles' sudden and unexpected visit. Although, as she said, it was good to see him, she couldn't quite fathom out why he'd just dropped by to visit her, as he had never done such a thing before. Yes, she had urged him to keep in touch, but that doesn't usually result in an instant visit. I felt myself sticking up for the guy, as I explained that he was probably just trying to build back up their relationship from its evident neglect. If he was driving north and vaguely in her direction, why not call in? However, she didn't wholly buy this, and I can't say I really blamed her. There were plenty of unusual things happening in both our lives and it was perfectly natural, I reckoned, for her to put a suspicious spin or interpretation on any out-of-the-ordinary event.

As for me, I'd woken at about eight o'clock that morning. I reflected that it was almost three weeks to the day that Lindsey had driven herself away from home never to return. I made myself a cup of tea and went out to the patio. The sun had seized possession of the blue sky and the warm air was tinged with the slightest hint of autumn—you know, that crossover of seasons so familiar to the English. I decided it was warm enough to have my breakfast outside and so returned to the kitchen to make myself a couple of bacon baps—the only food that I found a delight to eat at any time of day. With a refreshed tea mug, I settled on the patio and made the decision to have a lazy morning, starting with a doze in the warming sun. And why not?

Half an hour later that had all changed. I decided that I needed to do something, not just look at the garden. When you look at a garden superficially, all appears good, but on closer inspection, something always needs doing. A bit of weeding here, a bit of trimming there. I was limited as to what I could do from my wheelchair. I needed the right tools, and the ground had to be dry, which it was that morning. Lindsey had done most of the work, and I told myself that failing to maintain, even to my limited extent, what she had created was somehow disrespectful to her memory. Besides, I liked the garden to look good.

I don't know about you, but once I get an idea into my head, I have to see it through. On that morning I decided to change my plan and pop down to the large DIY store on the edge of Tiverton to buy some weed killer and a couple of garden tools that were in need of replacement. I thought I would also make a quick visit to the supermarket on the same retail park.

I locked up the house, set the alarm and backed my car out of the garage, where it always spends its time when I'm at home. I drove steadily to Tiverton, where I bought the garden items and a couple of plastic carrier bags full of stuff from the supermarket. I also picked up a newspaper. I spent about twenty minutes in the on-site Starbucks drinking a pretty good cappuccino. The trip gave me time to relax, think and move things forward.

It was about eleven twenty when I arrived back in the village. The first unusual thing I noticed was a police patrol car parked in the high street, between the pub and the shop. I recalled my plea to Goddard to up the police presence in the village. But the fact that the car was empty, just sitting there vacant, waiting importantly for its driver's return, made me realise it was not there on account of my request. The rest of the street was quiet, just the odd pedestrian, which was not that unusual, even on a Saturday morning. It would have been even quieter earlier on.

I turned into my close and round the gentle bends to the bungalow. I noticed my neighbour Craig in his garden again. We ignored each other. All looked as I'd left it save for the new Yellow Pages directory on the low wall to the drive. I parked the car in the garage, closed the electric door and pushed myself to the front door with my shopping on my lap. This was something I'd never found easy, but I'd mastered the technique over time. I glanced down the road the way I'd just come—the close was peaceful, warm and still.

I unlocked the door, turned off the alarm and pushed my way down to the kitchen where I deposited my shopping in a pile on the floor to sort out later. I noticed the room was a little stuffy and so I wheeled myself to the patio doors and opened them. The air moved gently on my face, fresh and invigorating, and I took a deep breath. I'd grown to like the bungalow even more than I'd anticipated. Sure it was different now that Lindsey was no longer sharing it with me, but it was still a pleasant retreat in a quiet road with the sense of space and privacy from the fields at the rear.

Then I saw the shoe.

It wasn't immediately obvious from the angle I was sitting. A dark women's shoe. Flat soled. Casual, informal. I could see just ten centimetres of it on the grass peeping out from behind a geranium-laden terracotta plant pot on the right-hand side of the gap from the patio to the lawn. I eased myself forward out onto the patio to the wooden table at which I'd had my breakfast earlier that morning. Through the verdant plants, I could see an abnormal block of pink. It was just visible and was new. I squinted, paused and then slowly pushed the wheelchair forward. The block of pink grew larger as I raised the angle with my approach and my view of the lawn expanded.

I reached the potted geraniums and looked down. I'd not been mistaken. It was a dark-coloured, feminine shoe with short leather laces that are purely decorative. Slip on for ease and convenience. It just lay there on the grass as if it were meant to be there. However, one thing was not living with the shoe. I pushed myself onto the lawn and looked down to my right. Lying on her back in her pink cardigan on the grass by the patio wall, staring up with lifeless eyes into the clear blue sky, was the anguished and wracked body of sweet old Edith Riley.

SIXTY-SIX

Despite achieving my thirties, I had never had to ring the emergency services for an ambulance before. It was pretty obvious to me that Edith was long past any hope of revival, but I'd seen people make such calls on TV cop shows and asking for the ambulance as well. Whether the dramas were technically accurate or not, I've no idea, but it seemed the right thing to do to copy the procedure.

I gave the guy on the phone most of the details he asked for. I say 'most' because he asked if I could feel a pulse, and I said that I didn't feel I should touch the body. It was evident to me, I said, even as a layman on such medical topics, that she was dead. No living soul could maintain such a static pose for so long. She was quite clearly going nowhere, at least as a mortal being. He didn't push it.

Once I had it confirmed that both the police and the ambulance were coming, I made my way back into the house, as there was something sinister about remaining next to a dead body. As I entered the kitchen, my first thoughts were to telephone Grace. I presumed this wasn't in breach of police rules and procedure, and I was certain in my own mind that Edith's death was something to do with the macabre sequence of recent events.

As anticipated, Grace was surprised, but immediately started asking exploratory questions. I heard a car pull up on the drive and the sound of a couple of slamming doors. I told Grace I'd call her back, but she said she would come straight over. I didn't try to stop her. I pushed myself to the front door and opened it. PC Gosling and PC Webster, the officers who had attended when I'd reported the burglary, were standing there.

I took them through to the kitchen and they stepped carefully out onto the patio and took a quick look at Edith's corpse from the patio itself, peering over the plants in the wall. I presumed they didn't want to contaminate the area for evidence but wanted to check that Edith was indeed dead. They evidently shared my conclusion. It wasn't difficult to reach. They consulted with each other in low voices before PC Gosling re-joined me in the kitchen, leaving PC Webster outside on the patio to use his radio, I presume to notify CID at Exeter station.

'May I?' Gosling asked, indicating a kitchen chair.

I nodded. 'Of course.'

He settled on the chair with his cap on the table.

'She is dead,' he said. 'PC Webster is calling CID now. The ambulance is on its way in any event.'

'You got here quickly,' I observed.

'We were in the village. There was concern about her as the shop was still closed at nine o'clock and no one had seen her. Mrs Hill next door had tried the bell and knocked on the door round the back, but couldn't get any attention so we were called.'

'Of course. I saw your car when I came back into the village.'

'Had you been out?'

'Yeah, just after a quick breakfast. Decided I'd pop into Tiverton to get some stuff from the garden centre and supermarket.'

'I presume she wasn't lying there before you went?'

I smiled weakly. 'I think I would have seen her, officer. I was out there for breakfast after all.'

PC Webster came in through the patio doors.

'They're sending Chief Inspector Goddard,' he said. 'He's on the way now. Fortunately he was fairly local and so won't be long. DS Ward is joining him with the usual team from Exeter.'

I nodded. It seemed to make sense to have him on board although I personally didn't think the already stressed detective would welcome another murder on his hands.

Gosling said, 'There must be a degree of urgency with the weather forecast as it is.'

'Why, what's the outlook?'

'A storm later today sometime,' Gosling replied. 'Tail end of one of those tropical hurricanes.'

'Hannah,' Webster said. 'Hurricane Hannah. Unless it moves slightly north, it will make landfall in Cornwall early this evening and then hit us here in Devon before moving east. Won't be as dramatic as it was in St Lucia, of course, but they reported on the BBC this morning that it would still have some bite.'

Webster sat down in the chair next to Gosling and opposite me. Lindsey's old chair. In answer to Gosling's next question, I went through my morning again. I confirmed I'd locked the house when I went out, but I said I couldn't be sure whether the side gate to the garden had been locked as I usually left it unlocked. PC Webster interjected that it had been unlocked as he had just inspected it. In my mind I could hear Grace admonishing me about my lax security on that front. I reflected on the fact that she'd warned me and I could only surmise that she'd been right to do so. This current situation may not have been what she had in mind when she'd said it, but it had been a gypsy's warning to me and I'd stupidly ignored it. Now I had a dead body in the garden, although thankfully not my own.

'Mind you,' I added, 'the garden's not exactly secure whether the gate's locked or unlocked anyway, what with the field over there at the back and limited fencing.'

We maintained some small talk until the doorbell rang. It was Grace. As she brought me through into the kitchen, the officers rose and I did the introductions. Grace offered us all a cup of tea as if it were her own house and, with positive responses all round, set about making a pot. I explained that Grace had been a close friend of Lindsey's and that she'd been very supportive over the last few weeks.

'She's been my rock,' I added and beamed at her.

'No more than a good friend should be,' she said.

By the time we'd finished our tea, bedlam took hold. Goddard arrived and, not long after, DS Ward and a whole bunch of professionals descended on the garden. An ambulance appeared. I've no idea what they all did, but some kind of white tent was erected over poor Edith, and from the kitchen Grace and I witnessed all sorts of comings and goings. Chaos to us, probably a well-organised and routine exercise for them.

Gosling and Webster departed, and Grace and I settled with Goddard and Ward in the sitting room, which, as the Chief Inspector correctly pointed out, was less distracting than the kitchen and the view of the garden through the patio doors. It all seemed very familiar.

I ran through yet again the events of the morning. I explained how I'd had my breakfast on the patio, had gone to the Tiverton retail park, had driven back, had noticed the police car by the shop and had returned home. I commented on how quiet the village had been and that I'd noticed nothing unusual at home until I'd seen what turned out to be Edith's shoe and then her pink cardigan through the plants and flowers in the patio wall. I told Goddard, as Ward rapidly noted, how I'd wheeled myself forward to look closer at what I'd seen and had found the body. No, I said yet again, but more seriously this time, I was absolutely sure that she hadn't been lying there when I had had my breakfast.

'When did you last see Mrs Riley, Mr Miller?' Goddard asked, giving me one of his piercing stares.

I gave it some brief thought. 'Would have been Wednesday morning,' I said. 'I volunteered in the shop and was there till gone lunchtime. I was going to help out yesterday morning, too, but in the light of what happened to Barney, I decided it was more important to get Grace away from here and we went to the seaside at Lyme Regis—I rang and told Edith, and she was fine about it. So, last saw her Wednesday, last spoke to her yesterday.'

'Barney? Who's Barney?' Goddard queried.

It then occurred to me that neither of us had reported the events of Wednesday evening to Goddard. Grace started to relate what had happened, but Goddard interrupted her.

'Why the hell have I not been told about this?' He said staring at me. 'You keep criticising me for slow progress, but you're hardly helping by not telling me important stuff like this.' I started to speak, but he just carried on. 'I told you right at the start to report anything unusual. First it's the break-in here, now this. Both pretty unusual events, wouldn't you say…'

'I apologise for that,' I said, holding up my hands.

'Apologies don't help me, information does—okay?'

I nodded as Goddard started to relax a bit. 'Right,' he continued, 'give me all material details about last Wednesday evening.'

Between us, Grace and I described the horrors of that occasion and Ward jotted it all down. I concluded with a defensive comment to try and respond belatedly to Goddard's outburst. 'As Grace just recounted, she did call the police and it will be on record somewhere.'

'Sure, but—yes, what do you want Wayne?'

I turned to look round as Goddard suddenly addressed a man who'd appeared in the sitting room doorway. He was one of the forensics team, dressed in white paper overalls that covered his complete body and head, leaving just his face showing. A white face mask had been pushed up on to his forehead. In his gloved hands he was holding a clear plastic bag that contained a piece of paper.

'Sorry to interrupt, sir, but we've found this. Thought you ought to see it straight away.'

He stepped into the room and passed the bag to Goddard. From where I was sitting, I could see what looked like a single sheet of A4 paper on which there was some brief handwriting. Looked like large capital letters. Goddard read it quickly.

'Thank you, Wayne. Leave it with me. Where exactly was it found?'

'Tucked inside her cardigan, sir. They're just taking the body away now.'

Goddard nodded. 'Okay, that's all for now.'

The detective left and Goddard looked at us both.

'This is not good news,' he said. 'As you've just heard, this note has been found on Mrs Riley's body. It's handwritten in large capital letters so at least a handwriting expert can look at it. I'm going to read it to you.' His eyes returned to the page and he adjusted his glasses slightly. '*Let the death of this stupid old bitch be a lesson to both Miller and Atkins. There will be no more messing about. Atkins is next. Be warned.*'

SIXTY-SEVEN

'I'm struggling to make sense of this,' Grace said, looking in turn at both Goddard and me. 'Why poor Edith? And why should I be next?'

'That's for us to sort, and sort quickly,' Goddard said. 'My main concern though is your safety—and yours too if it comes to it, Mr Miller. We need to find somewhere safe for you to go pending a resolution of this.'

'You needn't worry about me,' Grace said, 'I was a reservist in the TA, I can look after myself.'

'I think you'll find this is all a bit different, Mrs Atkins.'

'With respect, Chief Inspector, there's no clear endgame here, is there?' I said. 'What with Sandra Roberts' killer still out and about after a year, we might have to seek a safe haven for more than just a couple of days. That's right, isn't it?'

'Good point,' Grace said. 'My home is hardly off the killer's radar what with the skull, Barney and that person watching my house the other night.'

'What was that?' Goddard asked.

Grace told him about the person she thought she'd seen on the edge of Cowgate Street watching her house. 'It might have been Lindsey's cousin, Frank, of course, since he seems to be spying on Mike and me for some bizarre reason,' she said.

Goddard looked as if he was about to explode about not

being told about something yet again, but he took a deep breath. 'That is something I'll need to know more about,' he said. 'We need to establish not only who but why they were there.'

'And talking of who and why, you've had another unusual visit this morning as well, haven't you?' I prompted.

Grace nodded and looked at Goddard. 'Mike's right,' she said. 'I had a visit very early this morning from my cousin Charles, Charles Fairfax. Very unusual for him.'

'Why did he call in?' Goddard asked as Ward continued with his note taking, flicking over another page in his small book.

Grace put Goddard in the picture.

Goddard said, 'So that puts Charles in the area this morning then, doesn't it?'

'Guess so,' Grace said with a slow, confirmatory nod. 'I don't see that as relevant though. He was just playing good cousins.'

I glanced at Goddard to see if his body language indicated he saw it that way. He had, after all, previously interviewed Charles. But I couldn't pick anything up.

'And what about poor Edith,' I asked Goddard. 'How will that progress?'

'The initial view is that she died earlier this morning. They will come up with a more accurate time later today after the autopsy, but they're talking between eight and nine o'clock.'

'Will the post-mortem establish how and where she was killed?' Grace asked.

Goddard nodded. 'Yes, yes it will. The initial view—and this is confidential—is that she has been strangled. We'll know later whether or not she was moved after death.'

'Did anyone see anything?' Grace asked.

'Early days,' Goddard said. 'We've made some initial enquiries. A white van was seen entering the close, and there will be house-to-house enquiries. She was a very familiar figure around the village, and people like that can often move unobserved.'

'Poor Edith,' I said. 'She was such a lovely person. How come she's been dragged into all this?'

Goddard shrugged. 'Time will no doubt tell us that, Mr Miller. I would like you to attend at the station tomorrow, please, to give a full statement. It shouldn't take long.'

I nodded, 'Sure, no problem.'

'Anyhow, the priority issue is what to do with you, Mrs Atkins.' Goddard pointed to the exhibit beside him. 'We must take this threat seriously. It seems to me that you are not safe at your own home. Someone's already gained entry and could do so again. From what you said earlier, you obviously don't feel totally comfortable there.'

I glanced at Grace. She said, 'I don't mind battening down the hatches, but you don't seem to think that's a good idea, Chief Inspector.'

'Indeed, ex-TA or not' he said. 'Is there anywhere you could stay for just a few days while we get to the bottom of this?'

Grace looked at me. 'I'd like to be near Mike if that's possible. I could stop here?'

Goddard shook his head. 'That's not a good idea. You've clearly been linked to Mr Miller by whoever's behind all this. Staying here is not a good option. At the end of the day it's as unsafe as your own home.' He paused and there was silence.

'I've an idea,' I said. 'We could both go down to

Sidmouth to my place there. That's not too far, but it's away from here. What do you think?'

'That would work,' Grace said. 'Mike has a house in Sidmouth, Chief Inspector. Inherited from his late parents. We actually visited it yesterday and it would work well. I'm up for that if that's okay with you, Mike.'

'Fine by me,' I said.

Goddard thought for a moment and then said, 'Okay. Let's run with that. You gave me the address before didn't you, Mr Miller?'

I said that I thought I had, and Ward confirmed this.

'I'll arrange for you to have a couple of officers looking after you at your home, Mrs Atkins, so you can pack. You can then make your own way to Sidmouth. Please stay based at Mr Miller's house so I know where you are. And keep in touch. If you want to move elsewhere, ring me. Okay?'

'Sure,' she said, and turning to me added, 'Best if you drive over to me, Mike, and then you can follow me down.'

I nodded.

Goddard arranged for a patrol car to meet Grace at her home, and Grace said her goodbyes and left. I fixed up to give a statement in Exeter the following afternoon and Goddard returned to the garden activities that now seemed to be winding down.

As soon as the bungalow became peaceful again and I started sorting myself out some lunch, my mobile rang. It was Clifford Denning.

SIXTY-EIGHT

'Is it sensible to meet him?' Grace asked shortly after I arrived at her house.

I'd packed a bag, locked up the bungalow and driven the four miles or so to Tiverton. As I turned into her street, I saw a patrol car parked up outside Grace's house. Two male officers were sitting inside, looking pretty relaxed. As I pulled up on the road in front of them, the one in the passenger seat slowly unfurled his six-foot-four frame out of the car and came over to me. He asked me who I was and why I was calling. Grace had obviously seen the situation from a window and came out to assist. She advised the officer who I was and insisted that we would be fine on our own and that they could leave. The officer said he'd check with 'control' and take it from there.

With Grace's assistance, I clambered into my wheelchair and, as we made it to the house, the police patrol car moved away unhurriedly down the street. Once inside, Grace took me through to her kitchen, and I noticed the laundry room door remained closed.

Over a cup of coffee, I told her that Charles Denning had rung me and wanted to meet with me.

'How do you mean 'sensible'?' I said in response to her concern about my approach.

'Well, you know, I'd be concerned in view of his connection with the coven and his apparent desire to buy your house. We just don't know how far he's involved with all this.'

I nodded and sipped my coffee. 'He didn't say anything about the house.'

'What did he want?'

'He said he had something of interest to tell me. He said he knew more about Lindsey's death than he'd been able to say before. I don't know why he wouldn't say over the phone. I asked him of course, but he said he "didn't trust the telephone", even though it was a mobile.'

'Probably *because* it was a mobile,' Grace said.

I reflected. 'Mmm, possibly. Anyhow, the bottom line is that he wanted to meet face to face.'

'You must tell Goddard.'

'Well, that was the odd thing. He expressly told me not to tell Goddard that we were meeting.'

Grace looked distant, pulled gently at her bottom lip and then seemed to snap into a conscious state again. 'Thinking it through, I guess you've no option but to meet him. This might be the break we've been looking for.'

'I agree. It makes total sense to me. So I've arranged to meet him as he's requested.'

'When?'

'This evening.'

'*This evening*,' Grace said. 'Wow, that's sudden. What time? Where?'

'Well, it's seven o'clock—early evening, I guess. It's in Exeter anyway. Apparently he's down there for the weekend. The plan is to meet at the Thistle hotel in the city centre and go somewhere after that.'

'It all sounds a bit mysterious. I have to say, I get a bad feeling about this.'

'Agreed it is odd, but what choice do I have? If he

knows something, anything, about Lindsey's death, then we want to hear it.'

She gave me a long look. 'Well, I guess it's a public place, Mike. Just keep it that way, right?'

'Of course, but I'll be fine,' I said with all the reassuring tone I could muster. 'I'll have my mobile with me and if I feel at all uncomfortable I'll either ring Goddard or the local police or insist that we stay in the hotel bar. Don't worry about me. *You're* my main concern here. As soon as I'm through, I'll come on down to join you at Cliff House. So, make sure you put the kettle on.'

'Open the wine more like,' she said.

I smiled and gave her the postcode for the house so she could find it with her satnav. I took a key off my key ring.

'This is for the front door, Grace. Just make yourself at home. We're going to need some basic provisions.'

We spent much of the afternoon chatting, although the principal topic was never far away. Later she disappeared upstairs to pack. As I sat in the sitting room listening to her pottering about upstairs, I saw that the room was darkening. It seemed early. I looked at the carriage clock on the mantelpiece. Six o'clock.

I pushed myself to the sitting room window at the front of the house. The clouds were turning black and threatening. I'd forgotten about the threat of the storm, the remnants of Hurricane Hannah. Something caught my attention.

I wheeled myself hastily to the hallway and called up the stairs. 'Grace, look out of the window quickly. Corner of Cowgate Street. That bloke's there again. Quick!'

I heard her move hurriedly across her bedroom floor

above me. Silence. She walked to the top of the stairs and looked down at me.

'Too late. Missed him. What did you see?'

'I think your guy was back. At least there was someone there. Quite a large man standing near the corner of Cowgate Street. I couldn't see much of him from the angle I had, but someone was definitely standing there. Didn't you see him? You must have done.'

'No, didn't see anyone, but it would have only taken a second or two to move out of view. I might just go out there now and confront him if he's still around.'

'I don't think that's a good idea, Grace. He's bound to have gone by now.'

'He could still be there,' she insisted. 'He wouldn't know that he'd been seen.'

She walked down the stairs and opened the front door as I sat watching her.

Looking out she said, 'It looks pretty dark, Mike. Have you seen the black clouds—and it's just starting to rain.'

As she stood in the doorway, I told her about the storm—she hadn't heard about it on the weather forecast or the news.

'I'll leave it,' she said, closing the door. 'We'd better get going.'

She returned upstairs to her room and a few minutes later she returned and placed her suitcase on the hallway floor. She commented again on the blackness outside.

'It'll be fine,' I reassured her. 'It'll pass over in a handful of hours—might even freshen the air a bit.'

Grace locked up the house and then went round it again to 'double check' as she put it. Every room, window and door was revisited, and she admitted to me that after several years she had finally placed the hidden key in a different location and told me where it was for future reference. She'd arranged for new locks for the doors to be fitted at the end of the coming week.

'In all the circumstances, that sounds pretty sensible,' I said.

Once outside, she kept glancing down towards the corner of Cowgate Street as the rain started to pick up. We left at the same time in our separate cars with the joint intention of meeting up that evening at Cliff House.

SIXTY-NINE

You might think that I spent the journey to Exeter thinking about my stated meeting with Clifford Denning—you know, wondering about what he might have to say or what was behind it all. In fact, I was focused on Grace and whether she would find Cliff House okay. The weather was deteriorating fast, and the storm had forced an early evening. By the time I reached the outskirts of Exeter, the rain was falling quite heavily from a prematurely darkened sky onto my windscreen and streaked rapidly in the headlights of my car.

I knew where the Thistle Hotel was, although I'd never stayed there. It was an easy twenty-four-hour rendezvous point, and I could understand why someone might choose it as such.

At about ten to seven, I reached my destination. I pulled up and stared out at the rain now teeming down heavily on a bedraggled Exeter. I hated getting wet like this, but I knew that I obviously had to get out of the car before I could reach the comfort of the building's shelter. I counted to five and then went for it. I had a challenging meeting to prepare for and was fascinated to know what he was going to say to me.

*

I love my silver Mercedes SLK, but on this dreadful evening it let me down big time. I don't mind admitting that I called it a number of choice names. Even used the F-word, which is

337

pretty rare for me—in fact, I don't think I've done that since my lying bastard of a husband cheated on me.

I was heading east on the main road in a very rural location, some fifteen minutes short of my destination according to my satnav, when I felt the handling suddenly deteriorate. I knew exactly what it was and brought the car to a rest in a field gateway neatly tucked off the main road. It was getting dark, and the rain was appalling, thundering on the roof of the car and lashing off its windows. I started to get out of the car to go and change the wheel, but the weather was so bad I changed my mind. I picked my mobile out of my handbag on the seat next to me and rang the AA. It would be just as quick, and considerably more comfortable, to ask them to do it.

Sitting by the side of the road in a useless piece of junk waiting to be rescued while sporadic traffic splashes past you effortlessly to their respective destinations is indeed miserable and pathetic. I took the opportunity under the car's interior light to jot down in my diary some thoughts about our investigation, as well as a small shopping list for essentials that I needed to buy to at least see us through this evening. It had gone quarter to eight when my mobile rang. It was Mike.

'Are you settled in okay?' he asked.

'No. You wouldn't believe it, Mike, but I'm stuck in some godforsaken gateway with a bloody puncture. Typical, huh? The rain's so bad, I rang the AA about half an hour ago and they should be here soon—I'm less than ten miles shy of Sidmouth.'

'That sounds pretty grim. Well, stay in the car and lock the doors.'

'That's what I'm doing. So what's happening with you?

Have you finished your meeting with Denning already? What did he have to say?'

'He hasn't pitched up yet.'

'Really? Has he rung you?'

'No, not yet. I've tried his mobile but there's no reply. Goes straight to voicemail.'

'So what you going to do?'

'Well, I'm tempted to leave and join you, especially if you're stuck there with a puncture. I feel I should be with you—I'm rather coffeed out already. But, then again, there may be a good reason for his being delayed.'

'He should have rung and told you then. Give him another call.'

'Pointless really, I've already left a suitable message.'

'He can always tell you another time, surely?'

'I guess so. It's only that he was so insistent about meeting this evening.'

'Look, don't worry about me. I'm fine here in my little cocoon.' A sudden squall of rain lashed on the windscreen. 'I know, why not set a deadline? Say another half hour? Try his mobile again then and if there's no response, or he hasn't turned up, come down to Sidmouth?'

There was a pause. 'Mm, maybe that's the answer, if you're sure you're okay. I could always leave a message with reception when I leave. Yeah, I'll do that, Grace. If he's not here by say eight fifteen, I'll give it up. Can't sit here like a lemming all evening.'

'No, that seems to be my role. Anything else, Mike?'

'Er, no—not really.'

'What do you mean "not really"?'

'It's nothing.'

'Sounds like something to me. What is it?'

'Look, it might be nothing at all. Completely innocent.'

'Nothing appears innocent around here anymore, Mike. Come on, tell me.'

He paused, and then said. 'I had a call from Goddard fifteen minutes ago.'

'And?'

'He told me that he'd taken up one of the lines of enquiry I previously suggested to him—you know, in connection with poor Edith.'

'Go on.'

'He told me that he'd rung Martin this afternoon.'

He paused. A large lorry thundered past me on the road to my right, splashing rainwater and rocking my small car in its violent wake.

'And? What did Martin say?'

'Well, that's the thing, Grace. That bag of bones Sally told him that she hadn't been able to talk to him today—he'd gone out unexpectedly somewhere early this morning and she hasn't heard from him since…'

SEVENTY

The headlights were bright as they pulled up close behind me. Lit up the whole of the inside of my sports car as if I'd been spotted by a searchlight. Then the orange light bar towards the rear of the AA van's roof enlivened the night as it started to flash angrily through the rain. Progress at last.

The guy was friendly enough and I took up his West Country drawl suggestion of taking shelter in the passenger seat of his van while he fixed 'the blighter'. I watched him go about his task in the merciless rain, appreciating his effort and dedication in such conditions. I glanced at my watch. It was heading for eight thirty-five. Something caught my eye. I did a double take. In the passenger-side mirror, I saw a single headlight. At first I thought it was a partially obscured car coming up behind the van on the road, but it wasn't moving. It was a long way back. Difficult to tell the distance, but certainly at least a couple of hundred metres on this straight piece of road. I stared at it until I was totally convinced that it was indeed motionless. I couldn't take my eyes off it. I leant over to the door and eased it open slowly. The rain blew in on my face, but I looked out through the door and back down the road. It was still there, a single, stationary headlight.

I slammed the door shut again and looked at the AA man. He was putting the old wheel back into the boot and tidying up. I reached for my handbag, but realised I'd left it on the front seat of my car. I looked back to the door mirror.

It was black, impenetrable. I opened the door again and peered behind me through the rain. Nothing. No light, stationary or otherwise, only darkness.

'You getting out then?'

The suddenness of the AA man's query made me jump. I hadn't noticed his arrival next to the van.

'Sorry. Did I make you jump?' he said in a caring manner. 'I was just coming to tell you that I've finished. It's all sorted you'll be pleased to hear. But then you'd have seen that from here, wouldn't you?'

'Oh, thank you. That's great.' I remained momentarily in the front seat and he looked expectantly at me as the rain poured down. I was holding him up. 'By the way,' I continued. 'Did you see a headlight parked up some way behind us on the road?'

'Didn't notice anything.'

'It was a sole headlight a couple of moments ago—you know, like a motorbike.'

He shook his head and raindrops fell off. I wasn't being fair. 'There's been a surprising amount of traffic passing,' he said.

'Sure, but this one… okay, no matter,' I said, stepping down out of the van onto the soaking ground. 'But thanks anyway. I'll get off.' I insisted there was no need to wait as I had a call to make.

I dashed back to my car through the rain and hopped into the driver's seat. I closed the door and wiped my hand across my face to remove the excess water. My hair was soaked even from that short period of exposure. The recollection of the headlight came back to me, and I locked the doors quickly. As the AA guy backed away and headed off down the road with a quick, friendly cheerio on his horn,

I dipped into my handbag for my mobile. It was gone. I snatched the bag off the seat and quickly ran my hand around inside. Not there.

I flicked on the interior light and tipped all the contents of my bag onto the passenger seat. Still not there. Surely that AA man hadn't taken it? He looked so honest. I sat back in my seat and ran my hand through my damp hair, feeling annoyed that a seemingly trustworthy guy had taken advantage of me. This was not the time to be isolated.

With exaggerated force, I inserted the moulded key into the ignition and moved my left foot onto the brake. It kicked something. I felt it, heard it. Just a light thud. I flicked the interior light back on and looked down. My mobile smiled back up at me. Then I remembered. I'd spoken to Mike, of course, while I was waiting for the AA man. I couldn't have put it back in my bag. Must have put it down somewhere, and it had found its way to the foot well. Maybe when I got out of the car. Maybe before. I stretched down and rescued the phone from the floor, and almost caressed it like the prodigal son as it snuggled into my grateful hand. I was back in communication and back in control again.

I turned the ignition and the engine roared. With a couple of jolts over the rougher terrain of the gateway, I eased the car back onto the smooth tarmac of the road and put my foot down hard on the accelerator as the windscreen wipers tried their damnedest to give me vision through the downpour.

Five or ten minutes later, I reached the outskirts of Sidmouth with its welcoming orange street lights blurred by the rain. My mobile rang out a couple of notes to advise me that a text had arrived. I slowed and pulled into a petrol station with a convenience store in what was now a town street with houses either side of it.

I picked the mobile up from the passenger seat and found the text. It was from Mike: *"Still sitting here! I'm eating a burger, more for something to do LOL. Will give it ten and then leave. Get take away or something out of freezer for you. Will ring when on the way over or if he turns up. Looks like lost cause ☹. Mx."*

I felt annoyed with Denning and tapped out a reply: *"OK. What's he playing at? Leave as soon as you can. Car fixed ☺. Just reached Sidmouth. Rain's awful. Gx"*

I popped into the convenience store and bought the basics on my small list.

In the stormy weather, I needed my satnav to find Cliff House, and turned into the driveway at about five to nine. I looked at the imposing residence towering over me in the darkness, solid and silent. No lights of course, and the windows were lifeless.

I looked in my purse and took out the key for the front door that Mike had given me. I grabbed my handbag and the small bag of shopping, and opened the car door. The rain was as heavy as ever and the wind had really got up. I hurried round to the boot in quick, almost mincing steps, my left foot splashing in a puddle. I took out my case, slammed the boot lid and made my way across the drive towards the front door, pressing the button on the fob to lock the car as I went. The indicator lights flashed obediently. But that wasn't the only thing to flash. Way up in the heavens above me I saw a bright flash of lightning rip its awesome power across the distant sky. I reached the cover of the small porch roof above the front door and placed my case on the step. I carefully inserted the key into the lock and turned it. It was slightly stiff, but it eventually moved effortlessly enough, and I heard the metallic jolt of the mechanism and an almost imperceptible relaxing of the door itself, as if it knew it was now off duty.

Then the thunder echoed around me. Not close, but still present.

I opened the door and explored the inside wall with my outstretched fingers for a switch and found two on a single plate. I flicked both, and the hallway light and a lamp outside above the front door both came on simultaneously. I picked up my case, entered the house and gratefully started to close the door on the raging night.

When the door was all but closed and the view of the front gate and street was almost gone, a strong beam of light on the road caught my attention through the miserable darkness. A motorbike went slowly past in the rain. I made to run out to get a better view, but it was gone. I closed the door on the storm.

SEVENTY-ONE

I dumped my suitcase and the shopping near the front door and, after slipping my mobile into my pocket, left my handbag on a small antique table in the hallway. I rapidly drew all the curtains both in the hallway itself and the large sitting room that stretched the width of the house off to the left. As I did so, I tried to rationalise that the motorbike was perfectly innocent, a mere coincidence.

"*I don't do coincidences,*" I could hear myself telling Mike.

Mike. I telephoned him. The connection was very poor, but, as the signal came and went, he told me he had given up waiting for Denning and he was now on his way to Sidmouth.

'So what was all that about?' I said. 'If he couldn't make the arrangement he should have called you.'

'I agree,' Mike said. 'Anyhow, I'm making good progress despite the weath…'

The connection went again. Which was frustrating. Surely in this day and age, with people exploring Mars, they could fix a decent mobile signal to this house? I tried him again and got through for only a couple of seconds. Enough to hear his voice, but then he was gone.

I thought I would give it a few moments before trying yet again and popped the mobile back in my pocket. I looked at the long curtains covering the French windows to the rear. Behind them the rain continued to lash against the glass in erratic, powered jets. The wind gusted and blew as it funnelled its way through every opening around the house. In my mind's eye, I could see it tugging on waving trees and shaking the bushes as it made its destructive mark. Indiscernible cracks around the French windows whistled in harmony. I heard a metallic crash outside and guessed that the fragile patio table had given up the fight. It felt as if the wind were trying to lift the whole house from its very foundations with no respect for age or the natural order of things.

The curtains at either end of the room suddenly lit up with the brightness of another lightning flash, and this time I automatically started counting the seconds. I never made it to three. The thunderclap was terrifyingly close. It seemed directly overhead. There was no doubt that the storm was right over Sidmouth now and was giving its best. The only bright side was that if this was its peak, it could only start to improve. And the sooner the better as it was hardly helping the situation.

I extracted my phone, pressed redial and tried Mike again. I paced up and down the sitting room, my mobile phone pressed tight to listen to every sound that emanated from it. Suddenly I was through again.

I stopped my pacing and spoke loudly and clearly into my phone, 'How long you going to be, Mike? I think someone's followed me here.'

The reception continued to be poor and I pressed the phone even harder to my ear, keen to hear his reassuring voice.

'Did you say you were followed? What's...'

'Yes, *followed*. Please hurry. When will you get here?'

'Not long now, Grace. This storm's getting worse, I'm

sure of it. The roads are pretty treacherous...' He faded.

'Can you hear me, Mike?'

I moved nearer the front window with the vague notion that it would somehow improve the reception. It didn't.

'Just about, can you...'

'You've gone again. How long will you be?'

'I can hear you. The reception's never good in the house at the best of times... the police...'

'What? Mike, what did you say?'

'I said my reception's better.'

'Okay. You'd better ring Goddard just in case.'

'Ring who?'

'The police. Ring the police, Mike.'

'Okay. I'll ring Goddard as well. Just stay in the house.'

'I'm hardly going anywhere, Mike.'

'Don't let anyone in except the police. I will...'

'I've lost you. If you can hear me, ring me when you get here and I'll let you in. So how long will you be, Mike?'

There was a short period of silence and then in a very faint voice I heard him say, 'Not long, I'm about...'

But the line had gone dead. I tried redialling but it wouldn't connect. The lightning flashed again and the room lights flickered. Shit, what if the electricity cut off? I realised that the priority was to secure the house and quickly while the lights were on and I could actually see where I was going. See what had to be done to make me safe. The priority was surely the principal means of access, front, back and side.

I hurried into the hallway and across to the front door, my casual shoes moving silently across the parquet floor. I'd locked the door straightaway after seeing the motorcyclist, but now I placed the security chain across for good measure.

I noticed that there was also a solid bolt at the top of the door. I stretched up, but it was stiff and wouldn't move. Why the hell won't things do what they're meant to do? I thumped it with the edge of my right hand, but all I did was hurt myself. I was going to shift the bugger, come what may. A defiant piece of metal wasn't going to win. I placed my useless mobile on the antique table and looked around. The poker in the hearth caught my eye. I picked it up and used it to hammer the bolt into place, dropping the tool on the floor as I stepped back to admire my handiwork. At least something made me feel good. I'd won a battle, but not the campaign. Not yet.

I scurried out of the hallway, down the short passage, past the study door on my left and the cloakroom door facing me at the end, and into the kitchen on the right, switching the light on as I entered. The window on the left-hand wall looking out on the rear garden suddenly lit up again with a sustained flash, and some two seconds later the thunder gave its all. Although I knew I was safe from what was after all only noise, I cowered in the middle of the kitchen floor.

When the noise abated and the lashing rain took centre stage by drumming on the glass again, I crossed the length of the kitchen to the laundry room at the rear of the house. I opened the door and looked in. Empty and still with just the hum of a chest freezer. A single dark window with some scant decorative white nets. No curtains to draw. I glanced to my left at the back door to the garden and scanned it. I was certain it would be locked. I hadn't used it after all. I stepped towards it and tested it. And I was right—locked and bolted. I returned to the kitchen, leaving the laundry room door slightly ajar, and moved to the window. As I leant over the sink and lowered the Venetian blind in no more than a few seconds, I was able to take in the rain and the darkness and the force that nature was throwing at me. So far so good.

Facing the kitchen window in the wall opposite was the doorway through to the new lobby and the rest of the extension, which Mike's parents had built for his granny. It was shut. This door could be bolted from the kitchen side, but the bolts hadn't been slid across. As I stepped towards it, I suddenly had a vision of the door abruptly opening. Someone could already have got into the extension. I moved quicker towards it and slid both bolts home. The key was too stiff to turn and, after a few seconds of trying, I gave up. I turned and leant against it, as if leaning on it would make up for the lock. I knew it wouldn't, but crucially the act added to my feeling of success and gave me a moment to re-assess.

I glanced round the kitchen. Nothing more I could do in here. The lightning and thunder played out their sequence again. Still close, but I was becoming used to their violence. The lights flickered again and reminded me of why I was rushing round the house. I noticed a large torch on the work surface and made a mental note of its location—just in case. The threat of darkness galvanised me to hurry into the short passage, turning out the kitchen light as I went. I returned to the hallway. There I stood, panting. Where was Mike? Where were the police?

As I stood at the foot of the stairs contemplating the next door to check, I heard it. A crash. Someway off. It came from the direction of the kitchen. The way I'd just come. Certainly somewhere back down the passage. I listened intently and realised that the sound was of breaking glass. Surely the rain hadn't broken the window? How stupid a thought was that? I ran silently on tiptoes back across the hallway and retraced my steps down the short passage, pausing at the end. I listened again, poised to move in any direction. I glanced through the open study door to my left. The room itself was in darkness, with the only light flooding in from the passage. Its window looked out onto the rear garden. The lightning flashed again and lit up the sheltered patio and the study itself. Ironically, at that moment, the electric storm had done me a kindness and had shown me that nothing was disturbed. Nobody at the window. Nothing broken.

The cloakroom door at the end of the passage was ajar. I leant forward and pushed it. The door was oak, heavy and solid like the other internal doors downstairs, but it moved to my command and swung away from me into the small room. I flicked the light on. The window on the far wall was modern. Long, low and oblong. Too narrow to allow even a child through. Shut and secure. No problems there.

I stepped cautiously to my right into the kitchen doorway. Paused again. Listened, like a deer in a meadow. I heard a further noise coming from the darkness of the kitchen. I couldn't make it out. I eased forward and paused again. Listened. From that position, the side of the cupboard units prevented me from seeing down the length of the kitchen. With the light from the passageway, I could see the near end of the room and the opposite wall down as far as the extension door. It was still shut. I started to inch forward, but something made me stop and listen yet again. And then it was obvious. Despite the lashing rain on the kitchen window, I could hear the sound of the laundry window opening at the far end of the kitchen. I froze and strained to listen. Further noises. I leaned forward and, peering slowly round the end of the kitchen units into the gloom, I could just make out the distant laundry room door still ajar. The way

I'd left it. I suddenly felt a slight draught wend its way over me like the touch of icy fingers. Easing back behind the shelter of the cupboard, I heard the sound of someone scrambling over the sink unit. Some soap container or the like went flying.

Someone was in the house.

I turned and ran silently back up the short passage and into the hallway to the front door, but it was locked of course. Despite suspecting the exercise was pointless, I tugged on the bolt, but it refused to move. I glanced at the poker lying on the edge of the floor by the skirting board, but realised the noise I would make in trying to hammer the bolt would simply signal my whereabouts and take far too long. I picked up the poker anyway, and felt stronger. How had I got this so wrong? I was trying to make myself safe and secure, but in reality I'd made myself a prisoner. Trapped inside my own sanctuary.

With a killer.

I heard the sound of footsteps slowly cross the length of the kitchen floor towards the light of the passage. *Heading towards me.* I calculated that I had no time to attempt any exit from downstairs. I had to find a way out of the house. The stairs stood opposite me. The logic of seeking height to evade danger became overwhelming. The stairs themselves seemed to invite me upwards, calling me to disappear into the labyrinth of rooms on the upper floor. If I could find a window to open, I could jump out. They did it in films, didn't they? I pictured myself hanging from the windowsill and dropping nimbly onto the lawn below before making off into the safe veil of the rain. But what if I landed badly and twisted my ankle or broke my leg? I'd be at his mercy as he stood over me gloating in the privacy of the large garden as the rain sheeted down around us. The footfall snapped me back to reality. I could simply hide until either Mike or the police arrived. But they would have to be here soon. I moved quickly for the stairs as the sound of the footsteps left the kitchen and, still out of my vision, entered the passage leading into the hallway.

As I silently made the first step, the brightest of flashes outside was followed almost instantly by a tremendous clap of thunder right over the house.

And all the lights went out.

SEVENTY-TWO

With the sound of the thunder still in my ears, I took the first few carpeted steps up to the half landing where the staircase made a ninety-degree left turn to the next half landing. Very little light came through the hallway windows onto the stairs, and the area was almost pitch black with the curtains drawn. I had only recently been up and down these stairs when I'd visited with Mike after our day out in Lyme Regis, and I tried in my mind to picture its layout.

Placing the poker into my left hand, I held my right arm out in front of me and felt for the rear wall. Edging forward slowly I found it, angled myself and crept almost crab-like up the stairs while keeping a weather eye on the hallway below. The sound of the footsteps had ceased. He either was stationary or was moving silently to catch me up. My eyes scoured the darkness below me but I had to twist my head now and then to ensure I didn't stumble. My right hand and the whole of my right side from my shoulder down to my hip pressed against the wall. With each step, I feared the treacherous creak of a floorboard that would give away my position. I recalled Mike's comment that his parents had spent some two or three hundred thousand pounds modernising the house, and I trusted that quality new floorboards came with such a package.

It suddenly occurred to me that if another lightning charge exploded outside, my position would be lit up like a crowd at a firework display. I tried to up my pace as I turned left again at the second half landing on my way to the landing at the top. As I reached the last step, I ducked down low, maybe from instinct or basic self-preservation, but the timing was perfect. The lightning came again, immersing the house momentarily in bright light, followed a second later by the thunder, loud and close. From where I was crouching, my vision back to the hallway was limited. The flash of lightning had briefly revealed where the passage joined the hallway, but there was no one there.

My eyes were starting to become accustomed to the dark. I was now facing the front of the house, having taken a one-hundred-and-eighty-degree turn up the stairs. To my right at the end of the landing was the master bedroom with its large en suite. I remembered that, like the sitting room below, it stretched from the front of the house to the rear, where a set of glass doors opened out onto a small balcony overlooking the back garden. Just before it on the right was a smaller bedroom. I glanced back down the stairs. I thought I heard a noise in the kitchen, which threw me a little. I'd expected him either to have made for the stairs or to be searching round the downstairs rooms. Why back in the kitchen? I glanced to my left, hardly daring to move from my crouching position, although I knew I was pretty exposed there. But which way? The bulk of the landing was to my left. I could vaguely see two more bedroom doors facing me from that direction, and I recalled that the fifth was round the corner out of sight and next to the main bathroom. The nearest door was to a small airing cupboard. I toyed with the idea of hiding in there but was uncertain how much space I'd find. It might also be a noisy exercise, and I would be trapped.

I reached into my pocket for my mobile. But my

pockets were empty. I double-checked quickly, trying to retrace in my mind when I'd last used it. Then it came to me. I remembered that I'd left it on the hallway table when the front door bolt had picked a fight with me. Maybe I'd read that all wrong. Maybe it had been trying to save me, to stop me locking myself in. *Stop it!* It's an inanimate object for heaven's sake. *I'm in control.* A further noise sounded from down the passageway, and suddenly a beam flashed. He'd found the torch in the kitchen. It was powerful and vivid in the darkness and leapt out of the passage into the hallway like a search light, illuminating everything in its path. It waved and probed within its trajectory and then started to advance, flicking and flashing off the walls, creating fast-moving shadows. Relentless.

It was decision time. I eased to my right for about a metre towards the master bedroom, keeping low with my back to the wall. I was now beyond the stair wall. I glanced back over my shoulder as the view faded. The torch was playing round the hallway and suddenly turned up the stairs. I shrunk back behind the shelter of the wall. *Had I been seen?* The light threaded upwards with the rise of the staircase and then flashed around an arc of the landing ceiling. Bright, sharp, probing. Looking for me. *Whoever you are, look downstairs first.* I thought I could hear a footfall on the stairs, but the torch beam faded and I realised the bearer was walking towards the sitting room. It would be only a few moments before he came upstairs.

I raised myself up into a crouch and ran down the carpeted landing into the master bedroom, mindful that the man was now in the room beneath me. The carpet in this room was thick, but I was conscious that my weight might cause floorboards to creak. The room was dark but, as the curtains were open, there was sufficient light outside to guide me to the large windows at the far end. The lightning struck again and lit up the whole rear garden. I placed the poker on the end of the large double bed and moved towards the pair of balcony doors with their matching levered handles. There was a single key in a lock on the right-hand door. As I turned it, the incredibly well-timed thunder roared in the sky to comfortably drown out the mechanism's noise. This was going to work. I eased the handle of the right-hand door down, sensed the door give and tried to push it open. But the wind and rain resisted. I pushed harder, and the wider it opened, the wetter and colder I became. Keeping my feet firmly on the dry carpet, I leant forward into the misery and pushed the door fully open until it came back on its hinges and thumped against the house wall. The wind and the rain blew into the room, and I knew the countdown had started.

I turned, picked up the poker, and scampered back to the bedroom door, trying to move lightly on my feet. As I entered the landing, I saw light in the hallway, and the beam was clearly heading out of the sitting room and moving rapidly to the staircase. He would have to have been deaf not to hear the noise upstairs or sense my presence above him. As I moved towards the top of the stairs, I heard him come up quickly. The torch flashed and jolted ahead of him, but I remained sheltered where I stood. But not for long. Soon, very soon, I'd be in his path. Exposed and found.

I stepped to my left through the open door of the smaller bedroom and tucked myself behind it. *Walk past me, you bastard.* The torchlight grew stronger, and through the narrow crack between the edge of the door and the wall I saw him for a split second hurry by. A big man, but he went too fast for me to see anything more. I gave him two seconds to enter the master bedroom and then slipped out onto the landing and made for the stairs. I trusted that the open balcony window would delay him as he wondered whether I'd jumped out. I'd kept my feet dry and so there were no giveaway tracks. It would take a few seconds for him to make a decision. Worst-case scenario? He'd be searching upstairs realising it was a decoy although that would only antagonise him.

I turned down the stairs, glancing to my left in time to see the torchlight reflecting off the master bedroom walls as the man surveyed the room. I placed the poker in my left hand and allowed my right hand to hover over the banister for both guidance and support should I stumble in the darkness. I took the steps quickly, relying on my experience and judgement. I reached the upper half landing, turned ninety degrees to my right and then down to the next one.

As I took a step or two down the final flight, I paused. *Why was I running away from him?* I knew where he was, but he was looking for me. My advantage. And I had the poker. If I returned up the stairs and waited by the wall at the top, he would at some stage come hurrying out of the bedroom. I would be hidden—until I lashed out with the poker as he reached the top of the stairs. Time to go on the offensive.

I turned quickly, but in the darkness I miscalculated. I'd taken two steps, not one, down the final flight. My foot caught the riser and I started to fall forwards towards the lower half landing. Instinctively I stretched out my left hand to reach the banister for support and dropped the poker. It thumped silently down onto the stair carpet, glancing my left foot. The banister saved me from falling and I looked back up. Nothing. Then the poker completed its fall in the darkness and hit the hallway's wooden floor loudly. The torch shifted instantly towards the stairs, like iron filings drawn to a magnet. The beam became stronger and headed back down the landing, pointing at the floor ahead of the bearer. As it arrived at the top of the stairs, I turned and took the last short flight quickly before reaching the hallway floor. The man reached the top step and started his own descent, quicker than mine. He had the benefit of light, the confidence of the chase.

As he reached and passed the upper half landing, the torch flashed over me and I was in its full glare. I was a king to his bishop and he'd placed me in check. I snatched my mobile from the antique table and ran into the short passage towards the kitchen. I remembered that the door to the extension had two bolts. Could it be locked from the other side? If not, there was no way I could hold the door to prevent him from forcing it open. But even if I could lock it from the extension side, where then? He would be outside as quickly as I could make it outside. Wouldn't be hard. Either way I was going to get caught. And I knew what that meant—checkmate. And at the end of the day, there was no way that I could even slide the two bolts across and open the door before he would be on me in the kitchen. The back door in the laundry room, or even the broken window, were no real options either. There was just no time.

I heard him reach the hallway and, as he lined up with the passage, the beam of light hit my back, and my moving shadow patterned the wall ahead of me. He was metres behind me and gaining fast. Very fast.

There was only one option.

I ran straight ahead into the cloakroom and slammed the

door shut behind me. Slid the large brass bolt across. Leant back on it. A second later the door and my body shook with a dramatic thud as my pursuer crashed into it. I could imagine him shoulder-barging it, hoping that his strength and momentum would force it open. But the door was made of sturdier stuff. Three more times, he slammed his body against the door and each time it resisted. Lightning ripped across the sky again, lighting up the small cloakroom and drawing my attention to the window. I realised that not even a child could climb out. But then, the man on the other side couldn't climb in either.

Stalemate.

SEVENTY-THREE

In the darkness, I slid my back down the door and sat on the floor. Raised my knees up as I sought to steady my breathing. I tilted my head back on to the door and listened. Nothing. Finally a chance to reflect. Who was he? Evidently a large man—and strong. But then if this was Lindsey's murderer, it was established that he must have been strong. He had dragged her along the ground and killed her with considerable force. Slit her throat. So callous. It seemed to me that only this sturdy door stood between me and a similar fate.

It dawned on me that even if Mike were here, there was only a limited amount that he could do. I was annoyed with myself for not calculating the seriousness and nature of the threat. It was so unreal, so alien to me, but so deadly. Mike was a brave man, he'd shown that after all he'd gone through, and it came as no surprise to me that yet again he was willing to put himself second and come to my rescue, but this would be a game too far.

And where were the police? Had he been able to call them?

A sound beyond the locked door caught my attention. I took a deep breath to keep me still and listened. It sounded metallic, like someone unlocking the front door. Had he given up? Or was he coming round to try his luck at the window? My mind started to work on the options for me to escape. I concluded that the best bet was to wait for the police, but try them myself to see how near they were. I shuffled across the room to sit against the opposite wall and out of the sightline of the window.

Once again, lightning ripped through the sky to light up my temporary haven. I counted almost six seconds before the thunder rolled, quieter and more distant now. I looked at my phone. One missed call from Mike that somehow had escaped me. I started to call the police, but all of a sudden my phone lit up and gave me Mike's name.

'*Mike!*' I shouted down the phone. 'Can you hear me?'

'Yes, yes I can. You okay? Where are you? What's happening?' His voice brought a normality to the situation.

'I'm fine... well, sort of. I've locked myself in the downstairs toilet. He's here Mike. He's been trying to break the door down. Where are you? Did you call the police?' I pressed the phone hard against my ear, conscious of the poor signal.

'The police are on their way, Grace. Any minute now.'

'So where are you?'

'I've just pulled up on the road outside. I saw him Grace.'

'*You saw him?*'

'The front door flew open and someone legged it down the road.'

'Did you see who it was?'

'Sorry, no. He was a big man, wearing a balaclava. Dark clothes—is that what you saw?'

'I didn't really see him at all, Mike. Look, get after him. I'm fine for the moment.'

'Okay... oh, hang on. Here's a police car now. Look, Grace, I'll get them to go after the bloke. Come and join us, it's safe now.'

'Okay. And Mike?'

'Yeah?'

'Thanks.'

He rang off. A sense of relief ran over me. If the police could just get after him and catch him, everything would be resolved. But what were the chances of that? He had a head start. Was on foot. Lose the balaclava and he could melt into anywhere. Or hide up in a garden. But then they might summon one of those helicopters with heat seekers to find him. Better for him to keep going. Merge in a pub crowd. Anyhow, that was for the police to do. It was their job. But I would make sure they did all they could.

I stood up and stretched. Then the lights came on. I blinked and adjusted my vision. I had done it. What a story I had to tell.

I unlocked the door, opened it slowly and peered out. The passage light and the hallway lights were blazing again. I walked slowly up the passage and into the hallway. The front door stood open as Mike had said. I walked towards it. I wanted to run. To get out of the house. To find Mike and the police and contribute to the inevitable endgame.

As I neared the door, it suddenly moved. Pushed from behind until it stood marginally ajar in front of me.

And there was Mike. He was holding a handgun. And he was standing up.

SEVENTY-FOUR

The look on Grace's face was priceless. But it was one I'd seen before—more than once. On my count, five times. It was clear that she didn't comprehend. The cripple, the paraplegic, was walking on his own two legs. How could this be?

Grace took a few meandering steps sideways and sat down heavily at the foot of the staircase. I was surprised she'd made it that far from the state she was in. She stared at me with her pretty little mouth all agape. Her eyes flicked rapidly over me, taking in the unusual sight of me standing up and no doubt working it all out in her bright little mind.

Without taking my eyes off her, and passing my gun between my hands, I removed my leather jacket, revealing a plain white T-shirt. I threw the jacket across the floor towards the passage and then stood there waiting, looking at her.

She seemed to be willing herself to show no emotion. 'Mike, this is one hell of a deceit.'

'The standing up thing? Yes, it's true. I can walk.'

'So the riding accident was bullshit.'

'Yes. I'm fully able to do all the normal stuff. And free to do whatever I want. If I want to walk, I can walk. If I want to run, I can run. If I want to kill, I can kill.'

She stared at me, her surprise long gone and replaced with a look of total distain.

'Mike,' she said slowly. 'We trusted you....'

'You've got it, Grace. We wouldn't be here if you hadn't trusted me. But it all ends here.'

'Ends?'

'Oh come on, Grace,' I said. 'What do you think? Here seems a good spot, don't you think?'

'What to *kill* me? What have *I* done? And why here, in your parents' home...?'

'Fuck them. I saw them off years ago. Inherited all this, didn't I?' I waved my left hand generally around me whilst my right hand kept the Glock 17 trained on her.

'But I thought... the fire tragedy... the faulty cooker... that girl you were with ...'

I smiled. 'Oh yes, sweet Rosemary. The perfect alibi. Drugged with a cocktail and sleeping, but awakened enough later for more sex. And in between I'm off out down the fire escape at the back taking my motorbike out to the moor.'

'A motorbike,' she said and nodded as though the word was the key to everything.

'Yes, my irritating grandma bought it for me when I was eighteen. Our secret, she said, so I could get out more. I still keep it in a lock-up in Exeter – a consistently reliable place to park and allows me to swap over easily with my car. The magic of a motorbike is its speed, agility and, most importantly, its anonymity. A celebrity, or even a Mike Miller, becomes just a motorcyclist with a helmet and visor.' She continued to look up at me intently from the stairs. 'Some freaky pyromaniac I met in a pub taught me how to create innocent looking fires. You should have seen that caravan go up, Grace. Awesome. Quite took my mind off the screaming.' I paused a beat. 'I'll always remember that weekend. A well-accomplished mission to inherit a subsequent decade of wealth—the first part of my life plan.

Even got to screw a virgin, too.'

There was something cathartic about telling her these things I'd never told anyone before. It had all been bottled up in the secret part of my mind for so, so long. I wondered how she'd react. You don't hear many confessions like that, especially from a close friend.

She shook her head and said softly, 'You're a monster. Nothing less than a callous, greedy monster. You cut short two perfectly decent lives—the very people who gave you life and looked after you.'

'Oh sure, they gave me life, Grace, but not *a* life—not until after their deaths, anyway. Mother was unemotional—a cold, wet fish. Father was overbearing and remote. Always at work, never here, and when he was here would be working in that sodding office which at least kept him out of my way. What kind of life is that? I went to university to escape them, pretended I'd be a lawyer, too, just to get them off my back. But I set a goal to get rid of them within the degree's three-year course. That way I could live the life I'd always dreamt about—living here, as I wanted, with girlfriends on tap for my pleasure, and able to buy what the hell I wanted.'

'That's a nightmare.'

'So wrong, Grace. That's a dream: a solid, worthwhile, gold-plated dream. I have enough dreams for everyone. Most based on true events. I feel like these dreams make us who we are – and also make us do things, drive us on. That's how I see it, believe me.'

'*Believe you.* That's ironic, isn't it?'

'I had a plan, Grace, a life plan. A plan that would give me that life of pleasure without having to spend every day going out to earn enough for even an eighth of what I wanted. Toiling away like my father did. Stage one was to kill my parents. Stage two was a wealthy wife. And my plan was going so well. But it all started to unravel today. I should have listened to you.'

'I don't follow…'

'The garden gate. You kept telling me to lock it, but I wanted it left open. Having it locked made me feel trapped. Sounds silly with the open field, but that's how it was. It was my choice, and I got it wrong.'

'So Edith came into the garden to find you, then.'

'I was clearing my breakfast things from the table on the patio when she came round the corner of the house, I guess to ask if I could help out in her crappy little shop this morning. I didn't hear her stupid soft shoes on the paving. She saw me standing up. She tried to escape from me but no way could I let the old bitch get away.'

Grace's eyes flickered round my face. 'And writing the note was a desperate effort to mislead everyone.'

'Yeah, a touch crude, but I needed time and it created a reason to manoeuvre you down here, too. Put that idiot Goddard off the scent though, but I knew it was only temporary.'

'They'll know it was you, Mike. You're a dead man walking.'

'That's why I'm free to do whatever I want to do. But for Edith, I could have continued with my life plan. From stage two to stage three: find another wealthy wife for a short while and then become a widower. Then another decade of doing whatever I want. I have no doubt that I'd have given Byron a run for his money.'

'And here was I thinking that you loved Lindsey,' Grace said sarcastically.

'That would have made the whole of stage two of my life plan far harder to accomplish. But I'm not stonehearted, Grace, despite what you might think. I was attached to her, but I knew it was temporary. My mind was already working on who would feature in stage three. Might ideally have been you. But stage three wasn't meant to be like this.'

'You bastard. You absolute bastard.'

'Life's a bitch, huh?'

Her face showed she was taking it all in, sifting through it and seeing everything in a different light. Getting to grips with brand-new, shiny facts. 'So you involved yourself in my investigation for what purpose? To mislead me? To keep a close eye on what was happening? Or just to get close to your next victim?'

'Rather than just sitting around, I thought it best to keep in touch with the investigation, so your willingness to be involved worked out quite well. You made it very easy for me to mislead and have some fun. Writing diagrams to help me find false arguments and stir it all up. How right Martin was when he angrily accused me of that.'

'No wonder he assaulted you. He could read you.'

I nodded slowly and smiled. 'Sure, he could. But if I hadn't play acted in my wretched wheelchair, it would have had a different ending. But that wasn't an option. Anyhow, he won't cause me any bother.'

'You don't know him, Mike. He may have divorced me, but he hates your guts.'

'He was more perceptive than most.'

'He *is* more perceptive than most, and—'

'No, Grace. He *was* more perceptive…'

She sat forward as I presumed my emphasis on tense hit the target. I thought I'd reinforce the message. 'Do you really think I've been sitting in some godforsaken Exeter hotel waiting for Denning, Grace? He's irrelevant to all this. No, I swapped my car for the motorbike at the lock-up and I've been to visit your Martin. I've taken *full* advantage of my newfound freedom. Taught him what it's like to be a paraplegic. What it's like to be kicked about in delicate places. He gave me one final weird look, Grace, but never again. Taught that Sally a thing or two as well, especially what it's like to have your spare room defiled, like she did to yours.'

She just continued to stare at me.

'I'm untouchable now, Grace. Up until today everything was planned. The last ones were meticulously planned. Now I know that time is nearly up, I don't need to plan any more. I can simply get on with it. And I have. And I will.'

'You're no more than an animal.'

'Just a regular guy travelling through life, Grace. Just a regular guy, that's all.'

'There's nothing regular about killing people.'

'Possibly, but there's everything regular about wanting the best life you can create. Emotional ease and physical comforts. Everyone deep down wants it, Grace, don't they? You took money from Martin on your divorce to get the best life you could. As I said, people go out for hours to work for someone else to have the best wretched little life they can. Yes, everyone wants the best from life. I'm no different.'

'That's crap,' she said.

I studied her. She was different. Something inside her had gone. No warmth, no affection. 'Stand up, Grace,' I said.

'What?'

'I said stand up. Now.' I said more firmly.

She hesitated a second. 'Fuck you, Mike. You're a

pathetic yellow coward.'

'*Stand up!'* I yelled and fired three shots into the stairs behind her. Loud and sharp. She hardly moved.

'Impressive,' she said with strong sarcasm.

'I'm not fooling, Grace,' I said through gritted teeth. 'The next one will be in your leg, just like your ex had.'

'I'm hardly going to stand up if you do that,' she said, giving me a defiant stare. 'As ironic as clamping an illegally parked car.'

I moved the gun slightly downwards and aimed at her right leg.

'Okay,' she said, 'since you've asked so politely, but first, did you kill Lindsey's mum?'

I paused a bit, wondering what game she was playing at, but there was no need to hide anything now. 'Of course. Didn't want any unexpected marriage by Mary to a seventy-year-old toy boy to take Lindsey's inheritance from her, did I?'

'But I thought you were miles away in your bath when Lindsey popped out briefly?'

'Not quite true. I was by the back gate with my stolen, duplicate back door key. I often dream about what happened, although sometimes I'm some strange woman, whatever that might mean.'

'So you drowned her?'

'Yeah, something like that and then home pretty damn quick on the motorbike.'

Grace stopped cold and I felt a rush of power over her.

'I can't believe I didn't see you for what you are,' she said. 'I failed Lindsey.' Her face hardened into an expression I'd never seen before.

'Stand up, Grace.'

She slowly raised herself from the step, stretching out her right arm to hold the newel post as if she needed the support, although I doubted it. A feisty, strong woman. Not my sort after all, I guess, but what a woman.

'Mike?' she said firmly. 'Why do you want to kill me?'

She had such a beautiful face, the most wonderful complexion. Younger than her true years. Her pale blue eyes were stunning and, despite what was happening, remained so resolute. You would expect that if someone tells you they're about to shoot you with a loaded Glock, you'd display some degree of fear. But not Grace. Mind you the gun wasn't fully loaded: earlier that evening I'd rather hurriedly filled about half the steel-based magazine with its 9mm Parabellum rounds and pocketed a handful more from their box for when they were needed. Since then I'd released half a dozen shots. But still plenty left for my purpose. It only took one shot to kill, after all.

She placed her left hand on the other newel post, facing me some two metres away. Her arms were now both stretched out as if to support her. Reminded me of a crucifixion painting I'd seen in Greece.

'So what's the big deal trying to kill me, Mike? You've told me most of your sordid little secrets, so what's this one? Go on, tell me. Talking must help you somehow, or are you just showing off?' She hardly moved as she addressed me.

Did I owe her an explanation? I didn't owe anyone anything, but it definitely felt good to rub her face in her downfall. 'I've always liked you, Grace. You're a beautiful woman. And you're wonderfully rich. But you made it plain you didn't want me, just as you didn't want a war with Martin since you're obviously still attached to him. Messing about with that womanising Rob and giving me the two

371

fingers was the last straw. And if you're not going to fit into the next stage of my life plan, then you're not going to fit into anyone else's plan either. I always get my way, Grace. Only I control my life, no one else. Not you, not Martin, not Edith. So, as I said, it all ends here.'

She glanced down at the floor and then looked up. 'Call me fussy, but I'm just not up for marrying a mad serial killer. Now, let's sort this out properly. Put the gun down and go. I won't stop you. Killing me will just make it worse.'

'Worse? I really am free to do whatever I want, Grace,' I said. 'If I'm ever caught, four or five life sentences are as long as a single one in my book.' I paused, admired her exciting body one final time, and said, 'So, let's say goodbye, Grace. Oh, and sorry about what I did to Barney, sacrificed for more confusion and to satisfy the desires of the green-eyed monster.'

She shook her head. 'Are you trying to shock me? That's hardly a surprise at this point, Mike.'

'Turn round, Grace,' I said.

'Why, easier for you, is it? You're quite a man.'

'Suit yourself.' I stared into her gorgeous eyes and she somehow held my look. She remained stoic and defiant. I slowly moved my right hand that nestled round the stubby handle of the Glock. A reliable weapon. Could kill instantly—especially at two metres. I pointed it towards her. My finger tightened on the trigger.

'Besides,' she said quickly, 'this way I can see the person behind you.'

I smiled at her. 'Of course you can,' I said. 'Goodbye, Grace.' I started to apply pressure as I gazed into her eyes, conscious of the whole picture in front of me. There was a sudden noise, some movement and then I fired.

SEVENTY-FIVE

The shot was deafening. I closed my eyes. I remembered from my reservist training that bullets can travel at something like fourteen hundred feet per second. I also recalled that sound moves at about eleven hundred feet per second. And if those numbers were right, then surely I'd be dead on the floor before the sound even reached my eardrums.

Yet I was still holding the two newel posts. By standing up I was in a better position to find a way out of my dire position, but I had found it increasingly hard to keep Mike talking. The longer I was alive, the more chance I would think of a solution. The more chance of someone, or something, intervening. Someone must have heard his three earlier shots, surely?

And I was also conscious of loud noises in front of me. I opened my eyes. And then wider.

The bear-like man with wild hair whom I'd seen silently pushing the front door open had seized Mike from behind in a literal bear hug. On seeing my predicament, he'd sprung into action and had come crashing in through the front door, which was even now bouncing back to its original slightly ajar state. The bear had his over-sized right arm wrapped round Mike with his hand clasping Mike's hand and its gun in a desperate struggle. The gun fired again twice more and I was conscious of a splintering sound in the sitting room door. At the sound and sight of random shooting, I instinctively dropped in self-protection to the stairs, watching as the men fought and twisted in front of me.

With both arms wrapped around Mike from behind and secured on his hands and wrists, the bear lifted Mike off his feet and shook him hard. Mike's legs kicked and lashed out, the heels of his shoes landing randomly on the bear's knees and shins. The bear bellowed and shook him even harder. The gun fired again. I eased slowly forward. When I had been standing at the foot of the stairs earlier working on solutions, I'd seen the treacherous poker lying on the floor half tucked under the bottom of the stair carpet. I leant forward and bent down to pick it up, but a sudden crash caused me to stop and I looked up.

Whether the bear had thrown him or whether he had broken free of the hold, I don't know, but Mike had hurtled against the antique table still clutching his gun. The bear lumbered with surprising speed the three metres that now separated them just as Mike recovered his senses and looked up at the man descending on him. Mike raised his right hand, but the bear grabbed it as they came together and Mike was hidden from my view by the wide, leather-jacketed back of the bear. I watched them wrestle with grunts and groans at close quarters, working out how I could help. Although I was uncertain of the giant's identity, he was clearly friend, not foe.

I bent down again and picked up the poker.

And heard a further shot.

I looked up across the hallway. Both men stood where they were as if, like toys, their batteries had run out simultaneously. The bear took a single step back towards me, still hiding Mike from my view. And then, with incredible speed, he suddenly drew back his right arm and launched a violent punch. I couldn't see, but I calculated it had landed full into the left side of Mike's face because Mike crashed downwards. The gun clattered to the wooden floor and spun away until it came to a rest at the front door.

The bear took a further step back revealing the whole of Mike's body and I saw blood on the front of Mike's T-shirt. I stood up holding the poker. As Mike started to stir, the bear tipped forward onto his knees, twisted and collapsed on his back. His own leather jacket fell open, and my eyes were instantly drawn to a growing red mark towards the bottom of his light blue shirt. As the bear groaned briefly, Mike sat up and rubbed the side of his face. He gave his head a quick shake and looked around. I ran towards the gun, but Mike scampered quick and low across the floor, his right arm outstretched. As we both neared our mutual goal, I swung the poker down firmly at full stretch just below his wrist. He shrieked in pain but, with his other hand, grabbed my own wrist and used my momentum to pull me over his rolling body. I tripped and fell over him hard into the wall. The poker fell and clattered on the floor.

Mike picked up the gun with his left hand and, standing up, pointed it at me. 'You bitch,' He placed his right hand on his stomach and pressed on it with his left elbow.

I sat up and leaned against the wall. 'You don't blame me for wanting to live, do you?'

'You nearly broke my fucking hand,' he said. 'You'll suffer for that.'

He was silent for a moment as he coped with the pain, but his attention never left me. I needed to communicate with him. I glanced over at the bear and couldn't see any breathing. 'Who is he?'

'What?' he said, still rubbing his hand and flexing it

gingerly.

'Who's that?' I said.

Mike took a deep breath, trying to come to terms with the blow. 'Him? That would be Lindsey's cousin, Frank.'

I looked again at the bear. *Frank? He saved my life.* 'You've killed him.'

'Sure. Glocks are pretty powerful. Got this one from some dude in Manchester as a millionaire's self-preservation weapon. Doesn't preserve others though. But can't be helped. Everyone dies sometime or other.'

'Others will disagree with your logic.'

'So be it,' he said.

I looked at him standing there soothing his right hand against his stomach, the gun still aimed at me. The poker was out of reach, and I'd miscalculated its value. I needed to get the gun or talk him round to leaving me alone. Surely someone would call the police with all this noise. And how did Frank find us? I needed to keep Mike talking. He seemed to relish the opportunity to confess his so-called life plan. 'You might be a right bastard, Mike, but I've got to hand it to you. You've fooled a lot of people and planned everything in great detail. So, the final question is, how did you kill Lindsey?'

'Confession time, huh?'

'You don't seem in a position to go anywhere right at the moment. And you were keen to talk just now. Surely you can just tell me this. Go on, it will make you feel better.'

He stepped back the few metres to the staircase and sat on the step I'd occupied a few minutes earlier, which frustrated me—I wanted him nearer to give me some chance of doing something. I felt the pressure of my mobile tight in my jeans' pocket.

He looked across at me. 'Murder has to be well planned. I knew if I were going to bed a wealthy woman and then persuade her to wed quickly, I'd need a cast-iron alibi, else no inheritance. Sounds brutal, doesn't it? Don't confuse romance and love with a financial scheme, Grace. This was the latter in the guise of the former. Simple as that. Life can be a sod, huh?' He gave a Gallic shrug. 'A guy in a wheelchair was perfect—can hardly commit a violent murder, can he? So I dreamt up the horse riding accident and learnt to use the wheelchair. Gives an alibi for a whole host of imaginative options. Who's going to question it, especially when you're well-known in the village through being at the shop? *The guy in the wheelchair*. Not even my wife second-guessed it.' He paused as if reflecting. 'Mind you,' he continued, 'those things are a bloody nuisance after a while, but a private garden, net curtains and sun-glassed visits to Sidmouth and elsewhere give some respite. Our visit here had to be after dark, as no one here's seen me in a wheelchair. Having my adapted car in service over the weekend was belt and braces.'

'So where did Lindsey go all afternoon? She obviously didn't go to Julie's.'

'Hadn't been there since I knew her. You can make up what the hell you like about the dead, no one's going to contradict you. Say she goes out, works nights or whatever, who can contradict? You can trash whatever reputation you want. No, I feigned illness and, like a devoted lamb, she went to the pharmacy in Tiverton for me. I'd brought a bag of goodies back from here the day before. Lindsey never knew about this place. My secret haven for respite. While she was out, I put false number plates on her car and hid a bottle in the back and the rest of the bag in the boot.'

I studied him, glancing about when I could. I was totally alert. 'And…?'

'And then I persuaded her to take me to hospital sometime after two. I was in such pain, I said, I had to lie down on the back seat and leave my wheelchair. Should get an Oscar for that performance. Towards Exeter there's a farm track to a quiet copse that I'd discovered. She pulled in near there as I said I was about to be sick. When she came to help me out, I pulled her into the back with me and chloroformed her. Gloves and over-sized galoshes on, then hauled her onto the back seat and drove down the track to the copse. Trussed her up like an oven-ready chicken with the rope and duct tape from the bag, dumped her in the car boot and drove us to my Exeter lock-up. And there we stayed until evening. She probably got hungry, but I was okay with my sandwich and a couple of cans of beer.'

I wanted to stay calm, but my anger was getting the best of me. 'You animal.'

He didn't seem to hear me, as he was in full stride off-loading his secretive ego. More time won.

'In the evening I drove her to the wood. Parked where I'd planned. At exactly 10.29, as DS Ward would say, I rang the bungalow from her mobile. The answering machine I brought specially from here kicked in for almost its full three minutes. I rang off. And then I opened the boot. She looked pretty scared. I ripped the duct tape off her mouth. Despite her situation, we had this weirdly normal conversation until I explained what was going to happen. Then she tried to scream the place down and struggled, so I had to reapply the tape. She was shocked and frightened, I guess, but there we go. Anyhow, lifted her out the car, dragged her through the undergrowth to where Sandra Roberts was killed, and slit her throat. Pretty straightforward. All worthwhile for four million quid, wouldn't you agree?'

I tried to remain stoical as the images of Lindsey's dreadful last hours played out in my mind. Terrifying for her. It occurred to me that most of us don't know when we've entered the last sixty seconds of our life—but Lindsey would have known. I realised Mike was still talking and forced myself back to the problem in hand. 'So you nicked the cash from her purse?'

'It all helps, huh? Packed up the bag, swapped the number plates back, and trekked home across fields through the night. Saw nothing but a handful of rabbits. When I reached the wood behind our house, I sank the bag in a little pond there before returning to the house through the back garden. Then it was a matter of waiting for the police. Sure, my mind kept wandering onto the effect Lindsey's death would have on me and my wheelchair—that I would be free of it soon—but a tap-dampened handkerchief and pitiful expressions can usually win the day.'

'So why did you write the letter from C?'

'The letter was down to you.'

'Me?'

'Sure, you overhearing her talking to a Karl opened a rich seam of potential deceit. All corroborated by you. By the way, I finally found out who he is yesterday.'

'Who is he?' I asked.

'Karl Goldsmith. A posh party planner. My little darling was secretly planning my upcoming birthday. I told you she was an angel.'

If I had been holding the gun, I swear to God I would have shot him. *Keep him talking.*

'But Clifford Denning was the inspiration for the "C"

itself. And that weirdo Craig, too, come to think of it, and it proved a good alphabetical choice, huh? I'd researched the coven and saw it as a brilliant distraction. The baby skulls came from a London curiosity shop. I was just going to use the coven theory until you mentioned Karl.'

'So it was you in Cowgate Street, not Frank here.'

'Yeah, waiting for you to go to bed. After you rang me I returned on the motorbike to Exeter and then back to you in the Focus. You could hardly criticise the paraplegic for any delay, could you? It's great making stuff up, Grace, like pretending to see the Cowgate guy again. Faking the phone threat when some call centre salesman rang, so I could pull out my home phone and use a mobile only. Faking the theft of Dean's notebook after waving it around a busy pub and inventing whatever I wanted about its contents.'

Mike was like a child relating everything he'd done at school that day.

'What were the contents?'

'Just some innocuous argument within the coven. He decided to tell a pack of lies to the newspaper knowing the coven would find it hard to refute. Pretty vicious. No wonder he hung himself. Denning may be somewhat overbearing, but he genuinely wanted to buy the house. When he rang me personally earlier today, I accepted his improved offer over the phone. Gave me the idea of how I could go off and see Martin, though.'

I felt anger that I had been so taken in, but I had to stay focused and keep challenging him. 'How could you plan everything? Surely not everything went your way.'

'No, not everything. When my Exeter private detective, Jack, traced Ada but a few months ago, I messed up my first call to her. Which was challenging when she raised it when we went to see her, but I had the impression there was some kind of notebook that I thought might just add to the deception one way or another. Mind you, Grace, Lindsey's pregnancy was a shock. But the coincidence with Sandra was wonderful. A real coincidence.'

'And you made the most of it, huh?' *Where were the police?*

'Sure. A gift horse.' He paused a moment and scratched his ear. 'Karl got me thinking, though. No way would Lindsey have had an affair—'

There was a sudden groan. I looked at Frank and saw him move.

'*Christ, Mike, he's alive*! We need to call an ambulance quickly.'

I leaned sideways and dipped my right hand into my jeans pocket. The mobile caught in the pocket as I tugged it out.

He stood up and rushed over towards me with the gun pointing at my chest. 'Put it down, Grace.'

'I'm calling them else Frank's going to die.'

'Yes, that is the point.' He took a final step towards me, snatched the mobile from my hand and threw it back towards the stairs behind him. I was about to kick out with my leg, but somehow I felt the time wasn't right. Patience.

He turned round, took the two steps over to Frank and landed a hard kick on his prone leg. Frank stirred and turned his head slowly to look up at Mike.

'Help me,' he whispered. 'Please help me. Rosie needs me.'

'You're a fucking pain, Frank,' Mike said, bending down towards his face. 'A right fucking pain.'

Frank said nothing. I was weighing up options. Nothing

yet.

'Why the hell did you have to interfere?'

Frank coughed showing evident pain. 'So I was right,' he said in a weak voice. 'You killed Lindsey.'

'No, you were wrong. You accused me of having her killed. Did it myself, huh? Less risk—and cheaper. You want a job done properly, do it yourself.'

Frank groaned in pain and his hand moved towards the heavy bleeding on his shirt.

'Hurt does it?' Mike said.

'I knew you were up to no good, Miller. Been finding out all about you. I got here just in time.'

'Just in time to catch your death, Frank. That's all. A murderer can't inherit from his victim so no money for me, but then no money for you either.'

'Rosie will get it all.'

'How sweet. Not for long though, huh?' He looked across at me. 'Funny this, Grace,' he said. 'It was only an hour or two ago that Martin was lying like this at my feet. Mind you, he had a hole in each leg by then and was making a fuck more noise than Frank here.'

'Let him be, Mike,' I pleaded. 'Frank's only trying to help his sister.'

'And himself. No one's that altruistic.'

'You'd be surprised,' I said.

'Whatever. I don't give a damn any more.' He turned to Frank and pointed the gun at his head. 'Maybe the coroner will rule this one a mercy killing, hey Frank? Like putting down a bloody horse or a sick dog. Final words, Frank?'

'Go fuck yourself' was all Frank could summon and he closed his eyes.

Mike held the gun steady. I started to rise. I heard a

382

metallic click. Mike pulled time and again on the trigger with growing frustration. He cursed and detached the magazine. He struggled to dip his injured right hand into his pocket and pulled out a handful of bullets. Some spilt onto the floor. My mobile suddenly rang out at the foot of the stairs. Mike looked round at it. Clearly summoning some inner strength, Frank lashed out with his leg and struck Mike firmly on the knee. Mike buckled slightly and started to turn back towards Frank. I was now up and, recalling my military training of old, threw myself at Mike to catch him off balance. The gun, magazine and a shower of bullets fell to the floor from his hands. I wrestled with him on the floor, grateful that the poker had already weakened him.

I never heard Frank until a shot rang out. Both Mike and I stopped and I rolled off him, looking at Frank as I went. Frank was still lying on the floor, but now he held the gun, and the magazine was restored to its rightful place. With some difficulty he was pointing the gun at Mike.

'The next one's in your head, asshole.'

Mike lay still.

I stood up and walked over to Frank, who was clearly weakening. The gun started to slip towards the floor.

'I'll do it, Frank,' I said, and took the gun from him.

And then I heard it. Through the slightly open front door came the sound of sirens, moving quick and fast and heading our way.

'Here come the cavalry,' Mike said, looking across at me from the floor.

I couldn't bring myself to reply, but walked over to the door and peered out. Blue lights were flashing and reflecting off every wet surface down the street. The cavalry was indeed arriving. I looked round into the hallway, just in time to see Mike grabbing his jacket from the floor and running into the passage. I levelled the gun and fired, but missed. He was out of sight. I started to chase, but Frank called out in a croaky voice, 'Let him go, Grace. He's not worth it. The police will catch him. It won't be self-defence if he's got a bullet in his back.'

Maybe I sort of grunted, maybe I didn't—I can't honestly remember. But Frank looked dreadful. I crossed over to him, put the gun down on the floor and knelt by his side.

'You okay?' I asked looking into his pallid, hairy face.

He shook his head ever so slightly and closed his eyes.

SEVENTY-SIX

The electric blue flashing of emergency vehicles now came through the open door and curtained windows. I leapt up and crossed to the door. Opening it, I saw a white police van and a couple of patrol cars parking up on the road. Armed officers from the Firearms Unit dressed in ballistic vests were taking up defensive positions in front of Cliff House. For some reason, I wondered what Mike's parents would have made of all this. I suddenly saw DCI Goddard near the gate.

'He's not here Chief Inspector,' I shouted from the lighted doorway. 'But we need an ambulance urgently. He's shot Frank.' I felt myself under intense scrutiny from the officers and instinctively raised my hands.

Goddard appeared to give some instruction, which I couldn't hear. He walked briskly onto the property towards me and stopped a metre short.

'You okay, Mrs Atkins?' he asked with genuine concern in his voice.

'I'm fine, Chief Inspector, but Frank's pretty bad.'

'I tried ringing you a few minutes ago,' he said. 'Tried before but got the number down wrong for some reason.'

'Ironically your delay in calling was life-saving, but I'll tell you about that later. Is an ambulance coming for Frank?'

'It's been called.'

'So where's Mike?' I asked.

'You said he wasn't here—'

'He ran out the back on hearing your sirens,' I said.

'Guessed as much,' Goddard said. 'I've got some officers round there. Back in a second.'

Goddard went to speak to a couple of officers standing with weapons poised in the drive. They moved past me into the house. He took his mobile out and made a call. I glanced at my watch. It was heading for ten o'clock. I had won the battle and the enemy was in full retreat—but not yet defeated. There was more to do before I secured the checkmate.

A few minutes later Goddard returned to me. 'I gather he's got a motorbike and can walk after all.'

'How did you know?'

'Frank rang me this evening. He followed Miller down to your ex's place and then on to here. He lost him at some point, but was going to look for this place. He'd somehow found out about it. He was worried about you. How bad is he?'

'Not good,' I said. 'Looks like he's been shot in the stomach.'

An officer appeared at the front door and signalled to Goddard.

Goddard nodded back at him. 'Let's go in,' he said to me. 'The house is clear.'

As we walked into the house, Goddard said, 'Do you know if he's armed still?'

'No, I don't think so,' I said. 'He's left the gun here.'

'He may have another one.'

'I don't think so,' I said. 'He would have used it here if he had another one, believe me.'

Goddard nodded. An officer was tending to Frank, and in the far distance I recognised the sound of an ambulance.

I took Goddard down the passage and into the kitchen. He took a message on his radio as I sat down at the kitchen table and watched him.

He finished the conversation and came over and sat casually at the table opposite me. He looked tired.

'As you would have just heard, we've found his motorbike parked up round the corner. Frank gave us the details.'

I asked the question I had to ask. 'Have you been to Martin Atkins' place, Chief Inspector? Mike told me he had shot Martin. Is it true?'

Goddard nodded. 'I'm sorry, Mrs Atkins, but it's true.'

He told me that he'd had a report from officers who'd attended at Martin's house following the 999 call by Frank, who'd heard shooting and had then seen Mike leaving. He confirmed empathetically that Martin had indeed been shot in the forehead, and had a bullet wound in each leg. Sally was not in a good way and was sedated in hospital. In confidence, Goddard told me that she had been found naked, gagged and tied to the spare room bed. She'd been raped. Part of me actually felt for her. Whatever her part was in the destruction of my marriage, no one should go through what she'd gone through. I made a mental note to try to contact her, say something caring, positive and good.

Goddard asked me what had happened at Cliff House. I told him about my journey down, my communications with Mike, my efforts on his advice to make the house a fortress only to find myself then trapped in a prison. And, very generally, his confessions.

'He must have intended to keep you here while he killed Martin and then come for you. You've had a very lucky escape, Mrs Atkins,' he said.

'It was certainly challenging, but I always believed I would find a way through. Frank was great.'

'I presume you had no idea he could walk?' he continued.

'Certainly surprised me. He's played quite a role. But too full of himself, that was his weakness. We just need him locked up now and the key thrown away. What can I do to help?'

Goddard smiled. '*Please* leave it to us,' he said. He paused a moment. 'You told me just now that he confessed to strangling Mrs Riley in his garden. His story didn't stack up to me, and I had some urgent enquiries undertaken in Edinburgh today. You may recall that's where he said his horse-riding accident happened. Gave me an exact date the first time I met him. My sergeant noted it down—he notes everything down. No records at the hospital about Miller, let alone the alleged accident. Nothing, nothing at all. And I don't think he ever lived in Edinburgh either. Take away his apparent handicap and add the fact that he's a first-rate liar, then everything falls into place.'

'But he's killed so many people, Chief Inspector. And got away with it for so long.'

'That's why we have to stop him before he does it again.'

DS Ward entered the kitchen quickly.

'Sir, he's been spotted. He's on foot. Up towards some local church. They're not approaching him, just observing.'

Goddard moved quickly towards the door.

'Stay here, Mrs Atkins,' he said. 'One of my armed officers will stay with you.'

'I can come with you,' I said standing up.

'I said stay. This could be dangerous. Ward, get

someone in here and whatever she says, whatever excuse or story she tries to make, don't let her leave.' He winked at me and turned for the door.

Goddard and Ward left, leaving me on my own in the kitchen. As an armed officer appeared in the doorway, I started to pace up and down, picturing what might be happening on the quiet streets of Sidmouth and wishing I could be there to see justice done for Lindsey, Martin and all the other poor victims of that callous, evil bastard.

SEVENTY-SEVEN

I ran through the back garden of Cliff House and through a hole in the hedge onto the pavement, guided by the torch I'd picked up from the kitchen where I'd left it after the pursuit round the house. I paused to put on my jacket and still felt deep pain in my right hand from the poker blow. Once ready, I walked away at a steady pace. As I distanced myself from the place, I knew with growing certainty where I had to go. I knew the direction well and started to pace like an automaton without any thought for left or right. My feet just moved forward with the confidence and purpose of foxhounds following a scent.

I'd thought about my immediate future. I knew my options were limited—zilch in reality, I guess. Even Goddard would be able to solve the death of Edith. As Grace had hinted at, there would be DNA aplenty, forensics would conclude she'd been murdered in my garden, and the shopping centre CCTV would crucify me on timing alone. And the fact I could walk would suddenly ensure that Goddard saw everything about Lindsey's death in a different and correct light. And when that happened, all would unravel like a knitted jersey snagged on a thorn bush.

And I had of course confessed much to Grace, and indeed Frank, if he survived.

And I had no gun anymore. But then would I really take on the expertly trained police marksmen no doubt on their way to tackle me? Would I go down in some blaze of defiant glory like a modern-day Butch Cassidy? Would you have done that? Maybe you think I should have found somewhere to hide and evade capture. Sure, the option crossed my mind, but I would simply be delaying the inevitable: an ignoble arrest in a remote wood, a lonely cove or a hay barn on some godforsaken farm. Tired, cold, hungry. Not my scene. Not what I could face.

And I wanted to live.

Like I said, zilch options.

The chilled night air reminded me that life is seasonal—the circle of life and all that. And it was with this thought that my foxhound feet took me round to the beginning again. Seeking a known quarry. In my mind it was poetic, perfect. It drove me on. There was an inevitability about it all that embraced me, almost empowered me. Told me to see it all through there, at that precise location I had attended just once before.

I was just turning right off the pavement through a small lychgate into a graveyard when I heard at least two police cars approaching up the road. Sirens, bright lights, moving fast. Professional drivers. They'd found me.

Streetlights, which stretched around two sides of the low-walled cemetery, cast an orange glow that gave the area good visibility, especially now the rain had stopped, leaving the ground wet and glossy with random reflective puddles of varying sizes. I kept my torch on. As I moved down the narrow cinder path surrounded by ancient tombstones and stone crosses, I heard the sound of car doors slamming and felt the presence of several officers on the road behind me. I kept walking, not fast, not slow, but deliberately towards my destination.

I heard Goddard shouting to me to stop and raise my

hands. He had to be about thirty or forty metres behind me and close to the lychgate. I stopped and turned round slowly while raising both my arms so that the torch shone diagonally upwards, diffracting as it smudged the slate roof of the church itself that stood guardian over the whole area.

'I'm here, Goddard,' I shouted. 'I'm unarmed. The gun's back at the house. Come on over. I need to walk on three more metres then I'm stopping. Come and join me. I won't hurt you.'

And with that I turned round slowly, arms still raised, and stepped off the path. Moved slowly a few metres amongst the graves, the grass wet and soft beneath my feet, the air fresh from the rain and the storm. I reached my destination, lowered my arms and glanced back over my right shoulder. Goddard and two armed officers were heading warily towards me. Two guns were evident. I admit I felt for Goddard a bit, but then he was no different to all the rest. I'd fooled a lot of people and got myself pretty wealthy and comfortable without ever lifting a finger—just a murderous hand to remove those who had to die to fulfil my plan.

I stood and waited for them to approach me. Yes, stood. None of that wheelchair crap anymore. Felt good to be free of all that. I shone my torch down on the grave at my feet. Time had taken it further into the graveyard, so to speak, as the grim reaper had claimed many souls over the eighteen years or so since it had been dutifully dug and solemnly filled. The marble stone still looked new, and from what I could see in the beam of my torch, it was, uniquely, the only grave of this age to bear fresh flowers. Some sweet-smelling, colourful freesias.

I glanced up and held out my right arm as my left

gripped the torch in front of me. Goddard and the two officers now approached me at a steady pace, slowing when they must have seen I was going nowhere. The two officers still had their guns trained on me. Quite the violent criminal.

'It's over, Mike,' was all Goddard said when he was a couple of metres or so from me.

I nodded. Didn't look up. Looked at the gravestone emblazoned by my torch. I was now comfortable with my decision that I didn't want to run. Had come to terms with it. Goddard was right, it was over. I needed time out. I felt a strange feeling of relief, almost peace. No need to think, to scheme, to lie. Planning the next episode of my life was going to be easy. For the first time since school days, others would do that for me and I was going to let them for a change. School days. Standing here had taken me on that full circle. It was a curious feeling.

Goddard must have noticed my interest in the grave.

'This grave mean something to you, Mike?' he asked patiently, as if asking me about my hobby, which ironically made sense in a way.

I nodded again. 'It's where it all began,' I said slowly.

He moved closer and looked at the stone lit by my bright torch. I guessed he read the inscription—the name, the age, the date and the brief quote from the bible selected by distraught parents. *Suffer the little children to come unto me.*

'Tell me.'

'It's when I learnt that you could kill without being caught,' I said. 'When I learnt I could lie, and lie well. The coroner ruled death by misadventure, although there was some toying with the idea of suicide. Murder never even entered into their equation, but I knew it was murder. I'd been there after all, just me. But they didn't know that, did

393

they? And I never said. You're the first person I've ever told.'

'Why did you do it, Mike?' The same quiet, peaceful voice. He didn't need anything stronger.

'Revenge and jealousy,' I said calmly. 'No one was going to behave that way to me. Decisions about my life are down to me. I don't share that right.'

'What happened?'

'A fall from the coastal path above the cliff one evening, but I gave the push.'

'She was only sixteen, Mike.'

'I know, so was I. But no one was going to dump me and get away with it. I make the decisions and I couldn't bear the thought of her being with someone else. Surely you understand that? I sometimes dream she fell from a bridge, or a balcony—it's all the same thing, I guess.'

EPILOGUE

Apparently Mike's not mad. His grey-haired barrister, a learned silk, tried running that defence to get him off on manslaughter. Didn't work. The judge ruled that he's as sane as the next man. I keenly followed his progress through the English legal system as he was moved like a pawn down a well-worn, predictable route of procedure, solemnity and pomp. Meetings with lawyers, adjournments and hearings, and then days in a modern courtroom, permanently scrutinised by not only a judge and jury but also ranks of journalists and rubberneckers. A worldwide attraction put on show as if he were the bearded lady or the elephant man. Front page news.

He had his day—indeed weeks—in court. I had my day too, in fact, with hours of giving evidence under his steely gaze from the dock. There was only one way it was ever going to go of course. They don't let people like him get away with it, once they're caught that is. I had suspected that he intentionally stretched it out a bit with his not guilty plea, realising that daily outside trips to court are likely something he'll crave in future years. He'll desire a change of scene and even the mildest touch of a wider social world of which he was once a part, albeit an unwelcome one.

I ended up spending quite a lot of time with Chief Inspector Goddard. We've got on quite well, and he's not such a bad chap really. In fact, he let me in on me how closed-mouth Mike was when questioned, giving just a series of well-rehearsed "no comments". Goddard told me about how he had asked Mike what he found the most difficult: the loss of his parents in such a dreadful way when he was young, the brutal murder of his beautiful wife, Lindsey, or receiving a written mortal threat to his own life whilst in a wheelchair. Which had he found the most difficult to plot, plan and execute? All Mike did, as Goddard put it, was keep silent for a few moments until he eventually said, 'No comment,' as though he were finally intimidated by something.

In the end, there was plenty of evidence to put Mike away, including his Cliff House confessions and the indisputable forensic evidence regarding Martin, Edith, and the bag used in Lindsey's murder recovered from the pond. Mike's ended up with a whole life sentence, including a term for the rape of Sally, who's actually my friend now. Goddard admitted to me that it was good to have this success, especially after everything that happened with Sandra Roberts.

I thought they should put him in isolation with nothing and throw away the key. But during his first year or so, he wrote it all down. I'm sure it was his way of spewing it all out, as he'd attempted in the hallway on that dreadful evening. Maybe he saw it as a way to write the crime novel he always said he was working on, although I've no way of knowing whether that was ever true. Truth is an antonym for Mike in my dictionary. He sent the draft to me through our respective lawyers to get around my injunction against him, which meant he was unable to ask me about using the pages and pages of my police statements as the basis for my side of things. He said he would like me to publish it and take editorial control.

I wasn't sure what to do. I had been in contact with Frank, actually (who told me the unfortunate news that Rosie died), and I asked him what he thought while offering my condolences. He said I should burn the manuscript. I discussed the dilemma with my fiancé, James, who thought I should go along with Frank. I tended to agree, but then Mike would still have a copy anyway, and so deep down I knew getting rid of it wouldn't give me real closure. So I've edited the book, corrected a few things from my angle and put it out there as a dire warning to other women like Lindsey and me.

In particular the ending of Mike's original draft book was, if I may say it, total crap, but there was one part I wanted to reproduce here so you can see why I finally decided to publish the novel. And it gives me closure on that terrible year as a new and exciting chapter opens for me:

"*Anyhow in my view, dreams, like people, are unreliable. I dreamt of an entire hedonistic life, but it ended abruptly at thirty-two. I had started to dream of Grace settling down with me, briefly, in the way that Lindsey had. But she was not who she seemed to be either. With the way Martin had treated her, I thought she'd be weak, compliant, and desperate to please a new man as she regained her feet and repaired her damaged confidence. How wrong I was. She was stronger than I'd realised.*

"*I still dream. It's no different now than when I was free, save that, when I dream of my hedonistic life, I wake up sweating with the realisation it won't happen today or even next year. But some dreams make me look forward to the future and carry on within these stifling walls. Like the one where I'm eventually let back into society, as I'm sure I will be, even in my eighties. When that happens, I dream that Internet dating still exists so that I can once again find a wealthy princess to kiss and wed, temporarily.*"

Indeed, if he ever does get out, I'll be waiting for him.

ACKNOWLEDGEMENTS

I would like to thank my editor, Amy Butcher at Amy Butcher Content in Montreal, for her calm, positive, efficient and encouraging support and approach to my first novel as well as for her honest opinions and sound advice. You have been fantastic, Amy, and I could not have dreamt of a better editor!

I would also like to thank my good friend Rob Whitney of Rob Whitney Design in Lincoln, UK, for his creative contribution in terms of the cover design.

Thanks, too, to Craig Smith of Stuart Smith Photography and to Kay Gugliotta at Pink Frog, both of Lincoln, UK, for their very generous support.

Further thanks must also go to Detective Chief Inspector Tony Heydon of the East Midlands Special Operations Unit – Major Crime. Tony dedicated some time to assist me with particular and general research, as well giving me a real insight into his team's work, for which I am really grateful. Tony hasn't read the book yet so I hope I've got the technical bits right, Tony!

Finally, and actually top of the list, is my fantastic wife, Kim, who has encouraged and supported this endeavour, even when it has meant me being somewhat of a hermit. You are every real man's dream, and I love you.

andrew argyle

www.andrewargyle.com

COMING SOON

from andrew argyle

The Sir Guy Sterling thriller series.

Ex-SAS officer, Sir Guy Sterling, retired early from the army to inherit the wealthy Hofton Manor estate in Shropshire on the sudden death of his parents and sister in a tragic road accident.

As the seventh baronet, Guy throws himself into the responsibilities of the estate and its philanthropic tradition, but the desire to return to a more adventurous life remains ever present.

Supported by his fiancée, Sophie Litchfield, and his ex-sergeant turned estate right-hand man, George, Guy is tempted into a real world of missions, adventures and vicious enemies. He is the 'go to' person for government leaders, celebrities and even high church officials who have discreet issues that need resolving with cunning, tact, diplomacy - and illegal brute force where required.

All of this the English aristocrat and gentleman can supply with hardened expertise.

www.andrewargyle.com

Seek if you dare

A Sir Guy Sterling thriller – publishing 2016

The wife of a wealthy Premier League footballer is shot dead by a professional assassin. Although there are suspicions that the footballer may be behind the death, the Chief Constable of the West Midlands force has other information, which might link the death to a series of professional hits involving various celebrities and leading figures

Driven by the temptation of solving a family mystery of his own, Sir Guy is persuaded by his friend the Chief Constable to leave the comfort of Hofton Manor and to investigate the crime. But this clandestine assignment is to run alongside the official police enquiry, and Sir Guy finds himself in no little conflict with the choleric female inspector who thinks she knows it all - and has no problem telling Sir Guy of that.

The sudden and unusual disappearance of a TV celebrity's eighteen-year-old daughter brings a new and deadly twist, and one in which time starts to run out for both Sir Guy's reputation and an innocent girl's life.

The Son rises in the West

A Sir Guy Sterling thriller – publishing 2017

The Christian church has received into its care an incredible and historic object, which has massive religious importance. Unfortunately it came to light in an Arabic dig on Temple Mount and its global significance means its prospects of leaving Jerusalem are slim. The Archbishop of Canterbury turns to Sir Guy to assist in retrieving it and bringing it back to England in a less than traditional way.

However the Church and Guy are not the only ones who know about the discovery. A violent organisation, fighting all religion and thought to be long defunct, is hell bent on destroying the find and, through treachery, have learnt about Guy's mission.

And the stakes are raised even higher when, through good fortune and courage, Guy discovers something further of massive religious and scientific meaning that makes even the original find of minor interest.

But the relative safety of England is far away, and even any successful return is still fraught with secretive and mortal danger.

ABOUT THE AUTHOR

andrew argyle was educated at Shrewsbury School and Birmingham University. He is now involved in executive strategy and management and is a non-practising solicitor having been in private practice for over 25 years.

andrew has four children and lives with his wife, Kim, in rural Lincolnshire along with a multitude of animals including horses, Labradors and several cats.

andrew is a man of faith, and, aside from his writing, his passions are travel (particularly cruises), football and rural living as well as socialising with friends.

For more information about andrew, his books and his future publications, including social media contact, visit:

www.andrewargyle.com

Printed in Great Britain
by Amazon